monsoonbooks

PEARL

British by birth, Rose Gan first arrived in Kuala [Lumpur] and has been living and working between both UK and South East Asia ever since. Married to a Malaysian, and formerly a teacher of History and Latin in UK and Malaysia, Rose was also Vice Chair for Museums of the Indonesian Heritage Society, a guide and docent in Museum National Indonesia, Jakarta, and Muzium Negara and the Textile Museum in KL. In addition to lecturing to cultural associations, Rose has been actively involved with museum publications in Malaysia and Indonesia, both as a writer and editor.

Pearl is volume two of Penang Chronicles, a series of historical fiction that delves into the backstory of the British settlement of Penang. It is preceded by *Dragon* and followed by *Emporium*.

'At last, a novel which engages a crucial and fascinating period of British merchant imperialism and Southeast Asian history. Penang, meeting place of Malays, Bugis and Siamese, here too are freebooting English and a more staid company in Calcutta. Here are mixed marriages, innumerable cross currents with the Dutch in Java and Sumatra, Chinese and Tamil traders, Achenese sultans and a Burma too close for comfort. And in the middle of it all is Francis Light, founder of modern Penang, a man of his times and of history. Britons today are woefully ignorant of the legacy of maritime Southeast Asia in which they played such a key role. This novel is a good start to re-engagement with this region, a meeting place of races, religions and cultures.'

Philip Bowring, author of *Empire of the Winds*

'Rose Gan, in this fascinating and well-researched novel, skilfully provides the reader with a colourful illustration to the early life and times of Light and those historically connected to him. The author cleverly unveils Light's rise to the rank of captain and his travels to this part of the world while meeting the people who would set the stage for his lustrous future.'

Dennis De Witt, author of *History of the Dutch in Malaysia*

'As a veteran journalist who read History at university – and one who has remained fascinated with Captain Francis Light ever since – I find *Dragon* truly enjoyable. Ms Gan has carried out extensive research in creating the world of this novel. It's definitely a first of its kind!'

Wong Chun Wai, Star Media Group, Malaysia

'*Dragon* is a rare example of writing about the important country trade that existed alongside of the East India Company and, since 1661, increasingly independent of it. Rose Gan's well-crafted narrative has clearly been written following extensive historical research.'

Sue Paul, author of *Jeopardy of Every Wind: the biography of Captain Thomas Bowrey*

'*Dragon* is a richly imagined yet historically faithful account of the early career of Francis Light, the founder of modern Penang. We follow his journey from his clever revenge on a bully during his schooldays in Suffolk to his heroic service with the Royal Navy, from his apprenticeship as country trader with a Madras agency to his delicate negotiations with the Sultan of Queddah, which will set him on the path leading to the founding of Pulau Penang as the first British settlement in the East Indies. Along the way Light has to weather storm and shipwreck, survive betrayal by company officials, balance palace intrigues and interpret the signals of ambitious royal wives and widows – all the while navigating the cross currents of British, Dutch, Malay, Siamese and Bugis interests in the region, with only his wits, moral compass and ambition to guide him. A marvelous cast of characters populates this well-researched work of historical fiction, with just the right blend of the real and the imaginary.'

John D. Greenwood, author of the Singapore Saga series

'Swashbuckler or swindler, trader or statesman, the mere mention of the name Captain Francis Light in the state of Penang is bound to draw an array of clashing reactions. Known for establishing the isle as a British settlement back in 1786 under the name Prince of Wales Island, Light has been quietly acknowledged with opening the door to the eventual colonisation of what would later be Malaya. From his schooling days in Seckford's School to a premature departure for a life at sea, Gan explores the twists and turns of what Light's early life could have been in this historical fiction narrative.'

Andrea Filmer, *The Star*, Malaysia

'When you think of British explorers from centuries gone by, you tend to think of the likes of Sir Francis Drake, Sir Walter Raleigh, Henry Hudson and Captain James Cook, to name but a few. But what about Suffolk's very own Captain Francis Light? From humble beginnings in Dallinghoo and Woodbridge, to more prestigious times spent in the Far East, Light lived quite the life.'

Danielle Lett, *East Anglian Daily Times*, UK

PEARL

Penang Chronicles, Vol. II

Rose Gan

monsoon

monsoonbooks

First published in 2022
by Monsoon Books Ltd
www.monsoonbooks.co.uk

No.1 The Lodge, Burrough Court, Burrough on the Hill,
Melton Mowbray LE14 2QS, UK.

First edition.

ISBN (paperback): 9781915310002
ISBN (ebook): 9781915310019

Cover design by Cover Kitchen.

A Cataloguing-in-Publication data record is available from the British
Library.

Illustration on page 458: 'View of the North Point of the Prince of
Wales's Island, and the ceremony of christening it' by Elisha Trapaud
(1750-1828) in Trapaud, Elisha, *A Short Account of the Prince of
Wales's Island, Or Pulo Poonang, in the East-Indies*. London: John
Stockdale, 1788.

Printed and bound in Great Britain by Clays Ltd, Elcograf S.p.A.
24 23 22   1 2 3

For Mum and Dad, always with me.

No finer, greater gift than that,
when man and woman possess their home:
two minds, two hearts that work as one.

Odyssey: Book 6, Verse 163-7

Glossary

Malay

atap	palm thatching for roofs
bapak	father
bersanding	wedding celebration
bidan	midwife
bunga mas	gold tree sent by northern Malay sultans to Siam as tribute (lit. golden flower)
dastar	headcloth worn by Malay men
Ferringghi	Foreigner, particularly European (from Persian 'farang' - Frank)
gundik	concubine at Malay court
haram	forbidden
ibu, 'bu	mother
Jawi	Arabic-based script originally used to write Malay
Juragan	Captain of a small vessel, skipper
kafir	nonbeliever, non-Muslim
Kapitan Cina	Leader of the Chinese community
kebaya	Close-fitting woman's blouse worn with sarong
kota	fort
lanun	pirate, from 'Illanun' an ethnic group of Sulu (Philippines) famous as raiders
merantau	'roaming'. A practice of sending young men abroad to experience life beyond their home village
mutiara	pearl
Nona	title for non-Muslim woman in Straits, especially of mixed race/ European
nenek	grandma

padi	rice field, paddy
perahu	boat, also *prau*, or prow (English)
pice	Indian coin 1/100th of a rupee *(also pais)*
picul	a weight (the amount a man can carry across his shoulders) approx. 60 kg
pulau	island
sayang	darling, my love
songket	rich brocade silk cloth with gold and silver interweave
tengkolok	formal male songket headdress worn only by nobility at this period
toddy	fermented coconut palm alcohol
wakil	envoy, representative of a Muslim court
wayang kulit	shadow play puppet theatre

Thai

chong kraben	loose wrap around trousers worn by both men and women
Farang	European, probably from Persian *'farang'* (see *Feringghi* above)
lomphok	tall high-pointed headdress worn by Siamese nobles
luk kreung	person of mixed race in Siam
Khun	polite term of address for men and women
sabai	shoulder cloth worn by Siamese women
Phaya/ Phraya	honorific titles equivalent to Lord or Great Lord (*Chao Phraya*)

Place names of the Archipelago

Achin: (or Acheen), Aceh, north Sumatra

Batavia: present day Jakarta, in Java, Indonesia

Chao Phraya: the highest honorific title of Siam; also
                    Chaophraya, the great river of Bangkok

Cochinchina: Vietnam

Coromandel: the coast of SE India, now in Tamil Nadu

Fort St David: Cuddalore

Fort St George: Madras

Jangsylan: see Phuket

Johor: southern kingdom of Malay peninsula, under
                    Bugis influence

Ligor: Ancient province of Southern Siam, historically
                    the centre of the south; also known as Nakhon Si
                    Thammarat.

Malacca: The English version of the Malay Melaka. Both
                    forms are used, depending on the speaker

Mergui Archipelago: island chain off southern Burma

Pulau Pinang: originally Pulau Kesatu. Colloquially known as
                    Pulau Pinang because of the abundance of *pinang*
                    trees (areca palms). The British often
                    mispronounced it as Pooloo Penang, renaming it
                    Prince of Wales Island, but the latter never caught
                    on. Today it is either Penang or Pinang (Malay).

Phuket: In the 18th century, this southern Thai island
                    was variously known as: Thalang to the Siamese;
                    Ujung Salang to the Malays; Jangsylan (also
                    Junk Ceylon) to Europeans. The population of
                    the island was diverse. Malay was as widely
                    spoken as Siamese. All three names are used,
                    depending on who is speaking.

Queddah:	(also Quedah) was an Islamic kingdom in the north of the Malay Peninsula, bordering on southern Thailand. It was a vassal of Siam. Today, it is the Malaysian state of Kedah, substantially smaller than in the 18th century. There is still a sultan.
Riau:	archipelago off east Sumatra under Bugis rule
Selangor:	Bugis kingdom on the central west coast of the Malay Peninsula
Siak:	sultanate of East Sumatra
Thalang:	see Phuket
Thonburi:	across the Chaophraya river from Bangkok fort, the capital of Siam in the reign of King Tak Sin
Ujung Salang:	see Phuket

Peoples of the Archipelago

Achenese:	the people of Achin
Bugis/Buginese:	migrants originally from Sulawesi (Celebes) known as traders, navigators and warriors
Chulia:	Indian Muslim merchant community from the south east coast of India
Ferringghi:	Malay term for Europeans, a corruption of the Arabic *Ferringi* (Franks/Crusaders)
Hokkien:	migrants from Fukien province in southern China, mainly involved in trade
Minangkabau:	migrants from West Sumatra, known for their matrilineal culture

Orang Belanda: Dutch (*orang* = man)

orang laut: sea people, general term for the coastal Malays of the Straits (also orang Selat)

Orang Inggeris: British, English

Salateers/Salat: English term for *orang selat*, Straits Malays, also Celates. (Malay: *selatan* – south)

Samsan: Siamese Muslims

Serani: Christian Eurasians of Portuguese/ South East Asian heritage (from Nazareni)

Siak: migrants from the Siak kingdom of East Sumatra

Syed/Said: Arab traders, often from the Hadramaut (Syed, descendant of the family of the Prophet)

Teochew: migrants from Guangdong province in China, mainly involved in trade and agriculture

Malay Court titles

Bendahara: Chief minister of an Islamic Malay court

Laksamana: Senior minister at an Islamic court, similar to Admiral

Raja Muda: Crown Prince (lit. young king)

Temenggung: Senior minister of Islamic court usually responsible for security

Tengku/ Tunku: title at Malay court for members of royal family

Tuan: Malay honorific term of address, 'Lord'.

Tuanku: term of address reserved for a Malay sultan, similar to Your Majesty/ Highness (lit. My Lord)

Yamtuan Muda: Malay title historically used in Johor for Crown Prince

List of Characters

Francis Light: British sea captain trading in the Straits of Malacca
James Scott: Light's friend and business partner
Soliman: Light's adopted Malay son

Ban Takkien family

Chom Rang: head of the clan, governor of Thalang
Mahsia: Malay wife of Chom Rang
Lady Chan: Eldest daughter of Chom Rang
Phaya Pimon: second husband of Lady Chan, governor of Phattalung province
Lord Thian: Eldest son of Lady Chan by her first husband
Lady Mook: middle daughter of Chom Rang
Lord At: husband of Lady Mook
Lady Thong Di Rozells: youngest daughter of Chom Rang
Martim Rozells: Eurasian husband of Lady Thong Di
Marthina Rozells: their daughter
Felipe Rozells: their son

Siam

Tak Sin: governor of Tak, later King of Siam
Lord Chakri Duang: his adoptive brother, later King Rama

Queddah

Sultan Muhammed Jiwa: aged sultan of Queddah
Raja Muda Abdullah: son and heir of Sultan Muhammed

Raja Muda Ziyauddin:	younger son of Sultan Muhammed
Jamual:	an influential Chulia, 'The King's Merchant' of Queddah
Tunku Ya:	Laksamana under Sultan Abdullah

Bugis

Sultan Salehuddin:	Raja Lumu, first sultan of Selangor
Sultan Ibrahim:	son of Sultan Salehuddin
Raja Haji Fisibillah:	a visionary rebel leader, brother of Salehuddin

East India Company

Sir Warren Hastings:	The Governor-General of India
Sir John McPherson:	Acting Governor-General in 1786
William Fairlie:	Calcutta merchant, friend of Light
Andrew Ross:	sea captain, Council member, friend of Light
Elisha Trapaud:	British officer at the settlement of Penang

Suffolk

Margaret Negus:	wife of William Negus
Mary Light:	adoptive mother of Light
William Negus:	guardian of Light

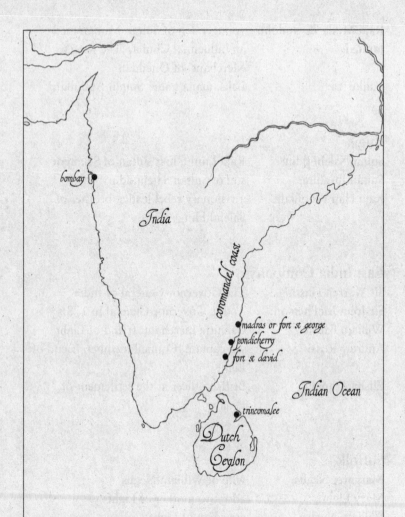

India and the Malay Peninsula
adapted from "A Map of the East-Indies",
produced for the East India Company by
Herman Moll, Geographer, 1736.

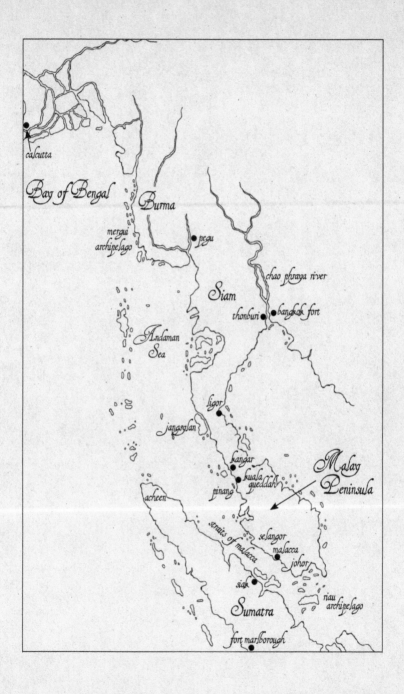

Contents

Prologue

Ban Takkien Village, Thalang[1]. 15th September 1756

The girl awoke with a start, the threads of a dark dream unravelling as she emerged into piercing sunlight. She lay there awhile, breathing deep and slow, in rhythm with the familiar 'tok tok' of the pestle on mortar wafting in through the open window without so much as a breath of air to accompany it. The sweltering heat of earlier had solidified into a thick wet binding that clung to her moist, sticky body. She rose unsteadily, swollen and sweat-drenched, dampening a cloth and pressing it to her forehead, her neck, between her breasts and thighs – but felt little relief. The water was as warm as her sweat.

Wandering onto the veranda where the house girls were pounding and peeling, chopping and grinding in preparation for the evening meal, she squatted down beside them, her belly resting on a cushion. The sky was a blinding blue, the air a little fresher outside. She settled herself in, taking comfort in the idle chatter of the servants. Picking up a basket of beans, she began pinching and trimming, grateful for something practical to while away the dreary humid hours of late afternoon.

---

1 The Siamese name for Phuket. It was also known as Jangsylan (or Junk Ceylon) by Europeans, and Ujung Salang by Malays.

'Rain's coming,' Boon murmured, glancing up at the sky. The girl raised her eyes to the heavens. Sure enough, amongst the patches of blue, white clouds were foaming, milk on the boil. She breathed out slowly, waiting for the welcome breeze that would herald the daily rains. But no cooling relief followed. Instead, the afternoon grew even more sultry, pressure rising and her head swelling as if to burst.

'You feeling alright, my lady?' Boon asked, noticing how quiet and pale she looked. She shrugged, returning a wan smile. Boon Lek, on the nodded direction of her mother, ran off to fetch some cool ginger tea; she gratefully sipped at it, pressing the terracotta beaker against her head and cheeks. Darker clouds were now scudding in, casting the grounds around the house in shadow. At last, the leaves began to rustle. The breeze picked up and became a wind. The longed-for shower was imminent, the rain moving in fast. Gathering up their utensils, the servants fled inside, but she shook her head at their proffered hands. The cool air felt soothing on her cumbersome body. She would sit a while longer.

Within minutes, however, the trees were swaying ominously, then leaves and twigs broke off and swirled around, like malevolent sprites. A great storm was approaching, no mere tropical downpour. Heavy drops of rain spattered the parched dust, turning the dry red earth to mud in seconds. Then the deluge broke.

Water hammered on the roof and ran in rivers through the compound, pulling everything with it. Their clay forecourt was already a pond, fed by rivulets bursting out of every spout and gulley. The afternoon became as night: dark skies shattered by blinding cracks and sheets of lightning, accompanied by shuddering thunder blasts. But only when the rising floodwater began to wash the veranda itself did the girl – already drenched – struggle to her feet, suddenly afraid in the face of the awesome power of nature.

A stabbing pain almost knocked her back to her knees as she straightened up, forcing her to grasp the door frame for support. Doubled over and groaning, she screamed, aghast at the sight beneath her, where a different torrent was now pooling. Her body was shedding its own downpour.

'Help me! My waters have broken!'

This was no ordinary September storm. For years to come people would speak of the unnatural force of that terrible day and night which took so many lives and destroyed so many homes, flooding tin mines and wiping out an entire rice crop. Trees were uprooted, houses blown down, children swept from their mother's arms, whole families drowned. Even those who remained safe did not pass unaffected through the jaws of the fearsome cyclone. Livelihoods were shattered. It took years for the survivors to rebuild and recover.

Some said it was a sign that the south was entering a time of dire misfortune, others that the Burmese were coming, which amounted to much the same thing. Another theory accused the Christian god of conjuring winds and rain to punish the people of Thalang for attacking a ship of the British Company in Tharua Bay. The crew had been massacred and all its goods stolen. The governor had blamed the sultan of Queddah, the sultan had accused the Siamese authorities. Who knew how it had begun? All that mattered was that they were suffering for it.

In the house of Chom Rang, leader of the Ban Takkien clan,

one of the richest and most influential Siamese on the island, that
night had another significance. During the storm, a child was born
to his third and youngest daughter, Lady Thong Di. It was a long
and difficult labour, made more so by the climactic conditions, a
terrifying background to the event, as well as a practical difficulty.
It had been impossible to bring a midwife from the village, for no
one dared to set forth in such weather.

Not that this bothered Lady Thong Di's Malay mother,
Mahsia. She offered up a silent prayer of thanks that the storm
was keeping away the village witches, for she had had the foresight
to employ a Malay *bidan,* who knew the proper way of birthing
a Muslim child. Mahsia tied her daughter's hair back with a
scripted headcloth containing sacred words to protect her through
her ordeal. But the household was uneasy; most of the ladies
in attendance were Siamese. They feared that if the propitious
Buddhist rites were not carried out, all the signs proclaimed that
on this awful night the child and mother might not survive.

Thong Di's older sisters, Lady Chan and Lady Mook, both
already mothers, were present – and they had little truck with
their mother's Queddah ways. They did, however, allow the
massage of the abdomen to help the baby work its way down.
They also approved of the steaming of the birth channel that had
greatly eased their own labours, supporting their little sister as she
squatted over the bowl of hot water-infused herbs and roots. But
they also insisted on the Siamese customary sprinkling with water
boiled in *pak plang* and *maiyarah,* then hung a plaited garland of
these same vegetables about Thong Di's neck.

When her pains reached intensity and they feared the child
might be stuck in the passage, they even sent out a few girls,

risking their lives in the lightning and the flood, to tie lengths of silk brocade around the roots of the *tahkian* tree, so that the *nang mai* would protect Thong Di in her labours. A sarong of sturdy cloth was then secured around the rafters and the two women sat behind as buttresses while the younger sister clung on and began to push. Meanwhile, Mahsia clucked and fussed and muttered prayers to counteract the pagan nonsense.

The windows and doors were all wide open to chase out evil spirits, but on that stormy night it resulted in the driving rain beating its path inside the house. Everyone was cold and damp. In an outer room, Martim Rozells paced up and down, as befitted a prospective father, ignoring the disapproving glances and muttered complaints of his father-in-law that he should be in the birth room holding his wife as she laboured. Martim had refused point blank. No self-respecting Christian man would be present at such a moment. Nor did he wish to observe all the profane practices that he was sure the silly women would be carrying out. He had instructed one of the Eurasian servants to pin a holy medal and a crucifix onto Thong Di's sarong as a talisman against the vagaries of childbirth and the evils of the spirits summoned up by the rest. It had been his original intent that one of the nuns from the mission would be present at the delivery, but the storm had put paid to that notion. Now all he could do was toss down brandy, say endless decades of the rosary, and chase out the Muslim fellow who had been sent by his mother-in-law to chant some misbegotten mantras.

In the dawn light, with a constant rain still beating down but the violence of the storm finally abating, a cooling breeze and a watery light found its way into the foetid chamber. And on that blessed portent of the return of peace after chaos, the baby girl finally entered the world. She was small but perfectly formed. Her first cries were strong. Smiles beamed all around. The little girl was fair skinned – so white that Thong Di wondered how such a pale child could have come from her own body. The baby's hair was sparse but what was there was brown. Her eyes were midnight blue. The women of the chamber gasped at this unusual little one.

'She will be a great beauty, Lady Thong Di!'

'She will win many hearts!'

'A golden child from a golden mother!'

The attendants all kept to themselves what they really thought. The baby was a *luk kreung*, a half breed, more *farang* than Siamese. Had she been born looking more like her dark pretty mother then she would be better able to fit in. But who would want a child like this for other than a plaything? She had been born in the night of the storm. It was a bad omen for sure.

Thong Di was delighted in her daughter, but unsure how Martim might react; he had hoped for a son. Yet no sooner had he seen the little child than he beamed with pride. His daughter was a beauty. She favoured his people. 'It is better to have a daughter first! She can look after her brother when he comes next!' he laughed.

Lady Chan and Lady Mook, the elder sisters, agreed with Martim. 'It is certainly far better to have a daughter,' they whispered between themselves. 'Men are useless, good for nothing but making babies and holding public office. And if she has no brains, she will have at least her beauty. She might even be chosen for her fair skin as a royal concubine!'

'Praise be Allah, the almighty and merciful!' whispered Mahsia. 'Thank God it is a girl! Easier to raise her in the true faith. My kafir son-in-law is sure to bother more about a son than a daughter!' She seemed to have forgotten how little success she had had in raising her own five children as Muslims.

As he buried the placenta beneath the ta-khian tree in thanks to the nang mai for a safe delivery, Chom Rang ruminated on the events of the night. He was worried about the losses he had sustained. The rice crop was ruined. Word had arrived that several of his boats had been destroyed with full cargoes and, most worrying of all, many of his labourers had perished. Who would now work his land and mines? But still, he was grateful for the gift of a girl. Female children were always good for the family. His sons were the opposite: spoiled wastrels, more interested in gambling, smoking opium and whoring than expanding the family fortune. His daughters were well named: Silver Moon, Lustrous Pearl and Shining Gold – his precious treasures. They had good heads for business, understood the intricacies of the political climate, and had married husbands who had brought great benefits to the family. All in all, he was a lucky man. He would simply have to raise rents and taxes to recoup his loss.

'What shall we call her?' Martim asked his wife as she was being wrapped in her binding cloth. It was good for the womb, or so they said. Martim had turned his back while the women worked, still embarrassed by the whole business of birth and confinement. But he already loved to hold his little girl, marvelling at her perfect tiny features and the tightly curled fingers that wound around his own.

Thong Di smiled. 'I shall call her Ma Li,' she told him. 'She is so white and fragrant!'

'Jasmine flower? So common! Half the girls in Thalang have that name!' he exclaimed.

'But none are so white and fair as she!' Thong Di reminded him.

'True. She is fair skinned, like a tiny perfect pearl. My little Mutiara! Yet, I believe we should choose a Christian name to favour her European features and my ancestors.'

A fleeting frown crossed Thong Di's brow. She was unsure that identifying her baby by name as a farang would be the best course of action, although she knew better than to openly oppose her husband. 'An excellent idea, Mah Tim. You must choose!' Whatever he named her, she would always be Ma Li in the house. And who could even pronounce his strange other name, Roh-Se-Las? Everyone called him *Khun* Mah Tim. It sounded Siamese.

Martim paused awhile to give the matter some thought. 'She should be named for my beloved grandmother. As was I. We shall call her Martinha!'

Lady Thong Di tried out the unfamiliar name. 'Mah-Ti-Nah? What does it mean in Portuguese language?'

'It is the same as my name, Martim, but for girls. I think it means warrior, the great god of war, something like that.'

She smiled. 'Ma Li will be a great warrior! I like it. We will baptise her Mah Ti Nah!'

'It is also the name of a great French saint, I believe. My grandmother was half French, you know? The daughter of the priest at the mission,' Martim added.

Thong Di shrugged. Saints, gods, spirits, holy men. It was all the same to her. This was Thalang. All races and people lived here.

Each brought their own gods and ways. The more the better.

'A strong name for a strong woman. That is my Ma Li.' She reached out her arms for her child and then settled the baby at her breast. Her fingers stroked the strands of baby hair on the delicate scalp. 'But we must still shave her head on the seventh day. It will help her hair to grow. Mother insists. It is a Malay custom …'

PART ONE

The Girl from Jangsylan

(1765-1767)

1

The Business of Matrimony

The Governor's Residence, Tharua, Jangsylan[2]. January 1765
The reflection in the cloudy mirror brought the merest glimmer
of satisfaction to Lady Chan's perfectly arranged face. Carefully
unfolding herself from her stool so as not to disarray either her
clothes or makeup, she resumed her serene appraisal of herself,
her eye more critical than vain. The agile fingers of her girls deftly
arranged her *sabai* over one shoulder, tweaking and smoothing
the heavy red and gold brocade of her skirt and bodice. They
adjusted the elaborate hair knot woven with fresh jasmine and
delicate pearls and crowned in gold. Final touches were added
to the bridal outfit: chains of gold and jewelled pendants about
her neck, then heavy ruby earrings. Bangles were eased onto her
wrists and ankles. Cloying fragrance was sprayed around, like
incense before a shrine.

And all the while, Lady Chan, skin whitened to a porcelain
mask and eyes kohl black, stared at this marble image of her
true self. It was exactly as she had planned. Without a doubt, the
guests would recognise her *erb-im,* the inner beauty and spiritual
perfection that would mark her out as a lady of the highest nobility.
She looked younger than her years, still ripe for marriage and

---

2 The European name for Phuket, also Junk Ceylon.

breeding, but with the added bounty of status, proven fertility and an aptitude for commerce and politics. Along with her undoubted beauty, Phaya Pimon was a very fortunate man indeed.

Her outer composure, however, belied the turbulent inner world of her mind's eye. A panoply of the past made its stately progress through her memory. Her younger self, a bride of fourteen, shy and love-sick, breathless with anticipation. So much for love, Chan thought. Her indulgent father had rejoiced when a young noble from Phang Na province had fallen for her. A marriage made in heaven, or so he had said. Naïvely she had thought herself blessed among her peers to marry for love. The handsome face and noble bearing of her late husband appeared before her in the mirror as on that other wedding day, twenty years before. Then the years rolled forward to the night she had cast him off for good. How to compare that charming boy to the bloated, wasted wreck of a man he had become, eaten up by disease and dissolute living! Better to marry for anything but love, she now knew.

It seemed to Lady Chan that marriage itself was little different from business and public life in general. Love belonged to a wholly other part of life and its private pleasures. If a man and woman were pragmatic and respectful towards each other, they could enjoy the fruits of both. In marriage, one side has something to sell, the other wishes to buy. What could be simpler? Agree a contract and form a partnership. As long as each enters the contract fully aware, then all parties can be satisfied. And just like commerce, a wise vendor or a sensible customer knows the other will never be constantly faithful to the terms of the agreement. For that is business! The thrill of the bargain lies in pitting one's wit against another's in the dealings to come. Exactly like marriage! Not that Lady Chan was in much doubt about the outcome of today's matrimonial contract; she already knew Phaya Pimon would be exactly where she wanted him. Most specifically, far away from home – at least in the near future – in his capacity as governor of a mainland province. She would be a virtual free agent on the island, able to make full use of her father's elevated rank and her husband's royal connections. And perhaps find discreet opportunities for love along the way.

The wedding party set off for Wat Tha Rua carried by uniformed bearers, as befitted the eldest daughter of the ruler of Thalang. Her esteemed father, Phraya Chom Rang, recently appointed governor of the island, settled back on silk cushions and acknowledged the admiration of the gathered crowds with impassive conceit, his face a study in inscrutable superiority. It was not often that an event of such opulent magnificence was seen in humble Tharua port. The locals were out in force, struggling to secure a vantage from which to gawp at their betters. How intensely gratifying to seal his gubernatorial appointment with such a propitious marriage, especially when it gave him the opportunity to flaunt his many successes in the face of the other noble clans of the island.

Despite the uncertainty of the times, the Ban Takkien had risen to the very top of the heap, all due to his genius. They were now the pre-eminent family on the island, their influence reaching as far as the southern Vice-Regency of Ligor itself: the current viceroy, his own second cousin, had personally appointed him governor of the island. The Takkien clan ruled supreme and unchallenged. To his delight would be added his daughter's imminent alliance with Phaya Pimon, the governor of mainland Phattalung province. The family was now unassailable. Not that he was himself insensible to the bitter whispers behind his back that his luck would soon run out if the Burmese attacked again. 'Those who rise too high have much further to fall', so his rivals warned. Chom Rang was unconcerned. Another invasion might even work to his advantage. 'When the floods arrive, bring a jar' or so they say. For how could the king at Ayutthaya interfere in the distant south if the Burmese embroiled them in hostilities again?

The procession reached Wat Tha Rua, situated on a hill facing east overlooking the bay. The temple buildings and grounds were lush with flowers, offerings and candles. Yellow cloth garlanded the stupas and statues. Pungent smoke from incense burners swirled in opaque clouds, mingling with the heady mists of ylang ylang and jasmine oils, those twin perfumes of matrimonial bliss. Gongs clanged, bells chimed, and chanting monks droned. The wedding party was crossing the threshold from the mundane into the divine.

Lord Chom Rang secured his high-pointed *lomphok* on his head and led his daughter into the shrine hall. It had taken months to reach this day while negotiations to decide the bride price had travelled back and forth. Complex consultations with astrologers had dragged on and on until a mutually auspicious date had finally been agreed upon. Meanwhile the couple was not getting any younger. Chom Rang had feared that Pimon might even pass away before this day was reached. Ever mindful of the price of everything, the governor could not help but calculate the cost of these extended celebrations. This time better be worth its promise, he mused, unlike Chan's first disastrous foray. Still, his new role as governor would offer ample opportunities to refill his personal treasure chests again.

His daughter was radiant, as he had expected, outshining every woman in her beauty and poise, with the exception of her sister, Lady Thong Di who – to her credit – had dressed simply so as not to court comparison with her elder sister on her special day. His youngest daughter was always impeccable in matters of etiquette. It was a pity that his middle girl, Lady Mook, had not done the same. She was injudiciously decked out in a gaudy brocade of many colours with too much paint upon her face, more dancing girl than noblewoman. Nor had the girl inherited the beauty of her Malay mother. Mahsia claimed she had Arab blood, accounting for her fine features and abundant dark brown hair. Chom Rang suspected it was more Chulia from the Coromandel. Poor Mook favoured her stocky father, with thick ankles and a moon face. But she had made a good marriage and was happy enough with her lot in life. Silly woman, though. She would never be able to compete. It was seemlier not to play the peacock when you only had the attributes of a common duck.

He glanced back at his wife bringing up the rear, his tempestuous Mahsia, still an attractive woman and a force to be reckoned with. Her public disdain for the occasion, muttering prayers to ward off the pollution of entering a temple, quietly amused him. Almost forty years on, she was as resolute in her opposition to Buddhist ritual as on the day of their own marriage. Mahsia was dressed in Muslim garb, her head shrouded in a vast *songket* shawl, refusing to allow anyone to see her face. No wonder his daughters were so spirited.

Chom Rang bowed his head to acknowledge the arrival of his sons with their wives, concubines and who knew how many children, and felt the usual acute pang of unfulfilled promise. How strange the disposition of his family! He had bred a weighing scale: Lady Chan and Lady Thong Di in one basket, his sons on the other side, and sturdy Lady Mook holding the fulcrum in balance. The girls were his treasures, and the boys, Tha Wan and Sa Ming, the bad karma of his existence. He blamed his wife, of course. She had indulged her sons all their lives. Thus, his family achieved the Middle Way; perhaps the Dharma decreed it should be so. He had accepted it long ago. Almost.

His thoughts were interrupted by the arrival of the party of the groom accompanied by the piping of flutes. Phaya Pimon came first, richly dressed in yellow silken *chong kraben* and a high-collared jacket of gold-edged blue brocade, sporting an impossibly tall *lomphok*. Undoubtedly, he was of noble bearing but still as ugly as a toad, despite his finery. Not that it mattered in the least, thought the governor. Princely lineage was more than sufficient to blind anyone to repulsive features.

The governor made his formal *wai* of greeting then stepped back to proffer his daughter forward. Lady Chan meekly took her place beside her future husband. Before the golden statue of the Lord Buddha, the couple bowed deeply, lit candles and incense, and arranged garlands of flowers around the lotus base. Then they fell to their knees in obeisance, touching their foreheads to the marble floor as humble supplicants, whilst chanting the invocation to the Buddha.

Mahsia hid her face, reciting her own verses even louder, hands uplifted to the heavens that she might shut out the recitation and beseech forgiveness for her attendance at this unclean event. But she could not resist peeping. With satisfaction, she observed when slaves bore in a weighty teak box containing Phaya Pimon's dowry gift, sizeable enough even to please her. When the time came, she unwillingly submitted to partaking in the ritual herself, initially feigning hesitation until her husband firmly gripped her arm, giving her no choice but to comply. Together they looped the rope of jasmine flowers around the new couple to join them and tied the silken cord around their wrists to bind them for the rest of their lives. Or until they divorced, Mahsia thought wryly. When the monks came forward to begin their long and tedious mantras, she retreated again into her private prayers, ignoring when the couple's foreheads were anointed with a dot of fragrant wax. That seemed close to forbidden magic to her. Her disapproval rose another notch.

Lady Thong Di was also conflicted by her presence in the temple. Martim had shuffled uncomfortably from the start until he had insisted on taking the children into the temple grounds to play 'so that they would not disturb the occasion'. It was an excuse. Her husband did not feel it godly to be witness to heathen practices, nor did he wish his children to be overly exposed to the ancestral beliefs. Her feelings were more complicated. For many years she had worshipped the Christian god and attended Mass at the mission. She had not entered the wat since her girlhood. Yet the familiar rituals and the awesome stillness of the Lord Buddha filled her with a peace she seldom experienced on her knees before the bleeding Christ on his brutal cross. It flooded her with guilt that Lord Jesus' great sacrifice for mankind did not touch her soul as much as the gentle inward gaze of the Enlightened One. Would she be punished for her sacrilegious thoughts? *'Dear God, forgive me. I have no choice. It is my sister's wedding day!'*

Her eyes strayed over to her children, Martinha and Felipe, chasing about outside with their many cousins, shepherded by Martim and a host of servants. Love washed away her self-reproach. They were different from the rest. Special. Touched by a golden brush. They would never belong in this wat. It was right for them to be raised the Christian way. Jesus welcomed everyone, whatever their colour, creed or language, as the priests told them. She had accepted estrangement for their sake. It was the price that must be paid.

Turning her focus back to the wedding couple, Thong Di shuddered inwardly at the prospect of her sister's coming intimacy in the bed of her new husband. Imagine Phaya Pimon touching her slender body, his gnarled hands on her smooth dusky skin, and his fleshy lips sucking on her tender mouth! Yet her sister, for her part, seemed almost to relish the alliance. Lady Chan was delighted to have landed the governor of Phattalung for a husband – even if she would spend very little time with him over the coming years. He could not join her as a husband should, for he must reside in his province at the king's command. Perhaps that was why Chan was so eager to wed him? All the benefits of a marriage without any of the disadvantages. Apart from tonight, of course. That she would be unable to avoid.

2

The Stones of Immortality

Tharua town, Jangsylan. February 1765

A few weeks later, when all the festivities had run their course, Lady Mook and Lady Thong Di were sent on a somewhat delicate mission on behalf of their father. Now that life had returned to normal, it was time to begin the task of ensuring that the business of this busy trading community continued to pass through the proper channels. By that, of course, Governor Chom Rang meant through his hands. Every transaction, import, export, raw material and item of produce must render its due portion to the new governor of Thalang, the expected compensation for the honourable lord who shouldered the onerous commitments of public office.

In the months leading up to his appointment, control had either been weak or non-existent. As a result, the regular collection of rents, taxes and duties had languished. It was time to rectify this sorry state of affairs. 'When the cat is not there, the mice are happy,' Chom Rang had reminded his daughters. 'In recent times, the people have made profit out of the state's loss. It is my noble duty, not only to reinstate the correct levies, but also to gather in back debts.' The governor spoke with no apparent sense of absurdity. He was enjoined to pay the royal treasury a set tribute. Everything else collected went straight into the governor's own coffers. But who of all 'people' had benefited more than Chom Rang himself during this recent interregnum? As a private citizen, he had lined his pockets for years on his many sources of undeclared income. He knew every devious trick to avoid taxation. Which made him the ideal choice for high office, of course. Who better than he to root out those who shirked their civic responsibility?

As a royal appointee, naturally, it was unbecoming for him to soil his own hands in commerce, nor could he rely on local agents – who would cream off goodly sums for themselves, the dogs. A nobleman had only one recourse – his family. His two sons would be his representatives, the public face, but they could never be trusted to be in sole charge. His preference as deputy was his eldest daughter, Lady Chan, his usual business partner, but she was still enjoying her first weeks of marital harmony at their country estate. Fate had gifted him two other daughters. This was the ideal time to involve them in family affairs.

Which found the two women early one morning making their way by bearer through the most insalubrious alleys of Tharua, heading for Chinatown. It was a distasteful journey. The stench from open sewers blocked by animal carcasses and human detritus jostled for entrance to their genteel noses with the alien reek of unsavoury food stuffs. Thong Di held a cloth soaked in perfume against her face; her sister had sticks of cinnamon and lemongrass bound in pandanus leaf. Despite the steamy interior of the litter, the sisters chose not to open the curtains. They wished neither to be seen nor observed, although few who witnessed their procession were ignorant of their identity. Rumour circulated faster than disease in this small port settlement.

At their destination, they stepped down into a street less squalid than the surrounding alleys. From upper windows, scantily clad girls with pale dreamy faces and dark hollow eyes leaned over to observe them. There was money in these establishments, even if it was coin shamefully befouled by degrading trades. Shrouding themselves with shawls, as much to hide from the vile sights as to disguise themselves, the sisters hurried through an unremarkable doorway into a narrow corridor, leaving their slaves and ladies out on the street. This was personal business.

It was gloomy and silent within in sharp contrast to the bright morning sunshine outside, as though neither light nor sound had ever penetrated this dusty interior. Up a rickety staircase they went, brushing against customers – more shades than human beings – who flattened themselves against the wall as they passed. They were led into a room overlooking the front of the building. Or rather not overlooking anything; the windows were firmly shuttered. It was always night in there.

Scattered candles cast dim pools of pale-yellow light, illuminating random objects. Flickering shadows from tiny burners sent thin fingers creeping up the bare plaster walls. The room smelt rank, of bitter-sweet odour, smoke, and the underlying stench of humanity. As their eyes adjusted, rectangular shapes formed themselves into mahogany beds inlaid with mother-of-pearl, an incongruous luxury in the bare and shabby chamber. No doubt, this was the best room in the house, meant for the rich to enjoy in private. In the middle ground, a low teak table rose before them, host to a tray of scattered paraphernalia. And lying on the bed, attended by a squatting, sullen-faced girl, was their brother, Tha Wan, dressed only in his loincloth. His neck was stretched back on a wooden headrest and his eyes were closed. By his side lay his pipe.

Mook waved her hand in imperious dismissal; the girl fled. Thong Di flung back the shutters. Sunlight darted into every unfamiliar corner, a starving animal searching out its prey. Tha Wan groaned, hands to eyes, muttering foul curses. He was awake but hardly sensible.

'Get up, miserable wretch!' Mook commanded. 'Your honourable father needs you. Matters of government await.'

'Fuck off,' growled her brother, rolling over and scrabbling for his pipe. His fingers fumbled, knocking it to the floor. It was an elegant piece, ornate silver bowl with ivory stem. The pipe of a man of wealth and status. Opium cared not from whence you came.

'You want me to send in the men to drag you out? If you come easily, we will take you home to bathe and change your soiled linens. And eat. You look dreadful. Have you been here all night?'

His answer was a shrug.

'If you choose the hard way, and we have to use force, you will be taken straight to Father. Who will be mightily entertained to see you, no doubt. Or perhaps you would prefer brother Sa Ming was given your duties? If they have become too onerous for you –'

Tha Wan's grunt was accompanied by his struggle to rise. The sisters did not assist him. With his feet finally planted on the floor, he sank his head into his hands and rubbed at his temples. 'Cease your prattle, you witch. I am coming. I will behave. I promise to be a good boy. So, your new role is nursemaid to your brother, is it? What an important responsibility! But, you're a woman. What else can you aspire to than minding wayward children? Look at you, with your thick legs and fat, piggy face! Who would want you for the only other thing a woman is use for?' He raised his ashen face, his lips parted in a feral sneer.

Lady Thong Di stepped forward and slapped her brother hard across his face. 'You're lucky Chan is not here today or she would have broken that pipe across your sorry head! I am somewhat gentler in my approach. But no less adamant. Lady Mook and I are here, not because we are your servants, but because we are the right hand of our honourable father. Lord Chom Rang requires you to put your name to several documents by which you are to assign all your rights as agents of the governor to me and my sisters. From now on, you merely act as go-between in matters of commerce and tax farming. Ladies of nobility do not dirty their hands with common traders and tin miners. But, as your hands are all already mired in filth, it shouldn't bother you one bit.'

Her brother's gaze speared her with darts of impotent rage but he possessed neither the strength nor will to oppose his sisters in any meaningful way. Tha Wan might be a pathetic and self-indulgent man but he was no fool where his own self-interest was concerned. In return for his compliance, he would be rewarded with wealth enough to drink, gamble and smoke himself to an early death. Her elder brother would never raise sufficient energy to free himself from either his opium cravings or his sibling oppressors. How beneficial the 'stones of immortality' were in maintaining the harmony of the family!

The sordid business of the day done, Lord Tha Wan was dispatched home to be bathed and restored. The sisters now intended to reward themselves for their successful undertaking. Why waste the visit into town without making the most of its attractions? Rumour had it that the market was a hive of activity, busier than ever of late. Traders had been running riot moving stock before the imminent imposition of even heavier duties. Merchants had flocked to Thalang in recent weeks, expecting easy terms. The central marketplace near the harbour was alive with more than the usual merchants, both foreign and local, all keen to take advantage of the current situation, which everyone knew was about to change.

The place was swarming, yet in moments a swathe was cleared for the noble party. People with money to spend were easily recognised. Lady Mook and Lady Chan insisted on alighting, having no intention of merely observing from the distance of their chair while their maids had all the fun. From then on, they browsed like other customers, closely flanked by their ladies and the anxious guards, all nervous of the possible dangers in such milling crowds. If anything happened to the ladies, their lives would be on the line.

A dizzying array of faces and costumes met them as they wandered, the entire archipelago on display. Siamese, Malays, Chulias, Arabs, Chinese, Javanese, Buginese, Achinese, Burmese, and many others they could only guess at, mixed cheek-by-jowl with local businessmen. Everyone was shouting at once in an organised hurly-burly of commerce: sing-song calls from vendors advertising wares, fierce arguments over prices, cries of feigned horror at exorbitant requests, the to-and-fro of bargaining, raucous laughter when deals were struck, curses vented when a sale fell through. Even more surprising in this polyglot mob, business was entirely conducted in a bastardised Malay that somehow did the trick. Everyone seemed to understand well enough. Barely a word of Siamese was spoken.

To amble about this hectic place was an experience unimaginable in the cool, calm halls of home. Despite the mire underfoot and the press of unwashed bodies, the unfamiliar din and the lack of any of the accepted courtesies, the noble ladies were visibly affected by the dynamic energy and ingenious spirit of the place, perceptible enough almost to be a living, breathing force. This was the lifeblood of these people, the common thread that brought them together in a language of commerce as old as time, an instinct shared by all. There was always money to be made, even in the humblest trade.

It seemed to Lady Thong Di that every item she had ever dreamed of – and some she had never even imagined – were located somewhere in the maze of stalls, the little bamboo shacks, and the wooden shophouses. Those who did not even own a cart, placed a mat upon the dusty ground and laid their wares out before them. And both rich and poor were not too proud to squat and browse. Luxury items and humble fare were jumbled together in haphazard harmony. One never knew quite what to expect. There was almost too much choice, the sisters agreed. It made their heads spin.

Selected merchants were usually invited to their home, bringing requested goods for their perusal. But here, the choice was limitless. There was much to tempt the idle shopper that would never have been on their list of needs. *'Buy now, one time only, never see again, this my last one, genuine copy, come pretty lady, your husband will approve, don't miss your chance, best price, made for the Emperor of China ... !*' Textiles, gold and silver jewellery, gemstones, pearls, copper goods, silverware, vibrant feathers, silk purses and beaded slippers, fine ceramics, perfumes and oils, birds' nests, spices, pretty song birds, and all manner of other luxuries were arrayed side-by-side with wooden items, woven baskets, terracotta pots, local fruits and vegetables, chillies, pungent roots, fresh fish and prawns, slabs of pork, live chickens and ducks, jars of oil, sacks of rice, pungent *kapi* and *belacan*, sour-sweet *nam pla*, dried fish and fermented beancurd. The smells and colours, textures and sounds bewitched their senses. It was impossible not to lose all sense of time – and all good sense itself – with such enticements on show.

In one corner of the square there were even people for sale, slaves of every race, age and gender. They stood or crouched in groups, some hostile, some traumatised, some acquiescent, some fearful, depending no doubt on the circumstances of their slavery. There were debtors either selling themselves or sold by their families; there were the desperate poor for whom slavery was a preferable option to freedom; others were criminals who had been spared the lash, or even worse. Of course, a number were also innocents snatched from nearby settlements by pirates. No one asked where the slaves came from. No one cared.

The children were the most wretched: dirty, tear-stained faces, matted hair, and eyes that had already seen too much. Lady Thong Di was sad but realistic. Slavery might be anyone's fate. Who knew what lay in one's future? Jesus said all men were equal in the face of God but that was the law of heaven. Here on earth, if your town was raided, your army lost the battle, or your ship was boarded, everyone knew what to expect, whether lowborn or nobleman. She thought about the slaves her family owned. It wasn't such a bad existence. They were well fed and happy, their lot much better than the average poor farmer. Life was cruel as well as kind. Better to accept and make the best of it.

The sisters wandered back and forth until their girls were heavily laden with cloth, bangles, feathers, and wooden toys for the children. Durians were in season; they filled a basket, sampling the different varieties first before making their choices. At another stall, they tasted little cakes, fried bananas, dumplings and pastries filled with meat and spices. They drank fresh coconut water from the shell and ate slices of its fragrant flesh until their fingers were sticky.

More even than the shopping itself, Thong Di was thrilled by an unaccustomed taste of independence. She was now a mature married woman, a mother herself, from a family of standing. A future role in the commercial life of the island had been bestowed upon her. From now on, a different life presented, one where she could enjoy a public existence without fear of scandal or reproach, like her older sisters. Thong Di was only just beginning to understand the possibilities that lay ahead for her. Best of all, on this most satisfying of shopping expeditions, she had paid out not a single coin. Every trader made the flamboyant gesture of refusing to take payment from the honourable governor's beloved daughters. They were grabbing the chance to make a good impression on the members of the ruling house. Future benefits were worth more than a sale.

By midday, hot and weary, the noble party headed for home, longing now for the silent pavilions of the governor's residence. The streets were busy at the height of the trading day hindering their progress, until their vehicle finally came to a complete stop, and then remained stationary for some time. Inside the sedan, the air was stifling, almost impossible to breathe. Sweat ran down their faces and necks, between their breasts and into every hot and sticky crevice. Lady Mook could stand it no longer. She thrust aside the curtain, fanning herself.

'Why are we waiting?'

Her ladies walking behind, clustered round. 'No one knows, my Lady. We cannot pass. There's too much traffic! Nor can we see ahead.'

Motioning for her sister to join her, they both gamely set forth, the guards hurrying to clear a route until they reached the bottleneck ahead, where the road from the jetty intersected with their path. A huge mob had gathered, swelling as they watched. There was no obvious way for their chair to pass until this crowd had dispersed. Thus, with little choice, the sisters carried on, their curiosity piqued to find the cause of so much excitement, until they emerged on the edge of an open field.

The crowd was arranged around its perimeter, held back by guards brandishing clubs. In the central ground a captive prisoner hung suspended from an upright stake, his body sagging at the knees. The man struggled helplessly against the ropes, jabbering hysterically. Solemn-faced judges in resplendent attire congregated about. A group of monks gathered to one side, chanting and banging gongs, their saffron robes shimmering in the heat of midday. Just then an officer thrust something into the prisoner's mouth; he gulped it down gratefully then began to quieten, slumping against his ropes, his head drooping listlessly. Someone had taken pity on him and slipped him opium to ease his passing.

Lady Mook and Lady Thong Di exchanged a horrified glance. It was impossible to retreat now, for the assembled mass had closed in tight behind. As rumour spread, more and more people flocked to witness the grisly event. 'We must stay here at the front or we may be trampled in the surge,' whispered Mook. 'Moreover, as members of the ruling family, it is fitting we should be witnesses to the act.' Thong Di winced and surreptitiously reached out for her sister's hand. Mook grasped it tightly. They had never before watched an execution.

A sudden outcry heralded the onset. One section of the crowd fell back as an enormous bull elephant with great tusks was ridden through a gap into the central ground. An expectant silence, heavy as the humid air, fell upon the people, curiosity tinged with repulsion. Meanwhile, the beast began its slow progress around the condemned man, while a slow drum thumped in time to the stately tread, a pulse of dread. Lady Thong Di placed a hand on her racing heart. She felt faint and nauseous. But she could not drag her eyes away.

The prisoner raised his head to stare the animal in the eye, then groaned deeply, but the drug had taken effect. He showed less panic now that the time had come – or perhaps it was futile resignation? All the while the elephant circled, his mahout whispering in his great ear, the animal's attention fixed trance-like on the victim. Then, all at once, as if he himself was in control, the beast charged, wrapping his trunk around the prisoner. With mighty force, he wrenched the man off the ground – still bound to the stake – swinging his huge head from side to side. Then he tossed the helpless body high into the air and skewered it on his tusks. The terrible screams were drowned out in the roar that burst from the angry animal, who continued to shake his head, the man writhing in agony, until the body had been loosened and the wretch tumbled to the ground, thick streams of blood spurting from deep wounds.

For long moments, the elephant stood motionless, staring down at his beaten victim who was already more dead than alive. Then he raised one colossal foot, which hovered for an instant over the broken and bleeding body, and stamped down hard. The man's head shattered like a broken egg shell.

Lady Thong Di closed her eyes against the appalling sight, but the image still burned. Earlier that day, she had observed a watermelon dislodged from a passing cart and tumbling to the ground. The bursting of the man's head resembled that sticky mess. Despite her revulsion, she found herself transfixed by the remains of what had so recently been a living man, now more akin to hunks of meat and offal on a market stall. Her prurience was keener than her disgust. The crowd demonstrated a similar reaction. Although some had fainted, several had spewed up, and wailing could be heard – no doubt from relatives of the victim – the initial horror also provoked a disquieting sense of exhilaration, even hysteria. Loud cheers rang out each time the elephant trampled on the body, followed by shouts and even laughter at the pulped carcass. It was as if they were watching an entertainment put on for their enjoyment. Or did they feign bravado to protect themselves from full realisation of the utter horror they had witnessed?

'What had the poor fellow done to deserve that?' muttered Thong Di. 'It is many years since such a method of execution was carried out, surely? I thought it was only done for treason!'

Mook shrugged. 'Something very bad, to be sure. Only the king sanctions such deaths,' she replied, her face pale, a cloth pressed to her mouth, as if fearful she too would vomit.

A bystander overheard them. 'The king – or the viceroy, do you mean? There's not much difference between the two these days. The governor can do what he likes with the Viceroy of Ligor in his pocket. That poor wretch was a business rival of Lord Chom Rang from Ban Lippon village. The governor claims he cheated him – who knows? He certainly got his revenge today, eh? A lesson to us all ...' A friend grabbed his arm and whispered something frantically in his ear. The informant drew back, his face a picture of abject fear. Who knew that these fine ladies were the governor's own daughters? The two men instantly vanished into the crowd.

'Is this the consequence of absolute power?' Thong Di asked her sister as they finally made their way home, the high spirits of the morning a distant memory.

'What do you think?' Mook replied. 'That man was right, though. More than anything, this act was a message to the people that the new governor will not be crossed. Those who do, face the direst of fates. Yet it is a dangerous precedent, all the same. A man can rise but a man can also fall. The people will not forget today. I pray it does not come back one day to haunt us. That, my sister, is the true consequence of absolute power.'

3

The Mangrove Swamp

Phuket Town. March 1766

'Cousin Thian! Cousin Thian! *Lanun*! *Sa Lat!* We have seen them!'

Lord Thian was deep inside his meditation when the frantic shouts of his young cousins dragged him from inner peace to raucous consciousness. How long had they been calling? His detachment from earthly thoughts had dulled him to the outside world. Might meditation sometimes be an unwholesome distraction from reality? An intriguing notion.

'Are you there, Cousin?' the urgent voices pleaded, hammering on the door.

Thian opened his eyes, gave himself a few seconds to gather himself, and returned to the present moment. The children had said 'Pirates'. Was this some silly game? Or was danger at hand? In a single graceful movement, he rose from his cushion and padded to the door, wrapping his robe tighter about his slender frame.

'Quiet!' he whispered as he opened the door. 'You will wake the household! Come inside –' The four children burst in, all shouting at once. With a finger to his lip, he made them stop and directed them to sit down beside him on the mat. 'Now, one at a time. Tell me your story. Where are these evil pirates?'

***

The track twisted down the cliffside through dense jungle strewn with boulders, fallen trees and dead ends. From the road above, the beach had seemed easily accessible, but the further they descended, the more distant it became. The roll and crash of waves, so loud from above, now faded away together with the bright late-morning sun. They found themselves stranded in a dank and shadowy world draped in coiled lianas that hid a myriad of potential dangers.

The children had known these forests all their lives. Before entering, they had rubbed their arms and legs in dirt against mosquitos and leeches and bound cloths around their bare feet. Dangers could come from above, below, and from any passing bough against which their shoulders brushed. Armed with sturdy branches, they cut their way, scrutinising the ground for ants and scorpions, the trees for snakes, and the route ahead for obstacles to their progress. They journeyed in silence, straining their ears for any unexpected sound.

The further they ventured inside, the more they realised that this was a riskier adventure than they had anticipated. Ma Li and Nilip had told their maids that they were going to Lady Mook's pavilion to play with Chai and Kaew, her daughters. Those young ladies had given a similar lie to their own servants. In fact, the four cousins had met in the spice garden behind the kitchen, from where they had cajoled fruit and banana leaf-wrapped rice. They had bundled their picnic and gourds of water in sarongs tied on their backs and set out, make believing they were carefree peasants off to work in the fields, the archetypal fiction of the upper classes.

The forest was alive with sound; even its silence hummed. Unseen monkeys high in the canopy mocked their stumbling progress, birds shrieked menacingly – but what worried most were the rustles and thuds, hisses and clicks, and other worrisome noises that they couldn't identify. Did tigers hunt this close to the shore? Might there be wild boar or rhinos, perhaps even a rogue elephant? Or a panther? Was that slight movement in the leaves a stalking leopard? And what about the crowded forest floor, a seething mass of insect life? Soldier ants could kill if enough decided to join the feast.

Relief brought excited smiles as they finally heard the thump of breaker on shore. A stronger sunlight now filtered through the trees and the way ahead thinned out. At last, they found themselves treading on sandy patches and then bursting out into the blinding sunlight of the muddy strand. For protection, they pulled cloths from their necks to wrap about their heads. Dumping their lunch on shady rocks at the edge of the beach, the eager band shrugged off their outer clothes and scampered into the water. If anyone saw them, they would be in serious trouble. But who would visit such a secluded cove in the heat of the day? Certainly no one who knew them would risk the midday sun.

Splashing into the foam, they laughed and played as children do. None of them could swim but they were in little danger, for they had chosen their spot wisely. The tide was on the turn but the undertow was gentle. This small lagoon, more like a pond, was protected by curved headlands on either side, and the mass of nearby Koh Sirae island. The sea was turquoise glass. Further out, where the deeper coral lay, the waters darkened into a glistening violet blue. The colours were fantastical, lustrous hues no jewel or textile could hope to imitate.

The afternoon passed in an idyll. They ate, they dozed, they bathed, they built houses out of sand – and ran about like wild things, an impossible liberty in the tightly restricted world from whence they came. They floated face down in the shallows, and disturbed darting minnows, burrowing crabs, iridescent needlefish. A flamboyant lion fish bobbed into view, a galleon in full sail, its spiky venomous fins causing a hurried exit back to the safety of the sand.

'Your nose is red!' Chai laughed, pointing at Ma Li some hours later when they were getting ready to leave. 'Your mother will ask you where you've been!'

Ma Li giggled. 'And you are black as rice farmers!' she responded. 'You think they won't ask where you've all been as well?' It was true. The skins of other three had deepened to tawny after only a few hours in the open sun, her brother Nilip, the darkest. The two siblings were not at all alike. 'I don't care. We just tell them we were playing in the grounds.'

'They will be angry at us!' Kaew was nervous of her mother's wrath.

'Let them be angry!' Ma Li, whilst giving the appearance of a dutiful daughter, had hidden depths. 'It was worth it. This has been the best day ever!'

Her little brother, Nilip, for Felipe was difficult for Siamese to pronounce, stared at his older sister in adoration. Whatever she said, he would stand by her. At seven, he was the youngest of the group, well used to playing only with girls. The other boys his age were studying with the monks. As a Christian, however, he remained at home to be tutored alongside the girls by a master whose fortuitous fever had presented them with today's golden opportunity.

The climb back up was harder than the scramble down, but their spirits were high. They were young and energetic and scampered up with little injury, apart from scraped knees and the occasional ant bite. Back on the path to town, Chai started up a folk song and they all joined in, dancing and laughing. But their moods changed when they neared the haunted woods, where the road looped around the edge of a gnarled and gloomy mangrove swamp. The locals believed that evil spirits drew in unsuspecting passers-by and fed them to the crocodiles. The children immediately fell silent and quickened their steps, for fear of attracting the attention of stray demons.

Thus, already sensible to danger, they were instantly alerted when noises emanated from the swamp, even before they saw any signs of life. Nor did it sound like malevolent spirits enticing them to their doom. No irresistible singing nor mellifluous voices whispered their names. This was harsh and guttural language. The speech of men.

As they rounded a bend in the road, a rickety bridge crossed a creek flowing inland from the sea to the main river. It was still low tide, so the inlet was barely a stream. Curious now, they tiptoed along the bridge to its centre, peeping through the slats. A narrow *perahu* was beached on the river bed, out of sight of both the coast and the inland road. They strained their ears to catch the distant conversation.

'*Alamaaaak* … !' shouted a voice, accompanied by a splash and the laughter of several men. Someone had fallen off the boat into the shallow waters. The men were speaking Malay, not unusual in Thalang, where more people spoke Malay even than Siamese. But when a Malay boat hid in the mangroves waiting for the turn of the tide and the arrival of nightfall, it did not usually bode well for the local inhabitants. These men were not there to trade or fish.

Chai mouthed: 'Pirates!' The others all knew instantly she was right. If they were caught alone on this road, they didn't stand a chance. Four healthy children would be a slaver's dream.

On all fours they crept to the other side, hearts in their mouths, expecting discovery any moment and the sealing of their fates. But they were fortunate. The men had neither seen nor heard them. Once clear of the bridge, they took to their heels and did not stop running until they reached the safety of the town.

'We should warn someone,' Ma Li considered. 'They're planning to raid the river settlements tonight. We must raise the alarm!'

'But they will ask how we know!' protested Kaew. 'Mother will find out where we've been!'

Ma Li was obdurate. 'People might die if we say nothing! Or be dragged off as slaves! A beating from your mother is nothing compared to that. We cannot let it happen!' Felipe burst into tears. It was all too much for him. His sister put her arm around his shoulders, while they gave the matter some consideration.

'I know what we should do!' Chai exclaimed. 'Let's tell Cousin Thian! He can say he saw the pirates himself. That way, no one will know we were there. In fact, once the story of a pirate raid goes around, no one is going to take much notice of us anyway!' It was the ideal solution.

***

'You're sure they were pirates?' Thian inquired. 'Perhaps it was local fishermen catching their sleep before the evening tide?'

The children thought awhile. 'But why would they be so far upstream against the channel? Surely they would stay on the beach under the trees where it wouldn't be so far to travel?' Ma Li suggested.

Thian knew the creek; she was right. Only those with something to hide would be in that location. 'Go to your pavilions. You're hot and sweaty. Bathe. Then lay down and rest a while. Leave this to me. There's been enough mischief for one day.' He looked down sternly at them. 'I am astonished at your deception. While I might expect it from your male cousins, who are imprudent and reckless, I cannot believe that you girls would shame yourselves like this. Chai and Kaew! Your mother would be horrified. And Martinha! To bring your little brother into danger. I thought you were a sensible young lady!' Thian was one of the few people in the family, other than her father, who called her by her Christian name. It had always endeared her to him.

The children's faces crumpled; a tear ran down Kaew's face. Little Felipe was already sobbing; Thian stroked his salt-dried hair. 'Come, little cousin. No tears. I will let you into a secret, you little monkeys. I used to do exactly the same when I was your age. We always went to the beach to play and were often beaten for it! But Cousin Thian is now a grown man. He must be serious and boring and chastise naughty children who do the same ...' Thian tickled them until they broke into giggles, wiping their cheeks and runny noses on the backs of their hands. He was never angry with them for long. 'Now run along and do as you are told for once!'

Thian was the eldest grandchild of Governor Chom Rang, the son of Lady Chan from her first marriage. At eighteen years of age – a man already – he was something of a disappointment to his ambitious mother. Lady Chan had once had high hopes for her son: he was handsome, intelligent and of excellent character, having inherited his father's physical blessings with none of his moral defects. She had regarded Thian as the perfect heir to her own father, for which role he had been groomed since early boyhood. His intellectual achievements were celebrated; he had studied at Ayutthaya with the finest scholars of the day. He had also acquitted himself with distinction in the martial disciplines.

Yet this golden boy had no wish to marry, be a warrior or involve himself in political life or commerce. Instead, he was determined to devote his life to his studies as a Buddhist monk. This announcement had come as a terrible shock to Lady Chan, who regarded the news with as much repulsion as if he had become a dissolute womaniser like his father and uncles. She had ranted and raved about his decision, but the boy had remained adamant. Finally, as a filial compromise, Thian had promised to first spend five years in the secular world. His mother had sent him to the family house in Phuket Town to oversee their mining interests, where the most alluring worldly temptations were on offer, hoping to distract him from his chosen path, but so far to no avail. When Thian was not working, he was either studying or meditating. He lived a quiet, contemplative life remote from the rest of the household. Perhaps her son's vocation might be the price that was demanded to atone for his own father's worthless life?

Today, however, he was to be roused from his hermit-like existence and thrust into the role of military leader. It was the seminal moment of his life. Who could foresee that misbehaving children, pirates up to no good, and a good deed done might stop a young man in his tracks and change his life forever? Such is the serendipity of existence.

Thian rode into the town at speed and summoned the militia. While messengers were sent to the riverine villages warning them to evacuate into the forest for safety, Thian led a ragtag assembly of locals armed with a modest assortment of weapons and iron tools. There was no time to wait for a military detachment from the fort at Ban Don. If they were to stop this raid, they had to make do with what they had: a gaggle of farmers, miners and a few veterans with military experience.

By now, it was late afternoon, the time the Malays call *petang*, when the languorous heat of day still hangs thick in the torpid air, and few eyes fail to succumb to the desire to drowse. Everywhere was quiet and still. Thian's force numbered about thirty men and boys. He dispatched the more experienced to approach on the turn of the tide from the direction of the sea, the rest he led to the bridge itself. The time for their attack was to be the exact moment when the heat broke. Like a shade dropping down on the window of the day, the heavy febrile air would all at once grow cooler, the fierce light would abate, and a sea breeze would begin to stir. And at that very instant, the twin assaults would launch.

From their vantage point on the bridge, they observed the men aboard the perahu. Those they could see moved idly about the deck, insensible to being watched. Others soon appeared, evidently from their naps, and joined in the unhurried preparations. There were probably ten or so in total, all armed with *keris*. No doubt they also carried guns. Thian himself bore a musket, as did a few others, but he did not wish for a running battle. Even though they outnumbered the sailors three to one, these Malays would be the more experienced fighters. They could not risk an extended struggle. Their only advantages were speed, surprise – and an unexpected attack from the rear.

Tension was high as the moments crept inexorably towards their deadline. Mostly they were farmers, fishermen and miners, humble folk defending their homes and fields. The reputation of the unpredictable *orang laut* was the stuff of nightmares for all such coastal peoples. The longer the men waited, the more time was afforded them to dwell upon the brutal fate that might await them on the blade of a deadly keris. Thian prayed that their nerve would hold.

Finally, the curtain of the day fell and the heat waned, all in one sudden instance. Thian directed his men to slither down the embankment into the creek, the water deeper now as the tide rolled in. The perahu bobbed in the rising current, momentarily occupying the sailors in their preparations, which was in Thian's favour. He could only hope that their other force was making its way from the seaward direction. Without them, they could not prevail.

His heart was beating so loud it was nigh impossible to believe that no one could hear it as they waded towards the boat, pressing themselves into the overhang of the bank. It would only take one sailor to venture a glance in their direction, and they would be finished. But their luck held. Moments later, a wild shout from the boat indicated that the raiders had spotted their fellow militia downstream, distracting all on board from their inland approach. Thian and his men thus took their chance, swarming over the side, startling their prey.

In minutes it was over. A few were killed or maimed on both sides, but the casualty list was relatively light. The pirates surrendered when they realised they had little chance of escape or victory. Thian demanded restraint of his men, for he was more interested in captives than dead bodies. They had to be questioned. He was not convinced that these Malays were simple slavers.

Under interrogation, the prisoners claimed that they were fishermen from Langkawi, an island to the south, a notorious nest of pirates, inhabited by locals who might fish one day and raid shipping the next. But few believed their story. Their dialects suggested something else. With rumours of Burmese activity threatening Siam's northern borders, it was likely that the Sultan of Queddah was biding his time for an opportunity to snatch the lucrative island of Thalang for himself. This might be a scouting expedition. Torture was applied, and following the excruciating flaying of a few wretched victims, Thian's suspicions were confirmed. They had indeed been sent by the sultan to reconnoitre an invasion. The men were executed and their heads returned to Queddah. Pirate or spy, the sultan was given an ominous warning.

The local men were fired up by their success and the bloodlust of their revenge, particularly when the people of the town received them back like heroes. Usually when raiders came, villagers took their most precious belongings and fled into the forest, accepting that when they returned their houses would be ransacked and burnt – and some of their friends and families would be dead or stolen away. This time, however, with adequate warning to prepare themselves, they had stayed and fought. It was an empowering moment for those usually helpless in the face of fate.

With mixed emotions, Thian left the town to its celebrations. Like them, he was carried on a wave of euphoria, but the lives he had taken weighed heavy upon him. His actions were contrary to everything he believed in. In his daily life, he would never even swat a fly or squash a mosquito between his palms. Yet today he had blown a hole in a man's chest and then ordered others to be decapitated, after witnessing their agonising torment. How could he justify that to his own conscience?

Nevertheless, he could not deny that it had been the right and necessary thing to do. It was paramount to safeguard the helpless people under his care. Duty to the poor and needy was essential to the Eight Precepts. But so was avoiding violence at all costs. He must now spend some time in contemplation to dwell upon the nature of leadership and responsibility set alongside his spiritual beliefs. Had he taken pleasure in the deaths of those men, or had he executed them only for a higher cause, whilst continuing to value their individual lives? The whole matter rendered him conflicted and less certain of his future than he had ever been. The most unsettling part was that he had a sense, perhaps for the first time in his life, that commanding this band of men had been as natural as breathing. His thoughts whirled back and forth. No longer could he find that calm inner centre wherein he was accustomed to keep the empty temptations of the physical world at bay. Nor did he wish to at this moment.

* * *

That night at dinner, the house was abuzz with reports that a huge fleet from Queddah had sailed up the creek only to be defeated by young Lord Thian and an army of local men. The children eavesdropped on the talk, out of sight of the adults on the veranda steps, having stolen from their apartments after they had been sent to bed. Everyone was eagerly awaiting the return of the hero of the hour, the saviour of the town. No one paid attention to the little ones.

'Chan will be so proud of her son!' Lady Thong Di exclaimed as the family waited at the dinner table for the return of their young nephew.

There were murmurs of agreement. This was a significant coup for the family, which was unpopular amongst many of the settlers. The tax burdens and levies on the poor miners in Phuket Town were onerous and Governor Chom Rang was regarded as exceptionally venal. Today, however, the handsome young scion of the family had earned the people's respect. The governor's family might take a high percentage of their tin and rice, but for once protection had been rendered in return. Had Lord Thian not been alert, they might have lost all. Perhaps their burdens were justified.

Lady Mook, however, was pensive. 'Chan will enjoy it, of course, as we all do. It was exactly the sort of challenge she had hoped for her eldest son when she insisted he wait before committing to the temple. She hoped he would find earthly distractions to replace his desire for study and contemplation.'

Martim Rozells laughed. 'I think she was expecting a rather less heroic form of distraction than leading the local militia! More in the way of loose women and gambling dens!'

'Even better if she can persuade him now to take up the warrior's life,' replied Lord At, husband of Lady Mook. 'This adventure might give him a taste for it.'

'Do you really believe there was an entire fleet? It seems unlikely. Were we in actual danger of a major attack?' his wife wondered.

'– if this town could sell rumour as fast as it makes it, we would be richer than Melaka!' The heads of all swivelled round and they broke into smiles as young Thian strode into the room. He was dusty and sweat-stained, but more spirited than usual; his skin had the glow of outdoors where usually it was pale from hours of study. 'Of course, there was no fleet! Just one perahu and a few wretched sailors. But, a danger all the same. They were looking for slaves. And anything else that they could steal. But most of all they were after information. We need to keep a close watch on Queddah in the coming months. Sultan Muhammed Jiwa is up to no good.'

'As usual. But we have enough to worry about with the Burmese,' Lord At responded. 'We would do better to court Queddah in these dangerous times. We might need them in the months to come.'

Martim scoffed. 'Queddah wants the island. You can court him all you like and Muhammed Jiwa will let you. He will do business with you. He will entertain you at his palace like royalty. But it won't stop him trying to pry Thalang from Siam when the time is ripe. And perhaps that is not such a bad idea? The governor himself agrees with me. He doesn't much care who is our overlord, as long as we are left alone to conduct our own affairs!'

Lady Thong Di lowered her eyes, embarrassed by her husband's words. As usual, he had drunk too much. Wine always loosened his tongue. There were things that one might think, but never deign to speak. Martim still did not understand Siamese ways. Her father might have spoons in many pots, but he would not be happy to hear them discussed so blatantly in the hearing of the house slaves. Once an idea was voiced, it became reality. And this reality was treason in the wrong hands.

Thian wisely stepped in to change the subject. 'I should bathe and change. Please, carry on. Eat. The food is already attracting ants!'

But they insisted he join them as he was, and recount everything from beginning to end, so he settled down cross-legged around the low table and eagerly tucked into the food. He had not felt this hungry for some time. He must take regular exercise in future and involve himself more in daily life. Indeed, there was much to learn from many things, not just books. Finally, he pushed his bowl away and sat upright, his audience eager to hear the story of the day's adventure. Even the household slaves gathered around the doorway to overhear at first hand the tale that was on everyone's lips.

As they had hoped, the four young children were not given the praise due for their accidental discovery. Their unorthodox day out was never discovered in the furore that followed the pirate incursion. Yet undoubtedly their action had saved many people from the slave markets, as well as the destruction of several villages.

Martinha lay wide awake that night unable to sleep, the conflicting experiences of the day running through her head. She imagined the capture of the pirates and what must have happened afterwards when they had been tortured and beheaded. Thian's account had been gruesome. She felt responsible for those deaths, even if they had been evil men wishing harm on the people of Thalang. Was it a sin to cause people to die? Or would God forgive an act if it was done for the benefit of others?

Other aspects of the dinner conversation also played on her mind. All that talk of war and occupation! The Burmese and the Sultan of Queddah! How was it that she did not know that they were living in such dangerous times? What had her father meant by wishing for a Malay overlord to conquer Thalang? There was so much in the adult world she did not understand. Martinha vowed to herself that from now on she would keep her ears alert and her mouth shut. Adults talked, both family and servants. That was how children found out what they were not supposed to know.

4

The Greatest City in the World

Ayutthaya, capital of Siam. November 1766

The rain poured down incessantly day after miserable day, but for the residents of the great city it was a blessing from the heavens. For four months, the largest enemy army ever assembled on Siamese soil had been camped outside their walls. An estimated 40,000 Burmese, arriving in a pincer movement from both the northern and the western coasts, had made their inexorable trek into the interior, laying waste to everything in their path, until they reached Ayutthaya. And waited.

Waiting is, of course, the very nature of siege warfare for, given time, all sieges must break. Think of Troy, that abiding exemplar. The invaders might retreat, unable to breach mighty walls or because their forces have been devastated by the diseases that run rampant when vast numbers of men live in insanitary conditions. Sometimes, disputes lead to fights which become insubordinations and finally mutiny, as bored, hopeless men take matters into their own hands. Alternatively, the besieged city sues for peace, after months of deprivations and despair, starved out when every last cat, dog and rat has been consumed, and epidemic infests each nook and cranny. Or the unthinkable happens – the walls are breached, and the enemy finally wreaks its revenge. The gods themselves would cover their faces at those consequences.

King Ekatthat was sure Ayutthaya would prevail and that the Burmese army would be broken on the great walls that had withstood for centuries. One of the largest cities in the world, Ayutthaya was situated on an island above the flood plain surrounded by water, thus blessed by natural defences. Inside the walls lived over one million inhabitants, with elegant houses, businesses, streets, parks and gardens, open spaces, palaces, and temples beyond number. Foreigners from all over the world had settled there, each in their own enclaves, from humble hovels to great buildings reflecting their own architecture, religion and cultures: Chinese, Japanese, Indian, Persian and European, alongside the peoples of the archipelago and Indo-China. Ayutthaya was a nation of its own. How could it fall?

The city was well stocked with food. Three rivers ran through it; there was access to the sea. Its water system was one of the wonders of Asia. The Burmese advance had been slow, giving time to pile up supplies that might last for months. The vast arsenal was full of weapons. Militia had arrived from every part of Siam, sending their best warriors to complement the royal armies. The Burmese could sit and wait as long as they wished, but the Siamese would outlast them. The enemy might launch an attack, but they would never breach the walls. In the end, patience would be rewarded. The king closed the gates with confidence that they could hold out indefinitely. It was the ultimate expression of Buddhist passive resistance.

A terrible price had already been paid for King Ekkathat's obduracy. Whilst Ayutthaya sat in cloistered seclusion, the surrounding lands had been devastated, their villagers either seized or slaughtered. The Burmese had carried off what they wanted until they made a wasteland.

And what they desired most was people. Thousands upon thousands of Siamese had been shipped to Burma. And still the king did nothing. His nobles, generals, the leaders from other provinces and all the court advisors begged him to take the battle to the Burmese king. No matter how large the enemy army, it was far from home and exposed. Forces could be raised elsewhere in Siam to surround the Burmese and cut off their escape to the coast. If Siam fought as one, and the forces in Ayutthaya advanced, the Burmese would be trapped inside a hell of their own creation, wherein they might be destroyed for good. But the king refused to listen. His walls would hold.

Perhaps he would be proved right. That year the rains had come early and lasted late; from July to November, the weather had been wet and cool. The Burmese found themselves living in a world of water. Their flooded camp forced them to abandon the perimeter of Ayutthaya and move to higher ground. The earth was a quagmire, the rice they sequestered mouldy and their vegetables rotted in the ground. Everything was damp: clothes, tents and bedding. Weapons rusted. Diseases multiplied. Throughout the camp, men died of fevers and infections of every type. Surely it was only a matter of time before they relented and returned home?

But King Hsinbushyin of Burma was as stubborn as his counterpart, even if the conditions were almost too intolerable to bear. How long could he keep the men here? It was impossible even to launch an attack in the current conditions. Fires were extinguished by the rain, their gunpowder was so damp it would not light. Any attempt to advance on the walls would end in men drowning in mud. They would be nothing more than sitting targets for the enemy on the walls. And so, the impasse continued.

One early evening, when the rain had slackened and an hour of daylight remained, Lord Thian took a stroll through the elegant streets from his lodgings south of the palace towards the section of the wall where his men patrolled. He was lost in thought. In his eyes, Ayutthaya was the pinnacle of human achievement, a city of temples and cultural treasures where the greatest ruler on earth lived. He had spent his formative years in its monastic schools. It was a microcosm of the entire world, a cosmopolitan environment where almost every race, language and religion on earth had its place, and peace and harmony reigned, driven by mutual cooperation and Buddhist law. One day, when this war was over, Thian intended to devote his life to study, prayer and contemplation. But, until then, he had cast aside his hopes and dreams to ensure that this beacon of Siam remained inviolable. Yet, for all his lofty purpose, these past months had been a trial.

He had brought a levy of men supplied by the Thalang government on the understanding that every district had done similar. Not so. Many provinces, unaffected by the progress of the enemy, had shut their eyes in a way that shocked him. Local rulers in the south were even setting themselves up as petty kings, taking advantage of the tragedy unfolding in the rest of the kingdom. Young Thian was learning a lot about the politics of men. His years of study had prepared him for a purer way of living little reflected in the realities of the world outside.

The young nobleman was thankful for his access to the great libraries, where he spent many hours whiling away the inactivity of the siege. His men were not so fortunate. When they were not on patrol, they had time on their hands, little interested in the cultural delights of the capital city. Instead, they gambled. They whored. They drank and, inevitably, they fought, either amongst themselves or with the militias from other provinces. Thian did his best to distract them, arranging daily training sessions, weapons practice, boxing bouts, races and other activities, but this was not what his men had come for. They were here to save Siam from the Burmese devils, not sit around wasting time. There was little news from the outside world. The longer they waited in inactivity, the more they feared what might be happening to their families and fields back home. Who knew if the Burmese had run riot over the entire country by now?

As he emerged upon the perimeter of the outer walls, Thian viewed the two distinct halves that now encompassed his world. On his right the glorious city shimmered in the golden light of dusk under a silver-grey sky warmed by a copper glow. To his left, a vision of hell. Misty vapours rose from sodden ground; the sky bulged dark with more rain threatening. In the far distance, the tents of the enemy circled the city on the ridges and knolls beyond the plain, a horde beyond number, settling around their cooking fires for another long night.

Across the river lay the first bank of Siamese defences, a new barrier erected during the wet season to delay any Burmese attempt to cross when the dry season began. It was also to prevent desertion, without much success; many detachments sent to hold this barrier had themselves defected to the Burmese. Whole bands of militia with their lords had crossed to the other side while the army inside dwindled. Every day more soldiers crept away under cover of rain or darkness. Thian sighed deeply. When he had left home with his eager band of men, they had been in pursuit of glory. Now they were as miserable and hopeless as the landscape itself.

'It doesn't improve, no matter how long you stare,' a cultured voice broke into his sombre thoughts.

Thian spun round to find himself staring at a man he knew by both sight and reputation, but to whom he had never been formally introduced. He did not move in this man's lofty sphere. It was Lord Sin Wachiraprakan, the governor of the north-western province of Tak, close to the Tennasserim Hills and the Burmese border, a region regularly affected by Burmese incursions. He was one of the few significant nobles to deliver an army for the defence of the capital. But Sin – or Tak Sin as most knew him – was known for more than that. Rumour in the city ran that, although his father was Chinese, Sin had been adopted as a boy by the Chancellor of Ayutthaya on account of his exceptional scholarship and character. Plucked from a monastery, he had been raised alongside his adoptive brother, Lord Duang, and was now the most talked about young noble of the day.

'Lord Sin! I did not see you there!' Thian replied, bowing in respect.

Sin laughed and clapped him on the back. 'I think we can dispense with courtesies in these circumstances. We are fellow soldiers at war. What's your name, young sir?'

'Thian, Lord. Grandson of Governor Chom Rang of Thalang,' he replied, with another polite wai.

'A southerner, eh? Not many answered the call. If I were you, I'd make a break for home while you still can. You should be guarding your own lands, not wasting your time in this impasse. But I applaud your loyalty and that of your men.'

His forthright comment came as a shock in a city where veiled language was the usual mode of communication. No one ever said what they thought – or thought what they said. Someone was always listening who could twist and turn your words. Paranoia was rife.

'I was a scholar, sir. I spent many years studying in Ayutthaya. It is my second home. One day I hope to resume my studies and become a monk. The city is worth everything,' Thian responded with feeling.

Lord Sin nodded with a sad smile. 'I, too, spent time in the monastery before I assumed my political responsibilities. And like you, it would be my greatest wish to return to that contemplative life. But we live in difficult times. It is not possible for honourable men to indulge their own hopes and dreams. We fight for those who cannot fight for themselves. I think we have much in common, Lord Thian.'

The older man offered a flask. Thian took a drink. It was sweet, fiery and welcome, although he did not usually take alcohol. 'Merely to protect you from the foul miasma. Medicinal.' Sin grinned. He was a handsome man, boyish of face, with an easy manner rarely found amongst those of the highest rank. 'We must talk again another day, young Thian. Thank you for your service.' And with a courtly bow, Lord Sin withdrew.

Thian had not been entirely honest in his reply. The idea of returning home to Thalang had indeed occurred to him, many times. Not because he feared death in battle but like his men he was anxious for Thalang. Had the Burmese sent a force south? Were they even now controlling the island? Was his family safe? Or had the Sultan of Queddah taken the opportunity to launch his own attack? The dilemma whether to place his family and dependants before the needs of a ruler far away was very real, particularly when the king himself seemed intent on doing nothing to protect his people. Yet this was the first time anyone had voiced out loud what he knew many were thinking.

After that first brief exchange with Lord Sin, Thian encountered the nobleman everywhere he went. Wasn't that the way of things? Yet, Thian was developing a presentiment that events might not be exactly as they seemed. Perhaps the oppressive atmosphere of containment was affecting him, but now he suspected ulterior motives in everything. These 'chance' meetings were more than mere coincidence, he was sure. Lord Sin had not touched upon sensitive matters with a comparative stranger by accident. He was being courted. Was Lord Sin shaping a rival faction that might potentially be in opposition to the king?

On most of their subsequent meetings, the conversation stayed on conventional topics: the weather, the food supply, the morale of the troops, reports of disease in the enemy camp, books they had enjoyed. On all of these occasions, however, they were surrounded by other officers or members of the court. Thian had the strong impression during these innocuous pleasantries that other conversations hung unspoken in the air, revealed only in a certain side look, the raising of an eyebrow, or a knowing smile. But it was enough to sensitise the younger man that he was being brought into Lord Sin's orbit of influence, both in the public and personal perception.

Thian's instinct was confirmed a few weeks later on another quiet night on the walls. When he turned a dark corner Sin was waiting, greeting him with a nod of acknowledgement. They were alone, the nearest guards well out of earshot.

'Well met, young Lord Thian! Have you eaten?' Sin greeted him as a friend, in the traditional way.

'I have, sir. Good evening to you.' Thian walked on, but a gentle, yet firm, hand stayed his progress.

'A moment, if you will.' Sin glanced around, inadvertently betraying suspicious intent. What he had to say was not for others to hear. Thian remained impassive; he had been expecting an approach and had been worrying it in his head for weeks. He would not be involved in treason. He would not defect to the enemy nor make a break for home. Yet, should a plot against the king be uncovered, would it now be possible to extricate himself from suspicion? The two men had been seen together in public often enough. His name would inevitably be mentioned as an acquaintance of Lord Sin. Had he been ensnared merely by association?

Sin smiled warmly with a hint of avuncular amusement. 'Do not be afraid, young man. Whatever is in your mind, you are jumping to very inaccurate conclusions. I do not intend to compromise your high moral code, sir.'

Thian did not reply but relaxed his guard somewhat and allowed himself to be led to a stone bench, tucked well out of sight of potential onlookers. Again, Sin pulled out a flagon but this time Thian put up his hand to wave it away. He must keep his wits about him. Lord Sin shrugged and took a swig himself. Wiping his mouth on the back of his hand, an unexpected touch of the commoner, he replaced the cork carefully before he began.

'The last time we met on the walls, I asked had you ever thought of making a break for home. Is your answer still the same?'

A long pause hung in the air. In his reply might lie both their futures. 'I worry for the fate of my home and family every day,' was Thian's oblique answer.

The flicker of another smile. 'That is not exactly what I asked you.'

Thian straightened up, pulling his shoulders back, military fashion. 'I will defend Ayutthaya and my king with my life,' he exclaimed, taking refuge in the conventional soldier's response.

'Fine principles, young lord, but sometimes pragmatism must take precedence over noble sentiment. You realise that we cannot win? This rain will end. The Burmese will attack. We will sit here like ducks on a pond waiting to be eaten. Ayutthaya will fall. Your magnificent temples and libraries, the statues and the treasures, hundreds of years of history and culture, all is on the brink of destruction. Do you wish to be part of that past – and die along with it? Or to be part of the future that saves Siam from the scourge of these devils?'

Thian did not speak, unsure whether he could have uttered a sound even had he found his voice. Darting a look to the right and left, he was relieved to find they were indeed alone. It was unlikely this conversation had been heard. If it had, it would be treason. They could both die in terrible agony merely for thinking such things.

But Sin seemed unconcerned. 'I understand. It is much to take in. Give my words some thought. Seek me out if you find yourself in agreement. I plan to leave soon and I would like to take a few reliable men with me. Siam's future will rest on us. There is no time to lose.'

'To oppose the king is treachery. To desert one's post is betrayal. If you try to leave, the Burmese will have you. Your only chance would be to join forces with them – and that is the ultimate treason. I will not consider such an act. How can you put your trust in me, a young man you hardly know? What if I take this knowledge to the king?' Thian asked when he finally found the words to speak.

Sin came close and whispered. 'You would not have asked that question had you meant to betray me. I've been watching you, brother Thian. I have surreptitiously asked the monks who have known you since childhood. You are a young man of singular virtue. You are highly intelligent and a brave warrior. But most of all, I do not think you are a fool, although you still cling to the ideals of those who have never had to face the choices that must be made when a nation is on the brink of annihilation. You are not the man to stand by and see a generation wiped out because of the foolhardy cowardice of one weak man. Thousands upon thousands of innocents, sacrificed to his blind stubbornness! What is the primary duty of a king? Surely, to protect his people, keep them safe, administer justice and enable them to live and prosper. Is it not the greatest crime willingly to lead them to destruction? I will not join the Burmese. But nor do I wish to throw away my life – and that of so many good men – when we could live on and take the fight to the Burmese elsewhere. Think on my words, Thian. But don't think too long. We need to leave before the rains end. Once the flood waters recede, the Burmese will come.'

'My lord! I must keep my oath! If I betray the king, it might mean the death of my family!' Thian protested, although he knew Lord Sin had spoken the truth. In his heart he had known it all along. Was his courage failing him – or did he really believe he was honour bound to his oath of fealty?

Sin hit back with his ace card. 'You are worrying about your family, should our attempt fail? Would you be more willing to break this vow if I told you that during the past months, whilst you have been sitting here doing precisely nothing, your island has been occupied by the forces of Queddah? It is now a Malay state. The Burmese assault gave the sultan the opportunity he was waiting for.'

Thian gasped, his worse fears realised. 'But what of my family? My grandfather is governor!'

Lord Sin shook his head sadly. 'I know very few details. Information trickles in through spies but the fate of a small island down south is of little interest to Ayutthaya. The king will barely have given it a thought. And yet, here you are, willing to risk all for the sake of a ruler who would sacrifice your people without a moment's hesitation.'

Thian could not deny that the same idea was running through his own mind. He might be the only family member left alive. Or would the Malays have enslaved the women and children? An even worse fate. 'I must return home. I must see if there is anything I can do to save my people!' he muttered. He looked Lord Sin straight in the eyes. 'What is your plan? How can we escape? If I can take my men with me, then I will join you. But what then? Do you intend simply to run away?'

It was a challenge to Lord Sin, an accusation that his plan was driven by self-preservation. The older man accepted Thian's right to call him out. 'The north is in Burmese hands. If we succeed, I plan to go south. Once we have united the southern provinces, I will raise an army of resistance. Then we will turn on the Burmese – and take our kingdom back!'

For the first time, the mask of Lord Sin's calm superiority slipped to reveal a fierce fervour. His eyes burned with passion and his face flushed red, his words spat out through gritted teeth. The change was frightening to behold, from cultured aristocrat to fanatic patriot in an instant. The passing glimpse inside the real man sent a chill through Lord Thian. Sin was plotting a new dynasty. The ultimate treachery. Yet it was no longer a matter of choice. He had to follow this man. It was the only chance his family might have.

A few nights later, Lord Sin and his adoptive brother, Lord Duang, led almost five hundred men out through the tunnels of the complex water system. A few weeks before, when the flood waters ran high, this would have been impossible, but as the weather turned, the levels dropped. Time was indeed running out for the capital. The escapees encountered few problems other than obstacles buried in the deep mud and sewage deposits through which they had to wade, and the hours spent in the dark, swirling water with only sputtering torches to guide their way. Soaked, filthy and exhausted, they finally exited beyond the perimeter of the enemy camp, across the river and the flood plain. If the Burmese had known of this particular access, they could have stormed the city months before.

'This tunnel is unknown to most, even the city engineers,' Sin had informed his officers, but only as they gathered to leave. 'It was created long ago as a royal escape route, through a shaft that runs beneath the river bed itself. It does not exist on any map nor is it mentioned in the records. It is said the architect and labourers who worked upon it were executed to prevent knowledge of it ever circulating. Tales of it are regarded as mere legend. Duang discovered it by chance years ago. I am the only person alive he has ever told, until this moment when I share our secret with you. That is why the route is so clogged in debris left from countless floods. No one has ever sent workers to clear it, for no one knows it is here. Other than the king, I suppose, and he does not intend to use it – for he believes his walls will never fail,' Sin added wryly.

Once out of the foul swampy tunnel, the men crawled across the intervening ground until they reached the cover of the forest beyond, grateful for the heavy rain and the hidden moon. Sin had chosen the night wisely. Behind them they could see the distant glow of the enemy arrayed in row after row of tents and smouldering campfires, and beyond that the lights of the city.

Suddenly from their vantage point, far off sounds of urgent activity reached them; there was a burst of gunfire, followed by piercing screams. The men fell to ground. 'What's going on?' someone hissed.

'A skirmish of sorts,' muttered another. 'Someone else is trying to make a break for it tonight, poor buggers. Still, all the better for us, eh? No one's looking this way now.' The men shrugged before disappearing into the trees. Lord Thian, however, continued watching until all his men were past, then hurried forward until he caught up with Lord Sin.

'There was another sortie from the city tonight. Quite a coincidence, don't you think?' Thian asked, his voice edged in suspicion.

Sin grunted. 'I know.' The nobleman walked on, indicating that the discussion was over.

Thian quickened up, placing a hand on his arm. Sin shook it off in annoyance. 'You knew that another escape was planned this night?'

Sin paused, staring straight ahead of him, before making a curt affirmative.

'You sacrificed all those men so we could escape unseen?'

Lord Sin spun round, eyes narrowing. 'At last you're learning, boy. Although we had a fool-proof escape route, a good general never puts all his hopes even on a certainty. An alternative strategy must always be in play. I suggested to someone that the tunnels of the water system might be a good way out. Even though I knew the Burmese had placed a guard on every exit. Except, of course, for this secret path.'

'You led other men to their deaths so that we might escape unseen?'

Lord Sin was losing patience. He grabbed Thian by the throat, pressing him back against a nearby tree. Although the shorter man, his grip was strong. 'You're alive, aren't you? Now concentrate on staying so. I want none of your monkish principles here. We are still in great danger. Your task is to lead your men to safety. Nothing more!' Sin relaxed his grip but kept his face mere inches away as he spat out: 'Just be grateful you were allowed in my party and that I did not choose to send you in the other group.' There was a warning in his words. 'They were dead men anyway. We must now survive to repay their sacrifice. One day you may have to make similar unpalatable decisions. Maybe sooner than you think. Wake up and be a man, *Lord* Thian!' With that, Sin brushed him aside and strode ahead to catch up with the rest of the force.

Thian barely recognised the man he knew in the Lord Sin he had just encountered. Glimmers of the steel and passion that drove his ambition had reared up once or twice before, but this was the first time Thian had tasted what Lord Sin was prepared to sacrifice to achieve his aim. His heart went out to the men who had been sent to their deaths, yet he was not insensible to the military rationale. The loss of those men had allowed five hundred others to escape. As Lord Sin had said, even now they were not out of danger. Who knew if outlying patrols were abroad that night? How far did Burmese control even stretch? Would they run into other enemy forces on their way south? Now was not the time to contemplate the rights and wrongs of what had happened. He would leave that for another day.

Clutching his weapons, he joined the other men as they trudged through the dense jungle, dulling their steps as best they could so as not to give themselves away. Five hundred men was a large number to make a stealthy flight through thick forest. But fate was on their side; no one was about. The canopy provided shelter from the worst of the rain and, although they were all wet and stinking, their hearts and spirits were high. After six months of waiting, they were on the move at last.

The trek south to Rayong took several weeks, foraging in the forest and moving mostly by night, unsure what they would find when they reached their destination. But Sin's instincts – and their sparse intelligence – proved correct. The south had not been part of the Burmese invasion. Indeed, several provinces had profited from the suspension of central control, and had declared themselves independent kingdoms, particularly Ligor, where Thian's distant relative had formerly been viceroy. He had seized this golden opportunity and had proclaimed himself King Musika of Ligor.

The outside world had moved on while the armies had been pinned down in the capital. It seemed to Lord Thian that the sacrifices they had made for Ayutthaya meant nothing to the lawless southern lords whose loyalties swung with the winds. His initial aversion to the pragmatic ruthlessness of Lord Sin was gradually replaced by a growing admiration, almost hero-worship. The regular soldiers had been the dupes of both king and aristocracy, sold a myth of loyalty, service and duty by those who would abandon those same qualities in an instant for the sake of their own aggrandisement.

The fraternal commanders of the tattered army of the Five Hundred, Generals Tak Sin and Chakri Duang, established an initial base at Rayong, on the invitation of an association of Chinese Teochew merchants, an unexpected source of support. Their leader was one Zheng Low, a distant relative of Tak Sin's birth father from the same village in China. Accommodation was provided for the officers in Zheng's own merchant house, while the ordinary troops camped on the edge of town, supplied with abundant tents, food and water. Rayong was a busy port; there were plenty of welcome distractions for the tired men as they recuperated from their ordeal. It seemed almost impossible to comprehend that they had survived with only a few minor casualties, and were now free to enjoy the fruits of their brave action.

The first priority was to raise money to fund a campaign, the second was to recruit more men. Without both, ambitions of uniting the south and driving out the Burmese were mere fantasies. The first was achieved with relative ease; this same Teochew association, comprised of rich émigré businessmen whose influence stretched to all such communities throughout Siam, was prepared to provide the gold and silver required.

Thian was overwhelmed by the generosity of Zheng Low and his associates. Although Tak Sin was Chinese, none of the others were. This act of altruism confounded him. Might the Chinese not have had more to gain by supporting the Burmese invasion? They had never enjoyed a good relationship with their Siamese masters. Why should they have sympathy for the fate of the dynasty? One morning, whilst breaking fast with the generals, Thian commented on their good fortune at meeting such charitable benefactors.

Lord Tak Sin was amused. 'It is true that by birth I am Teochew and that Zheng Low is my distant relative, but there is more to his munificence than you have understood. The Chinese are rarely given to liberality unless they see clear advantage for themselves. Nor do I impugn them when I say this. It is the very reason for their singular success at making fortunes even in the most challenging of circumstances. Chinese see opportunity where others disdain to dip their hands. I know this, for I share some of that expediency myself, no doubt inherited from my father's people!'

Lord Duang broke in. 'The Chinese are prosperous but they are much harried. They see an opportunity in supporting our cause and are willing to fund an army and a long campaign which will cost them a vast amount of gold. It is their wish that the next king of Siam should have Chinese blood.' He glanced meaningfully over at Lord Tak Sin. Duang, the direct opposite of the charismatic Sin was a thoughtful man, intelligent and able, renowned for his brilliance as a military commander. Where Sin was boyishly handsome and charmingly mercurial, Lord Duang was heavy set and solidly reliable. But the two men, close in age and friendship, were inseparable, and of one mind.

'But in what practical way can the Chinese gain? I thought that profit was their driving motive. If they give away a vast fortune in gold, where is the return?' Thian continued.

'Of course, the Chinese live for profit,' continued Lord Sin. 'But in the long term, a migrant people need more than money to survive. They wish to partake in the nation's affairs and have a role in the political realm. If we succeed, I intend to make full use of the Chinese community. With the greatest respect, Lord Thian, the Siamese nobility care little for the welfare of their people. They deem it their right to profit from the misery and labour of the poor and wretched. Even their loyalty to the king – as has been proved of late – is a moveable commodity. I will put an end to provincial aristocrats who govern provinces merely to fill their own pockets at the expense of traders, farmers and miners.'

'Provincial aristocrats like my grandfather, you mean?' Thian interrupted sharply.

The two men smiled at him. 'Like every noble family, ours included,' replied Lord Duang. Despite his inscrutability, Duang had all but confirmed that the final intent of this campaign was the removal of King Ekkathat and the installation of his own adoptive brother as the next king. The past weeks in the forests had stripped away all pretence.

Thian nodded solemnly in agreement. 'We are all guilty. We cannot vanquish the Burmese unless we look to our own faults. It is time for a new way.' He could no longer deny the venality of his class nor its exploitation of those less fortunate. In the past it had seemed a fact of life to which he had given little consideration. He had, of course, meditated on the inequities of existence in a metaphysical sense. But what was the use of the contemplation of the evils of the world if one did nothing to effect change in one's present existence? It was not enough to hope that these unfortunate souls might enjoy a better karma in a future life.

But first, there were other matters to attend to. 'I need to return to Thalang with my men,' Thian ventured. It had been on his mind for days; this seemed as good a time as any to broach the matter.

Lord Sin weighed up his request. 'I know you're eager to go home, but who knows what you will find there? Stay here and fight. Once we have an army, we will drive all invaders from the south. Including those from the Peninsula.'

Thian dropped to his knees, joining his hands in a wai, his head lowered. 'With respect, sir, that could take several years. First, I must discover if my family has survived. My men are also worried for their wives and children. Every day counts; it is months since the Queddah attack. But I shall return. This I promise. It would be an honour to serve you in delivering Siam from the foul Burmese menace. And one day, I hope, I will bend the knee to a new king, one who will be worthy of the name, my Lord.'

Less than two months later, Ayutthaya fell in an orgy of unparalleled violence and destruction from which it was never to recover. A new dynasty was already on the rise.

5

Revelations

The still atmosphere hung heavy with moisture; not a whisper of breeze stirred the late morning. Distant thuds and strident voices from the frenetic activity on the river below leached through the humid air. Ships and perahu, junks and barges, every manner of sailed and oared vessel speckled the muddy waters around the busy river jetties. Like worker bees, bare-chested labourers scurried about, loading and unloading, stacking and baling.

On the terraced slopes above the port, where the homes of the foreign merchants and court officials clustered like gilded birds of prey, a stench – ripe in sewage, rotting fish and stagnant mud – permeated all things until the smell became one with the natural world itself. The sun, reflecting off the sludgy brown-red water and the shabby timbers of the warehouses, struggled to glorify the day, despite the cloudless blue sky above and the dense green forest beyond. Limbun was a dreary, noxious, cheerless place. Martinha longed for home.

She did not fully understand why her family had uprooted so suddenly, propelled from the elegant mansion in Phuket Town to this drab river settlement. Vague rumours of the Burmese, those fanged *wayang* demons of her girlish imagination, circulated amongst the household servants – but that terror had not come to pass. Now the whispers said that Queddah itself had launched an attack, and that Thalang was now subject to Sultan Muhammed Jiwa. Her grandfather was no longer the governor. But no one seemed overly concerned. Her parents even seemed relieved.

Had she raised her eyes past the pulsating commercial activity on the wide and sluggish river, past the swampy mangroves on the opposite bank and over to the distant valley beyond, she might have experienced an appreciation for the picturesque beauty of Queddah, one of the most fertile kingdoms of the Peninsula. In the flat plains of Langgar, Lepai and Hutan Kampong lay a vast expanse of *padi*, a tranquil rice-growing centre that fed the entire region and beyond. If she contemplated the number of vessels and the amount of trade that changed hands in the vibrant emporium itself, she might have understood the allure of Limbun. Queddah was truly blessed, with an age-old industrial and commercial past, together with a developing agricultural wealth. But children are not interested in commerce and economy. They do not understand the enticements of wealth and power. They like neither change nor the unknown.

A bullock-cart was plodding along in the direction of their neighbourhood, following the winding path that led from the harbour to the houses above. Martinha had been idly observing its progress, now disappearing and then reappearing according to the contours of the hillside. The vehicle particularly caught her interest because of one of its two occupants. Even at a distance, under his wide-brimmed hat, the passenger was a foreigner. His clothes marked him out: coat and breeches, shirt and stockings, but she could also see his skin, almost translucent in the bright sunlight. Martinha had seen farangs in Thalang, but rarely close up. Her curiosity was piqued.

To her surprise, the cart came to a halt outside their compound and the man climbed down, conversing with the guard at the entrance. Martinha watched him take off his hat, mop his face with a cloth pulled from around his neck, and dust down his clothing, which was stained and creased. These white foreigners were not known for their cleanliness. It was said they seldom bathed and stank of body odour. His face, now exposed, did not appear white at all but a puffed up, swollen red; his hair was a strange yellowish fuzz, like dirty *kapok* fibre. The man was tall and portly, his nose was straight and long, and even across the dusty yard, she could see his eyes were pale. Martinha thought him quite repulsive.

A servant was padding down the steps towards the stranger, bidding him wait in the spreading shade of a rambutan tree whilst he informed the master. The man caught Martinha's eye and waved over, his mouth breaking into a friendly smile that softened his sharp features, making his light eyes dance. Martinha ducked down behind the wooden rail and backed away into the shade of the veranda, suddenly bashful to have been caught staring.

'There you are, Ma Li.' Her mother appeared behind her, using her familiar name. 'Come, your tutor is waiting inside.'

'Someone's come to see us. A farang. Look, *'bu*!'

Thong Di stared over at the man, her face instantly concerned. 'We must call your father. Go inside, it is not seemly.' And her mother escorted an unwilling Martinha back into the house for her lessons.

Before the unexpected appearance at his private residence, Martim had been working on his correspondence, his mind already uneasy, plagued with worries about their current situation and what was happening back home. The real purpose of their migration to the dubious shelter of the mainland had been to strengthen the ties of the Ban Takkien to Queddah in view of the uncertain political climate in Siam.

It was not, however, the reason they had spread abroad on leaving. Martim had long been a frequent visitor to Queddah with an existing office at the river port of Limbun in his capacity as a merchant. It was a perfect excuse for the family's presence there. Any other clan member visiting the kingdom would have raised suspicion. Furthermore, he was Eurasian. Christians would undeniably find themselves particularly targeted by the Burmese if they attacked Thalang. Other Eurasian families had already abandoned the island, trickling down the coast to Queddah, where there was always a welcome for merchants, whatever their race or religion. There was even a Catholic mission at Limbun itself. So, it raised no suspicion for Martim Rozells to take this precaution. But the initial fears of invasion from the north had been unfounded; the Burmese had not come. Instead, within weeks of the departure of the Rozells family, the Sultan of Queddah had launched his own attack. Thalang was now Ujung Salang – a Malay island.

The new occupiers made little material difference to the islanders. Trade still flourished at the ports, tin was still mined and exported from Phuket Town, and fishermen still sailed the local waters. Life went on much as it always had. Why would it not? The island had always been as much Malay as Siamese. Conflict was to nobody's advantage. In fact, it was generally believed that life was better now. For one, piracy had reduced since many of the raiders were vassals of the sultan himself. Furthermore, the worst excesses of the powerful Siamese noble families had been contained by the new Malay governor. Chom Rang's secret alliance with Sultan Muhammed Jiwa – strengthened by Martim's mission at the Queddah court – had been perfectly judged. Whilst Chom Rang might have temporarily ceded his gubernatorial office, it had been a small price to pay for independence from Ayutthaya. The threat of the Burmese had been a gift. The former governor would in time be offered his old position back. It had all been decided ahead.

Chom Rang believed himself to be a master strategist who had manipulated the situation to the benefit of himself and his family. Martim and Thong Di, however, did not share his confidence. To underestimate Sultan Muhammad Jiwa would be a mistake. The astute old king, in his fifty-seventh regnal year, knew every gambit known to man. He played politics with the dexterity of a *wayang kulit* puppeteer. Were they allies or willing hostages to ensure the future loyalty of the Ban Takkien?

As is often the case when one fears the worst, however, it is from an entirely different direction that the devastating blow arrives. The unlooked-for arrival of this visitor, a farang captain based in Tharua port, indicated news of some urgency. Had something happened in Thalang? Was this a warning for them to evacuate?

Martim crossed the main room to greet his guest, sending a fleeting look towards his startled wife that betrayed a similar disquiet to her own. Thong Di hovered by the shuttered window, peeping through the slats to observe the two men. Martim knew many foreign traders, but he had never before entertained one in their home.

The two men apparently knew each other well, exchanging formal greetings in Malay. Martim invited the stranger to mount the steps, remove his boots, and take a seat, a sign that he was welcome. A bowl of scented water was proffered for him to wash his hands and feet, and drink was set down as refreshment. The man seemed familiar with local custom; his Malay was fluent.

An eternity passed as Thong Di peered out, straining her ears to catch the muttered conversation, but the men's voices were low and sombre. Eventually, after a long pause, Martim lowered his head, appearing to gasp for breath, his hands joined as if in prayer. Unable to bear the tension further, Thong Di pushed aside the curtain and stepped outside.

'What has happened, my husband?'

The two men spun round, startled by her appearance. Martim visibly gathered himself, offering a curt introduction: 'This is Kapitan Sakat with news from Thalang.' The farang bowed his head, nervously fingering the brim of his hat, his expression subdued, no gracious words or smile in response.

'What news?' she demanded urgently, her hands pressing on her heart, fearing the worst.

Sakat took a step backwards, turning respectfully away, while Martim advanced, his grave face and watery eyes confirming her suspicions. Drawing her aside, he whispered into her ear: 'Your honourable father is no longer with us. He has begun his journey to his next existence ...'

Thong Di's screams pierced through the lazy buzz of the morning air, stilling the children and shocking the servants. Neighbours peered out, dogs stopped barking, even monkeys held their chatter. The grief-struck woman fell to her knees, tearing her hair from its tightly arranged bun until it hung in strands about her face, all the while screaming and wailing pitifully.

Martim was at a loss. This manifestation of his usually tranquil wife was unknown to him. He tried to embrace her but she slapped away his hands. Kapitan Sakat, his face now even more florid than before, came over to offer his hip flask, but she knocked it to the ground. The children rushed out, crying without even knowing why. Finally, when Thong Di had succumbed to exhaustion, her voice cracking, her ladies gently eased her to her feet and guided her back inside the house. One brought a sedative infusion, another encouraged her to sip. They stroked her forehead and bathed her skin in cool water until she finally fell into a fitful, feverish sleep.

'*Bapak*! Why is mother crying?' Martinha finally choked out, eying the visitor with a malevolent stare, as if he was wholly responsible for her mother's sorrow.

Martim crouched down to his children's level, placing an arm around each and hugging them close. 'Your grandfather has passed away. Mother is very sad. She loved him very much.'

Felipe wiped the tears from his eyes. 'Was he sick? Did he have a fever?'

Martim shook his head. 'A bad man hurt him.' The two children paled in fear at the thought of a violent death for their beloved grandfather.

'Was it the Malays? Or have the Burmese come?' Martinha gasped. Perhaps the unthinkable had happened. The new Siamese army must have been defeated and the enemy had invaded her home.

Again, her father shook his head, sighing deeply. 'No. It was a Siamese. Do not worry about the Burmese. General Tak Sin has taken the south and is marching north to Thonburi. We are safe. Everyone at home is safe.'

'Except for grandfather,' Martinha added.

'Except for grandfather,' Martim repeated. An assassin had despatched Chom Rang in the dark of the night, disappearing without trace. The former governor had been found in his own blood-soaked bed, stabbed many times. A brutal, bloody death. Rumour and supposition were all they had by way of explanation. His father-in-law had enemies, of course, not the least from the other noble clans of the island who resented his meteoric rise and autocratic rule. It was even possible, Martim thought, that his alliance with the sultan had been discovered and that he had died for this perceived betrayal. Just as his plans had come to fruition, had Chom Rang been felled either by old vendettas or the consequences of his own machinations?

From that morning on, Thong Di, forsaking her Christian faith, retreated into the Buddhist traditions of her childhood. Despite Martim's protestations, she shaved her head and refused all food but tiny portions of rice and steamed vegetables. Garbed in white cloth free of adornment, she spent hours chanting ritual prayers and making offerings of flowers, incense and paper objects before a shrine dedicated to her father. In the absence of the monks at the temple and without the support of the rest of her family at such a time, she had no other means of grieving. The children crept in to her room and sat by her as she prayed, but she seemed oblivious to them, so they crept out again. No one was sure how long Thong Di intended to keep up this excessive display of grief. Excluded from the traditional ceremonies carried out in the ancestral shrine at Thalang, Thong Di was alone in her abject sorrow, unable to pass through the natural stages of mourning that the complex rites allowed. She was stranded in a foreign culture, in a nowhere land of guilt and shock.

* * *

The arrival of her mother, Mahsia, many weeks later was the catalyst that finally turned the tide. Unannounced, and accompanied only by a few of her closest companions, Chom Rang's widow returned to her homeland after her long and self-imposed exile. Although in deep mourning herself, she had come to terms with her loss. From the day Mahsia was reunited with Thong Di, her daughter at last began the journey from her twilight existence back towards the light.

One afternoon, the two women were resting through the hottest hours of the day on a low wooden bed piled with velvet cushions, in the shady space between the poles of their stilted house. The children lay on mats nearby, playing with a tiny kitten. Calm had been restored to Thong Di's soul as Mahsia soaked up the balm of her native land.

'You look brighter today, *sayang*,' Mahsia stroked her daughter's pale face. Thong Di had lost weight, sharpening her already fine features. Her eyes were deep ponds of welling tears.

'It is unseemly for me to dwell on my own grief, *Ibu*, when you have lost your husband,' Thong Di whispered back. She spoke Malay, the language of her childhood, her mother's tongue.

Mahsia sighed deeply. 'We had many years together. Good years. Your father loved me, *nah*? Imagine that?' She laughed ruefully. 'My first husband, Mahum, was a weak man, full of bitterness and envy. He was a Siak who had the luck to marry a beautiful Queddah girl of higher status than himself. When my wealthy father died, I was his sole heir. My husband and his family treated me cruelly. Then he went and died, the stupid man. His younger brother moved in and took everything. He demanded I become his second wife, pretending concern for my welfare. My son Kamal and I would be nothings in the house of my own father!'

Thong Di had never heard her mother speak of the past. The story of her first marriage was entirely new to her; she doubted even her elder sisters had heard it. With bated breath, she willed Mahsia to continue, afraid to interrupt in case her mother fell silent.

'I was a fiery young woman in those days!' Mahsia grinned, despite the single serpentine tear that snaked down her cheek. 'I had an older cousin in Ujung Salang who had married a Samsan of Tharua. One night, I sneaked out with Kamal and my servant Anom. I had gold hidden in my sarong. For years I had been squirrelling it away, just in case,' she added, the gleam of triumphant memory in her eyes.

Her daughter suppressed a giggle, the first time she had smiled in weeks. Mahsia caught her eye and together they shared a much-needed moment of joy. Her mother had never changed. She had lived her life her own way. That was why Father had loved her so much.

'I arranged passage on a perahu owned by the son of an old retainer of my father, may he rest in peace! Imagine the journey up the coast at dead of night and through pirate-infested waters, hiding my few trinkets of gold! My cousin was shocked when we turned up at his door. He was furious at my treatment and welcomed us in. He made a home for us at Tharua with his family.'

'But how did you meet my father?' Thong Di exclaimed, unable to contain her curiosity.

Mahsia tilted her head and pouted, still vain in her old age. 'I was a very beautiful girl. Dark curls and flashing eyes. Your father saw me in the market and was smitten. The rest ...' she clucked her tongue and gave a throaty laugh, like the beguiling girl she had once been. 'He was quite the catch, you know, the younger son of a rich Siamese family. How could a girl resist him? I was lucky. I found my future in a man whom I could also love,' she added. Rare indeed in either community.

'But what happened to Kamal?' Thong Di ventured. She had a step-brother she had never known!

The smile on Mahsia's face died away. 'He stayed behind with my cousin's family when I married your father. It was better for him to be raised in a Muslim home. Then he grew up and went away. Last time I heard, he was in Johor.' She stopped speaking, far away in her memories of the child she had lost. To think her mother had borne this tragedy through the years while the rest of the family were in ignorance! Thong Di filled up her glass and sat back down, allowing her mother the time to recover her composure.

'It was a good marriage,' she finally muttered. 'Better than most. Even though I struggled with all that *haram* Buddhist nonsense! Yet, women are well treated in Ujang Salang. I'm glad my daughters grew up in Siamese ways. A noblewoman has no freedom in Queddah.' It was an unexpected reproach from her mother, who had always vainly protested that the girls should be covered and stay at home, probably more for form's sake than because she really believed it. Who better than she to appreciate that a woman without agency was at the mercy of the world, no matter who her father was?

'But why have you returned after so many years, *'bu*? Why have you left your other sons and daughters for a place that treated you so ill?'

Mahsia raised her palms to heaven as if in prayer. 'Your father is gone. My children are grown and married. They do not need me anymore. And I want to die with my own people. With my own God, Allah be praised! I waited out the forty days since your father's death. I performed the *tahlil* for his soul – and then I left. I cannot stay for months while your father's body lies in state without a decent burial. I cannot watch them burn him at the cremation. And I have no place there now he has gone.' Her voice tailed away. Thong Di well understood the dilemma of belonging in two opposite worlds. Would she one day find herself alone in an alien place? Might she too have to choose between her traditions and her children?

'But we are here, mother. We shall never abandon you. You will always have a home with us!' Thong Di smiled, taking her mother's hands in hers.

Mahsia nodded as the two women both fought back tears, then feigned annoyance to mask her tumultuous emotions. '*Aduh!* So now I have to put up with all your Christian nonsense, I suppose!'

The children had been listening in, Martinha particularly captivated by the romance of her grandmother's former life.

Drawn by the sound of laughter, a rare commodity in recent weeks, they climbed onto the wooden platform and curled up on the cushions in the embrace of their mother and grandmother. The kitten leapt around until it grew tired, purring in their arms. For the first time, Queddah felt like home.

6

Two Birds with one Stone

The Royal Palace, Alor Setar, Queddah. January 1767

Sultan Muhammad Jiwa Zainal Adilin Mu'adzam Shah II perched on his golden lotus throne, one leg bent and the other hanging down, whilst his *laksamana* droned on in the background. The hall was crowded: senior officials, advisors, retainers, bondsmen, guards and foreign visitors. As the morning eased towards midday, the languid heat intensified. Draped in heavy formal garments, bodies dripped in sweat. Torpor settled over all. It was the time of day when everyone began to think of refreshment, a shady spot, a comfortable cushion, and a doze. The perfect time to take an audience by surprise.

The sultan appeared to be the most somnolent of all. So still was the old man's body that, to an observer, he seemed to have nodded off, his drooping forehead resting on his palm. One could be mistaken. The sultan's black, bird-like eyes were not closed, but buried deep within the folds of the dark wrinkles that encircled them. He might be ancient and wizened, his body as frail and delicate as a moth – but his mind was still as active as men a quarter of his age.

The people of Queddah regarded Sultan Muhammed with an awe that bordered on deity worship, unbecoming for a Muslim ruler, but the sultan encouraged it all the same. His subjects thought him immortal. He was reputed to be more than one hundred years old – which he was not – but he saw no reason to counter this inaccurate belief. The sultan had reigned for more years than most of them had lived and showed no sign of slackening. It seemed to him that this alone was justification for their simple-minded devotion. Furthermore, the support of the ordinary people was his strongest weapon against the constant treachery of those who surrounded him at court.

In his long life, many had tried to unseat him and, so far, all had failed. Even as his courtiers fawned and flattered him in his own palace, the men he had raised up and who had made fortunes from his largesse, were plotting and planning his overthrow. It was ever thus. The sultan thrived upon it. Let them think he was an old man struggling to keep up with the demands of his responsibilities. Their over-confidence would destroy them.

There were always threats: the jealousies of his family, the ambitions of the nobles, the land-grabbing of the Bugis, the machinations of the Arab Syeds, the schemes of the Siak sea lords, the demands of his Siamese masters, the distant threat of the Burmese, and now looming on the horizon, the destructive arrogance of the *Ferringhi*. He alone could move these players around the stage, pitting one against the other, holding the world in balance. And so, he let them underestimate him and make their little plots, while he listened and he planned.

His latest challenge concerned his son, Abdullah. It amused him that, against conventional wisdom, the survival of his son had not helped secure the future of his lineage, but had instead thrown his court into even greater intrigues. Whilst he had remained without legitimate heirs, members of his vast extended family and his sons by palace *gundiks* had patiently awaited his inevitable death to seize the throne. But then, relatively late in his life, he had been blessed with two healthy boys in quick succession, Abdullah and his half-brother, Ziyauddin. Two more wives and a host of new uncles were added to the pot. The result was even more widespread conspiracies. Different factions formed around the two boys (who could be more easily manipulated), as well as those who favoured older, more tested relatives.

Only a few years before, the sultan's half-brother had staged a coup, along with various disaffected courtiers. It had failed, but the sultan had not forgotten the danger presented by counsellors who wielded so much authority on his behalf. They needed restraining. The heir he personally favoured, Abdullah, needed support. Sultan Muhammed had the perfect solution.

Raising his hand, he feebly motioned for the conversation to end. 'Enough. It is already lunch time. I need to eat.'

His counsellors salaamed and backed away. His attendants advanced to assist him from the throne to his own apartments. But the sultan had not quite finished. 'One more thing. I quite forgot to mention it. How scattered are the thoughts of old men!'

The room reassembled, impatiently waiting for the sultan to continue. 'A fleet is being readied to carry my family and all the Queddah nobles to Selangor. Prepare for a magnificent occasion! For in three months, the daughter of my old Bugis friend Raja Lumu, the new Sultan of Selangor, will marry my beloved son, Raja Muda Abdullah.'

The entire assemblage caught its communal breath. Faces either paled in shock or flushed with anger. But not a sound was uttered as Sultan Muhammed took the proffered arms of his attendants and made his way to his private apartments, a half smile curling in satisfaction on his lips. '*Sambil menyelam minum air,*' he muttered to Agus, the Javanese manservant who had been with him since his youth. Two birds with one stone, indeed: he had curbed the power of the Siaks, whilst placating the Bugis of Selangor, in one fell swoop. That would keep them on their toes.

* * *

A few weeks after her arrival in Queddah, a formal invitation arrived for Mahsia and her family to attend the wedding feast of Raja Muda Abdullah and his new Bugis bride. It was an occasion of staggering importance. Who would have imagined a few decades ago that those upstart Bugis raiders from far off Celebes island would one day carve themselves a kingdom along the Straits of Melaka? But the sultan of Queddah had played a deft hand. Internal rivalries were already breaking the Bugis into rival camps; he would hobble their nuisance for good by driving his own wedge between them.

The festivities were to be held in Selangor. The Rozells family would travel down the coast in Martim's ship alongside the royal fleet, a great honour extended to very few outside the nobles of the court. Had the Rozells family been nurturing any concerns that the death of their patriarch might have an adverse effect on their safety, this summons suggested otherwise.

Sultan Muhammed Jiwa had been informed of Mahsia's return almost as soon as she arrived. Little ever escaped the old sultan's notice. He had spies and informers everywhere, handsomely rewarding those who did him service. Not long afterwards, the sultan had singled out Martim to enquire about his mother-in-law's welfare with what appeared to be genuine affection and concern. Sincere condolences were extended on the loss of Governor Chom Rang, 'his old friend' as he called him. And now this prestigious invitation had arrived. The Takkien links between Queddah and Ujung Salang seemed to be holding.

Preparations for their attendance, however, were complicated by the fact that the family was still in mourning. Mahsia told her daughter it was out of the question to be presented at the palace in plain attire. It was essential to dress finely in respect of the two sultans, the occasion itself, and their own family pride.

'Daughter, you cannot wear white cotton cloth. It is an insult!'

'Then I shall wear white silk,' Thong Di shrugged.

'Pah! You cannot wear white silk either! White is a royal preserve, forbidden for commoners,' Mahsia exclaimed. 'And you must cover yourself fully with a shawl. Imagine if the sultan should see your shaved head, like a plucked chicken. So shameful!'

It was Martinha, sitting quietly nearby enjoying the spirited chatter, who spoke up. 'Why not wear black then, like a Christian in mourning?'

'Clever girl!' Thong Di exclaimed. 'What would we do without you?'

A large quantity of black songket was ordered. Seamstresses worked long hours to complete the garments; even Martim and Felipe were to be clothed in traditional Malay court attire. It was a great expense, but no one quibbled: the outlay was worth its weight in gold. Martim frequently attended court in his capacity as a merchant and representative of Ujung Salang, but a personal invitation to a royal wedding was something only extended to those with close ties to the ruling house.

On the evening before their departure, Mahsia revealed another unexpected gem. They were eating dinner and speculating on the coming events when she suddenly interrupted: 'Of course, it is to be expected that the sultan would invite me. I am, after all, a relative.'

Everyone fell silent. 'A relative? Of Sultan Muhammed Jiwa?' Martim gasped. 'How do we not know this?'

Mahsia dismissed him with a wave of her hand. 'How would you know? I told no one.'

'Not even father?' Thong Di exclaimed.

'Especially not your father. I did not want to be caught in the middle between my husband and the sultan!'

'So, you are a royal princess? Tunku Mahsia?' Her daughter was fascinated.

Mahsia scoffed 'My title is Wan Mahsia. My father's mother married a commoner, although she was the niece of a former sultan. So, her children had the title 'Wan', which passed down to me. There are so many of us, it doesn't mean much. But yes, I am distantly related to Sultan Muhammed.'

'Did you know him personally?' Thong Di asked, curiously.

'Personally? How does one know a sultan, personally? He knew of me, of course. In fact, he arranged my first marriage. At that time, he was keen to appease the Siaks against the Bugis so he looked about the court and married off any eligible young royal maidens to their young bucks. My father was delighted. The sultan rewarded him very well for his only child,' she added bitterly.

'But will the sultan be angry that you ran away?' Martinha

blurted out, and then blushed when all eyes swivelled on her. Would her grandmother be offended? She was only voicing what her parents already feared.

Mahsia chuckled. 'I'm sure he was furious at the time! But that was many, many years ago! And now the Siaks are out of favour and he's marrying his son to a Bugis princess. Everything has changed. Don't worry, I can manage the sultan. To be honest, I think he once had his eyes on me, but I wasn't important enough,' she added, assuming an unconvincingly demure expression. The old woman was full of surprises.

* * *

Sultan Salehuddin, formerly the Bugis leader Raja Lumu, presided as a most gracious host at the wedding of his daughter Tengku Puneh to Prince Abdullah of Queddah. His star was rising, the marriage a significant mark of his acceptance as the newest ruler of the Peninsula. Not that he was naïve to Sultan Muhammed's motives. This alliance was built purely on self-interest. Muhammed Jiwa wished to exploit the divisions of the Bugis factions, control his over-mighty Siak lords, and give notice to the court of the danger of conspiring against his son and heir.

The whys and wherefores were inconsequential, for now the security of the whole Straits rested on a finely balanced knife-edge of contrary coalitions, with Selangor at its centre. And Sultan Salehuddin relished his moment. Sultan Muhammed might privately regard him as a lowly *parvenu* of humble origins whom he would drop in the blink of an eye should it later serve him better; Salehuddin himself intended to act much the same should the opportunity arise. For now, however, it was enough to be an anointed sultan whose authority could never be rescinded. This marriage was a mere stepping stone towards his even greater territorial ambitions. One step at a time. Until he was in the position to take it all.

Flanking the richly hung dais where the bridal couple presided like golden statues, the rival sultans sat on their respective thrones, from time to time acknowledging each other with a regal nod. Sultan Muhammed Jiwa inwardly assessed his rival Salehuddin. The new sultan was a man in the prime of life, his sturdy build betraying his Bugis origins. Although no one could call him tall, Salehuddin was of imposing stature, with the broad shoulders and the thick limbs of a warrior. To Sultan Muhammed, this indicated common birth, lacking the refinement of those raised to lead. Salehuddin's nose was bulbous and his lips were fleshy, features without the delicacy of royal blood bred for generations by good diet, a life of ease and wives of extraordinary beauty. Although clothed in a sumptuous chequered silk sarong shot through with gold, and a high-necked shirt trimmed with gold appliqué, it was not enough to mask the Bugis sultan's lowly origins, patent in his poor table manners and slovenly carriage.

Salehuddin's keris, however, caught the old king's eye. Wrought of astonishing craftmanship, its sheath was a complex floral patterning of embossed gold inlaid with rubies, resting on its distinctive flange. The Bugis knew how to forge a dagger, Sultan Muhammed would give them that. But he disdained Salehuddin's style of *tengkolok*, the flopping triangular peak not at all majestic, in his opinion. It revealed the vulgar taste of a commoner.

Switching his attention to the bride, Sultan Muhammed felt

similarly unimpressed. Tengku Puneh was unfortunate to favour her father, although her broad hips suggested easy childbearing, an essential consideration in a royal wife. Abdullah, slender and fine-boned, gave nothing away in his serene expression – but the sultan wasn't fooled. Beneath his composed exterior, Abdullah seethed. He thought his new bride ugly and inferior. His father didn't care. He had told his son to be a man. At night all birds are grey.

He cast his gaze over the guests gathered on banks of cushions, their food set out on the carpets before them. Most were helping themselves with gusto to the exceptional assortment of fish, meats, crustaceans and platters of spicy vegetables that surrounded triangular mounds of fragrant yellow rice. Many rarely tasted such delicacies. Most people, even those of means, ate a simple diet of dried fish, rice and greens. He himself was accustomed to pick like a tiny bird – but an array of delicacies would always be set before him.

'Where is Wan Mahsia?' he asked of his man servant Agus, whose eyes were still sharp enough to see to the rear of the crowded room.

'Near the entrance at the back with her family, Tuanku.'

'Call them to scatter rosewater and petals over the wedding couple. Then bring them to me.'

The Rozells family made their way through the lines of cross-legged diners, aware that their progress from minor guests to a personal audience had been widely noted. Martim felt a surge of relief. This was a significant moment that would go a long way to securing the family's safety in Queddah.

Before the sultan, they followed the lead of Mahsia herself, who knelt before him. But as they were trying to find the space to do the same, the old king broke in: 'Stand up, my dear girl! You are too old for such things! A simple bow will suffice! Your family, also!'

Mahsia bowed, her hands placed palms together and raised above her head, before stepping forward to kiss his outstretched hand; Martim knelt on one knee, his head lowered; while Lady Thong Di led the children in a deep wai. It made the old man chuckle. 'All manners of respect shown to me in one family! How very charming! Come closer, my vision is poor. Let me look at these beautiful children!' Martinha and Felipe were pushed forward, shy and embarrassed. The sultan touched each in turn on the cheek. 'The boy will be strong and handsome! The girl is fair. She will marry well!'

Next, Mahsia introduced her daughter. The sultan complimented Thong Di's elegant beauty and offered his condolences on the death of her father. Martim he already knew; for him he had a ready smile. He complimented him for his excellent choice of wife and for his well-brought-up children. Then he turned to Mahsia.

'So, Wan Mahsia binte Wan Ibrahim Kamalaruddin, it is many years since we have seen you at my court. And may I say, those years have treated you well. Still the beautiful girl of my memories!' It was an auspicious opener. The sultan did not harbour any anger towards her.

'Great King, you are too gracious! I do not deserve such generous words. To be admitted before your glorious presence is enough for a sinner such as I!' Her reply was formal, framed in the courtesies of the palace language.

But Sultan Muhammed Jiwa was in a good mood today. His plans had been accomplished. His Siak lords were already sulking; he had not finished with them yet. 'Nonsense, dear lady. You had every right to leave. Your unkind treatment at the hands of your husband's family was shameful. I should have intervened long before you were driven from your home by those brutes. You are a woman of great courage and spirit. I am delighted to welcome you back to your homeland. May you never leave your native soil again!'

Mahsia bowed and began to pour out her thanks to the sultan. He raised his hand to stem her grovelling flow. 'Furthermore, I believe your husband's family retained your marriage portion, which by rights belongs to you. Your former brother-in-law and family are now in exile. They were involved in a plot to overthrow me, the devils! That was the thanks for all they had received at my court, not least one of the pearls of my kingdom in marriage! Their lands were confiscated. It seems fitting that I now return them to you and to your children.' The sultan had raised his voice so that everyone could hear the conversation. He was using the opportunity to warn disgruntled courtiers what they could expect should they dare to oppose him again.

Martim was astonished. Mahsia was now a wealthy heiress in her own right with a fortune that would one day pass to his own wife and children! This was beyond his wildest dreams. Their position at the court of Queddah was secure. How ironic that the death of Chom Rang had been the impetus for all this!

'Herewith I bestow upon you the title of Tunku. This exception is granted in honour of the celebration of my beloved son's marriage and to express my humble apologies for the shame that you have endured at the hands of Siaks!'

There was an intake of breath at the blatant accusation, directed at one of the most influential factions, especially insulting in the presence of Sultan Salehuddin's court. The latter, savouring the rich food, his attention rivetted on the proceedings, appeared mightily amused. His alliance would be all the stronger for this turn of events. He noted the displeasure of the Queddah nobles. Muhammed Jiwa had better treat Selangor kindly. If not, he knew exactly who would value his support.

As if from heaven, the Rozells family found themselves the benefactors of a magnificent windfall, raising them from lowly merchant settlers to the nobility of Queddah. But they were merely convenient pawns in a much larger game. The eyes of many at court were turned upon them now. That was not always a blessing.

PART TWO

A Marriage of Convenience

(1772-1774)

7

The Price of Failure

Francis Light, former Royal Naval officer, now country trader plying the waters of the Andaman between India to the Straits in his search of fame and fortune, had not lingered at the court of the sultan of Queddah despite the accolades and gifts that the old king had showered upon him. Following the disastrous failure of his bid to establish a Company outpost there – for which the entire blame was unjustly laid at his door – he wished to put distance between himself and the bitter memories of that debacle. The slur to his reputation was already resounding throughout every port in the region. His name was mud in British circles – even local allies were abandoning him as yesterday's man. Such is the fate of those who fail. In the face of that humiliation, it was unsurprising that he was eager to embark upon his new joint endeavour in Jangsylan with James Scott, and lie low while he concentrated on rebuilding his depleted resources.

Light's recent poaching of a band of European mercenaries from the service of the Sultan of Selangor on behalf of Sultan Muhammed Jiwa of Queddah – and the disputed haul of cannons they had brought with them – had cost Light another valuable ally. The Bugis were now literally after his blood, thus the southern Straits was all but closed to him. In one fell swoop, his prestige had been destroyed. Siam and Queddah were now the only lifelines remaining to him.

Before he departed for his new life, however, there remained the not-insignificant matter of his arranged marriage to young Martinha Rozells. Her mother, Lady Thong Di, had offered her daughter's hand, Sultan Muhammed had approved, so Francis Light had grasped the straw. It was undeniably a most appropriate alliance to secure his future position in Jangsylan, for Lady Chan herself had initially suggested it. A marriage that forged a bond with his two remaining allies? Who could spurn such a happenstance?

Nevertheless, Light's enthusiasm for the marriage was as slight as his need for it was great. Martinha was a child. They barely knew each other. He disapproved of arranged marriages. Once he had even been attracted to the girl's own mother, surely the most disturbing factor of it all. Yet, what choice remained to him? Marriage was the obvious next step for a man of his age. Furthermore, familial relationships were a significant bond in these parts where dealing with relatives was always preferred to outsiders. This union would ensure he remained centre stage in the commercial life of the northern Straits, a major consideration in view of his decline everywhere else.

Thus, he would swallow down his distaste. A beggar such as he could not afford to turn up his nose at a whiff of the improper. For what business did a trader have with high principles? He would never have gone far in his chosen profession had he bothered about virtue. As his options narrowed, so must his moral compass widen. He would be a fool even to let such considerations enter his head.

By the time Light and Scott returned to the fort at Kuala Bahang, the motley band of mercenaries was joyfully ousting the previous Company residents. The *Triton* had already sailed with most of the Madras contingent, apart from Monckton and Fairlie, who had remained to finalise the particulars of the withdrawal. Hythe at least was gone. It was probably for the best. Light could still not guarantee to hold his temper should they meet again.

Back at Scott's house, Francis prepared to inform Martinha's family of his decision to wed their daughter before his imminent return to Jangsylan. He planned to visit Merbok so that he might formally plight his troth and spend some time with his future wife. Privately, he desired the whole damned business to be resolved as quickly as possible. Martinha would remain in Merbok for the time being while he embarked for the island; he would send for her later. In the meantime, he had more urgent matters on his mind than romancing a girl.

'Where's that damned Soliman?' Light's temper was not improved by the composition of the letter to Lady Thong Di. The more he tried to find the words, the more he regretted his decision, despite all the justifications in its favour. Tossing down his pen, he shouted again for Soliman, the foundling who had become his right hand. He needed the boy's help with its wording 'Sol? Where are you hiding, you wretched boy?'

But Soliman could not be found. In fact, Light realised that he had not seen him since his return, a most unusual occurrence, for the boy normally clung to him like a limpet. By the time evening fell and he had still not been located, he began to worry. At the mosque where the boy attended classes, he was informed that he not been seen since the day before. Nor could the house servants explain his absence. It simply wasn't like the boy. Soliman never took himself off alone for long.

A search party was organised to scour the settlement and finally Soliman was located, left for dead in a filthy drainage ditch on the outskirts of the town. Had it been the rainy season, he would surely have drowned. The boy had been badly beaten; several bones were broken. He was dehydrated and weak from blood loss, but still alive, drifting in and out of consciousness.

Light himself carried him through the streets, at first too concerned for his survival even to contemplate how this dreadful attack had come to pass. Bursting into Scott's dwelling, he ordered the table cleared and gently laid Soliman down, easing away his shirt to assess his condition. Although many years had passed since his days as surgeon's assistant in the Royal Navy, the lessons he had learned had not been forgotten. From the recesses of his mind, the instinctive memory of the healer took control. Meanwhile Scott had fetched a local woman, a midwife but the nearest to a doctor he could find. 'Francis, let this woman dress his wounds –' Scott began.

'No, leave it to me. I have experience in these matters,' Light insisted, all the while running his hands delicately along Soliman's right arm from shoulder to palm, tracing the impossible angle of the damaged limb. Soliman was moaning softly but his eyes remained closed. The lad had taken a brutal pounding. Livid bruises had formed. His face was bloody and his lips badly swollen. It was difficult to gauge the full extent of the damage beneath the layer of dirt and blood.

'Get some water,' Light muttered to the woman – or to anyone present. He was too far within himself to be aware of others, running through all the possibilities that a real doctor would consider at such a moment. 'Clean him up! And try to make him drink. He's probably suffering from heatstroke added to everything else.'

Suddenly Light took a firm grip on the arm, jerking it in a violent movement. A loud popping sound, accompanied by a piercing shriek from Soliman, caused the onlookers to shudder. The arm snapped back in place with a bony click. 'Not broken, thank God! Just out of its socket. But he has broken ribs. It's too soon to tell if there is rupture so we must watch for signs of internal bleeding. His skull has taken a heavy knock. He is concussed. His brain has received a fierce shaking. Expect some vomiting ...'

With the skills acquired in his youth, Light dressed Soliman's wounds, binding his ribs tightly before carrying him to his own cot. By his side he remained for the next two days, tending to Soliman's every need, wiping up vomit and changing dressings, praying to whatever God might listen for his precious boy to recover.

Soliman for his part could shed no light on the attack. He had been startled from behind and beyond that had no recall. Light did not need to investigate further. He was convinced that his dear boy had been punished for his sake. The loathsome Hythe had arranged this assault on the eve of his departure in revenge for the beating he had received at Light's own hands. Not that Hythe would have done the deed himself. He would not have taken the chance that brave little Sol might have fought back. Doubtless he had paid a few sepoys to carry out the heinous deed.

'If I ever have the misfortune to meet you again, Charles

Hythe,' Light promised as he knelt by the boy's side. 'If we ever meet again, you pitiful, cringing coward, I swear that I will kill you with my bare hands. That is my promise. It would be worth chancing the hangman's rope to put an end to your miserable existence.'

8

Raja Sehari

Merbok, Queddah. August 1772

Martinha Rozells slammed down the book she was reading in frustration. English was the most ridiculous language, impossible to pronounce, unfathomable to spell, and unpleasant to the ear. She hated it almost as much as she disliked her tutor, Père Michel, the ancient French priest sent to Merbok to live with her family so that they could hear Mass regularly. The nearest mission was Alor Setar, so they made do with this doddery old fellow, who was as hard of hearing as he was rigid in his disciplinary fervour. Her mother had asked him to give daily English lessons to Martinha and Felipe. They lived in dread of it.

Her displeasure was fuelled by more than her dislike of the language alone. Since her mother and grandmother had taken her aside and informed her that she was soon be married, she had become withdrawn and sullen. The English captain who had brought his little Malay son to dinner? He had been little more than a curiosity to her, an opportunity to observe a farang at close quarters. It had never occurred to her that his visit had been for him to appraise her as a potential wife. In fact, she and Felipe had suspected that their lady mother had been his interest. After all, the captain and her mother were of a similar age, and he had been an acquaintance of her father. Furthermore, as a merchant trader, he would probably be mostly absent, so their peaceful life could carry on much as it always did.

But to discover that she had been the object of his desire all along? The very idea filled her with disgust. Captain Francis Light was at least thirty, a veritable old age to a girl not quite sixteen. He was also large and hairy, just like all Englishmen. His nose was long and his feet and hands were big. How could her mother force such a man upon her?

Martinha rose from her table to pace about her room, unspent emotions and pent up energy coursing through her young body. Life was either tediously dull or bitterly tragic. Her fate was either to be confined to endless tedium in the middle of nowhere with nothing but boring studies and her little brother for company, or married to an older man and sent far away, where she would have even less freedom and must submit to the unwanted attentions of a man she couldn't bear. Such was the life of a young woman. Her grandmother had told her enough stories of a similar ilk. History was repeating itself. Mother had been blessed to marry a good man like her father. How she wished she might be so fortunate!

Martinha viewed her face in the mirror from a variety of angles, objectively aware of her own delicate, pale beauty, wishing in her petulance that she had been born fat and ugly. Then mayhap every man who saw her would run away and leave her well alone. She threw herself upon on her bed, slipping the pages of a poem from beneath her mattress. It had been a gift from Aunt Chan, her mother's elder sister, concealed amongst a parcel of trinkets. Martinha had kept it well hidden; her virtuous mother would not approve of its erotic imagery. The more worldly Lady Chan, however, had deemed it appropriate that Martinha should learn something of the affairs of the heart now that she was approaching marriageable age.

The poem was a short extract copied from *Lilit Phra Lo*, that famous tragedy. It described the moment when Prince Lo first encountered the two beautiful sisters, Princess Phuan and Princess Pheng, the daughters of his enemy. The sequence was heartbreakingly poignant in respect of the dire fate awaiting all three. This was how love should be! Passion so encompassing that even death itself could not shake it. Not to be a piece of cargo traded like a bale of exotic silk.

Her brother Felipe had been bereft at the news that his precious sister was leaving, although Martinha suspected his response was driven more by jealousy than sorrow; he felt abandoned in this backwater while his sister was escaping to join the adult world. But like so many girls before her, Martinha would meekly do her duty. It was what her mother wanted. It would make her grandmother happy. She had been told it would 'save them all', although she failed to understand how her marriage might accomplish that. Yet she understood filial piety. There would never be any doubt that when the time came, she would do her duty.

The first time Martinha met her future husband – other than the short visit he had made to Merbok weeks before when she had been a mere child at the dinner table and he had taken little notice of her – was at the grand *bersanding* on her wedding day. It had been Light's intention to visit Merbok to formally ask for Martinha's hand in the European style, but Soliman's injuries had prevented him. Thus, there had been no attempt to court his young bride, now relegated to a minor player in the arrangements. Instead the traditions of the Malay court had predominated, where contact before the day between bride and groom was deemed unnecessary. The official betrothal had been delivered on Light's behalf by court officials who themselves negotiated the dowry – provided by the sultan himself – and the gifts from the groom-to-be. For this was to be a customary wedding in all its forms, other than those pertaining to Islamic custom.

The palace took the place of the bride's own home. It was there in the women's quarters that Martinha was prepared for her role as 'Queen for the Day' with pampering that would have befitted a royal consort. While her grandmother clucked around and her mother drifted about, a somewhat subdued and distant figure, Martinha was primped and cossetted, bathed in perfumed waters, and her skin rubbed with fragrant oils. Her hands and feet were hennaed in swirls and motifs that were strange and primitive to her. She was aware of her mother's discomfort and her grandmother's pride, but with a distinct sense of dislocation. It was as if the entire proceedings were happening to someone else. What did all this have to do with her and the Englishman?

When all the tedious preparations were complete, Martinha was eased into the red songket wedding costume. The silken brocade, heavy with golden thread, weighed her down as much as the occasion depressed her spirits. Then came the jewels, gold necklaces, strings of pearls, rings and bracelets, anklets and earrings, finished by an elaborate hair arrangement, interlaced with jasmine flowers. Finally, the outfit was completed by a headdress comprised of dozens of little golden pendants, each tipped with a tiny pearl. Every time she moved her head, she tinkled. The burden on her neck was formidable.

Martinha was led by her attendants to a dais festooned in

swags of yellow cloth, where her groom already awaited on his grand bridal chair, *raja sehari*, the King for the Day. A man she barely knew and cared for even less. Moving at stately pace, she passed through a phantasmagorical dream where little made sense and where random, unconnected actions whirled about her. But this was real. This was her fate.

It was impossible to catch more than a glimpse of him. The golden head adornment obscured her vision; she could neither turn nor lift her head for fear of dislodging the fragile coronet. As she made her way through the throng, eyes demurely downcast, *kompang* drums beat her arrival, and music and singing welcomed her. Her attendants lowered her gently into her seat, but her vision was restricted to her lap and the knees of the man seated next to her. His sarong was the same fabric as hers. He had long legs. He was her husband. The hall fell silent and a holy man began the invocation; the guests either mumbled along or bent their heads in silent prayer.

A hint of pressure against her arm. 'Greetings, Martinha. Have courage. The day will be long but it will end,' a low voice murmured. He spoke in the language of her mother, an unexpected courtesy, an attempt to comfort her. For that she was grateful. At least he was a kindly man. As carefully as she could without disturbing the cumbersome headdress, Martinha nodded her acknowledgment and returned the pressure. It was the first time they had touched.

By the time the rituals and feasting were over, and the dances and music performances complete, many hours had passed. Throughout all that time, although the guests had in their turn processed forward to sprinkle rosewater and potpourri, neither the bride nor the groom had been given food or drink. Martinha was lightheaded and her limbs felt numb. She wondered whether she would faint away completely. When the moment finally came for the couple to be led to the bridal chamber, she would not have been able to rise and walk for herself without the aid of her ladies. As her new husband had said: the day had indeed been long but it had at last come to an end.

The door swung closed. They were finally alone, heavy teak silencing the sounds of merriment and festivity. The world had vanished. The cosmos was this room. The two halves of the universe must meet on this night, as her mother's people believed. A man and a woman must cleave to each other and become one flesh, according to Christian teachings. Moments before, her mother and her grandmother had removed her headdress and the heavy *selendang* shawl, the ropes of pearls, and the many items of jewellery. They had embraced her and whispered blessings, before slipping away. Now Martinha stood alone before her husband, face uncovered, still clad in her robe – and wondered what came next. The Scriptures did not clarify that.

'Well, then, my little wife. Thank God that's done. Let's eat. I am so very hungry.' Francis tossed away his *dastar*. The elegant keris worn tucked into his belt, he placed more carefully on the table, momentarily admiring its gold and jewelled sheath. 'It's a beautiful piece. The sultan gave it to me as a wedding gift. It's of Bugis origin. They make the most astonishing weapons. I expect it amused the old fellow to give me something he had stolen from his enemies!'

It was not at all as Martinha had anticipated. Francis pointed to the large velvet cushions set around a low table piled with food, fruit and dainties, indicating that she should join him. Momentarily she remained standing, unsure of herself, and then, recognising her own hunger and thirst, she lowered herself down gingerly. Francis filled a plate of food for her and poured out a glass of rosewater. 'Here, Martinha. Eat. You're very pale. It will make you feel better.'

Better for what, she mused to herself? Yet despite herself, Martinha found herself enjoying the food, for she was indeed very hungry. Her husband smiled tentatively over and followed her example. They ate in an uncomfortable silence.

'Would you like some more rice? Cake? Fruit?' Francis kept adding items to her plate. He was trying to make a connection but she simply did not know what to say in reply. Instead, she accepted each new helping with silent affirmation.

When they had finished all they were likely to eat, Francis rose and strode over to the window where he stood turned away, hands behind his back. He was tall, she thought. And strongly built. His shoulders were broad, his hips slim. He looked ridiculous in Malay garb. Europeans always did. But she rather liked his brown and wavy hair, tied in a bow of velvet. She wondered if it was as soft as it looked.

'Martinha?' Suddenly spinning round, he caught her in the open act of staring. Her head dropped, bashful to meet him eye to eye. 'Martinha? My dear, we must talk. Do you understand what I am saying? Please, speak to me. Help me to understand you.'

She was unsure what he meant. Raising her eyes, Martinha looked directly at him for the first time in her life. His was an earnest, open face with strong lines. His eyes were blue green, the colour of the sea at midday. 'I do not know what to say to you,' she answered truthfully.

'Then, ask me a question. Surely there are things about me you would like to know? Ask me anything.' He sat down across from her. 'Martinha, we need to get to know each other, for we are married now.'

Martinha paused, then tilted her head at him. 'What must I call you?'

At that he broke out in a warm smile that caused his eyes to sparkle playfully. 'Why, Francis, of course! After all, it is my name. And I shall call you Martinha, unless you wish me to use another name. It is your choice.'

She considered his comment carefully. 'Francis. I will call you Francis. My mother calls me Ma Li. It means jasmine. My father called me Muti, his little pearl. But I would like you to call me Martinha. After all, it is my name,' she added, revealing a hint of her true spark. 'And now I ask you another question, correct?'

'Indeed,' Francis replied with a courteous bow.

Her words tumbled out, spilling thoughts that had spun around her head all day. 'Why did you want to marry me? When you came to our home that time, you hardly looked at me. Did the sultan order you to take me for a wife?' she asked boldly.

It was Light's turn to give her questions careful consideration. Martinha had brought him straight to the crux of the matter and deserved an honest answer. 'It was not the sultan who suggested it, although he was happy to agree. I married you because your mother asked me to. She feared the sultan might force you to marry a man of his choosing. She wishes to keep you safe.'

Martinha gave him a piercing stare, lightened by the flicker of amusement that graced her lips. It reminded him of her mother.

'To save me from marriage to an older man I do not know, my mother marries me to an older man I do not know. Is that the measure of it, Francis?'

Her acuity caused him to laugh out loud. She grinned back, emboldened by his reaction. Where he had first seen a little girl, he now recognised a clever, shrewd young woman of spirit. It was not for the first time in his life that he had underestimated well-brought-up maidens. A fleeting memory of poor Marianne Lynn crossed his mind unbidden.

'Dearest Martinha, you have inherited the wisdom of both your mother and your aunt. Perhaps I am a more suitable choice because I was already known to your family, if not to you. I am also a Christian, which your mother feels is more fitting in your husband. And I hope I am a gentleman. I promise never to do you harm, Martinha. You are now my wife and I will always keep you safe.'

It was sweetly said. If not love, it was at least kindness. 'Well, Francis Light, it seems we are now married and must make the best of it. I, too, will make a promise. I will carry out my duties as a good wife. If my family approves of you, then I accept the wisdom of their decision, for they have my best interests at heart,' she replied cautiously. But in her head, Martinha wished he might have said more. Perhaps that they might one day find love?

She rose, aware that now, with night falling, he would expect her to offer herself to him. Her mother had told her to begin to undress and he would know what to do next. Standing before him, she fumbled with the brooches that held together the front of her *kebaya*, her fingers betraying her anxiety. But Francis stayed her hand, taking her fingers in his own. She shot him a troubled look.

'No! It is too soon, Martinha. I do not intend to make demands on you tonight or any forthcoming night until we know each other better. For now, it is enough that I can keep you safe. In time, when you are a little older and fondness has grown between us, then we will become man and wife fully. But not yet. Nor has this wedding, as splendid as it was, been conducted accorded to Christian rites. Frankly, I had little idea of what was going on. One day soon, we will marry properly and then all will be as it should be between us. Until then, you are my betrothed. Let us begin our courtship first.'

Francis dropped her hand and stepped back, to give her space and time to consider his words. 'Where will you sleep then?' she asked him, still trying to comprehend this unexpectedly courtly action.

'These cushions will do for me. I'm a sailor. I've known harder beds. Tonight, I wish for us to become friends. Let's simply talk. I want to tell you something of my life and I want to hear about yours. And then we will retire to sleep – separately. Is that acceptable to you?'

Martinha smiled, a wave of relief coursing through her body, bringing the colour back to her cheeks and the light to her eyes. The great weight was lifted. Now she was lightheaded, not with fear and exhaustion, but with happiness. 'But what of tomorrow? Will my mother expect me to have become a woman? Will people gossip if I do not carry a child?'

'I doubt you would be with child by the morrow anyway!' Francis grinned. 'Martinha, what we do from now on is between you and me alone. The opinion of others does not matter as long as we are of one mind. Now, if you will excuse me, I am going to strip off this sarong and sit here in my shirt and breeches. Please feel free to disencumber yourself from some of those beautiful but burdensome robes. Then let us refill our glasses with this excellent rose water and spend a pleasant evening in chatter.'

Martinha jumped up with the easy grace of the young, no longer the silent and sombre maiden of the hours before. She unfastened her kebaya with much more dexterity than her nervous fingers had allowed her earlier. Beneath she wore a blouse and, along with her sarong, she deemed it acceptable clothing in the company of her betrothed. Thus, they settled down around the table, all barriers disappearing. They talked until Martinha's eyelids began to droop and she stifled yawns behind her hand.

With deft charm, Francis lifted her up in his arms while she giggled shyly, and he laid her softly on the bed, covering her over and placing a chaste kiss upon her lips. 'Good night, sweet Martinha. Sleep well. This has been a good day.'

As he arranged a sleeping place for himself on the pile of velvet cushions, Francis heard the rustle of the bedcoverings as Martinha sat back up. 'Good night, Francis,' she whispered, speaking to him for the first time in her halting English. 'May God bless you always.'

***

Soliman wandered about the palace grounds, sampling the lively entertainment that was set to continue throughout the night. The atmosphere was joyful. Not only had a wedding taken place, but peace had been restored after the turbulence of the past few years.

Even the rise of the Siamese was preferable to the disorder of the Bugis and the intrigue of dissident nobles. The palace of the sultan was triumphant.

For a time, the boy sat and watched the *wayang kulit* performance, a rare treat that he would usually savour. But tonight, his mind wandered from the entertainment. He had spent an entire day on his feet, his ribs were aching again, and his head was throbbing. The milling crowds made him feel uneasy after weeks of quiet convalescence. Drifting away, he lingered on the fringe of the cock-fighting circle, crowded with eager gamblers fervently shouting and encouraging their birds. But that also failed to catch his interest – so he moved on.

Eventually he found himself in the grounds outside the pavilion where the captain and his new lady were spending their first night together. There he sank to the earth to sit cross-legged in the shadows, heartsick and despondent. In his hands he played with the finely wrought silver keris that Captain Francis had presented him that morning to complete his costume in traditional fashion. Light had told him he was old enough to bear a weapon. If he was ever attacked again, he would now have the means to defend himself. But Soliman knew what it really meant. Captain Francis was casting him off to fend for himself. The man he regarded as his father now had a wife and would soon have children of his own. Soliman was almost a man. He had his own keris. He was expected to make his own way in life. For who was he, when all was said and done? Just an orphan boy. After all, he had never called Captain Francis *'Bapaku'*.

9

Duplicity

From the moment the launch left the jetty and began its way along the lower reaches of the estuary to the sea heading towards the English ship moored in the bay, its progress was followed carefully by the captain of the *Blake*. The oared ceremonial vessel of ornately carved teak, replete with silken hangings, was not a sea-going boat but a barque meant for ferrying people of significance in comfort along the river, or for their transfer to a ship. It was a royal craft, bearing the red trade insignia of Siam. What might be the reason for a visit from the governor's office – or the king's military command? Light doubted it would be a social call.

During their early months in Jangsylan, Light and Scott had remained aboard ship close to the island but ready at any time to hoist sail and depart should the hostilities of the land boil over and draw them in. For, in King Tak Sin's desire to reclaim the island first from the Malays and latterly the Bugis, his army had swooped down in an orgy of brutality. Malays, Samsans, Eurasians, Chulias and Europeans alike had perished, many of whom were mere random bystanders, their misfortune to be in port at the wrong time. The local Siamese had been largely left unscathed, other than the inevitable retribution visited on those who had most obviously collaborated with the enemy. Since the involvement of Light and Scott with various rival factions on the island and beyond was common knowledge, neither could take the chance that they themselves might become targets of the purges. Thus, they had remained offshore throughout.

Yet, the king – or rather his deputy, Lord Duang, the commander-in-chief of his military forces – did not intend to be overly vindictive. Punishment was one thing, but the new regime understood the politics of the island. Who could blame traders for their fluctuating loyalties in the face of so much uncertainty? It was inevitable that they would ally with whoever was in power, blown by the contrary winds of necessity, for conflict is the death knell of commerce. Too much violence against merchants would only damage the economy of Thalang, which was far from the king's intention.

More far-sighted than previous inward-looking rulers of Siam, King Tak Sin was himself very much interested in access to the trade of the Straits and the rest of the world through this little jewel of an island in the south. It was essential that business should continue to flourish under Siamese rule as quickly as possible. It had been enough to sacrifice a few scapegoats to demonstrate the ruthlessness and intent of the new king should his authority be challenged. Now the time for reconciliation had come.

A new superintendent from the mainland, Khang Seng, had been installed in the independent-minded southern region, a member of the same Chinese Teochew merchant community that had funded King Tak Sin's rise, and, of course, of which he was a member himself by virtue of his birth. This appointment had served as both a sop to the Chinese and a warning to the nobility. For the time being, the latter was to be denied political power.

Their previous venality had shown them incapable of loyalty to the sovereign. It was now beholden on them to win back their king's trust.

The strictures of living aboard had been of little consequence to Scott and Light, who spent much of any year at sea. Between them they now owned seven vessels employing a number of local and European captains servicing the ever-hungry market for opium, weaponry and cotton. Light was one of the leading suppliers, making regular forays to Madras for guns, opium and cloth, where he would trade in tin from Thalang and rice from Queddah, along with his other specialities: pearls, elephants, tortoise shell, ambergris and horn. Scott, meanwhile, concentrated on the southern waters and the lucrative China and Arab trade between Malacca, Riau and Aceh. Light's reputation may have taken a beating, but Scott had kept himself in the background of the political intrigues, thus was still regarded as unaligned and interested only in profit, qualities preferred by both the Bugis and the Dutch. Light and Scott were indeed the ideal partnership.

Their offshore commercial enterprise might be thriving, but they were still to find their feet in Thalang itself. Superintendent Khang Seng was a solemn-faced merchant, the very epitome of inscrutability, who did not personally favour the new farang agency, nor did he look kindly on any European merchants. Whilst allowing their trade, he was punctilious in his application of the law, restricting the liberties that Light, Scott and others had been accustomed to enjoy for so long. Light himself regarded Khang Seng as an out-and-out villain, as did many of the local Siamese, who disliked any attempt to limit their activities. His opinion, of course, was somewhat partial predicated on the fact that since his arrival he was no longer able to abuse the local system as he had done in the past.

The regional governor himself was suspicious of Light's close relationship with the Sultan of Queddah. He was also inclined to mistrust any merchant who was hand-in-glove with the Ban Takkien clan. Little had been heard of late from Lady Chan. Initial rumours suggested that her family might have been amongst the victims of the Siamese invasion but Light doubted that. With her eldest son a leading young army general, she must have been manoeuvring her position long before the royal armies landed. She might even have been secretly in contact with the invading force all along, despite her relationship with the Bugis governor. That would have been typical of this most duplicitous of ladies. But, wherever she had been in recent months, she had kept a low profile.

These matters occupied Light's mind as he watched the launch approach at its slow and steady pace. Tharua Bay was a calm and sheltered mooring, protected as it was from the monsoon winds by a chain of outlying islands. But therein also lay its danger. A sailing ship could not escape at speed, especially on a day such as this when there was hardly a breath of breeze. Nibbling on his bottom lip in thought, Light considered various possibilities. His men were armed, but stood down. The sails were hauled in preparation, and the anchor part-raised. They might have to make a run for it if this boat contained soldiers sent to arrest him. But surely, a vessel of this opulence would not have been required for such a commission? Unless it was a trap. But who could say? One could be the enemy on one day and an ally the next in these waters. It was important to keep an open mind – with a pistol close at hand.

A Siamese herald announced the arrival of a senior military commander, a representative of King Tak Sin himself. The officer was an elegant, impossibly handsome young fellow, of a manly type of beauty found only in the East. His skin was smooth, his hair like polished ebony; he was tall, slender and serene of expression. Everything about this man spoke of privilege, rank and breeding. He was likely well placed in the new dynasty, possibly of high aristocratic rank himself.

There was much formality in the initial welcome, with bowing, exchanging of gifts and refreshments, during which both sides had the opportunity to take account of each other whilst giving the impression of exchanging pleasantries. Finally, they reached that crucial juncture in Asian negotiations, often overlooked by Europeans who deem excessive etiquette a sign of weakness. Englishmen charge straight to the point, barrelling in with bombast and arrogance to claim the upper ground. But in the East, one needed first to take the measure of a situation in order to tease out the chinks in the other's armour. It was unseemly to rush into business until the niceties were accomplished. These courtesies could be misleading; behind the restrained smiles and diplomatic compliments might lie a sudden change of direction.

'My Lord, your presence honours my humble vessel!' Light said as they settled down in his cabin, hastily put to rights by Soliman and a few crewmen. Although the young officer gave no indication of disdain for his surroundings, Light felt ill-at-ease in the cramped and cluttered space. His guest had the look of a man used to lofty halls and shady corridors. It immediately cast him in a position of disadvantage, even though he was on his own territory. Light wished he had arranged for them to sit on the open deck.

'The honour is mine, sir. My sincere apologies for arriving without notice or invitation. It is an unforgiveable breach of etiquette,' the officer replied. Unless you are planning on throwing me in chains and hauling me off to a dungeon on the island, Light thought to himself. 'But first may I introduce myself properly? Whilst I am indeed a military officer and the representative of King Tak Sin, founder of the glorious Thonburi Dynasty, scourge of the Burmese, and saviour of Siam, my reasons for visiting today are more directly connected with Thalang itself. For I am in fact a son of this island and it is in the interests of its prosperity and security that I am here. My name is Lord Thian, a member of the Ban Takkien clan. I believe we are related: my mother is aunt to the Lady Martinha.'

For a few beats, Light struggled to comprehend this relationship, and then the mists cleared. This must be Lady Chan's eldest son, the young man who had survived the terrible events of the siege of Ayutthaya and had thrown in his lot with the new king.

'We are cousins by marriage, I believe? This is an unexpected pleasure, my Lord! How are your mother and stepfather? For I have not heard from her of late. With the recent troubles in Thalang, I have had concerns for her wellbeing,' Light inquired tentatively.

Thian smiled, revealing white, even teeth. 'She is well, and recently bore another child, a daughter. My mother is a formidable woman, Captain. Age and the demands of motherhood do not daunt her. She has withdrawn for her confinement to the family estates for the time being but still leads the family enterprises with the vigour of a man half her age!'

'Please give her my congratulations on the safe delivery,' was Light's guarded reply. 'I look forward to renewing our acquaintance when she has returned to society.' It was unlikely Lord Thian knew the full extent of his relationship with his mother.

'You may soon pass on your good wishes in person, Captain, for my visit today is partly to invite you to our family home. It has come to my mother's notice that you have been living aboard ship since your return. She hopes that you will soon settle in more comfortable quarters on the island. It is her firm belief that, together with Captain Scott, your presence in Tharua is most beneficial to our trading community. Furthermore, she wishes to facilitate your enterprise in any way she can, for reasons both of personal relationship and mutual benefit. Do not fear the Siamese government. Please feel free to come and go as you see fit.'

Lady Chan had landed on her feet again with her usual feline grace and the many lives with which she was apparently endowed. Of course, she had survived the purge. Was there ever any doubt? She had probably been in contact with the new king through her well-placed son, even as she had been conspiring with the rebel king of Ligor, the Bugis of Selangor, and the Malays of Queddah. Like her father before her, she always had a finger in every pie. And still amidst it all she found time to bear more children!

'I am honoured at the invitation, my Lord. Captain Scott is currently in Malacca but I will inform him on his return. He has family on the island and will be glad to return home,' Light answered.

'Several families, or so I am told,' Thian grinned. His placid exterior concealed a lively spirit and an easy manner. Light responded by rolling his eyes in amusement. The formality between the two men was easing.

'But would Superintendent Khang Seng be amenable to this arrangement? He has been cautious so far in accepting my approaches,' Light asked with circumspection. He did not wish to be caught between opposing forces.

'Do not concern yourself with the superintendent. Chao Phraya Khang Seng is regional governor with far wider responsibilities than our little island alone. Our Great King has indicated his intention to appoint a governor for Thalang itself, one more acceptable to the people now that the island has been returned to Siamese control. I assure you that the new governor will be delighted to support your commercial activities in every way.' It was a remarkable piece of intelligence that no doubt hid even more than it said, as was the Siamese way.

Light decided not to prevaricate; he suspected Lord Thian was not a man to take offence at the more direct approach. 'So, the new governor will be a local appointee?'

Thian shook his head. 'Not exactly. But as close to local as is possible. The king has chosen Phaya Pimon, the current governor of Phattalung province, my mother's beloved husband. My stepfather is a man of great experience and good character, well known to the people of Thalang. Naturally, this is a great honour for our family.'

It was a stroke of genius. Lady Chan would be the effective future governor of Thalang! King Tak Sin was exploiting his trust in Lord Thian at the same time as he embraced the talents of the

Lady of Thalang herself.

'An excellent choice, if I may say so! May I offer you a taste of something stronger than tea, my Lord? It seems fitting to celebrate this good news with a glass of brandy.' Lord Thian accepted; another positive indication of his character in Light's opinion.

They turned to family matters and spoke of Light's recent marriage to his young cousin, Martinha, still at the family home in Queddah until it was deemed safe for her to return to Thalang. Soon he intended for them to set up house together on the island. Martinha would be happy, for she missed her island home and her Siamese family. Lord Thian himself had not seen her for six years; she had been a little girl when he had taken his leave for war. That led them on to military matters. Light was curious to hear of the many triumphant campaigns that Lord Thian had fought with King Tak Sin. Thian was curious about the sea engagements of Light's naval days. The two men exchanged their personal witness of war.

'Captain Light –'

'Francis, please. We are cousin brothers and, I hope, will become good friends,' Light insisted, now that the atmosphere between them had relaxed into the camaraderie of comrades-in-arms.

'Cousin Francis, then. There is another purpose in my visit today. I have a business proposition for you, one that is entirely separate from any that my mother might propose. This request comes from the king himself. He has personally asked me to engage your services.'

Light was astonished. How had the king of Siam even learned of his existence? Nothing and no one of significance escaped the eye of the royal court, it would seem.

Thian continued. 'The north is still unsettled, for the Burmese continue to cause nuisance. Another invasion is imminent. It has come to the Great King's notice that you have access to large quantities of armaments from India, and a plenitude of powder and cannon. What are you willing to supply for us?'

Light feigned deep thought, although he already knew his answer. 'As much as the king desires,' he replied with a flourish.

'Despite your amity with the Sultan of Queddah? Surely he will not approve of you giving aid to his enemies?' Thian countered with rapier-like acuity.

Light bowed his head in acknowledgement of the question. 'The sultan need not be told. And if he were, he would not be surprised. Sultan Muhammed is the master of strategy, as is your king himself. The prime aim for all is to maintain the balance of power. It can be argued, that supplying weapons to his enemy to keep him occupied elsewhere is the best distraction to safeguard the kingdom of Queddah from interference. And what does the sultan have to fear from King Tak Sin anyway? He sends the *bunga mas* tribute regularly to acknowledge his fealty.'

'He also sends it to Burma,' Thian broke in with a knowing grin.

Light conceded the point, hands raised in mock surrender. 'Which proves my point entirely. Sultan Muhammed Jiwa wishes to maintain the status quo.'

'Then it seems we can do business, Cousin Francis. Now, perhaps another measure of your excellent brandy to seal the agreement?'

***

The following day, Light received another unexpected visitor, this time from the sea, rounding Cape Yamoo shortly after dawn. The watch observed the boat curiously. Although it was a humble local vessel, it was early in the day for a trader to be about, so its presence was reported immediately to the captain. The vessel was a simple flat-bottomed sampan with rounded cabin, of a sort common in Malay and Siamese waters, used mainly for sailing up and down the coast and from island to island, conveying local goods to larger markets. But the stealthy manner in which it had used the cover of the pre-dawn to enter the bay – possibly from the direction of Ko Yang Rai island where it had probably spent the night – suggested subterfuge.

The clandestine visitor was none other than Temenggung Dajati, the head of Sultan Muhammed Jiwa's military forces, a man well known to Light. It was a risky endeavour for a highplaced minister to sail so close to the jaws of Siam. Once the niceties had been performed, and the temenggung had taken refreshments, he presented Light with a personal message from the sultan. Light took the ornate brass cylinder from its velvet bag and eased out the letter, excusing himself to read it alone in his cabin. Once there, he summoned Soliman whose assistance in these matters he always valued.

From the ruler of Queddah, the Abode of Peace, to our dear son Captain Lait, Dewa Raja

When you left us for Ujung Salang, everything was peaceful. Mr Monckton remained as the Company representative but has done nothing of value for us since.

*He despoils everything that he touches. Out of courtesy
for the authority he bears from the Governor of Madras
and because of our admiration for you, we have ignored
his dreadful conduct, nor will we say more about it at
this time. However, on the next occasion that you present
yourself before us, we will further discuss his misdeeds.*

*We eagerly await news of our dear son in Ujung
Salang for reports have been concerning and we long to
hear that you are safe and thriving. Furthermore, two
merchants of Queddah, Nakhoda Mir Amin and Fakir
Lebai, who departed some time ago with our cargoes to
trade in Ujung Salang, have still not returned. Thus, we
have despatched Temenggung Dajati to request our son's
support in assisting these merchants in their return to us.
May our son help overcome our difficulties, as you have
done on so many occasions.*

*The Temenggung has been informed of all our other
news. Our son may speak freely to him.*

*Written in the Dalawal year of 1187 AH, on Thursday,
24th day of the month of Dzu'lhijjah.*

Light's report would disappoint the Sultan. Although his two
merchants had not been killed, their goods had been impounded;
they were currently mouldering in a prison on the island. It would
require a sizeable ransom to negotiate their release – and the loss
of their cargoes. The sultan probably already suspected as much.

The real purpose of this missive lay in the final sentence. The
temenggung was in possession of further intelligence that he had

been instructed to impart personally; a senior statesman would not be required merely to deliver letters. The danger of a royal minister falling into the hands of the Siamese indicated that the sultan thought it was a risk worth taking. Light called Soliman to attend their discussions; he did not wish to miss anything of the significant 'other news' that Temenggung Dajati had to relate. If it was so secret that it could not be committed to a confidential mail, it must be highly sensitive indeed.

Returning to the temenggung, Light bade him divulge the information. With an elaborate play of politeness and courtesy, taking many winding routes to reach the heart of the matter, Dajati finally came to the point. It was all Light could do to restrain himself from laughing out loud at the audacity and perspicacity of the old king. Sultan Muhammed Jiwa wished to purchase weaponry from the British, which he intended to sell on to Burma. The cargo was to be transported direct from India to Burma via Mergui, so that no Queddah connection could readily be made. The Machiavellian sultan was already stirring up the pot against the rise of Tak Sin, and securing a new ally in Burma, just in case. Would the intrigue never end? But when all was said and done, Light had nothing to lose. More guns meant more profit. He would now be the main supplier of armaments both to Siam and Burma. The sultan would be heartily delighted at that piece of intelligence.

It was many months before the transactions were completed. Not that the armaments were difficult to source, even in the vast quantities that Scott and Light required. No questions were asked in India when they obtained two shiploads of weaponry, enough to launch a war, and then moved them across the Andaman Sea. The tedious delay, however, resulted from the usual waiting around for the suitable sailing season. But the two men did not waste their time stranded in Madras and Calcutta. They had arrived with lucrative cargoes from the Straits to advertise the debut of their new agency.

There were many old contacts to meet, for the new trading company intended to drum up significant interest in the port of Jangsylan, a landing that had been somewhat neglected by English traders of late. The general opinion of the day held that Siam was hostile to outsiders as recent history had borne out.

But Light now planned to challenge that assumption. He described how, despite being surrounded by 2 000 armed Siamese in a tiny thatched house on the coast near the port, Scott and he had been left unscathed, whilst terrible atrocities had occurred in the settlement about. They themselves had personally witnessed captives being roped together and trodden under foot by elephants. But the Europeans had largely been unharmed. They had never been the target of the new regime. Furthermore, the new governor was most open-handed in his desire to attract foreign merchants to Jangsylan. They only had to seek out Scott and Light Esquires for introductions and they would be free to operate, on payment of their usual commission, of course.

This version of the past year's events put about by the two partners might not stand up to the closest scrutiny – but who but they would know different? Nor was it entirely fiction. Terrible punishments had indeed been dealt out on the island. Scott and Light had come through dangerous times untouched. As the rumours grew that the ubiquitous Captain Light had managed to charm his way into yet another previously obdurate market, the disappointments of the Monckton affair soon began to recede into the distance.

It was now all about the advantages of Jangsylan: a free port, already long established, with links to the fabulous wealth of Siam and an ideal landing across the Andaman, well away from the pirates and the Dutch. There were even whispers of a new route to China that Light was personally recommending across the narrow Isthmus of Kra by land and river to the east coast and the South China Sea, bypassing the dangers of the southern Straits entire. The idea was gaining in momentum. Suddenly Light again found himself the man to watch.

10

A Servant of Two Masters

Thonburi, Siam. February 1774

The following year, while Scott sailed for Burma on the *Blake*, loaded up to its full 250 tons with guns on behalf of the sultan of Queddah, Light took the overland route from Thalang to Thonburi to personally deliver a similar consignment, at the invitation of the King himself.

His journey was by way of a surprisingly accessible track long-established for trade goods, particularly tin. This long-established tin route was ideal for heavy loads. Pontoons loaded with weaponry were floated across the narrow northern channel between the island and the Phang Na mainland, where teams of elephants dragged the great pallets across a well-cleared pathway to the mining town of Takupua. There they continued via the Khao Sak Pass down to Phanom, to be loaded onto river boats and transferred to the sea at the port of Ao Ban Don.

At the jetty, ships were waiting to transport the goods north across the gulf to the Chao Phraya river, while an elegant royal launch stood ready for Captain Light himself. The trek across country had taken seven days in all; it would have taken weeks to sail south through the Straits and up the eastern Peninsula. But more crucially – would a cargo of weapons have survived the sea route? It was hard to imagine that the Dutch or the Bugis, the

Illanun or the Siaks – or any other random *orang laut* – would not have got wind of such a treasure in their waters. This was the safest and most secretive method of shipping such commodity.

The trek had been a pleasant enough experience that gave Light the opportunity to see more of the interior than his usual business allowed. He was impressed by the efficiency and apparent security of the route, which was not plagued by robber bands as one might assume in this dangerous land. King Tak Sin's control of the south was total. Riding on elephants, however, was not entirely to Light's taste. He was much relieved when they at last reached the river, his bones having been shaken for days on their lumbering backs, sliding around at great heights above the ground. He longed for a horse.

As he embarked the official vessel at the port, an unexpected welcome party awaited. Lord Thian was aboard, sent by the king himself to make the honoured guest feel more at home in the company of a man already known to him. Nothing seemed to have escaped the attention of this most charismatic of rulers. After a welcome bathe, change of clothes and a hearty meal, Light settled back to enjoy the journey in the company of Thian, whom he had already come to admire. They had three days of pleasant journey ahead.

To Light's consternation, however, Lord Thian appeared somewhat distant in his manner towards his guest, formally polite but avoiding the inchoate friendship begun in Thalang. The reason for his detachment revealed itself the following day as they strolled on deck. It was a fine morning, the seas were placid, and a pleasant wind propelled them towards their destination. They walked in a silence broken only by stilted observations on the weather and the current that only brought their mutual awkwardness into sharper relief. Finally, Lord Thian broke the deadlock.

'My cousin, Lady Martinha is still in Queddah. You have been settled at Tharua for a long time. When do you intend to send for her? There has been talk. The family disapproves. Your treatment of her is dishonourable.' The directness of his questions was an indication of the extent of the insult the family felt. Within both Siamese and Malay cultures, such neglect was unforgiveable. He had supposed Martinha and her mother would have understood his reasons. But people talk. Rumours spread. Traditional attitudes are hard to surmount.

He opened his mouth to reply but Lord Thian continued. 'Furthermore, it is known that you keep a mistress in Tharua. Does that not strike you as an affront to your wife's family, who are also close by? I am disappointed in you, Captain Light. I had thought you a better man.'

Light interrupted, rattled by the inquisition. 'I am in the midst of building a new home for my wife. My current living arrangements as a guest of Captain Scott and his concubine are not appropriate for a lady of such high birth. It is my intention to send for Martinha when the house is complete.'

'Not even one visit in well over a year? For a man who sails up and down the coast, it is lacking in basic courtesy for a new husband not to make at least one call upon his wife! Martinha has been abandoned, or so the common gossips say.'

'We are not yet married, Lord Thian, or at least not by our lights. When she is a little older and everything is prepared for her in Thalang, then we shall be wed under Christian rites. Until then, it is fitting that she stay with her mother and brother at her grandmother's house.'

Lord Thian raised one arched eyebrow. 'That still does not explain why you have not at least visited.'

Light suppressed his annoyance. It was nobody's matter but his own. Yet, in the East that was not the way where marriages were concerned. You marry a girl, you marry her entire family. They did not hesitate to interfere. 'I have written regularly to Martinha with my news and good wishes. Furthermore, as you well know, I have spent the past many months in India securing weaponry for your king. Pray tell when I had leave to make sentimental visits to Queddah? Or would you prefer I had risked your cargoes in the Straits merely for a romantic interlude?'

The tension between the two men led to a period of silence, during which both stared out across the water considering their positions. The next few moments would be crucial; they could either set aside this issue or it would remain a permanent obstacle to their friendship. For the second time, it was Lord Thian who breached the impasse.

'You have made your case, Captain. I allow there has been little time for lovemaking of late. But once this duty is fulfilled and you have made your name as a favoured merchant of the Great King, then it will be the time to mend all misunderstandings. Do not wait too long, Francis. It is not the Siamese way.'

The use of Light's personal name diffused the friction of the moment. But the warning was clear. Lady Chan was not pleased, nor was her sister. Despite how he was viewed by Thonburi, it was the ruling family of Thalang who would make or break his future on the island. Light nodded tersely to indicate his acquiescence, although raging internally that his private life had been so openly flaunted in public. The allusion to his private arrangement with Madame Chipat was also humiliating. His personal affairs had nothing to do with his marital plans. What man didn't keep a woman behind the back of his wife in this part of the world? How else was a man to cope with months of distance between himself and his marriage bed?

But Light knew better than to give voice to his emotions. It was not the Siamese way. Lord Thian was, in his fashion, rendering a service by reminding him that things were done differently than how they perceived Europeans treated their women. Light bowed to the inevitable and swallowed the resentment that his movements would always be observed and noted. What had he expected? It was a salutary reminder of the need for vigilance at all times, especially when playing the double game.

Back in his cabin, he opened the letter that had been waiting for him when he had embarked. It had been sent from Queddah direct to Lord Thian to pass on to Light. That alone proved the extent of the family's communication lines. He had scanned it the previous evening and thrown it down, for even then it had piqued his unease at how badly he had managed the affair. The short note had been written by Martinha in halting and awkward English, the first time she had done so. The artless pathos of her stumbling ill-formed sentences said volumes more than the usual formal notes she had sent in her own language. Lord Thian was right. His absence had been too cruel on this young woman.

My dear Captain Francis,
I hop you are well. I am well. My mother send good wish.

I try write English so you understand. I lonely. Please come soon. Here everbody talk talk. Say you no want marry with me. I pray every day. Soon you come. Take me home Thalang. I seventeen. Old enough, Francis.

Your little wife

Martinha Rozells

***

The breathtaking spectacle of their transfer by royal barge from the sea along the Chao Phraya river was a mere foretaste of the magnificence to come. A new capital was rising on the west bank of the mighty river, with ambitions to become an even greater city than the glorious Ayutthaya in whose image it was recreated. That so much could be achieved in a mere six years? It staggered belief. Light had seen many cities in his time, but few were on the scale of Thonburi. Rome may not have been built in a day but the Siamese king looked set to create a wonder in less than ten years. It encapsulated the Age of Tak Sin, that singular general who had already defeated Burma, reduced Cambodia and Vietnam, and had now set his sights on Laos. No objective seemed beyond his grasp, his very name alone sufficient to strike fear into the hearts of his enemies. Thonburi would proclaim his glory to the ages.

A series of landing bridges loomed ahead, six exquisite Chinese pagodas of green granite, glistening like polished jade in the brilliant sunlight. The party disembarked and processed along a white marble pathway towards a complex of buildings ascending like a vision of a heavenly paradise. Four smaller towers girdled an identical but towering central *prang*, as tall at least as the main mast on a sailing ship. Carved in finely wrought lattice, in tier after tier of figures, flowers and patterns, the complex created a bewildering effect that appeared as delicate as lace, yet was sculpted of solid stone. Atop the soaring stupa stood a great seven-pronged spear of shimmering gold. Light stared in astonishment, his mouth gaping. He had never seen the like.

'Magnificent, is it not?' Lord Thian could scarce keep the pride from his voice, doubting that European cities had anything to rival the glory of Siam. He imagined these westerners came from dark, squat, ugly places, barren of the inspiration that came from knowledge of a higher existence.

'Indeed, sir,' Light gasped. 'Is this the new palace of the king?'

Thian was amused. 'This is Wat Chaeng, a temple complex. The palace stands in its grounds. But the temple is the focal point. For what are we but insignificant specks in the eye of the Buddha? Even a king must know his place.'

Not for the first time, Light was intrigued by the philosophical gulf that existed between west and east. In Europe, the purpose of great buildings – even those of religious significance – was to humble. Thian's explanation suggested the opposite, that they were salient reminders to the powerful of their own feet of clay. Yet Light was not entirely convinced that Tak Sin's construction projects were quite as noble in intent. 'Did the king build this? In so short a time?' Light wondered aloud.

'There was a humble temple here before, Wat Makok. Our fledgling forces visited while we were struggling to drive the Burmese from Bangkok Fort across the river. Dawn was breaking when the king led us to the temple where we prayed for many hours. King Tak Sin believes that this was the moment our victory was sealed. We returned to the battlefield and expelled the Burmese in an astonishing rout. Afterwards, the general vowed to rebuild the temple in splendour as a living embodiment of the new Siam arising from the ashes of disaster. It is now Wat Chaeng, the great Temple of the Dawn.'

Strolling around the complex, Lord Thian proved to be an eager and well-informed guide. He indicated the hundreds of statues arranged around the perimeter of the base, intricately sculpted figures of ancient warriors and mythical beasts. In recesses too many to count, golden Buddhas wrapped in yellow silk, stood silent and serene, contemplating the new city out of jewelled eyes. Climbing to the higher second terrace, the two men craned their necks and screwed their eyes up against the sun to observe the great statue of the God Indra, set inside a deep alcove far above, riding the three-headed Erawan, like a guardian at a gateway.

'Each side contains a similar statue of the god on his three-headed elephant. He surveys the four directions of the kingdom, for Indra is the special deity of the kings of Siam.'

'Indra is a Hindu god, is he not?' Light asked, curious how a Hindu god had found a dwelling inside a Buddhist shrine.

Thian bowed his head in agreement. 'All deities have their place in the cosmos. Lord Buddha sits serene at the centre, flanked by the fiery gods of the pantheon. See, at the very top of the stupa, the highest point of all?' He pointed upwards to the soaring steeple, shaped like a trident with seven teeth. 'That is the seven-pronged fork of Lord Siva. This great temple represents Mount Meru reborn, surrounded by the four towers of Phra Phai, the God of the Winds. There is much symbolism here. It harnesses the energies of the universe –'

'And creates awe in the hearts of all who observe it,' Light answered, reflecting his own emotional response to the grand spectacle. Although he grasped little of the complex worldview of Buddhism, he understood the message, despite Thian's alternative more altruistic argument. Great buildings were statements of power and authority the world over. Yet few were as beautiful as this.

'I fear you are a cynic, Captain Light,' observed Thian. 'You do not share our beliefs. Yet, you are not entirely wrong. King Tak Sin is a devout Buddhist but he is also a shrewd student of the minds of men. You must conquer the spirits of your enemy first. Once it is accepted that you are indestructible, so will you be.'

They continued on their tour, ascending higher and higher on the precarious spiral stairway to the very topmost level of the stupa itself. From there, Thonburi lay spread before them: the broad serpentine Chao Phraya river thronging with traffic winding its sinuous way to the gulf; the new fortress to their right; and on the opposite bank the older Bangkok fort, scarred from its many recent battles. Beyond that, the river swept through a flat, green plain across the vast hinterland and beyond. The four winds blew in every direction over territory that belonged to the new dynasty, or lands that would soon be crushed beneath its heel.

'What is your king like, as a man?' Light wondered out loud. Lord Thian had been with Tak Sin since his rise had first begun in the dying days of Ayutthaya. If anyone knew the man behind the myth, it would be he.

Thian did not answer for a while, struggling to put into words the dichotomy of the man he had known set against the distant god-king he had now become. 'Lord Tak Sin was always formidable. It was as if he could see inside your soul and knew the man you were even before you knew yourself. In public, he was charming, gregarious, witty and dignified. In private, he was quicksilver: irreverent and audacious, but cruel and heartless when he deemed it necessary. I knew from the beginning he would be both a dangerous enemy and a perilous friend. Nevertheless, first I came to admire him, then to believe in him, and finally to love him. He has changed my life, set me on a wholly different path. I cannot imagine what would have become of us all without him.'

His testimony was honest and revealing nor did Thian shy away from the darker depths of his ruler. Perhaps all great men are thus: able to inspire but also capable of terrible brutality. 'And now? How does a comrade-in-arms, a man with whom you have shared the deprivations of siege, flight and campaign, become a remote, all-powerful ruler before whom you must abase yourself?'

The question brought a wry smile to Lord Thian's handsome face. 'Sometimes, in his private chambers when he is relaxed, the king allows that other man to escape for a while. Then I remember what it was that first drew me under his spell. But moments like that are becoming increasingly rare. I have watched a man transform little-by-little into a deity. His human side is fading away. It is awe-inspiring but also terrifying. I imagine it is the only way a mere man can possibly assume such a mantle of responsibility,' Thian observed.

'Are you afraid of him?' Light asked bluntly.

'We are all afraid of him. It would be foolish not to be. And yet, I also worship him. Look how Siam rises, stronger and more vital than ever! It is only seven years since Ayutthaya fell. Only a man of transcendental wisdom could achieve so much in so little time.'

They looked out again over the impressive vista, over the many constructions that had turned the muddy banks of a sluggish river into a mighty city, and on the human ants scurrying far below, all driven by the will of this one man. 'But what if he should overreach himself? For after all, he is but a man. Can power such as he wields not drive a man to ...' Light stumbled. He did not have the words to express himself in Siamese 'There is a word in Greek, a language we study as children in England. It is the language of philosophy and thought. The word is "*hubris*". The Greeks believed that if humans became too powerful or vain, they come to think themselves as great as the gods. That is the sin of hubris.'

Thian listened carefully, lost in contemplation. There was still something of the monk about him, Light thought. 'We call it "*mana*". It is one of the poisons. I have observed it even in the most devout masters who believe they have already been transmitted and are now one with the Buddha. What did your Greek gods do when they encountered hubris?' he asked, fixing Light with his piercing stare. It seemed that this matter had already been eating at his soul. He was searching for an answer.

Light pulled a face. 'I was never much of a Greek scholar, but I recall a few of their stories. If I remember correctly, hubris was punished most terribly. Yet rarely with death. It amused the gods to repay the sinner with an appropriate and lasting penance, as a salutary reminder to all mortals who dare fly too close to the sun. But I fear that this conversation has strayed into murky waters,

Lord Thian. I do not accuse your king of prideful behaviour.'

Thian bowed his head. 'Of course not. It was idle chatter. I still enjoy discoursing on abstract principles, although there are sadly few opportunities for such diversions in my current role. You are quite the thinker, Captain Light. I have enjoyed listening to your thoughts most particularly. I desire to know more of the learning of the West. We must return to these matters again.'

Light broke into a hearty laugh. 'Well, I must say, I have never been called a thinker before! My old headmaster would be most amused to hear that Francis Light had been disputing with a learned Buddhist monk!'

They began their descent in a lighter mood, discussing the vast new construction projects, the forthcoming audience with the king, and the entertainments that were planned for the next few days. But the conversation lingered, casting its shadow over the day. Light began to realise that he was consorting with a ruler whose authority was limitless and arbitrary. He must tread carefully in his dealings with the mighty Tak Sin.

For his part, the conversation had awoken the concerns that were already stirring in Lord Thian's soul. The floodgates had been further breached and a trickle of water were seeping through the dam. This was the first time he had put into words the disturbing metamorphosis of Lord Tak Sin into the Mighty King Borrommoraja. But once let out into the light of day, it was nigh impossible to stuff a thought back into the deepest crannies of one's soul. It would be easier to trap a plague and halt its spread.

Their audience with the king took place later that day in a great hall swathed in yellow silk, surrounded by an open portico that looked out over the gardens nestling in the shadow of the temple itself. The room was lined with officers of state, military commanders and noblemen. The king sat high upon his golden throne, remote and silent. Light followed Lord Thian in solemn procession, heads bowed as they advanced into the awesome presence. At the steps to the throne, the two men prostrated themselves, an abasement essential in Siamese court ritual. Whilst they lay face down, bearers carried samples of the weaponry Light had brought loaded onto gilded biers. Light dared not move, awaiting some form of sign from Lord Thian that it was permitted for him to rise. For far too long it seemed as if the moment would never come.

At last Thian murmured; they rose to their knees, heads still bowed. The ceremonial was taking its toll. Light, already somewhat nervous at the prospect of an audience with the king, now felt the first uneasy presentiments of fear. A mere speck in the eye of the Buddha, Thian had said. What if the king had learned of Scott's secret trade with the Burmese king on behalf of the Sultan of Queddah? What if the muskets were deemed poor quality? What if some negative reports from Thalang had reached the king's ears? His life would be forfeit in moments. Such was the sobering reality of prostration at the feet of the ruler of all Siam.

A man clad in formal robes by the throne, descended the steps. He bowed to them both. Lord Thian introduced him. 'Bow your head to the great Lord Chakri Duang, general of the armies of Siam and right hand of king Borrommoraja IV, the Great Tak Sin!'

Light bowed lower, at a distinct disadvantage from the lowly position on his knees. Lord Duang was a tall man, broadly built by Siamese standards, with a strong face etched in character. By the merest gesture of his right hand, he indicated that they should stand, then led the way to the array of weaponry. Choosing a musket at random, the general scrutinised with the eye of a seasoned veteran, weighing it in his hands, then raising it as if to fire. He nodded and moved on, selecting another gun and repeating the procedure several times. Nothing was said. The hall remained in silence. Light's heart was beating hard and his knees felt weak. He had never felt such irrational fear.

'It is good. You have fulfilled your contract admirably, Captain,' Lord Duang finally announced. Relief coursed through Light's body, as enervating as his fear had earlier been. A cold sweat settled on his skin, his head aching dully. 'Please follow me. The king wishes to meet you in person.' And with that, Light was led to mount the golden carpet step-by-step, until he stood in the actual presence of the king, but on a lower tread.

King Tak Sin was smaller in the flesh than Light had expected, which was probably inevitable, for in the minds of most people, the new king had already reached godhead. Few mortals ever live up to their reputation. His features were pleasant, almost boyish, but his eyes penetrated deep. Light shivered, despite the heavy atmosphere. He had never before experienced such supreme power.

'Captain Light, it is good to meet at last,' the king's voice was mellifluous. Should he answer? Was it permitted to speak in the presence of the king?

Tak Sin observed him impassively, and then suddenly his face broke into a benign smile. 'You may speak. Or how else are we to know each other?'

Light bowed again to mask his uncertainty. 'Great King,' he

began, the correct official modes of address quite disappearing from his brain. 'Forgive me, for my knowledge of your language is limited. You do me great honour to receive me.' He hoped that would be sufficient humility, even for the great king of Siam.

'I am eager to learn more of your nation and its place in the world. I believe a relationship between Siam and Britain might be beneficial to us both. Generally, I am unimpressed by your countrymen, Captain Light. I find them treacherous and ignorant, but I hear positive words about you. This consignment of arms has been well received. It seems to me that we can do more business.'

More business. Now that was a concept Light could understand. 'It would be my honour to serve you in any way I can, your Highness.'

'Good. Then we can enjoy a fruitful relationship. I have great need of armaments, for there are many pressing demands on my military. Continue with this regular supply. If matters progress to our satisfaction, then we may be willing to allocate a coastal settlement for the sole use of the British Company. But that is for the future. For now, my mind is taken up with military matters. Later, when peace is attained, we shall talk more.'

'As you wish, your Highness. Your generosity is endless,' Light replied and bowed again deeply, preparing to make his leave, backing down the first steps gingerly.

'Wait! There is one more thing,' the king spoke again, his right hand raised. 'We would bestow a title, so that all may know you are an appointed servant of the King of Siam. From this day you shall be known as "*Chao Phraya Raja Kapiten Baang Ken*". Henceforth, you will be the leader of the hat-wearing European community of Siam.'

'I am not worthy!' Light responded, delight glinting in his eyes at this unexpected benefaction.

'Perhaps, perhaps not,' was the king's enigmatic reply. 'For now, we put our trust in your good faith. Your wife is a close relative of our beloved Lord Thian. Your new family holds a high position on the island of Thalang, which is very dear to our heart. You are in a unique place to bridge the gulf between East and West. But take caution, *Chao Phraya Kapiten*. One who flies high, may fall far. Much rests on your continued loyalty. You are now a vassal of my realm and, as such, your foremost duty is to Siam. Remember that.'

It was a warning. He could not be the servant of two masters. The passing mention of his Siamese family might indicate high regard but was also a reminder of what would be at stake if he crossed the ruler of Siam. The lion had unsheathed his claws, as was to be expected. Light was stepping forth on a narrow bridge with scarcely a handhold.

All the same, two kings and two titles. How strange life was! The boy who once upon a time could not gain a naval commission for love nor money, was now ennobled in the Indies by two rulers. He had also all but been offered a British base in Siam, something that had once seemed impossible. Aceh, Riau, Queddah and now Siam, four kingdoms formerly resistant to European advances had all been his for the taking, if not for the intransigence of his own nation. Yet, he doubted even now whether this achievement would be recognised in Calcutta for what it was. A hard journey still lay before him to win back the Company's trust.

11

Hostages to Fortune

Merbok, Queddah. March 1774

As her second wedding day approached in a swirling complexity of mixed emotions, Martinha finally allowed herself to believe that a future with Francis – this foreign man she hardly knew – might actually happen. Her bridegroom had made a deep impression two years ago at their first ceremony at the palace of the sultan, but the disappointment of the subsequent separation still lingered. Despite clinging resolutely to the belief that Francis would soon return, as the weary weeks had passed with a paucity of news – other than an occasional letter to her mother with mere cursory inquiries about his young wife – her surety had been undermined. Furthermore, she had suffered the ignominy of becoming a source of local gossip, even mockery: the girl abandoned by her ferringhi captain following her wedding night. Gradually, Martinha's confidence had been chipped away until she too had come to believe that Francis Light might have found a new life without her, turning his back on Queddah and all its encumbrances for good.

Her mother refused to doubt Captain Light, her optimism founded more on pragmatism than good faith. If Light dared offend the family of Lady Chan, he wouldn't last long in Thalang. Thong Di also believed Francis to be a man of honour, upon whose word they could rely. But even her resolve had been tested of late. Some months after Light had sailed for Thalang, a letter had arrived from court. Sultan Muhammed Jiwa had arranged a marriage for Lady Thong Di, the not-unexpected consequence of her thwarting his plans for her daughter. It would be a bitter irony if she was punished for the sake of a marriage that was already destined for divorce.

Thong Di's new husband was an aged courtier of Queddah, important to the sultan in his constant battles to control his wayward nobles. In fairness, it was not the most intolerable of alliances. Dato' Seri Yahya Ismail was an old man who already had several wives and a number of sons. Her elderly bridegroom had no interest in more children, thus made few intimate demands upon Thong Di. Yahya Ismail did, however, relish the verdant lands in the rich rice fields of Merbok that belonged to his new wife's mother, and had wasted no time in moving there with his brood. Several new residences had been constructed to accommodate all the wives, children and grandchildren of his extended family. The once quiet idyll was now a bustling kampong; Tunku Mahsia, Lady Thong Di, Martinha and Felipe were relegated to a small *atap* house in the grounds of what had once been their home. As the fourth wife, and at thirty-four considered long past childbearing age, Thong Di's status in the household was minor, to say the least.

Tunku Mahsia had not taken well to their new living arrangements. Demanding to make her case before the sultan himself, she travelled to the new palace at Anak Bukit despite her advanced years. There she secured an important concession: her daughter's new marriage notwithstanding, her lands would pass directly to Felipe on her death, for he was the legitimate male heir of her late father. The sultan even provided a document as proof of his agreement.

This turn-of-affairs naturally aggrieved Dato' Seri Yahya, whose sole purpose for accepting the marriage had been the tempting inheritance he had presumed Lady Thong Di brought with her. He had set his sights on Merbok for one of his sons. Mahsia's act of defiance brought its own retribution, further exacerbated by Thong Di's refusal to give up her Christian faith. As punishment, the padre was dismissed. She and her children could no longer attend Mass, but Thong Di remained obdurate in her prayers and in raising her children in the Faith. She paid scant attention to the traditional restrictions of Malay custom towards women. As a consequence, the family was mostly ignored, their food rations cut to the bare minimum, and access to their wealth denied. They were pariahs in their own lands.

And then, just as their life seemed mired in despair, true to his surname, Francis Light turned up again, bringing a glimmer of hope. He arrived in grand style, loaded with silks, pearls, precious jewels and many other delights. He even brought a rare novel for Martinha to aid her English studies. It was the celebrated *Clarissa,* which Francis ruefully admitted he had not personally read. The bookseller in Madras, however, had assured him that it was well enjoyed by ladies everywhere. Francis hoped it would instruct his new wife about the life of an English gentlewoman, which unlikely status he naively hoped was to be Martinha's new station. To her wry amusement, even with her rudimentary grasp of the language, it did not take long for the clever girl to realise that well-born English girls were just as much hostages to fortune as their counterparts in the Straits.

His arrival gave Francis the opportunity to inform the family of recent events in Thalang. The situation was now much improved. Since their first marriage ceremony, he had been caught up in the tumultuous events on the island, so dangerous that he and Scott had spent months aboard ship, afraid to land for fear of the terrible outrages that were being perpetrated by the Siamese army. Happily, peace had now been restored. Lady Chan and family were not only safe, but her husband had recently been appointed governor of the island. Moreover, Light himself had been called into the service of King Tak Sin and had visited Thonburi in the company of Lord Thian himself, where he had received the great honour of a formal title. Thus, all was now well. It was safe for Martinha to return to her homeland, where he had already ordered a suitable house to be built.

Sheltered in their sleepy hamlet, in one fell swoop the Rozells family suffered the shocking news of the violence in their homeland, then moments later learned of their family's fortuitous preferment. Martinha's heart soared to hear of beloved Cousin Thian, whom she had not seen for many years. He had even sent a marriage gift, a golden brooch of rubies set in a circle of diamonds. She intended to wear it on her wedding day.

Yet even as her dreams had finally come to fruition, there was still sadness. Her mother and grandmother would not be allowed to attend the ceremony in Thalang. In the eyes of Dato' Seri Yahya, Martinha was already married, thus he would not allow his own wife and mother-in-law to attend a Christian ceremony of which he heartily disapproved. Martinha was unsure when, or if, she would ever see again the women she loved most. Thong Di refused to comment on their imminent separation. She had made her choices long ago.

But one matter still troubled her, that of the future safety of her son. For who knew what might happen to a Christian boy set to inherit a large Queddah estate? On the evening before their departure, Thong Di raised the matter with the couple as they enjoyed the cool, night air.

'Felipe must return to Thalang with you. As yet, he knows nothing of my decision, nor will I tell him until the very last moment. I have not even packed his belongings in case the servants suspect and inform my husband or the oldest wife. That old hen rules the roost. She sets the maids to watch my every move. Everything I do or say is noted. Captain Light, my son must escape this place, for I fear he is in even more danger now that the sultan has formally made him heir. Take him to my family in Thalang. They will keep him safe. This I beg of you!'

It was a complete shock to Martinha, who sank to her knees at her mother's feet, clutching her hand. 'We cannot leave you alone, mother! You and *Nenek* will pay dearly if Felipe leaves without permission!' she gasped.

But Thong Di's mind was made up. 'I cannot suffer more than I do already, sayang. To know that both my children are free will be enough reward.' She turned to face Francis, placing a hand upon his arm. 'I entrust to you my daughter and my son, my two most precious jewels. My sisters will take him in when you reach Thalang. But I pray you watch over him like an elder brother. He is a gentle boy with little understanding of the world.'

Light well understood Felipe's predicament, but her request was tantamount to an act of disobedience against both her husband and the sultan. 'But what of his inheritance, Lady? Surely it would then be forfeit?'

Thong Di shrugged. 'What of it? Either the Sultan will honour his promise, or he won't. But I fear that something may happen to Felipe long before that day should he remain here!'

Martinha let out a cry. 'You mean he might be harmed?' Francis did not comment, his sombre face acknowledging the truth of Thong Di's conviction.

Nor did her mother spare her. 'In the dark of night men have been krissed for much less than a fortune, I can assure you, my daughter. You are soon to be a wife; you can no longer remain naïve to the ways of this cruel world.'

Francis knelt down beside Martinha, taking Thong Di's other hand in his. 'My lady, I swear you need fear nothing in respect of either of your children. Your son and daughter will always be safe with me. Felipe will join our household; he must stay with his sister. I will teach him the business of my trade, for Martim was a fine merchant, and it is an honourable profession. Whatever becomes of the inheritance, as long as a man can earn his own fortune, he will never want for anything.'

Martinha's father, Martim Rozells, had been a Eurasian merchant of Jangsylan – and a personal friend to both Francis Light and James Scott, known to Light even before he had real dealings with Martinha's family. It had been a genuine affection. Martim, an uncomplicated and straightforward man, an unusual quality amongst traders of that or any region, had welcomed Light from the first and generously introduced him to remote locations not generally visited by Europeans. Martim's sudden death some years before had been a shock to everyone. He had seemed such a hale and hearty fellow, if somewhat fond of food and drink. But weren't they all?

That night, as they retired to the small chamber set aside for them, Francis asked Martinha to tell him everything that had occurred since he had gone away. His negligence was unforgiveable; he had paid little mind to what was happening in Merbok in his absence. Now he must redress the situation. At first, she shook her head. He insisted. 'We are man and wife. There must be no secrets between us. I cannot protect you if I do not know the truth. Has this family done you harm?'

Martinha breathed deeply, recalling the humiliations of the past two years. 'They have been unkind. They drove us from our home and treated us little better than servants. We were forced to eat rice and vegetables with hardly any meat. They ignored us, mocked us, spurned us, but we have not been harmed. It was not pleasant, but it is their right. You know how it is, sir.'

What could he say? He doubted if such things were much different back in England when a widow found herself forced by circumstances to take another husband. She was at the mercy of her new family. The Rozells were Christian outcasts with no place within the society of Queddah. Who better than he to understand what that meant?

'The men did not touch you?' Light resorted to the only thing he could control. Martinha was his wife. If her modesty had in any way been compromised, he would have recourse at court against Dato' Seri Yahya.

Martinha shook her head. 'They looked. They made comments. They did what men always do. But no one was fool enough to touch me. They all know you stand high in the sultan's regard. The women were the worst. They said you had abandoned me. They laughed at me for being a spurned wife.' Martinha put on a brave face while Francis winced at his failure to protect her. Lord Thian had been right to chastise him. What had he expected when he left? Had he even given a single thought to how the girl might feel, or what the inevitable gossips would say?

'It is to my shame that I have neglected you. I am a thoughtless, selfish fool. I promise you will never want for anything again. And worry not about your mother and grandmother. I shall protect them. The sultan needs me. I will find a way to set them free. But for now, we must concentrate on you and Felipe. That will give your mother some comfort for the time being.'

His declaration broke through the reserve that still existed between them. Martinha smiled; tears ran down her cheeks. Francis thought he had never seen anything quite as lovely as her innocent, trusting beauty. He drew her into his arms and kissed her, not the gentle peck he had given her before, but the embrace of a man and woman on the very edge of passion. This unconventional relationship, forged on misunderstanding and blighted by absence, was stumbling its way to love.

'Soon, Martinha,' he whispered. 'Soon we will marry in the sight of God, and then we can be one,' he muttered in her ear, his face burying in her thick hair. Martinha relaxed into his arms, an unfamiliar loosening washing over her. Strange, bewildering sensations flooded her veins. Would that Francis were not an upright English gentleman! They were married already. Surely God would not mind? It was fortunate indeed that she had acquired the habit of patience.

12

Crossing the Threshold

Our Lady Free from Sin, Tharua, Jangsylan. April 1774

It could not have differed more from their earlier marriage ceremony in Queddah, but it was a confusing mélange of contrasting traditions all the same. Light recalled George Doughty's sedate but joyful wedding in Suffolk with its polite conversations and genteel celebrations, conducted with the usual English propriety and restraint. But a Christian wedding amongst the Portuguese Eurasians of Tharua was a different animal altogether, a riot of colour, noise and contradiction.

The day began in muted fashion with a Buddhist ceremony, the bride and groom clad in Siamese attire bedecked with chains of jasmine, as befitted a scion of the greatest family on the island. Then, following a quick change from silk to muslin, Martinha reappeared in white, veiled and pure, for the ceremony in the Catholic chapel, fittingly named, 'Our Lady Free from Sin'.

Francis had little experience of Catholic rituals, other than the usual Anglican prejudices for the incense-laden jiggery-pokery of Rome, but even the most fervent Latin or Irish would have found little to recognise in this noisy, colourful extravagance. The whole port town was out, the hot, steamy air humming with expectation. Everyone knew Light and his best man, Scott. The entire settlement wanted to be part of the singular event.

The walk to the chapel afforded the two friends a relatively private interlude in the midst of the hectic day. Scott privately wondered to himself if Francis quite knew what he was letting himself in for. The mayhem of the celebration only served to underscore the very different worlds that now drew in his friend, each one with its own particular obligations and responsibilities.

'I cannae deny you brush up well, Francis. You almost look the fine young English gentlemen you desire to be!' Scott joked, jabbing his friend playfully in the ribs as they strode along in their European best: tricorne, shirt and stock, jacket and breeches, buckled shoes and stockings. It was a wicked burden in the heat to dress for an English salon.

'Nor have I seen you so well combed and turned out in many a year! How do you find breeches these days, Scott?' Light riposted. He was as merry as a cricket, sunnier in manner than Scott had seen for many a day. Perhaps this marriage was not merely one of expediency?

'The very devil. These breeches constrain my vitals in a most unpleasant way. It does a man no good to have his ballocks so confined! But you seem very pleased with yourself, my old friend. Could this be love, eh?' Scott added, while nodding blithely in acknowledgement at grinning passers-by.

Francis was affably bashful. 'She's a charming girl. Spirited. I have to admit, sir, she has quite won my heart. It's a most excellent turn of events, James. To think, I almost refused to wed her! And now, my little pearl brings me such sweet happiness!'

'Not to mention the support of the most influential family in southern Siam! Don't pretend that's not part of your high spirits, y'devil!' Scott reminded him. 'You have a charmed life, sir.'

Light scoffed at the remark. 'Charmed? I don't believe in luck. Anything I have won, comes solely from the sweat of my own endeavours against a tide of ill-luck. I deserve this moment, Scott. Frankly, I deserve much more. And I intend to win all the prizes, just you wait and see,' he promised with a hint of the old obsession slipping through the genial mask of lovesick bridegroom.

It was Scott's turn to show a touch of cynicism. 'I wonder how your friends in Bengal will view this new alliance? I thought marriage with the locals was frowned upon in those lofty circles? And a Catholic wedding to boot. Your currency was not very high to begin with, laddie. Popery may put you quite beyond the pale.'

They were nearing the church doors, flung open to receive the wedding party, leaving Light little time to expand other than to offer an opaque response. 'There are many ways to skin a cat, Jamie. This wedding is for Martinha and her lady mother. The ceremony in Queddah was for Sultan Muhammed. As for me, I am a still a member of the Church of England in whose eyes I never will have been married at all. I believe it is still approved in Company circles for their officers to keep local women? For if not, there are a lot of gentlemen from Calicut to China who have offended the governor-general.'

Bursting from the church, nuptials complete, the bride and groom, the wedding party, and what seemed the entire population of the port, processed into the grounds of the governor's mansion, where tables had been set loaded with mountains of food: fierce devilled chicken; aromatic beef flank stew; spicy *acars* and fried vegetables, heaped on mountains of yellow rice; followed by egg tarts, sugee cake, and platters of fruit. It was the traditional Portuguese wedding breakfast, or rather a version of it with a distinctively Straits flavour.

Musicians on their guitars, *rebanas* and bamboo flutes sauntered around the grounds while local girls whirled their embroidered skirts and flashed their eyes, for all the world like Portuguese maidens dancing the *branyo*. Everybody sang and clapped along, especially to the old favourite '*Jinkli Nona*'. Not to be outdone, Francis took Martinha's hand and joined the mêlée. The tranquil gardens of the governor's mansion had never seen such merriment. Meanwhile the governor and his family watched impassively from the shady pavilion above. It was impossible to know what they made of it all.

From their vantage point, Lady Chan and her husband, Governor Phaya Pimon, looked down in beatific tolerance. The occasion was a double blessing: their niece Martinha was making an excellent marriage, beneficial to the family, but the occasion also brought an added opportunity. After the brutal years following the Siamese re-occupation, many settlers – especially Christians – had fled Thalang. Today served as notice that the island was ready for business again. The governor was extending his generosity and tolerance to all, even to the extent of welcoming foreigners into his own family. Such an event announced that the previous cosmopolitan life enjoyed on the island was set to return.

'The farang has something about him, there is no doubt,' remarked Governor Pimon in lofty fashion. He had recently met the famous English captain, fully expecting to dislike him. Not only was he suspicious of Europeans, but this one – or so his spies informed him – had once shared an intimate relationship with his wife. But oddly enough, Pimon had discovered that he rather admired the fellow. He could even appreciate why his passionate wife had been attracted. For who could blame her finding comfort in the arms of a handsome adventurer during all those years alone? 'It is entirely possible that in time the king may see fit to offer Thalang as a British concession, with the understanding that Kapiten Light be its Superintendent. That resolution would suit us very well, I think, my dear?'

His wife turned her inimitable gaze upon her husband. He was aging rapidly. She doubted he would last much longer. Some might say the cosmos was aligning in her favour. 'That would suit us to perfection, my dear husband. And, even if the king does not see fit, the day may still come when there is a British establishment here. For who knows what may happen in the years ahead? Our king has many aspirations. He has spread himself thinly throughout Siam and its vassal neighbours. Such ambition may bring unforeseen consequences that could serve Thalang very well,' she observed obliquely.

Pimon shot her a warning look. 'We wish our mighty king every success and long life,' he proclaimed, whilst lowering his voice to mutter: 'Do not discuss such matters in public hearing!' Lady Chan waved her fan with nonchalance, little concerned at his trepidation. No one here would talk. They were her people.

Meanwhile James Scott, furnished with a flagon of whisky which he was liberally splashing into willing glasses, wandered about the revelries. It was the sort of abandon that appealed to his Gaelic nature. His attention was caught, however, by one guest who did not appear to be enjoying himself. It was Soliman, curled up beneath a nearby tree, looking a little worse for wear.

'I wondered where you'd hid yourself, boy!' Light's adopted son rarely imbibed alcohol, out of some notion that it was unseemly for a Malay, although in Scott's experience, most Malay lascars loved nothing better than sinking a few jars of grog. But it appeared tonight he had drunk deeply, if the rolling of his eyes and the heavy odour of toddy on his breath were anything to go by.

'Go 'way,' Soliman muttered, turning his face towards the tree trunk.

'What's up, lad?' Scott crouched down and reached out a hand. He was fond enough of the little Malay boy. Who would not be? Soliman was gifted and hardworking, utterly devoted to Light, and had been their local saviour on many occasions. 'Something bothering you? You've a face on you like you've lost a pound and found a farthing.'

'Leave me alone,' was all the boy would say.

Scott sat down by Soliman's side, swigging from the jar. 'You must be the only fellow here who thinks this wedding is a bad idea. Well, other than me, that is,' he added.

Soliman's ears pricked up. He swivelled round, curious to learn what Scott meant. 'Why you no approve? I thought you like Nona Martinha.'

Scott offered his jar. Soliman drank and grimaced. 'Oh, I like the lass well enough. Her mother, too. And young Felipe would make such a good pal for you, if you'd let him. It isn't about not liking them. I'm just unsure whether in the grander scheme of things, this marriage won't be a stone around the good captain's neck. Ignore me. I'm a pessimist by nature. What's your reason, lad?'

Soliman shrugged. 'Why things have to change? I like it before. I can look after the captain. Why he needs a wife?'

Scott chuckled at the comment. 'Every man needs a wife, my boy. A fellow cannae be happy all his life! But Soliman, my lad, you're not a little child any more. I've seen you hanging 'round the girls in town.'

Soliman pouted. 'Girls, different-lah! Why he needs a wife? Wife only nag, nag.'

This was not the question the boy was really asking. 'I know this is hard for you. But Francis was always bound to marry one day. He now has a wife and a new brother and no doubt there will be children soon. You cannot expect any different, boy. It doesn't mean the captain cares any less for you. He's done right by you all these years and he's not the sort of man to drop you now he has a family of his own.'

'I will never be his son now,' Soliman whispered.

'You never were his son before,' Scott reminded him bluntly. 'Do you know who Francis' father is?' Scott suddenly diverted the conversation.

The boy looked up. 'He has no father.'

'Oh, everyone has a father, Sol! A great man was his father but he gave him to another man to raise. And do you know something? That man raised him better than any real father would have done. When Francis took you in he saw something of his younger self. You will always be his Soliman.'

A solitary tear ran down Soliman's face. He scrubbed it away with the back of his hand. 'Is not the same. Now he has Felipe Rozells. He no need me anymore.'

Scott shrugged. 'It's up to you, boy. You either accept what life gives you or you don't. But promise me something. Don't just haul up and run because you think you have no place here. Talk to Francis first and tell him how you feel. If you can't stand to be around now that the captain has a family of his own, then fair play to you. But let him know. You may be surprised at what he has to say. Is it a bargain, Sol?'

Soliman looked up at Scott through thick lashes jewelled with tears. 'I promise, Captain Scott. I will not run away. But I will not stay either. It's time for me to be a man. I must make my own way in this world. I will talk to Captain Francis first. We will part as friends. I promise.'

Scott nodded and pulled himself to his feet, ready to take his leave. Soliman called him back. 'Captain Scott. Thank you. You nice man. You drink and whore too much but you still good man. My friend, too.'

It was late when the newly married couple finally took their leave and were conveyed by bearers to their new home set in a clearing of towering angsana trees on a gentle slope above a bubbling stream. It was a pretty spot. Their spacious two-storey wooden house with a red-tiled roof was raised on stilts wrapped round by a wide veranda. Francis had spared no expense, having ordered furniture from Madras, ceramics from China and elegant Siamese cabinets made to measure by local craftsmen. With an efficient household staff supplied by Lady Chan and well-tended grounds, Martinha was a fortunate young bride.

But all that passed her by as they climbed down from the sedan and dismissed the servants. Francis had held Martinha's hand throughout the short journey, but they had exchanged few words. Now at home, he swept her off her feet and set off up the steps at a lively pace. She laughed and leaned back against his shoulder. 'It is a custom in my country,' Francis informed her with a grin. 'A bridegroom must carry his bride across the threshold of her new home.'

'Why?' she asked. 'Do English people fear evil spirits like the Chinese?'

Francis shrugged. 'I have no idea. But I suspect it might be because in our culture it is thought seemly for a bride to resist her husband's advances. A decent woman is not supposed to enjoy earthly pleasures. Thus, her husband must ensure she will not run away!'

Martinha was amused. 'So English men must force their wives? Do they know nothing of the ways to please their women?' she teased. Francis burst through the door of their bedroom with a show of force. It made her giggle all the more.

'I'm not entirely sure such comments are fitting for a maiden, Martinha. Nor should a young bride taunt her husband about such things. I will have you know that this Englishman is very proficient in the arts of love. You need have no fear, sayang. You will be well pleased, I assure you!' And with that, he set her down gently on her feet by the ornate bed richly ornamented in red silk. 'Do not be afraid. I promise to be gentle.' His tone changed suddenly from boisterous lad to tender lover.

Martinha raised her eyes to meet his own, shrugging off her veil to reveal a forward and alluring gaze. 'I am not afraid, Francis. I am so very happy. This is the best day of my whole life!' she whispered, reaching out to smooth back a lock of his hair that had escaped its ribbon.

Francis lowered his head to kiss her. She was so tiny and perfect, a little pearl indeed, but her body beneath his hands felt lithe and strong. Martinha was deceptive. She might appear the shy, innocent virgin but her artlessness hid a young woman eager to experience the world. She responded fully to his kiss, her arms sliding round his neck, drawing him closer to her body in invitation.

Clothes fell away as if by magic, apart from the interruption of the removal of his breeches, bringing a peal of unladylike laughter from his wife, as he struggled to pull them off, his shirt still hanging clumsily from one arm. And then they were free of all encumbrances, falling to the jasmine-scented sheets, burying themselves in each other with passionate abandon. Later, lying back, legs tangled and damp bodies curled, Francis marvelled at the path his life had taken. From Suffolk village, the bastard child of some unknown lord, through shipwreck and war, by intrigue and double-dealing, and a myriad of other adventures, he had always chased the unattainable. And on this night, he realised – with a sense of unfamiliar peace – that the dragon had his pearl at last.

PART THREE

Wedded Bliss

(1775-1782)

13
Merantau

After a protracted honeymoon of many months, during which Francis stayed close to home establishing his company and playing the bridegroom, at the turn of the new year he returned to sea with a vengeance, more than ready to slough off the land and its responsibilities. Since then he had been back and forth around the Straits and over to India, eager to announce his return to the scene after his fall from grace in Queddah. There was much to do and the time was ripe. He had written to Warren Hastings proposing Jangsylan as the ideal site for a British base – and finally there was interest in the prospect. Light must strike when the iron was hot and rebuild his reputation, especially now that he could boast the support of governor Phaya Pimon and the favour of the Siamese king. Surely the pragmatic Hastings would not waste such an opportunity on account of grudges from the past?

There was another more personal reason for his eagerness to escape the family home. Not long before Christmas, Martinha had suffered a miscarriage, a six months' babe, a little boy, with no apparent defect other than being born too soon. They had both felt the loss deeply, their mourning expressed in different ways. Martinha had become remote and sad, unable to move on from her grief. Light struggled to know how best to support her, until it was apparent that what she needed most was her mother. Thus, he had taken her to Merbok, where she was now recovering in the bosom of her family. Meanwhile his lonely anguish had no other outlet than the bottle and the beds of other women. So, he had run away to sea. For where else would he go?

Soliman was sorely missed. When the boy had first approached him a few days after the wedding, his intentions came as no surprise. Since the marriage ceremony in Queddah, Soliman had become increasingly moody and difficult. At first, Light had attributed it to his age; the boy was nearing seventeen by his estimation. It was not an easy age for any young man, replete with mixed emotions and driving passions. But he soon realised that jealousy lay at the heart of the matter. Soliman felt excluded from Light's new family, his isolation made even more acute by the presence of Felipe, a boy of similar age who seemed to him to be bound to take his place.

**

'Captain Light? I want private talk. May I come in?'

Soliman entered the office on a cool morning after heavy rain, when damp mists seeped off the forest and the air was fresh and clear. Light had been engaged in wading through a pile of correspondence neglected since before his wedding.

'Of course, you may! I'm more than ready for a break from all this tedious paper work. Felipe? Be a good lad and sort through my mail. Deal with any minor matters and order the rest for my attention. I wish to take a walk in the fresh air with Soliman and blow away the cobwebs.'

Felipe glanced up from his paperwork, smiling. He was a willing assistant and learning fast. 'Certainly, sir. I will translate where necessary for that will speed your progress later.'

Light acknowledged Felipe's efficiency with a nod, then indicated for Soliman to proceed him outside. The ground was wet underfoot but he decided nevertheless they should take a stroll to evade the ears and eyes of the servants. He had an inkling what was to come – and suspected that there might be tears.

Soliman led Light out of the house and across the compound, towards the path that meandered to the river. It was muddy, clods of red earth sticking underfoot. Light was glad for his sturdy boots. 'I used to be your translator,' Soliman observed, as they picked their way through ruts and puddles, pulling the back edge of his sarong between his knees and tucking it into his waistband with practised ease. His feet were bare but his steps were steady. He always moved with grace, even unshod.

'You are still my translator when I need you to be, Soliman. But you are also many other things. I have more need of you elsewhere than behind a desk. Felipe has a job to learn. For now, that is all he can do to earn his keep. It is not a competition between the two of you. Soliman, let's not beat about the bush! Come on, lad, spit it out! What's eating at your bones?'

They had come upon a large flat rock overhanging the stream where local women washed clothes. The sun was already piercing through, the rain clouds evaporating as the heat rose and the blue sky unfurled. Insects buzzed about, kingfishers skimmed for tasty morsels, and iridescent dragonflies hovered curiously about the intruders. Light and Soliman were alone amidst a natural world as busy as any city dwellers venturing out after the rain. Soliman squatted down, picking idly at pebbles and tossing them into the foaming stream that was still struggling to disperse the aftermath of the deluge.

'It's time for me to leave, Captain. I am a man now. I must make my own way.'

Light took off the cloth he wore loosely round his neck and folded it carefully to use as a cushion. Then he sat beside Soliman, his knees pulled up around his chin. 'I never could get the hang of this squatting that you all do with such ease. My English bones are far too stiff,' he remarked with affection.

Soliman glanced across, a sad smile brightening his sombre mood. 'You need to practise more. Or maybe your legs too long?' There was still a glimmer of his old sense of fun.

Light did not prevaricate. Soliman would avoid the direct approach, so he must take it to him. 'Soliman, is this because of Martinha? Are you telling me you have no place here anymore because I have taken a wife? My marriage doesn't signify, you know. Nothing has changed between us. You are still my Soliman!'

The lad shrugged in that ambiguous way of his. 'It will never be the same again, Francis. You know that. Before it was you and me. Now you belong to others. Is good. You need a wife. A man must have children. I understand. But still it makes me sad. So, I have decided it is time for "merantau". For both our sakes. It is our way.'

Merantau. Young men of the archipelago had always left their home villages to seek their fortune in other parts. It was the essence of the dynamic forces that had shaped these people. Sometimes they returned home. Sometimes they did not. Light could not deny that in Soliman's culture, his decision was an appropriate and natural response.

He smiled sadly. 'It is our way, too. Why do you think I came all this way across the seas, leaving my family behind? The world over, young men sail off to find their fortunes. But for you and I, it is even more difficult. I know you wish you could be something that this world will never let you be. I understand better than you think, Sol, for I am such a man as you. I believed I did not belong where I was born. Even though I was loved, both by my benefactor and my dear mother, it was not enough. I left to forge my own way in life, certain that this was the only way to prove I was the equal of those born more fortunate than I. Was I right? Who knows? Once one embarks upon such a step, there is no return. One must then follow that course until it ends. Had I remained in Suffolk, would I be a happier man today? Would I be a better man? I don't know. I sacrificed my beloved family for a dream that even now is still beyond my grasp. And they let me go without recrimination, knowing they might never see me again.'

Soliman sighed. 'Is the same. I am sorry I did not talk with you before. It is not just because you have a new family, Francis. I must become a true Malay. You understand? I can never be an Englishman. I must be what I am.'

It was a simple statement of fact but an inspired perception for all that. Whatever bitterness had eaten into his heart these months, Soliman had given it much consideration and had come to his own conclusions. And for the most part, he was right.

'When you are young, it is natural to be constricted by the opinions of other people. No matter how much a boy is loved, at some point he pulls away from filial ties, eager to experience for himself what the world might offer. For those like you and I, who have no parents of our own, it seems even more important to force this world to stand up and notice, for we believe no one else will. Let me tell you something I have discovered in my own "merantau". You are already who you need to be before you leave. Else you would not wish to go. Use all the gifts you have been given and make your life richer for it. Go with my blessing, Soliman. But do not stay away! I expect to see you regularly in and out of every port in this region!'

They both laughed, an easy peace between them now the hardest part was done. 'I'm not going to the other side of the world, as you did. Of course, we still be friends. I would like that very much,' Soliman added shyly.

'Friends?' Light exclaimed. 'Goddammit, Sol, we're more than that! Don't be so formal! You do not have to be a son, to be my son. I do not have to be a father, to be your father! Nor shall my boy leave me with nothing but a sarong and a keris to his name! Do you think I will send you out in the world without a penny in your pocket?'

Soliman shook his head fiercely. 'No, sir! You owe me nothing! You have raised me these ten years' past and given me everything a boy might desire!'

His objections were greeted with amusement and a healthy measure of disregard. 'I myself remember a similar conversation years ago with Squire Negus – how strange life is! The wheel of life, indeed. It is not about what I owe, Soliman. It is about what you deserve. Here I am, setting up a trading company, and in my household is the most competent young sailor that I know. He speaks many languages – which he reads and writes just as well – is clever and brave and knows as much about these waters as I do, maybe more! What kind of fool would I be if I let such a talent slip through my fingers?'

The clear, honest gaze of Soliman pierced straight into Light's heart. How he would miss this young man, whom he loved and trusted more than anyone he knew! And yet, he could not deny that Soliman would have his uses as a free agent in the Straits, for he could go where no white man would try. Even as he felt the sorrow of their imminent parting, the businessman in Light could not but speculate on the advantages that Soliman might bring in the future.

'You want me to work on your ships? With another captain?' Soliman guessed.

Light held up his hands. 'No. That is not my intent. I'm going to give you the *Eliza* and you can choose your own crew. It's high time you became an independent trader, contracted to carry out business on behalf of Scott and Light Esquires ...'

'The *Eliza*?' Soliman gasped. 'You give me my own boat?'

'I do indeed. She's a perfect vessel for you, a little padewakang such as a Malay might have. Juragan Soliman – it has a certain ring to it, don't you think?'

Soliman burst into delighted laughter, shaking his head back and forth in wonder. 'I am to have my own perahu? I can do my own business and be an agent for you as well? It is my dream! I promise I will make money for you. Lots and lots of money.'

'Make it for yourself, boy. That's the best way to make money for someone else. But there are other things you can do for me. Imagine where you might trade? I've a burning desire to worm my way back into Riau and Selangor. The Bugis have the Dutch on the run. I want a part of that. You, my little captain, are the perfect man for the job. You even speak their damned lingo!'

Just as the sun cleared the last damp dregs of the storm, Light's gift wiped the lingering tentacles of bitterness from Soliman's soul. Scott had been right. He should have known the captain would not let him down.

'Is perfect. *Sampurna*!' Soliman exclaimed. 'I will be your spy in every port. I can learn many things for you!'

Light rested his hand on Soliman's arm. 'You're not my factotum anymore. You are a trader first and foremost. But keep your ears to the ground, lad … for knowledge is everything in these waters.'

***

And so, Soliman sailed off on his own boat, now renamed the *Harimau* in remembrance of his long-dead pet. Since then, they saw each other from time to time, and true to his word, Soliman always had nuggets of intelligence, as well as useful new contacts in unexpected places. But he was missed, especially now when Light needed support. Scott was a close friend, but he was not the man to comfort another in his time of emotional need. Light needed his grown son to recover from the loss of his baby.

14

Betwixt Grief and Joy

The letter had taken an inordinate amount of time, even allowing for the usual misfortunes that might blight the *ad hoc* postal service. After lingering months in Bombay on missing the sailing season, it had eventually been despatched to Madras, where no one had taken the initiative to pass it on to one of the many captains who plied the Andaman route. It had then found itself sent to Calcutta until – this time by a stroke of happenstance – it had been added to a Company delivery carried by Captain Lindesay on the *Speedwell* bound for Tharua. Did this reflect the current low regard in which Captain Light was held in Company circles? Or was it the casual vagary of fate that chose at whim how deeply to turn the knife of sorrow? But at length, the letter did arrive, bearing the marks of the many places it had lingered, in a wallet of mail from India, crumpled in a corner at the bottom of the bag. It was a miracle that it had found its way at all.

The message he had always feared. The message he had known would one day come. Uncle William had died two years' past of a seizure brought on by a rigorous hunting session. He went much as he would have wanted, full of the elation of the hunt – and a copious helping of spirits. Penned in no-nonsense fashion by Aunt Margaret, it went straight to the point, as was her way. Squire

William had died suddenly, they were deeply saddened but took comfort that he had not suffered or lingered. He had reached the decent age of sixty years and had been a good man. They were all in deep mourning.

Francis had been left the sum of one thousand pounds; Mary Light had been provided with a generous bequest. Aunt Margaret hoped that Francis would take consolation from the pride that Squire Negus had felt in his achievements. He had always been uppermost in his patron's thoughts. Mrs. Negus promised to watch over his mother, for it was what Squire William would have wanted. The two women were both well, if permanently clad in widows' weeds, for in truth, that was what they both were now that he had gone.

The paper fell from his hand to the floor to which he sank, falling on his knees, wracked with a sorrow so visceral that he could only gasp for breath. Light might have half-expected such sad tidings in almost every mail that arrived, but found himself wholly unprepared all the same. The squire had not been a healthy man; he was corpulent and choleric, too fond of red meat and brandy, given to over-indulgence in all things. Yet how could the world have turned these past years without his stout heart beating?

Two years? Where had he been on that fateful day when the Squire had fallen from his horse, already cold? He thought back upon it. In June of '73, he was recently arrived in Queddah, at the very beginning of that sorry business, still sending fruitless letters to Calcutta, obsessed with claiming a settlement for the Company. How could he not have known? Surely some otherworldly sense should have told him that, half a world away, his father – for the squire would always be that – was no more. It seemed that every moment between that time and this had been squandered in futile undertakings, in self-seeking, and in frivolous pursuits. There had been little consideration for those back home, other than infrequent letters, saying little of his true heart, but filling the lines with vain boasts and idle chatter. He should have told Uncle William that he had been the single most important person in his life, save for his mother. That he could never repay his love and generosity. That he would not now be the man he was had he not had the unfathomable good fortune to have been his ward. It was now too late. Those words could never be said this side of the grave.

At first, Light laid his head on his desk and sobbed like a baby. Then charged with irrational anger, he swept the table of its contents, kicking out at chairs and ornaments like a petulant boy. Finally, he resorted to the equally infantile behaviour of the tormented man: he reached for a bottle, and when he had drunk his fill, went off in search of a woman.

Felipe Rozells witnessed the display at a distance, peering through a crack in the open door, and then retreating to the veranda where he could watch through the window, unwilling to embarrass Captain Light in his distress. He worshipped his brother-in-law, the very epitome of what a man should be. To see him brought so low was a pitiful sight. Something very bad had happened. Perhaps ill news from Merbok?

As the captain staggered from the house, Felipe salvaged the letter from the floor. In moments, he understood the nature of the sad tidings. Relief coursed through him. Nothing bad had happened to his family. Then shame that he had read the captain's private correspondence. But it was too late now. Captain Light had taken himself off into the night, and Felipe was concerned for his safety. Tharua was a port town after all and a drunken man out of his mind with grief would not have his wits about him. Even a man of note, such as the captain, might meet with trouble in such a state.

Picking up a stout stick by the door, just in case, Felipe charged into the night, hoping to pick up the Captain's trail. It was not difficult. Only one path led to Tharua. Where else would he have gone? Nor would the inebriated man be moving at speed. Even so, by the time the boy caught up with his brother-in-law, Light had reached the outskirts of the settlement. It was fortunate indeed that Felipe sighted him when he did, for Light almost immediately ducked off the track down an obscure alleyway that ran behind the wooden shanties lining the road.

It was only then that Felipe considered both his own plight and what he intended to do next. He had never been out alone at night in the port, nor had he ever had any wish to do so. Felipe was a gentle soul who shrank away from conflict and danger. The back lane was in total darkness; it was dank and foul, littered with abandoned objects, and it led him further and further away from the comparative safety of the main street. The night was total, purple-grey swirling clouds blurring the starry firmament and blotting out the moon. A storm threatened offshore, distant rumbles announcing its arrival from the sea. Episodic flashes of sheet lightning cast a momentary and terrifying light, as intimidating as the darkness itself. Felipe's imagination created robbers, pirates and even demons, lurking in every nook and cranny. But still the brave lad stumbled on, carried only by the staggering footsteps ahead that were punctuated by the occasional bang and subsequent oath. Where was the captain heading?

A rapid knocking on the door of one of the hovels brought Felipe to a sudden halt; he scrambled back into the darkness to observe. A scraping sound announced the opening of rickety wood; faint candlelight shed a distant glow. It was enough to reveal the captain's destination. A short, muffled exchange and then a young Siamese woman stepped into the light, reaching out a hand to draw him inside. Felipe stared in horror. This was no chance encounter with a local harlot. Captain Light knew this woman. He had been to this dwelling before. She was his *mia noi*, his mistress.

* * *

It had seemed to Martinha for so very long that she would never raise her head again after the loss of her baby boy. The initial news that she had been carrying a child had taken her by surprise despite the fact that no other subject had occupied the household since her marriage quite as much as whether or not she was pregnant. Furthermore, it was not for want of opportunity, for Francis was an eager lover and she a willing wife. Yet, all the same, when her bleeding ceased and she complained of feeling tired and nauseous, turning her nose up at spicy food, she had been astonished to learn that she was to become a mother.

At first, she had been in denial, wishing it had not happened, for she feared that the wonderful idyll of her romance with Francis would now come to an end. She would grow fat and slow and he would be loath to touch her. But impending motherhood brings its own irresistible emotions, even more powerful and lasting than amorous love. Soon she had become entranced with the miracle in her body as her slender, girlish frame ripened and bloomed into fertile womanhood. Francis had been equally captivated; she need not have feared. Many was the night he lay with his head upon her belly, whispering sweet nonsense to the little child within.

Joy had been ripped from them in one terrifying moment. A trickle of blood, and then a cramping pain had left her in no doubt. The child was coming – with months to go. It could not be held back. After a short and wretched labour, Martinha had delivered a tiny perfect baby boy. He had never breathed. His eyes had never opened. It was the moment when she first learned the true extent of the sorrow that life might bring. Neither the death of her father nor separation from her mother could compare to the pain that wrenched her heart that day. It was a dagger that both pierced and left embedded its cold, hard, irretrievable shard.

Francis had tried his best but his ministrations had been clumsy; they intruded into her personal grief. She knew he was in agony too but it was impossible for her to bear his pain, for she could not get past her own. Every time she saw him, he reminded her of what she had lost, the child in his image, the manifestation of their love that never was to be. She had failed her husband in the only thing that she might offer as a wife, for if she could not bear a healthy child, what sort of woman was she?

His instinct had been to return her to her mother and grandmother in whose tender care she might find peace, and his instinct had been right. As much as she knew she was abandoning Francis, unless she found her own way to the light, she could never be the wife he needed.

It had been a slow and painful process, but gradually she accepted the fate that God had decreed. It helped to hear the stories that Thong Di and Mahsia told of their own lost babies. She had never known her mother had suffered twice: a baby miscarried in its early months and a full-term child stillborn. Mahsia herself had lost children: one to her first husband and others to Chom Rang. Nature always had its way. Time healed the worst of the pain. One day she would hold a beautiful baby in her arms and that would be her reward. At last, Martinha began to look forward while vowing never to forget the little boy whose future had ended even before it had begun. She would pick up the threads of her life and return to Francis.

And just as she was contemplating writing to Tharua, she received an unexpected correspondence from the self-same place. It was from Felipe. He never usually wrote to her, although he regularly kept in touch with mother. In consternation, Martinha ripped the letter open.

Dearest sister,
I hope you are feeling better now and that the time spent with Ibu and Nenek has been a balm to your spirits. I pray for all three of you daily. Martinha, I think it is time to return. Captain Francis is very sad. He has begun to drink too much spirits and it is not good for him. But there is more. I know he would want to tell you this himself but I fear he does not wish to worry you, so keeps it from you. His uncle William has died. This news has been a further burden to his already sorrowful state. I am worried for him. He is alone in his great grief. Only you

*can help restore him to his usual vigour. Nor would you
wish for him to leave port in this frame of mind. It will
affect his ability to think clearly. I have sent this letter
with Soliman. He awaits you on the Harimau. Please
come home. I miss you, too.*

Your dear brother, Felipe

Her brother's letter unleashed a storm of activity where
for months Martinha had been numb to life. Some measure of
recovery had already taken place in the weeks of quiet seclusion;
the floodgates now poured forth in one eruption of decisive
endeavour. In the midst of it all, she had quite forgot – or perhaps
had chosen to ignore – her husband's needs. Now he had been laid
low by a further grievous loss. It was her turn to be the rock for
him. And in the outward turning of her thoughts, she finally eased
her inward sorrow.

Of course, she would return to Tharua and be with Francis
at his time of trial! She scanned her brother's earnest words,
suspecting they hid a multitude of meaning, for she knew Felipe
would not have taken such action lightly. Her first instinct was to
race out of the house and leave immediately. But almost as soon
as the urge arose, another idea struck her. An inner voice recalled
her other dilemma: how could she leave her mother and Nenek
Mahsia alone again?

Her grandmother's health was fragile. She was old now, her
decline more rapid of late. The straitened circumstances caused
by Thong Di's second marriage and the concomitant humiliation
of her family had hit the grand old lady hard. Martinha feared
her broken heart might simply stop beating, especially should she

leave them for a second time. And then Mother would be totally alone. Unthinkable.

'Where is Juragan Soliman?' she inquired of the manservant who had brought the letter. 'Has he waited? I must send a reply.'

The servant eyed her suspiciously, but decided her request was harmless. He nodded. 'Then bring him here. Call for refreshments whilst I write my answer. You may go now.'

It was as simple as that. Martinha dismissed her maid to bring the food and in the short time they were alone, she outlined her plan to Soliman. He understood immediately.

'I will return after dark. Be ready. We will not have long. Bring only what you need.'

While the arrangements were easily made, sneaking out her mother and an old lady of almost seventy, was a tall order indeed. Their only advantage was that in the evenings they were largely left alone with only a few servants who mostly kept to their quarters. As their dwelling was at a distance from the main house, little passing traffic would observe them.

After dark, as agreed, Soliman slipped through the door, as silent as a shade, to find the three women ready and waiting, having spent the afternoon sewing jewels and coins into their shawls. Apart from a few important documents, there was nothing else to salvage. It was enough to be free of the place.

Old Mahsia did not complain, even though her bones were stiff and frail. She crept from the house at an unexpected speed, the brunt of her weight supported by Soliman. Swathed in their darkest cloths, they disappeared into the trees where several crew members waited with a makeshift sedan. They lifted up the old lady while Soliman attended to Lady Thong Di. Martinha walked behind, flanked by another lascar.

And so, began the terrifying trek through the dark forest. Despite the well-trod path from Merbok village down to the river, at night the jungle was a forbidding place of flickering shadow and sudden movement, unexpected shriek and menacing rustle. To add to their distress, the wind had lifted, causing the trees to surge violently, stirred by contrary gusts. A relentless rain poured down, limiting what little vision they already possessed. The men still plodded on, so Martinha simply had to trust they knew where they were going.

Soliman recognised her apprehension. 'One of the men is Samsan,' he whispered. 'He recognised me at the jetty and asked after Lady Thong Di. It seems he used to work your land before his family was evicted because they are Siamese. He holds you in high regard. I took the chance of asking him to be our guide. He knows the way even in the dark, my lady. Do not worry!'

Martinha breathed a sigh of relief. Do good things, and good things will happen to you. That is what her mother would say. It was a Buddhist principle that she supposed Jesus would also share. 'We must pay him for his service. He has taken a great risk,' she insisted.

'Already done, ma'am,' Soliman replied softly. 'Rain is troublesome but it helps. Makes it hard to follow. And no one will be about on such a bad night. By the time they know we've gone, we'll be far away at sea.'

The inclement torrents did not feel like benefit as they struggled ankle deep in mud and water, soaked to the skin and wearied to the bone. The jungle swallowed them up but it would only take a momentary lapse in concentration for any number of unpleasant fates to befall them. Martinha's slippers were most unsuitable; they chafed and blistered her feet and gave no support either from the water or the rough ground. Eventually she kicked them off and carried on barefoot. She girdled her sarong into her waistband, male fashion. Lady Thong Di could not bring herself to do the same, struggling on with her dignity still retained. The cumbersome fabrics weighed them down, their hair streamed about their faces, and yet the endless journey continued, step after sodden step.

It was still relentless dark when the forest began to give away to scrub and they found themselves descending the slippery path to the river whose level was rising fast; the jetty was already partially submerged. The men lowered Tunku Mahsia into the arms of awaiting sailors, who laid her on a small skiff for transfer to the *Harimau*, anchored in the deeper water. The rest of the party gathered on the wooden dock, exposed and as miserable as could be, but hopeful now that safety was in sight.

There were a few anxious moments as the old lady was raised to the vessel and the skiff returned for the rest of them, but eventually the ordeal was over. The sailors shook themselves off and set to punting the craft downstream, making use of long poles to avoid being dragged into narrow inlets, until they found a fast current and caught the prevailing winds. By the time the first streaks of dawn broke through, they had made the open sea, where they slid into the grey mantle of a watery world, the shore of Queddah slipping steadily away.

In the cabin, Martinha made her mother and grandmother as comfortable as possible, peeling off their sodden garments and wrapping them in soft cloths and blankets. Mahsia was uncomplaining but exhausted, shivering and wan, sipping at a warm glass of tea. She soon fell into an unsettled sleep, already showing signs of fever. Her chest was constricted, her breathing laboured and shallow. Thong Di sat by her mother's side, pale-faced but resolute, suddenly older and frailer than Martinha had ever realised.

'Rest, mother. I will sit with Nenek,' Martinha whispered. For once, her mother did not demur, grateful to curl up on the floor, immediately asleep. Martinha held her grandmother's hand, but sleep soon claimed her too, slumping half onto the cot, and half on a low stool. The subsequent hours were spent recuperating in this fashion, dozing and then nibbling at the sailors' humble fare.

By the time they put into Tharua two days later, the two younger women were much restored, although Mahsia was sick with a hacking cough and persistent fever. Yet in her lucid moments, she shrugged off their concern. 'It is better to be free and dead than spend one's days in a living hell!' she proclaimed gamely. 'I do not intend to die this time, yet if I should, it will be in the knowledge that we escaped from that black-hearted old rogue Yahya Ismail!' she cried. 'Worth dying for!' was her dramatic assertion.

Soliman sent runners to announce their arrival the moment they reached port. Even before they disembarked, Light was charging through the curious crowds, dashing wildly this way and that, desperate to greet his family with Felipe close on his heels. Martinha watched them from the deck, her heart so full that she feared she would faint for joy. Francis did not even wait for a gangplank, but bounded in one sure-footed leap from harbour to boat, while his wife gasped at his audacity. 'Francis! Be careful!'

she shouted her arms outstretched to save him.

He caught her in his embrace, swinging her off the ground. 'You ask me to be careful? When you three ladies have just escaped the clutches of Queddah? Madam, I bow to your reckless bravery!' And he kissed her in full view of all the crew and onlookers, causing a ripple of embarrassment to run through the crowd. Such public displays of affection were rare, particularly amongst decent society. But even Lady Thong Di and Tunku Mahsia smiled with indulgence. There was a time and place for everything and it seemed appropriate that love be the sentiment of their deliverance.

'It was Soliman who made it possible! Without his support, we would never have been able to escape!' Martinha called Soliman over. He had been lingering in the background.

Light threw his arm about his adopted son. 'This young man has saved my life more times than I can remember. Now he has saved my entire family. We owe him more than we can ever repay. Soliman, what can I do to show the extent of my love and admiration!'

Soliman smiled, delighted by the public recognition of his place in Light's affection. 'Until the day I leave this world, Captain Francis, it will never be enough to settle my debt to you. My joy is in your family reunited.'

Light called Felipe over and with one arm round Soliman and another around his brother-in-law, he chatted with the ladies as the sailors prepared to offload the arriving party onto waiting carriages. As the merry group began their journey homewards, Light whispered into Felipe's ear: 'And my eternal thanks to you, young fellow, for rescuing me from myself. I am doubly blessed.

You have more than proved your place in my household – and
my heart.'

Felipe responded with a shy shrug. He hoped above all that
Francis might settle back to peaceful family life now that the
entire household was restored. No more trips to the back alleys
of Tharua in future. Would that the captain's wandering eye was
now fixed where it belonged for good.

15

Undercurrents

Royal Palace, Thonburi, Siam. September 1777
If his first visit had brought a chilling intimation of how dangerous it might be to cross King Tak Sin, Light's second audience proved even more disturbing. In the intervening years, Thonburi had continued to rise, a wonder to behold. Yet behind the ostentatious grandeur and the obsequious ceremonial, disturbing ripples of unease criss-crossed the capital. Not a single word of dissension was ever spoken, yet discord was in the air, a living, monstrous creature hovering above the rooftops, breathing suspicion into every crevice and cranny.

The beast dwelled in impassive looks and downward gazes, in shared silences and backward glances; it exhaled from every pore and dripped from every fountain, it watched and waited in claustrophobic anticipation. It was much more than the paranoia of a king. The city teetered on a tightrope where rumour, fact and outrage distorted the public conscience until even the most disparate elements of society were of one mind. The king was mad.

During the royal audience, King Tak Sin proved as amenable to Light as on his earlier visit. He spoke again of a Company settlement, this time mentioning the Mergui archipelago, describing its ideal location as a potential British outpost and the mutually beneficial prospect of a future relationship between the two kingdoms. Yet, just as before, there was no firm talk of treaty. Mergui was a mere sweetener dangled before the British whom Tak Sin knew would be little interested in the northern port, particularly as it was still under Burmese rule. The British were being played for the fool, useful as a valuable source of much-needed weaponry and enticed from alliance elsewhere by a prospect largely based on thin air.

Ominous portents warned that intimate connection with the court of Siam was highly dangerous. At whim, Tak Sin swung from genial ruler to frenzied tyrant. For some time, the king had been obsessed that he was a reincarnation of the Lord Buddha on the final stages of his Enlightenment, endowed with powers beyond the human realm. He spent many hours withdrawn in meditation, fasting until delirium. On the increasingly rare occasions when he appeared in public, his behaviour was unpredictable, given to sudden acts of inexplicable violence.

Whilst in conversation with several venerable abbots – who had once been his own teachers – the king had announced that he was able to fly. Afraid that he might try to demonstrate this irrational claim from one of the higher tiers of the shrine, the holy men remonstrated with him, begging him to refrain from such imaginings. Tak Sin was seized by rage at their disbelief and ordered them to be flogged to death before the entire court. This atrocious act lost him the support of the monastic community, even if it was loath to publicly condemn him.

During a private dinner with Lord Thian, Light raised the matter of the king's sanity, but the younger man closed down the conversation. Where once he had discussed his patron, now he would no longer even speak of him, let alone reveal an opinion. As a leading general, Thian was rarely in the city these days, preferring the less capricious existence of war, where life and death had simpler parameters. He was close to Lord Duang. The foreign campaigns were going well. Siam was reasserting its rightful place in the region. Beyond that, Thian would not say.

Instead they spoke of easier things. Martinha was back in Thalang; Francis and she both hoped soon for the blessing of a child. Thian teased Light on the necessity to spend less time on the high seas if he wished to achieve that particular goal. Light countered that he could hardly use that as an excuse to King Tak Sin for any delay in the musket supply! The family was enjoying its reunion. Although Mahsia's health was fragile, the old lady was back to her redoubtable self, badgering all and sundry, her tongue still spiky as aloes. Young Felipe, once more answering to 'Nilip' now back in Thalang, had found his place in Light's agency. The boy had proved unsuited to the sailor's life, but was a meticulous administrator with a fine eye for detail, a gift for languages and a natural flair for business. The family was settled and prospering. Lord Thian should try to find time to visit; they would be honoured by his presence.

'My mother constantly begs me to return but the military campaigns are endless. There is never time. And it might cause talk –' but he cut off that thought instantly. 'Perhaps next year? If you ever manage to conceive this child that you so long for, that is!'

Why might visiting his home be suspect? Thian was shrewd. He sensed the way the wind was blowing and undoubtedly knew what was happening at home. If allegiances were ambiguous in

Thonburi, how much more uncertain would they be far away in the independent-minded south? If there was to be rebellion, it would most likely arise in Ligor and Phang Na. Should a man so close to the king spend time in the southern region, would his visit be adjudged to have ulterior motives? Might the pretext of spending time with family in reality be meeting with disaffected parties, this young general who had the trust of armies in the palm of his hands? His loyal service of the past ten years would count for nothing if Tak Sin had a single doubt. The deranged and paranoid king would destroy him in an instant – and take down his entire family with him.

On board ship a few days later, Light penned a carefully considered letter to Calcutta. It was a masterpiece of ambiguity. While he overtly promoted links with Siam under the guise of making a bid for Mergui, his mind was fixed on a different agenda. The British should be primed if Tak Sin fell. Jangsylan could be theirs for the taking. This time, however, his approach would be more circumspect. Either Hastings would see through it, or would take it upon himself to suggest the more amenable location, one that would avoid tangling with Burma.

Written this 22ⁿᵈ day of September 1777

Dear Sir
It has been my recent honour to attend an audience at Thonburi with the Great King who in his conversation expressed a strong desire of cultivating a Friendship with the Hon'ble Company and showed great uneasiness at no English vessels having come to his Port of late. He said

*his soldiers would attack Burmese Mergui this season
and if they took it they would give it to the English.
Mergui is an excellent location, being only eight days'
land journey from Bangkok, as well as lying close to an
area rich in Tin. Furthermore, for the Southern Straits
become more dangerous every day as the Bugis and the
Dutch struggle for control, close ties with Siam would
offer up an overland route to China that would remove
the necessity for the long and fraught sea journey around
the Peninsula. Our China vessels might discharge their
cargoes on the East coast of Siam, from whence a short
land route to the West exists over which our goods might
be hauled. I have traversed the route myself several times
and find it surprisingly amenable; it was originally laid
down for the transport of Tin. From Mergui on the west
coast, our cargoes could be despatched to India at the
saving of many weeks at sea. An outpost in Siam would
be entirely free of Dutch menace, not to mention the
marauding of the many pirates and privateers that are
found amongst the Salateers.*

*In the meantime, the King was most grateful for the
supply of armaments. He wishes to be commended to you,
Sir. There is much more trade to be had in that quarter. It
is a fruitful partnership, indeed.*

Your servant,

Francis Light, Captain.

Light set down his pen and blew across the paper, reading over
his carefully chosen words. Did it convey his full intent? Hastings

would baulk at the suggestion of Mergui, for entanglement with Burma would be avoided at all costs, but he would have to agree that his general point was well made. After a mere cursory glance at a chart, it was likely that Hastings would himself conclude that the cross-country route was just as accessible from Jangsylan – it was in fact closer – and would shorten travelling time further. If the governor-general was half as shrewd as Light thought him to be, he would seize upon a preference for Jangsylan, in which case Light would have to inform him that, although it was indeed the better option, securing it as a Company establishment would only be possible if the British were prepared to provide a strong military presence, much as they had done in Madras and Calcutta. Should the decision to display a show of force came from Hastings himself, it would be easier to make the case.

On his next trip to India, Light intended to pay a personal visit to the governor-general with the hope of achieving this outcome. Meanwhile, Thalang was already primed. But that had been a year ago, and much was still the same. Tak Sin continued to strike fear in the hearts of the court, the northern wars consumed his armies and Light plied his trade around the Straits, still walking the precarious line between two royal patrons.

16

The Turn of the Wheel

Tharua, Jangsylan. January 1778

It seemed to be the season for endings and beginnings, or mayhap Light was reaching the age when those two opposing forces, life and death, were constantly tapping on his shoulder? As the New Year turned, death claimed old Mahsia. She closed her eyes one night and simply did not reawaken. Despite the painful absence of farewells, fate had ultimately been kind to her. Ever since her return from Queddah, her health had been poor; the family had known it was only a matter of time. In the end she had not suffered, still as lively and cantankerous as ever until her final day.

Then, on the heels of that sad loss, the heavenly wheel turned once more, and Martinha discovered she was with child again. It surprised no one. That was how life was: one family member departs, a new one arrives, the generations each on their allotted course. Much rested on this baby. Until a child was born, a marriage in these parts was on precarious grounds but once the gift of parenthood was forged, the union became a living, breathing bond, stretching down into the ages. The family was consoled in their bereavement. Mahsia, Chom Rang, Martim and Light's unknown parents would now live on in this tiny child.

Their daughter was delivered safely in October, a winsome child, sturdy and pale-skinned, with blue-black eyes and a charming dark-gold floss wisping on her tiny scalp. She was every inch an English baby, a novelty that fascinated the household. Even the midwife boasted around the town that had she not pulled the baby from her mother by her own hands, she would not have believed it could be Nona Light's child.

Francis was in love from the first moment. This little mite was the only flesh and blood he had ever known, the link that connected him to his unknown past and the longed-for future where he might at last belong. Her given name was Mae Sarah – Sarah May in English – which suited Martinha well, for within the wholly Christian name she heard the echoes of her grandmother, Mahsia. It was a fitting name to reflect the very different worlds to which this little child belonged.

The Lights threw a convivial celebration for little Sarah's baptism, a lively blend of the Ban Takkien relatives, English sea captains and members of the local Eurasian community. Tables were set between the trees for shade. They were lucky with the weather, for it was still the rainy season, although beginning to edge towards the fierce December heat. Today the sky was unrelenting blue, the air heavy and still with a likelihood of a storm by afternoon.

Children dashed about the tables, chased by numerous servants, while the adults ate and drank abundantly, grouped in their usual cliques according to the self-imposed boundaries of language, race and religion. Light circulated, easy with all parties, while Martinha and the baby remained on the veranda, surrounded by her maids and the ladies of the family. It was unwise for a recent mother and a new-born to mingle freely as they were more vulnerable to infection. For who knew what might be running through the community of Tharua?

'What d'you make of this American war?' William Lindesay asked the men of his table: Scott, David Welch, Edward Wilson and Lars Petersen, all captains in the employ of the Jangsylan agency. 'They say the Yankees have the army on the run. Might the colony fall?'

Scott chuckled, always one to enjoy a British disaster. 'All the better for us either way. Anything that damages the western trade will be a bonus for the east. And should the entire colony be lost? Well, where will they then go to source damn near everything?'

The loss of the colonies would only raise the profile of the Company. Light leaned in, resting his hands against Scott's shoulder. 'Don't count the Frenchies out! If they declare war in America, you can be damned sure they'll take the fight out here, for this is what they want most of all, a piece of the East Indies pie.'

'I heard tell their fleets are on their way already. Mark my words, the Coromandel will be threatened before the year is out,' added Edward Wilson, a morose but highly experienced Indiaman captain who was usually well-informed.

'Without their damned help, those Yankees would have been ground down long ago, the treacherous dogs,' David Welch added, swigging down his port. 'It will do 'em no good, mind. The Yankees have a mind to rule themselves. They'll take French help and then kick the lot out by the arse. But, can you see a bunch of common rebels prevailing in the long run?'

'We can but live in hope,' Scott poked the fires of their British egotism, his comment greeted with a round of jeers. He raised his hands as if to ward them off. 'Gentlemen, remember where you are!' he grinned. 'But all nationalistic sentiments aside, we must appraise the benefit in all this. For the next few years, I'd put my money on guns, gentlemen. For that is one trade which will never be short of business!' The catcalls turned to cheers and another round of passing the bottle. They were merchants first and foremost. The exploitation of the current state of affairs was their bread and cheese.

'Joking apart, sirs,' said Light. 'What little I have read of the new-formed Congress and their Continental Army would suggest these rebels are a cut above your usual bedraggled hordes. This fellow Washington is proving quite the statesman. I wouldn't bet against him. America's a vast wilderness, impossible to hold from Europe without a tremendous investment of men and money. We fought there in the '50s, Jamie and I. The cost of that engagement was monstrous in lives and money. This struggle could be even more protracted, for these Yankees are on home ground. They are even forming bonds with their native peoples, so I hear.'

'One man fighting for his own soil does the job of ten Redcoats on a paltry King's shilling. Did the Jacobites teach you Sassenachs nothing?' Scott reminded them.

'You damned well lost, Scott! Have you forgotten Culloden, man?' Wilson countered with pompous satisfaction.

'A tiny nation of stout hearts against the might of England? Think what we might have achieved had we but a continent to recruit from!' Scott snapped back in not-quite-jovial tones.

The others nodded their agreement. These men were realists above all. Their existence allowed little room for blinkered flag-waving. 'Tis so, in every land. A man would rather die than be the slave of another nation. And who would blame him?' Light reminded them.

Captain Lars Petersen, a bearish Dane, red of face and eyes of duck-egg blue, spoke up. He had the look of a man who had once been a beautiful boy, but time and tide had left him paunchy and grizzled. Until then he had been a mere observer in the conversation. 'Let them all shoot themselves into the next world if they so wish! War doesn't put food on the table or clothes on your children's backs. My home is where I take my boots off. Let's drink a toast to Fortune above all, for there's money to be made in these waters, and bad news will only bring us more!' Light clapped him on his back while the inebriated sailors found yet another reason to charge their glasses.

Taking the opportunity at that juncture, Light slipped away to join his wife above, and to check on his daughter. Little Sarah lay awake in her basket, her eyes fixed on some invisible point to her right. Her little face was deep in concentration, a furrowed wrinkle on her brow suddenly replaced by a look of surprise and a dribbly smile. 'I think she recognises me!' Francis was delighted at her response, chucking his little girl beneath her chin.

'Perhaps,' was Martinha's indulgent reply as she stroked the downy cheek. 'I'm sure she knows our voices. But she often stares into the distance, as if listening to someone. It occupies her and seems to calm her down. My girls say it is her guardian spirit, her Mae Su.'

Thong Di, batted away the suggestion with her fan, in an impatient gesture oddly reminiscent of her own mother. 'Nonsense, Martinha! You should not listen to these village tales! It is her guardian angel sent from Heaven to protect her.'

Martinha and Francis shared an amused look. Was there

much difference between a spirit or an angel? The baby was not crying. As all new parents, they were thankful enough for that. Shortly afterwards, Martinha and her attendants took the child within to feed and settle; Thong Di joined them, leaving Francis to the other members of the family. It was the opportunity he had been waiting for.

'Phaya Pimon, Lady Chan! Our humble home is magnified by your presence!' Light bowed.

'It is our pleasure, Captain. To welcome a child is always an occasion to rejoice!' Pimon replied, turning to his wife, who held out an exquisite tortoiseshell box. Inside was a golden bracelet embossed with a floral pattern, each pistil studded with a tiny ruby. 'For little Mae Sarah,' she announced stiffly, for the name was difficult for her to pronounce, her rendition more like 'Mae Sa-Lah'.

'An extravagance, dear lady,' Francis replied. 'My daughter is a fortunate little girl to own such precious jewels at only two months old!'

'Come, sit by us, sir,' Pimon patted a vacant chair. 'It is high time we talked.' He checked the surroundings; all the women had left and only a few of his retainers stood by. 'The situation in the City grows more "interesting" by the day. Moreover, my sources tell me that the Superintendent of the South is dissatisfied with loyalties in the region. He intends to limit European shipping in our ports. This will not be popular in Thalang.'

'It will not be popular in Calcutta either, sir,' Light interjected. Even in this safe location, they guarded their words carefully.

'There is an appetite for change in Thalang, Captain. This may be our moment.' His eyes were alive with meaning.

'There is always appetite in Bengal, sir,' was Francis' obscure response. 'But appetite needs feeding, Lord. Is there meat for the table now?' The Siamese governor nodded his approval.

His wife smiled beatifically. 'That is no longer the problem, my dear Kapiten.' Lady Chan had finally joined in the conversation, although she was likely its driving force. 'It is time indeed to set the table and serve the meal. When the time comes, can you guarantee the support we require?'

If his experiences in Aceh and Queddah had taught Light anything, it was that there was no such animal in politics as a guarantee, particularly where the Honourable Company was concerned. But, as ever, Francis did not let facts become an obstacle to opportunity.

'Without a doubt, sir. The need for an establishment has never been so great. The time is ripe for both parties, you have my word on it!'

'Excellent! Excellent!' Phaya Pimon clapped his hands in satisfaction. 'Your Siamese is very good, sir. I hear you are working on your writing, too?'

Light pulled a wry face. 'I struggle. Young Felipe is a patient tutor but I fear he has a very stupid pupil. He has me writing endless exercises, like a schoolboy. But I am determined to improve, although it is a very difficult language for a wooden-headed Englishman, I fear.'

His answer amused them both. It was always good strategy, Light had found, to encourage gentle mockery of clumsy English ignorance. But in truth, he was working hard on his written Siamese, and 'Mr. Nilip' as the locals called him, was proving as useful a teacher as he was a secretary.

***

The year was not yet done with death. October brought the news of the passing of venerable old Sultan Muhammed Jiwa, who had lived so long that many thought him immune to death. Scott had been in Queddah at the time and hastened back. The sultan's heir, his son Abdullah, was installed, although rumours were already circulating that this was not a popular choice. The young man was arrogant and feckless, not even half the man his aged father had been. Some parties favoured his younger brother, others his uncle. Another son by a palace *gundik* had his own faction.

The Light household was saddened by the death of the old king, for he had been good to them in his fashion; the sultan even referred to Light as 'my son'. But, like Mahsia, it had only been a matter of time. The palace vultures had been gathering for years, waiting on this very event. And Abdullah's ineptitude could be even more useful if handled with caution. The new sultan would have need of external support against the viper's nest of the Queddah court, as well as his other enemies. It offered Light another opportunity, should his plans for Thalang fail. A man must always have an escape route, no matter how comfortable one felt with the current situation.

Hot on the heels of the christening, came a letter from old George Doughty. For once it had been short and to the point. He was writing on behalf of Mary Light to inform Francis of the sad passing of Margaret Negus, now at peace with God and her dear William. It had been a cancerous growth thus her death had been a blessed release. The poor woman had suffered much with Mary Light her constant companion throughout her final trials.

His mother sent her fondest regards and wished him to be assured that she was well, as hearty and strong as ever, but missing her dear son.

Poor mother, all alone now. What chance was there that he might ever hold her in his sight again in this life? These further sad tidings cast a damper on Light's spirits that even the infectious chuckles of his darling daughter could not mend. In the end, all was dust. Every single one of them would one day pass; their struggles and their joys would count as naught. The year had truly been bookended by loss, even if the joy of parenthood had been at its heart.

17

The Debt Wife

When the trouble in Thalang began, it seemed innocuous enough. Superintendent Khang Seng made his regular visit as Thonburi's appointed representative and formally announced that a series of restrictions was to be placed on foreign traders. In future, they would sell their goods through government-appointed officials only, at strictly controlled prices favourable to the state. This regulation was not new; it was the traditional system, happily ignored for generations by the merchants of Thalang. With monotonous regularity, previous governors had attempted to reinstate it with little success. But this time, Superintendent Khang Seng supplied military support and a team of meddlesome officials to oversee the implementation, with powers independent of the Thalang governor. Subsequently, some European merchants were arrested for infringements and badly used, their cargoes impounded. Many foreign vessels chose to stay away.

Light and Scott viewed this development with wry indifference. Where other captains moved out of their quarters to live aboard their ships moored offshore for safety, they remained in Tharua, conducting their affairs much as before. They had a well-established local office: Nilip Rozells, plus a Chinese accountant, and a number of loyal secretaries. It seemed unlikely that their interests would be affected. Governor Pimon was in their corner, and they were also intricately linked with most of the local businessmen for whom these regulations were also an unpopular burden.

To counteract the prescriptions was not difficult, despite the government scrutiny. It required only a modicum of inventive misdirection. Their agency, in apparent good faith, supplied a limited amount of goods to the government officers at the imposed prices. These officials, who had no means of knowing whether this was the full extent of the usual transactions, took receipt of the commodity and offered it for sale on the local market at vastly inflated prices in order to earn revenue for the state, and, naturally, a cut for themselves. The government men viewed their office as a personal treasure chest.

Behind their backs, Light and Scott flooded the black market (ever-present in tax-despising Thalang) with an excess of the same goods at much more affordable prices. Thus, they reaped their usual profit and destroyed government sales in one fell swoop. There was much subsequent dismay at the Treasury when they were unable to sell the goods they had purchased. It appeared there was no local demand. Superintendent Khang Seng was furious.

One late afternoon with dark clouds gathering and an ominous wind whipping up, Light was overseeing the speedy offloading of a cargo of rice on the harbourside, a special order from the Superintendent's office to address food shortages on the island, caused by the decline in foreign trade. Light was driving the bearers hard. The rice sacks must be stowed before the heavens opened and everything was spoiled. It was a rare to find the Captain himself dealing with such a task but, given recent developments, he wished to closely supervise the activity.

'Phraya Ratchakapitan – ?' Light spun round to find a young Treasury official approaching him.

He held up his arms in protest. 'Before you begin poking your nose in where it does not belong, this is a special delivery by order of the Superintendent himself. It does not fall under the proscriptions. I have the papers in order here. See? Seventeen hundred bags to alleviate local shortages. No coin involved. This is an agreed barter in exchange for seven hundred *piculs* of tin to be supplied from the Treasury within three months.' Light was abrupt, in no mood to truck with petty officials.

'Honourable Kapiten, you misunderstand. I am Nai Thalakang. Although I am attached to the Royal Treasury, today I am here on a private matter. Perhaps I could have a few words with you, if you would do me the great honour?'

Light took a better look. He vaguely recognised the fellow, a scrawny, nondescript individual with the prideful look of the bully. For once, however, he did not have his usual swagger; today his face was pale and pinched. Light's first instinct was to chase him off but changed his mind. Perhaps this 'favour' could prove useful in the future.

Abruptly waving him away, Light snarled: 'I am too occupied at present. Wait for me by the *raan*. I shall be along by and by to take a drink. We can talk there, but I warn you if you think to waste my valuable time!'

Nai Thalakang bowed low, profusely thanking the captain and assuring him that to waste his time was not his intent. Meanwhile, Light turned back to the job in hand, and only when the last sack was stowed and the warehouse bolted, did he remember the appointment. Some time had passed. Fat droplets of rain were already falling, spattering the cobblestones. Glancing up, he assessed the sky. It would be a fierce but short-lived downpour. There was time for a glass of tea and a chat with the loathsome fellow while he waited out the shower.

Taking shelter towards the back of the open stall, where a modicum of shelter was provided by the awning, Light called for a pot of tea and a tot of rum. A rat ran across his feet, another refugee from the deluge. He kicked it hard, sending it flying into the gulley outside, already streaming with rainwater. 'Damn, bloody, filthy rats,' Light muttered, although his insult might have been directed as much towards the Treasury official himself. 'So, sir, what's your problem? I suppose it isn't official business or you would have been bothering me at my office as you usually do.'

Nai Thalakang stared morosely into his empty teacup. Light had not offered him anything stronger – but he had the look of a man who needed it. 'Phraya Ratchakapitan. I have a favour to ask.'

Light groaned. 'I might have known! And what might this "favour" be? I presume it involves some cost to me? And why exactly would you think me disposed to help one of your miserable band?'

The young man grimaced. Light wondered if he was about to vomit, so wan did his countenance appear. 'I have incurred a debt I am unable to repay. I bought goods from a Chinese trader called Wong on a promissory note. But I have been unable to sell them at any profit and ...'

'... you were hoping to pay the fellow from your profit, I take it? But no one now wants to buy your goods. Is that the long and short of it? I know Wong. He'll take it from you in flesh if you don't honour your debt, young man.'

'He gives me only two days! If I cannot pay, he will report me to the Superintendent for corruption! It carries a death sentence!'

Light sighed. He could imagine the scenario, the little toady throwing his weight around, trying to cheat a wily Chinese businessman. Thalakang deserved to be brought to justice. The restrictions were unfair enough without the venality of the officers presiding over them. Yet to have some leverage over a government official was always useful. Nai Thalakang was no doubt relying on that. 'How much?'

'Six *bahars*.'

It was not an enormous sum – but a significant one for a man who could not pay. 'Do you have collateral? You're not from Thalang. How do I know you won't take the money and disappear?'

'I pledge my wife. I send her to you. She is your wife until the debt is paid.' Thalakang spat the words out. The lines were rehearsed – he had known it would come to this – but it cost him much to say it, nonetheless.

'Your wife, you say?' Light shrugged. 'I already have a wife.'

'She is very beautiful,' Thalakang admitted grudgingly.

Light laughed out loud in disbelief. 'You? A beautiful wife? I find that hard to believe.'

'Sir, it is true. Amdaeng Rat is very beautiful. Everyone says so. I am a very lucky man,' he replied without any sense of irony.

'You have children?' Light asked. Debt wives were commonly pledged for surety in such matters, but he did not find the practice to his taste. To take a mother from her children was un-Christian, in his opinion.

The wretched man shook his head. 'No children. Only married short time.'

'Foolish wretch!' Light interjected. 'Still a bridegroom and you offer your bride to pay your debts? What kind of man are you?'

'A desperate man, sir. But I do not want Wong to have her. He will take her if I cannot pay. He will abuse her, pass her round his friends for sport! You are a good man, Ratchakapitan, everybody says so. She will come to no harm with you. And I *will* pay you back. This I promise. My wife is very dear to me.' Nai Thalakang joined his hands in a desperate prayer, begging Light to help him.

He groaned. 'Come to my office tomorrow morning. We will draw up the papers. Your wife can join my household.' He pointed his finger threateningly at the official. 'But, I warn you, sir, I want more than your wife from this agreement. Do you understand me? I want your cooperation in future – and I am sure you know what I mean by that. When my goods are inspected, you better turn a blind eye, if you know what's good for you. These are my terms. Take or leave them!'

'Thank you, thank you, Ratchakapitan.' Thalakang sank to his knees, grasping the hem of Light's jacket and bringing it to his head in obeisance.

'Get up, you damned fool!' Light shouted, shaking him off, much as he had done with the rodent. 'Do you want the whole damn island to know your business?'

The entire island probably already did. Nothing was hidden in Tharua port. Not that it was of any significance to Francis Light.

It was enough to have a Treasury man in his pocket. Everyone would approve of that. Except for Martinha. He doubted that she would be as accommodating when she heard the news about his acquisition of a beautiful new 'debt' wife.

18

The Chulia Merchant

Anak Bukit palace, Alor Setar, Queddah. June 1779

A courtesy visit to the new ruler of Queddah was long overdue, with the added bonus that it provided Captain Light with the perfect excuse to escape the brewing unrest in Thalang. Sultan Abdullah Mukarram Shah II had been installed earlier that year following the passing of the long-lived Muhammed Jiwa. It was high time for Light to pay his condolences and pledge his commitments to his successor.

The court of Queddah now had a distinctly different face. His audience with the young king bore little resemblance to the crowded gatherings of previous visits. Where Muhammed Jiwa had surrounded himself with a vast assembly of nobles, officials and retainers, Light found a relatively small select group, mostly comprising relatives, supporters and personal bondsmen. His father had kept his enemies close at hand but Abdullah preferred to surround himself with flatterers. The new king's grasp on Queddah was unlikely to be as firm as his father's.

Presiding was Abdullah's chief merchant, the unpopular and divisive Jamual, a Chulia of dubious character with powers greater than the Bendahara himself, who was roundly despised by almost all the significant men of Queddah. So sinister was his influence that many believed he had cast a spell over the impressionable young sultan. Abdullah saw in him a brutal ally to keep the opposition in check but failed to recognise that even those inclined to support him were by now repulsed by the venality and cruelty of his new advisor.

Light and Abdullah knew each other well; the younger man had always been impressed by the English captain. The sultan welcomed him warmly, receiving his gifts with grace and genuine pleasure. The usual back and forth of courtesies was exchanged before Abdullah turned to the role that Light might play in his administration. He was eager to resume the mutually beneficial relationship that Light had shared with his beloved father. It was hoped that Light would regard Queddah as one of his favoured ports through which he might channel an abundance of his trade, in return for the usual preferential inducements that Light had enjoyed in the past.

'It would be my greatest wish to continue the close ties between us, *Tuanku*,' Light agreed, as eager as the sultan to re-establish links. 'Although I have been residing in Thalang with my wife's people, I still fondly regard Queddah as my second home. In fact, my other purpose here today was to ask permission to return. Thalang is not the ideal place for my growing family. There is much unrest and uncertainty.'

Abdullah smiled, clearly jubilant that all was not well in the north. One less threat to preoccupy him. 'Our spies have told us of the recent unfortunate events there. It seems many merchants no longer feel safe in Tharua port. On the other hand, Queddah is a peaceful place. We welcome traders who respect our values and bring mercantile opportunities to our jetties. You may be assured that Queddah will always be open to you, Kapitan Lait. Have no fear,' Abdullah replied.

At that juncture, Jamual leaned over to whisper furtively in the king's ear in an unusual breach of etiquette. He even rested his hand upon the sultan's person, stalling his response. It was a revealing indication of the extent of the Chulia's overbearing authority. Abdullah frowned, then asked a further question. Jamual's answer seemed to satisfy the sultan, for he rested back against the cushions of his throne, his earlier arrogance restored. The king's merchant returned to his place at the sultan's side, and meekly folded his hands below his belt, yet all the while fixing Light in his ominous stare.

The sultan spoke again. 'My advisor reminds me that the matter of your family inheritance still remains unsettled. We have learned that Tunku Mahsia has recently passed away. May Allah give you fortitude to bear this great loss! She was a significant landholder in Merbok, an estate currently under the care of my loyal friend Dato' Seri Yahya Ismail. However, it appears that her daughter, Dato' Seri Yahya's wife, abandoned him of her own volition, leaving him bereft. Her flagrant act amounts to *khula* in our law, a divorce agreed by both parties. Of course, this affects the inheritance and dowry, which cannot now be granted in the wife's favour in view of her desertion. It is the decision of this court that by her unseemly behaviour she has forfeited her rights to her mother's inheritance. Tunku Mahsia's lands in Merbok have been granted to her son-in-law Dato' Seri Yahya Ismail. We would be most unhappy to learn that your visit was an attempt to countermand our decision.'

Light chose not to point out that the estates had been left, not to Lady Thong Di, but to Tunku Mahsia's grandson, Felipe, thus never part of any marriage portion, inalienable by divorce. He also did not produce the document granted by Sultan Muhammed Jiwa that guaranteed Felipe's rights. Such arguments were futile. Acquiescence was more beneficial in the long run. Abdullah was beset with the same problems as his father, but lacked the resources and ability to play his father's masterful game of intrigue. Soon enough the sultan would be desperate for Light's support, with much less than the old king to gamble. Sacrifice a pawn to take a king.

'That was never my intent, Tuanku! It is entirely fitting that the matter of the lands should be settled in this manner. My only concern is the status of Lady Thong Di should she return to Queddah. I assume that if the divorce is granted on the terms you have described – terms of mutual agreement – then we do not have a problem.'

Sultan Abdullah waved his hands in a gesture of magnanimity. 'My dear Kapitan, I felt sure we could easily solve this troublesome matter! It is with great pleasure that I grant you and your family permission to return to Queddah. It was always my father's wish that Kuala Queddah should be the seat of your trading factory, as it continues to be mine. Perhaps now we may find terms agreeable to this end at last. This has been a most propitious visit, Kapitan Lait! So many matters resolved at once. As a further token of my welcome and a promise of our future alliance, we will arrange for a fine house to be your residence. I fear the port will simply not do for a young family. You must be housed in the style of a noble of this court!'

His largesse pleased Abdullah almost as much as it satisfied Francis Light. No lasting damage had been done by the unfortunate events at Merbok. Abdullah had been more than willing to set that incident aside in the hope of future British support. It was the same old story of peninsular politics, the pendulum swinging back his way again. This time Light did not intend to squander his advantage.

On his way out a short while later, he found his way barred by a pair of impassive guards: 'Follow!' He never argued with spearmen armed with long keris. The guards led him to another part of the palace complex, to a teak pavilion hung with expensive carpets and richly adorned with silk-upholstered divans, more like the quarters of an Ottoman pasha than a Malay noble. They waited outside on the loggia, a cooling breeze wafting in across the valley from the distant river. It was a most well-appointed spot.

Jamual took his time to arrive. When he strode imperiously up the steps, the guards backed away, heads lowered in deep obeisance, to take up their watch beyond earshot. Light observed the performance with cool disdain. The king's merchant was trying to intimidate him. An invisible sparring match was imminent.

'Captain Light, it seems appropriate that we should get to know each other since the sultan holds you in such high regard despite your family's flagrant insult to one of his nobles.'

Light grinned and made a mocking bow, even adding a flamboyant hand gesture to rub salt into the wound. 'Does my arrival cause you such distress, *Tuan*? It was never my intention. In truth, before this moment, I hadn't given your feelings a single thought!'

His derision caused a flare of something most malevolent in the Chulia's black eyes. Jamual was a tall man, broad of shoulder and big-bellied, standing head and shoulders over most men of the court. Light drew himself up to his full height – and matched him eye to eye. Jamual sneered, rubbing at his thick beard, his long nose curving in disdain. 'I know your type of man, Captain Light. In twenty-five years of trading in these parts, I've met more of your kind than I care to remember. Your arrogant swagger means nothing to me. You are sailing in dangerous waters, Englishman. You already ruined your chances with your English Company. The Sultan of Selangor has a price on your head. I now hear talk you have betrayed the King of Siam. Be very careful how you deal with me.'

Light crossed the distance between them, quick enough for Jamual to take an involuntary step backwards and for his guards to point their spears. He held up his hands, laughing broadly. 'My word, sir. For some inexplicable reason my presence here has severely rattled your nerves. I can only presume that, despite your words to the contrary, you fully appreciate how influential a man I am. Fortunately for you, I intend to cooperate with your administration, for I believe it to be in both our interests. But a word of caution, Tuan. The more you alienate the sultan from his lords, the more fragile your position grows. Don't threaten me, sir. Or where will you be when all else fails and you are looking for a place to hide?'

And with that, Light bowed again – this time more curtly – and dismissed himself. Jamual was as coarse a blackguard as he had ever seen, but he was also a man running scared. His threats were empty. Everything Light had seen this day brought him great optimism for the future. Queddah was in turmoil, a seething morass of discontent, with only one way out. And he would be that way.

19

A Whiff of Treason

Light's residence, Tharua, Jangsylan. August 1779

The trickle of poor folk to their compound finally drove Martinha to demand answers from her brother. For a week, Tharua had been a powder keg. European captains were staying safely aboard ship. Reports of summary arrests were circling the port; the household was abuzz with rumour. Francis, typically, was nowhere to be seen, off on one of his never-ending voyages, which Martinha suspected were as much to keep him at a distance from what was looming as they were trading missions. The sea was always his favourite place of escape.

After a few days, however, the occasional tin miner had become a constant stream of workers lining up with paltry bundles of metal scraps, waiting patiently in the hot sun for their turn to climb the steps and make their payments. Martinha decided enough was enough. She appeared to be the only one in ignorance. Sending a maid to call Felipe inside, she waited for him in her parlour.

'Is this important, sister? I'm very busy this morning.' A distracted Felipe burst in, flustered and mopping at his brow. Her little brother, now raised to a position of responsibility in the business, had begun to treat her like the wayward child.

'It is the very nature of your "busyness" that intrigues me, brother,' Martinha snapped back. She was pregnant again; the steamy morning and the din of so many visitors had given her a queasy headache. 'What is this about? Why are all these people in and out of our compound? When did we trade in tin by the thimbleful?' she asked him bluntly.

Felipe frowned. Her brother did not disseminate easily; it was obvious from his expression that he did not wish to enlighten her. Before he had time to fob her off, she continued: 'Do not think you can keep secrets from me, Felipe! You may be the big man in this office, but I am the owner's wife! I insist on a full explanation here and now – or I shall go out there and ask one of the Chinese labourers myself!' Of the two, Martinha's will had always been the stronger. He would not hold out for long. 'I mean it, Felipe! I shall!'

Her brother flung himself down onto a chair, rumpling his hands through his wiry hair. 'Captain Francis told me not to cause you worry!'

Martinha scoffed away his reply. 'I am already worried, Felipe! And I shall continue to worry until I know what is going on!'

He gave a disconsolate shrug. 'You shall like it even less when you know ... Alright, alright! Superintendent Khang Seng has taken it into his head that insurrection is planned on the island. For some reason, he believes that Captain Light may be involved, along with Uncle Pimon. Thus, he has ordered that no one should deal with our agency.'

'What?' Martinha gasped. 'And no one thought to tell me?'

'The captain said he would make a decision when he returned. But he has not yet been apprised of what has happened of late.'

Felipe admitted with a wince. He was worried. Perhaps he should have taken more decisive action by now?

'And these people? Why are they selling tiny amounts of tin? Surely that is against the Superintendent's orders? Will they be in trouble?'

'They are hungry, Martinha! Captain Light supplies rice direct to the administration in return for tin. He has imported almost two thousand bags, but Superintendent Khang Seng now refuses payment, so the rice is rotting away in the stores, nothing but food for rats and weevils. The people are desperate enough to risk his ire. They come to buy their few bags and pay in tin scraps. They do not support the Superintendent. They favour Captain Light,' he added.

'They favour whomsoever supplies them food when their children are starving, you mean,' Martinha reminded him, shaking her head and mulling over what he had said. 'The Superintendent will retaliate.'

Felipe nodded. 'But I do not think he has been informed yet.'

'His spies are everywhere! He knows, you can be assured of that. If we continue with this illegal private trade from our own home in such public fashion, we are playing into his hands! And furthermore – for I do not believe the Superintendent took this notion without some provocation – what exactly is going on? Are you telling me Francis has been conspiring with Uncle Pimon to rebel?'

Her brother's pained reaction was enough. 'My God, Felipe!'

'It was little more than talk. Just an idle proposition in view of the unpopularity of the government officials and the discontent in Thonburi. For who knows what will happen if the king falls?

But the Superintendent has no proof. It is naught but speculation on Khang Seng's part.'

'The Superintendent does not need proof if he has a whiff of treason. There are purges everywhere! What of Francis?'

'The *Bristol* is due in any day. I thought to wait on his decision,' Felipe gasped wanly.

Martinha dashed from the room with Felipe in her wake, heading for Francis' study. 'Is there anything in this house that might incriminate?' she asked, her mind racing with possibilities.

Felipe ran behind. 'I don't think you should read the Captain's correspondence.'

'Felipe! Is there? Either you tell me or I ransack this place myself!' Martinha shook him in her desperation.

He held his hands up in defeat and indicated a small metal sea chest jammed under a cupboard. The key was on a ring inside the desk drawer. He dragged out the sturdy box, inserted the key, then riffled through the documents within. They were mostly private letters but in their midst was one that Felipe selected and passed stony-faced to his sister. She scanned it, her face paling. It was an undated copy of a missive sent by James Scott to Warren Hastings, signed by her uncle, Governor Phaya Pimon.

> *Dear Sir, Governor Phaya Pimon promises to hand over the island of Jangsylan to the English should the Honourable Company formally agree to furnish sufficient military support to repel any subsequent Siamese aggression. The terms as follows ...*

'Burn it! Burn it now!' Martinha demanded. 'This is a death

warrant, Felipe! How could Francis be so foolish as to keep a copy?'

Felipe struck a tinder to light a candle, holding the letter to the flame, his hands trembling, as if any moment Khang Seng himself might appear. 'The captain wanted to have something over the governor. Just in case. He doesn't entirely trust your aunt.'

Even Martinha appreciated the wisdom of that. 'Then he should have kept it on the ship!' She paused, her mind racing. 'Never mind, what's done, is done! We need to act. Have we a ship in port?'

'Aye, the *Speedwell*.'

'Send a runner to inform Captain Lindesay. In the meantime, I shall organise Mother and little Sarah. Pack all Francis' documents and records, plus any coin we have – and the tin. We shall stay aboard until Francis returns. You, too. I will not take any more chances!'

The *Speedwell* was an uncomfortable berth. Although Captain Lindesay offered Martinha the luxury of his own cabin, as it also served as the ship's trading room, it was a cramped and cluttered space for two women, numerous maids, and a fractious toddler. The rest of the household had to bed down where they could. But in the light of the news from the island, few complained. Lindesay established one condition: no women on deck. They must stay below. He did not want the added distraction of keeping them away from his men.

Thus, Martinha found herself cloistered with Amdaeng Rat, the woman Francis had somehow acquired as a debt wife. It did not improve her general mood or disposition towards her husband. Debt wives might be a relatively normal part of island business, but the presence of the willowy beauty was an irrational annoyance, even more so now that she was pregnant again. The girl was docile enough – although given to slyness in Martinha's opinion – but her very existence seemed to be a challenge.

It was well she had acted swiftly. The next morning, a message reached the *Speedwell* that there had been an attempt on Chao Phraya Khang Seng's life. The musket ball had missed, a stroke of luck for the unpopular royal representative. He had already left for the safety of the mainland but the attack had further raised tension to boiling point. Governor Pimon had taken his family to their Ban Takkien estates, hunkering down there with their own well-armed guards to wait out the emergency. Scott's wife had disappeared into the interior with her little ones to stay with relatives. One by one, everyone was deserting the port.

By the afternoon, they learned that the Light residence had been completely ransacked; a mob had set it alight after plundering their possessions. Martinha did not believe the perpetrators were locals. Under the guise of public disorder, Superintendent Khang Seng had sent men to search the property and find evidence of treason. The people themselves would not have done that to Captain Light. He was their defender, while the protests in the lanes and alleyways accused Khang Seng of tyranny and corruption, some even calling for anyone who heard to come and free them from his rule, be they Burmans, Malays or Christians.

Into this hotbed of disaster, sailed the *Bristol* and the *Blake*, Light and Scott together to the rescue, taking immediate action on being informed of the ill tidings. The three ships moored in convoy out in Sapam Bay from where they transferred most of the household to the larger *Bristol*.

That evening the officers gathered for a plain dinner of curry, dahl and chapatis, washed down by plenty of ale and Dutch gin, a convivial gathering despite the tension. The ships had guns and the company of several other European vessels moored nearby. The Siamese would not dare to attack such a fleet, nor would they wish to engage the ire of several European nations.

There was even a guest aboard, one Dr Johannes Koenig, a German botanist who had travelled from Bangkok with the intent of exploring the southern coastline in search of specimens. He had been dissuaded from his plan in view of the emergency, so had agreed to join them in their offshore exile on the understanding that he would be allowed to take a small boat to nearby islands for his botanical expeditions, accompanied by armed lascars.

'How much danger is there, Captain Light?' Koenig asked. 'Is this as serious as it sounds?'

Light laughed off their predicament. 'Khang Seng is a devil and a fool to boot. He has made shambles of it all! The Superintendent levels unproven accusations of treason, whilst himself terrorising the inhabitants to such an extent that he has incurred their wrath. They complain of tyranny, corruption and bad management, the very evils Tak Sin was determined to eradicate. I fear Khang Seng has gone too far. Let's sit this one out. I suspect the honourable Superintendent will soon be recalled, quite likely beheaded, and things will settle back to their normal calm, by and by.'

'I was recently in Thonburi, Captain, and heard tell of your excellent relationship with the king. He is most taken with you, sir. That will surely stand in your favour,' Koenig began.

'One would hope so, dear doctor. But we must not be complacent. There are rumours that not all is well at court. So, we must wait and see, I'm afraid.' Light tapped his finger to his nose in conspiratorial fashion.

'Whichever way the wind blows, that damned Khang Seng will fall!' Scott added. 'Either Tak Sin will hold him to account or the south will rise up against him – and if the latter happens, it's open season in Thalang. The people will not stand for it. They will find their own solution, mark my words!'

'So, there is some truth in the rumours of rebellion?' Koenig was a clever man. He might play the genial scientist, but he had made his own conclusions.

The two captains smiled into their glasses. Light ventured a cautious reply: 'I would not go so far as that, good Doctor Koenig. But if Siam falls, with Burma on its frontiers, where else would the people of Thalang look for support, but to external "friends"?'

'The Company, you mean?' Koenig attempted to force an admission.

'In one form or other,' came Scott's oblique response. 'So, take heart, doctor, and be patient. This misfortune may yet be lined in silver.'

* * *

The conversation in Light's cabin, however, was less agreeable. Martinha was waiting for him when he returned from dinner. He appeared to be in merry mood, while she was weepy and brittle. He could not convince her quite so easily that this was a passing crisis.

'We have lost our home, Francis! And we might have lost much more had I not had the good sense to burn that letter and evacuate the household. I saved your ledgers, your chests of money, and quite possibly our lives! Pardon me, if I do not understand how you were calmly able to spend the evening carousing with your friends!'

Light pulled off his shirt and splashed cold water over his chest, finishing by pouring the jug over his head. It was a hot night and the cabin was airless and clammy. 'I had to put on a front before the other captains, Martinha! The last thing we want is for them to flee the sinking ship and condemn Tharua to the backwaters of the Straits forever. Sayang, I am more regretful than I can express for what you have had to endure! Do you think I would have stayed away so long had I even an inkling that Khang Seng would go so far? He is a perfidious dog!'

'I read the letter! You were planning treason!' Martinha cried.

'It is not exactly as it seems. That letter was a mere proposal to Hastings to demonstrate that the local community looked favourably on a future British presence. You have little experience in these diplomatic negotiations, my dear. One uses many inducements to garner interest sufficient to bring all parties to the table.' But the shocked expression on his face revealed the danger he had placed them in, even while his words attempted to deny it.

Martinha sat down by him and took his hands in hers. 'Francis, if the letter had reached the wrong hands. What then?'

He closed his eyes, shuddering at the thought. 'We would all be dead. I should have kept it on the ship. It was a terrible oversight. Without your good sense, God knows what might have transpired.' His bonhomie of moments before quickly dissipated. It had been a smokescreen to conceal his inner distress. Martinha wondered what it had cost him to play act throughout dinner, whilst bearing the weight inside of what might have been.

Francis pulled her into his arms, fondly stroking the swell of her small belly, already beginning to show. 'Our son! That I might have endangered him!' he whispered, his eyes shining with emotion. 'Martinha, I was in Queddah when Scott found me with the news that Thalang was on the edge of chaos. I thought we would have had more time. I still believe if we hold firm, the island will be ours, but I would never risk the safety of my family. Arrangements are already in place. That is why I visited Sultan Abdullah. I am sending you all back to Queddah. I have arranged for a decent accommodation and –'

'We are returning to Queddah?" she gasped, aghast at the suggestion. 'But, how can we? We cannot go back there! We stole off in the dark of night. Dato' Seri Yahya will insist mother returns to him! We cannot escape the tiger by asking the crocodile for help!'

Francis smiled and pushed a strand of hair from her face, running his thumb along her cheek. 'Lie down, Martinha. You must not fret. Let me tell you what transpired, for things are not as bad as you might think.' He described his meeting with the Sultan and the price they would have to pay for his support. 'I fear your mother will be disappointed to have lost her ancestral home.'

'It was hardly ancestral. Muhammed Jiwa gives and Abdullah takes away,' Martinha scoffed with a matter-of-fact pragmatism that surprised him as she rolled onto her back to stare up at the low beams above her head. She watched a beetle scurrying along, intent on its own cares. 'Felipe has no interest in the estate. If mother is free and we can settle back in safety, then it is well worth the loss. Francis, I had no idea! I'm ashamed to say I harboured bitter thoughts, blaming you for leaving me in ignorance.'

He began to loosen the fastenings of her kebaya, his mind already occupied on a wholly different direction. 'Which I did in truth. And for that I humbly apologise. It's high time that I learned to appreciate the intelligence and courage of my dear wife, along with all the many other talents she possesses.' His smirk was laced with desire. 'From this day forward, I hereby promise never to keep you in the dark again, dear lady. Unless, that is, to do the things that are always best done in darkness ...'

Martinha stayed his hand just at the point where he had freed her breasts from the confines of her blouse. He glanced up at her, a quizzical expression in his pale blue-green eyes. He looked tired, and not a little inebriated, their moist sleepy softness showing he had drunk rather more than he admitted.

'One other thing, sayang.' A lascivious man would agree to anything. 'Before we leave for Queddah, you should return poor Amdaeng Rat to her family. I know her husband's debt is still outstanding but she's a free woman all the same. It is against our custom to take a citizen from Thalang without the consent of her husband or father. We have already lost so much, Francis, I don't think her small debt will discommode us that much more.'

He lowered his head to nuzzle lustily at the exposed brown nipple, smiling against the tender flesh – and recognised her checkmate, worthy of Lady Chan herself. Martinha was proving to be a force to be reckoned with. He would need to watch his step. 'An excellent idea, my love. Tomorrow, I will instruct Lindesay to arrange for her return.'

20

Clutching at Straws

Alor Setar, Queddah. February 1780

The residence granted by the sultan, a roomy teak house in the elegant Queddah style, required substantial renovation for the particular needs of the family. Martinha and her mother welcomed the activity to ease them into the reality of their new life. Neither had wished to return to Queddah, but they were determined to make the best of it.

Francis was back and forth to Thalang where his business flourished despite the precarious times. Many traders chose to stay away, thus even basic commodities were in short supply. For merchants with the temperament for it, much profit was to be made in perilous days when prices inevitably rose due to scarcity. From their ships in the bay, Scott and Light continued their trading activities, interspersed by regular runs up and down the Peninsula.

Scott had been in and out of Achin and Malacca. Poor Dr Koenig had near died of the remitting fever after one too many trips into the mangroves gathering specimens. When it had appeared that he was near the end, Scott dropped him off in Malacca, only to find that the intrepid fellow rallied and made a remarkable return to health. So typical of swamp fever: it either killed you in days or took you to hell and back after which you miraculously regained your normal equilibrium – until the next time. Light was regularly troubled ever since his serious bout years before in Sumatra.

The Lights were not the only refugees to arrive in Kuala Queddah during those months. In the aftermath of the unrest, the Superintendent – on the command of the king himself, so he claimed – had ordered all Christians to leave the south, on pain of death. Traders had taken to their ships and had largely been unmolested, but the poor Portuguese Eurasians, the easiest of targets, had found themselves largely abandoned to their fate. In dribs and drabs, they made the long trek down the coast to reach the comparative safety of Queddah. They were a wretched people, ever buffeted by the winds of fate, their very presence in Siam the result of a similar desperate exodus from Malacca after the Dutch arrived more than a hundred years before. Yet again, they were displaced and searching for a safe place to belong.

On one of Francis' increasingly rare stopovers, Martinha asked him to intercede with the sultan on their behalf. She wished to gain his permission for the Christian refugees to settle in the port town. Sultan Abdullah had no objections. The Serani community were known to be industrious people who kept to themselves and caused little trouble. Mostly they were involved in trade, although some inevitably worked the land or ran general stores, or stalls selling food and cakes. The sultan allotted them a section of the port in which to build their humble shelters – and made it generally known that they were not to be troubled by other residents. Martinha and Thong Di became their benefactors and were highly regarded by this vibrant community of settlers. Light approved of his wife's involvement in such charitable works as a worthy outlet for her energy and intelligence. It would keep her from dwelling too much on what she had lost – or interfering in matters pertaining to his business and political ambitions, about which he preferred to keep her in ignorance, despite his earlier promises to the contrary.

**

Thus occupied, the weeks advanced until the birth of her second baby – another daughter, healthy and bonny, thanks be to God. The ladies of the church fussed over her and when her time came, there were no shortages of midwives to attend the delivery. Martinha even had the expertise of a few nuns formerly of the Tharua mission. She weathered her ordeal with little problem, other than a nagging regret that she still had not given Francis a son. But she was well and cradled in the love of her mother and her friends. For that she gave thanks to the Lord. The child was born on December 13th, the feast of St Lucy, and in the absence of her husband, Martinha gave the child the name Lucy Ann, although the baby quickly acquired the nickname Lukey in the household, for the maids seemed incapable of pronouncing any European name as it was meant to be.

The child was several months old before her father even met her. His wife and baby Lucy Ann thrived, which gave him much joy, but Martinha privately suspected all the same that Francis would have preferred a boy. He seemed much fonder of his little Sarah – now babbling in a polyglot of three languages – and never spent more time than necessary with the baby. Whenever he saw her, he would smile, pat her head, then pass by. He always seemed preoccupied these days, his mind elsewhere, already planning another voyage – this time to India. Was he tiring of the mundane tedium of family life?

Days after his arrival, Francis finally revealed what was on his mind. He had not wished to worry her until he was sure she was strong enough. One evening when both children were asleep, Martinha joined her husband on the veranda, plumping up the cushions on a cane chair and gratefully sinking down, accepting a restorative glass of port. It was a clear and starry evening, the moon so silver-white that it shone as bright as day. Cicadas competed loudly, filling the night air with raucous chirruping, rivalled only by ribiting frogs from the nearby pond.

'No wonder little Sarah would not sleep! It's noisier at night than day!' Martinha observed as she sipped at the glass of rich red wine.

Francis chuckled, reaching over to take her hand in his. 'This is the first time we've been truly alone for so long. I have missed our talks, Martinha!'

She smiled over fondly, somewhat reassured by this unexpected declaration. 'Francis, I have so much to tell you about the church and all the many projects mother and I plan for the settlers –' she began.

He held up his hand. 'All in good time, my dear. I am truly delighted you have so much to occupy you, particularly as it seems we may be here for some time yet. But I must inform you of events in Tharua. It is not good news, I'm afraid.'

Martinha paled. 'Has something happened to Aunty Chan or Aunty Mook?'

'No, no, nothing like that. They are well and settled at

Ban Takkien with the little ones. No, this matter concerns me. Unfortunately, the king has rescinded his protection. All my lands and properties are forfeit. It is no longer safe for me even to trade out of the island. Under penalty of death.'

She gasped. 'But why? I thought the tensions had eased!'

Her husband shrugged evasively. 'The king is mad. Every day a new whim. He recently executed the son of Lord Duang for some imagined slight. He has threatened to kill every Christian in Siam. We can expect more refugees, I'm afraid.'

'The people of Thalang would never allow harm to come to you.'

'Perhaps,' he muttered darkly. 'But not to worry. Tak Sin cannot last much longer. Things are afoot, to be sure. Any new dynasty that seeks to replace him would be unwilling to alienate the Europeans, for there will surely be anarchy if this government fails, with each province seizing independence. It will all turn out in our favour, I expect. Meantime, our business thrives, thank God. Scott is still running everything from the *Bristol*. So, all in all, we cannot complain. At least I shall be here with you and the children in the months to come.'

'When you return from India, you mean,' she reminded him tetchily. 'Francis, why must you leave again so soon? Surely it can wait?'

Light pursed his lips in thought before replying, measuring how much to reveal. In the end, he decided to be as honest as he could for once. 'I must meet with Hastings in person as soon as possible. There's war in Europe and the Americas and now it has spread to the Indies. The damn French have allied with our local Indian enemies. The entire country is in flames. They say a huge

French fleet is on its way. Hastings needs an Eastern establishment now more than ever. But he must be willing to promise more than just a trading contract. I can bring him Thalang if he'll commit military forces. Face-to-face, I believe I can persuade him this time.'

Martinha kept her thoughts to herself. Since their escape from their home on the island, hours before it was attacked and destroyed, she had worried every time he had sailed for Thalang. Now he was completely out of favour in some way she could not quite comprehend. If Francis was in exile, why was Scott afforded leave to continue trading there? Surely both men had crossed the line in their allegiance? Why had Francis been singled out? Or did the king feel more slighted because he had forged a personal bond with her husband, which he may perceive had been betrayed in some way? Whatever the truth of the matter, she had not been given the whole story, of that she was sure. Something else had transpired that Francis was keeping from her.

Yet even in the face of this disaster, her husband would not abandon his dream to wrench control of Thalang and make it a British establishment. Or was that his only chance of retaining what had once seemed to him like his own private possession? Martinha sipped at her port and said a silent prayer that this governor-general in Calcutta continued to remain obdurate to her husband's propositions. They had built a new home in Queddah and she and her mother had surrounded themselves with a close community that needed them. They belonged here. Martinha had no desire to uproot her family again in search of a dream that seemed as far away as ever it had been.

Yet she smiled serenely as he laid out his plans, boasting of

what he would say to Hastings and how he would undoubtedly
win favour in the Council who were surely clutching at straws
now that war was looming. He spoke of the cloths and trinkets
he would buy for her and the gifts he would bring back for the
children. It was as if this journey was a pleasure trip when she knew
it was naught but a last-ditch attempt to save his reputation. The
benign expression on her face masked her inner concern. Francis
would always do what Francis would do, whatever anyone else
said. There was never any changing him once his passions were
aroused. It was her role in their marriage to temper his reckless
enthusiasm and – if she could not – then keep her wits about her.
Never would she allow a repetition of the danger they had faced
in Thalang.

21

Chowringee

Calcutta, August 1780

There was much to be done. Light had arrived heavily laden with a lucrative cargo, for profit was even now his foremost priority. To benefit from the current instability in the region was imperative particularly after the mishaps in Jangsylan. In India, war was raging on every side. Local rulers had taken the opportunity of the French threat to rise up themselves. Or had it been the other way around? Either way, Hastings had his hands well and truly full against the unholy coalition of the Marathas of Bombay, the Nizam of Hyderabad, and Hyder Ali of Mysore. Bombay and Madras bore the brunt of the hostilities, the bulk of the India trade now directed through Calcutta. Not only were these wars a huge burden on the Treasury but important supply lines had also been crippled.

Which was good news for those bringing vital commodity from the East Indies. As soon as he docked, Light sent messages to various agencies and acquaintances; word would circulate rapidly through the thirsty grapevine of this commercial hotbed. Business was always done by means of an invisible network whose tentacles writhed and burrowed throughout the city, as pervasive as the now-uprooted jungle upon which the city had been raised.

His secondary concern was to secure a private meeting

with the governor-general, a daunting task at the present time
with Hastings so preoccupied. Would he spare time for a lowly
merchant captain? But Light's mind was made up. If no response
was forthcoming, he would use other means. He knew enough
people of note around town who might be prepared, in return for
an inducement, to propose his suit direct to the Council itself. If
all else failed, he intended to sit outside Hastings' office day and
night until the governor-general relented. Time was of the essence;
he must seize the chance to reach Hasting's ear before unfortunate
rumours of his current difficulties in Jangsylan got there first.

As was often the way in India, an old acquaintance proved
invaluable. A gracious reply came swiftly back from William
Fairlie, whom Light had known in Queddah during the Monckton
mission of '72. Young Fairlie had then been a wet-behind-the-
ears junior writer who had hung around Light, shrewd enough
to realise that he had much to teach a newcomer about the East
Indies trade. Since then they had corresponded irregularly, enough
to maintain a slender acquaintanceship. Light rather liked the
fellow. The note was a cordial invitation for Light to stay at his
house at Chowringhee, where the fashionable people built their
residences. It was not for nothing that Calcutta was known as
'The City of Palaces'.

On the drive from the harbour along the Esplanade and
then by way of the new imposing fort, they skirted the airy open
Maidan and saw the best of this fast-growing city that changed
each time he visited. To think, not long ago, tigers were hunted in
the same forests that had been cleared to build this ordered and
splendid urban English landscape, set amidst the very heart of the
East!

Fairlie's home was not the grandest in Chowringhee by a long way for many of the residences there were more akin to stately homes, but it was a fine place for all that. Set in a meticulously tended garden, the spacious double-storey pukka residence – clad in white against the fierce sun – was light and airy, fronted by a breezy colonnade, the interior furnished sparingly but in exquisite taste.

Flanking the lofty entrance stood two vast blue and white ceramic vases, embellished with the dragon and the pearl. The boy had listened well and now, having risen to the top of the mountain, he had acquired the tastes to befit his station. Light's wooden house in Queddah paled into insignificance by comparison.

'Francis! How perfectly wonderful to see you again! Welcome to my home! I see you noticed the vases? I collect Chinaware, these days, don't you know? And I have you to thank for my little pastime. I haven't forgotten our time in Queddah. Come in, come in, you are most welcome!'

It was a very different William Fairlie from the gangling youth of almost eight years' prior. Then he had been a quiet, thoughtful young writer eager to learn the business and to take advantage of every opportunity presented. His determination had obviously paid off. William Fairlie was now a 'name' about town, a successful merchant and Council member, who had recently established his own trading concern with a Mr John Ferguson, another well-connected Scottish merchant of Bengal. Messrs. Fairlie, Ferguson and Company was already showing signs of becoming an institution in the city. All this and still only twenty-six years old!

'My dear Fairlie! You're quite the Nabob, these days. What a splendid property!'

They shook hands, the burly Fairlie pumping Light's up and down with obvious affection. 'Not a bad little house. She shall do for now, but when you see some of the other "chateaux" of my neighbours, she is quite the humble dwelling!'

After a brief tour, Light was shown his allotted room, a cool, high-ceilinged chamber with its own balcony giving out onto verdant gardens. He was offered a bath – a luxury in itself – prepared by a turbaned manservant who would be at his disposal throughout his stay. Refreshed, shaved and rested, Light put on his second-best frock coat for a pre-prandial bracer on the spacious marble terrace that wrapped around the rear of the ground floor. It was early evening, the sun just beginning to set. Unseen punkah-wallahs wafted fans; unobtrusive hands set down drinks and dainty snacks. A cool breeze carried scents of jasmine as the heat of the day melted into the balmy warmth of night.

'I've invited a few friends for dinner. Thought they'd like to make your acquaintance. There's interest in you here, Light. You'd be surprised how far your reputation has travelled. Memories are short. No one mentions the Queddah debacle these days. Your recent successes in impenetrable Siam quite trump any residual mistrust. It's a well-established fact that the Straits must be our next adventure. India's become nothing more than a rod for our backs. It's all taxation and rents and the government breathing down our necks, lapping up every penny. China's where real fortunes will be made – and the Straits are the key. We cannot let the Dutch hold us over the proverbial barrel any longer. This could be your moment, Francis. I hear you're well placed in Jangsylan ...'

Light considered his response. To let down one's guard merely because he had been lulled by an amiable host and plied with luxury would be careless. Although he liked Fairlie, he did not know his ulterior purpose. No young man who had accrued such wealth could have done so without a fair helping of calculation and ruthlessness. Perhaps this was all mere pretence. 'You're right, William. The signs are good. I am forging myself quite the little fiefdom in Thalang, or rather Jangsylan as you call it. I believe it to be an excellent prospect for a British factory. I hope to present my case to the Council.'

'No time like the present, sir. Hastings is beleaguered on every side. He'll grasp at any straw that's offered. I wish you well of it and hope that when you're Superintendent of your own establishment, you'll keep your old friend Fairlie in mind! We could do much business, I'll warrant!' He raised his glass; they drank to future opportunities, each man still stepping carefully round the dance floor.

'Before the others arrive, Francis, I wanted to mention something that might be of interest to you. I'm sure you recall our old friend Hythe?'

A shadow immediately darkened over Light's face. The very mention of that despised name made his hackles rise. 'That bloody wretch! Is he in Calcutta now? For if I run into the filthy bastard, I cannot vouch to keep my temper!'

Fairlie chuckled, his sturdy jowls wobbling. He had added a goodly amount of weight over the years. His ruddy complexion and portly frame made him appear the elder, although Light was his senior by near fifteen years. 'He was in Calcutta for a time, trying to insert himself in his usual unctuous fashion. His type are thirteen to the dozen here, Light. Only nincompoops like Edward Monckton would be taken in by them, and even the Honourable Edward ditched him, after being warned off by other more astute fellows. No, I thought you might like to know that I proposed a promotion for Mr. Hythe a while back. He is now in Bencoolen, which seems to me to be an ideal gutter for such a rat as he, would you not agree?'

Delighted at the unexpected news, Light could not help but show his gratitude. 'It could not have happened to a more well-deserving servant of the Company!' he declared. 'Good God, Fairlie, I owe you much for that intervention. For I swear, there was a time when I was ready to hang for that bastard!'

'He's not worth the cost of the rope, my friend. None of us liked him back in Queddah, you know? But I was too insignificant to have an opinion worth a sparrow's fart in those days and all the rest were toadies to Monckton. The way I see it, one must never let lowly scum such as he be the cause of one's downfall, however much one would wish to beat their damn brains in. For that is exactly what they wish for. Play the long game, Francis. Wait patiently, like a cobra in the grass, and strike when the opportunity presents itself. With any luck, Hythe will already be mouldering in his Sumatran grave by now. If the pestilences there don't get him, then he will have surely drunk himself into the ground. For what else is there to do in that godforsaken backwater?'

The fate of Charles Hythe was leaven to their budding friendship. Fairlie meant to make use of him, no doubt, but he had proved his fidelity. This revelation was intentional. Fairlie had set out to destroy Light's enemy to win Light's trust. One good turn deserves another. And for his part, Light fully intended to take advantage of Mr. Fairlie himself, who was well connected and had more ready money to invest than he knew what to do with.

'This is a fine house, Fairlie,' Light observed as they recharged their glasses. 'It must take an army of servants to keep it running smoothly.'

Fairlie shrugged. 'Well, I have a staff of sixty or so but it's a small household compared to some. Two hundred servants would not be thought excessive in the palaces around here, you know? It's a nice little property, for now. But as one rises, one must be seen to live the part. Except for Hastings, of course. Belvedere might be another Blenheim on the outside, but the man lives like a country vicar. They say he eats and drinks sparsely and is in bed each night by ten! He buys only two new coats per year, merely to keep with fashion. Hastings' a strange bird, for all his power and authority. But enough of the governor-general. You'll hear nothing but Hastings over dinner. He's on everyone's lips, even more than usual these days. I'm damned jaded with the subject, to be frank!'

Fairlie had piqued his interest but Light took the hint and allowed the topic to be dropped. He would return to it over dinner. 'I take it there is by now a Mrs Fairlie? Will your good lady be joining us?' Light queried tentatively. It was always important to make an impression with the wives, he had learned.

His companion pulled a wry face. 'No Mrs Fairlie "as such" at the present time. But I usually have a *Bibi* around the place, if you know what I mean?' The two men laughed knowingly. 'Of course, many of the older fellows have local wives, mostly Anglo-Indian women. They're Christian so there's none of the usual

Hindu or Mohammedan mumbo jumbo. I hear you've a Eurasian wife yourself now? All very respectable, I'm sure, but the fashion in India is changing, I must warn you. These new government officers and their little wives shipped out from England have very narrow minds, if you ken my meaning? They generally disapprove of too much intermingling. It's becoming the preference to marry white and keep the pretty brown girlies for recreation only.' Fairlie winked knowingly.

With an uncomfortable sense of being slighted, even if the remark had been made obliquely, Light responded gruffly. 'I'm not actually married either, William. Martinha and I merely have an "understanding" of sorts.' It was a gracelessly misleading comment, which he instantly regretted, but in his half-hearted attempt to clarify, he inevitably made it worse.

'I will admit there were some local rights in Queddah – a Muslim ritual, and then another traditional jumping over the broomstick in Jangsylan, but not a proper Anglican wedding,' he went on, aware that he was dissimulating. But, as Rome was not proper Christianity, he was hardly actually lying. 'I have two bonny little daughters, sweet things of whom I find myself inordinately fond.' Light added as if to make amends for his callous betrayal of Martinha.

'These mixed children are beauties, there's no doubt. I've a couple myself. Bring them up Christian and they'll be snapped up on the marriage market when they come of age,' Fairlie remarked. 'Fellows forget the mixed blood if the girl is fair and nubile –'

The demeaning remark hit Light fair and square in the gut, almost as if he had been actually punched. This was how the world would see Sarah May and Lucy Ann. Only at that moment did he fully appreciate the casual cruelty of such prejudices. Over his years in the Straits, he had become unaccustomed to such opinions, being so infrequently in the company of British gentlemen for other than the mercantile exchange. Throughout his own life he had raged internally against the injustice of his own birth, only to realise in so brutal a fashion that he had thoughtlessly bestowed that curse – perhaps an even greater one – upon his dear children.

'The girls have standing in Jangsylan. Their mother's family has both Siamese and Malay noble connections.' Yet his defence came somewhat too late to redeem the situation. 'They are not the children of some portside doxy, sir,' he added with a hint of truculence.

It made little odds with Fairlie. 'That might do in an East Indies backwater, Captain, but it won't pass the muster in India, I'm afraid.' The noise of guests arriving brought a welcome distraction from the sour moment, both men grateful for the escape route. 'Ahh, I think I hear the first carriage. Come, let's meet our guests.'

22

An Audience at Belvedere

Belvedere Palace, Alipore. September 1780

The days passed in a social whirl: dinner parties, visits to the Harmonic Tavern, a trip to the Whist Club where fortunes were lost at the tables in mere minutes. Light even attended a performance of *Julius Caesar* at the New Playhouse, a guest of honour in someone's private box. It almost felt that he had been magically transported back to London high society, had it not been for the cloying heat and the preponderance of Indian servants, who were distinctly more subservient and ubiquitous than their English counterparts. His other sense of dislocation was in the class of gentlemen who enjoyed this good life. For the most part they were hard-nosed businessmen with origins far beneath the station to which they had grown accustomed. Unlike London, Calcutta was a fluid world where birth only counted so far; after that, it was your ability to rule the system that accorded success and approbation. But prejudices still remained. He would be well to consider that.

As Fairlie had pointed out, at the current moment, much of the conversations at dinner tables and gaming tables centred around the governor-general himself. Scandal stalked the controversial Hastings, even though he was the least provocative of men in his private life. It was said that he had recently stopped drinking alcohol and that he took daily cold baths, all for the sake of his health. That alone suggested a man of very odd notions. His hosts took much delight in redressing Light's ignorance of recent events, and indulging in the favourite Calcutta pastime – gossip.

It was common knowledge that Hastings had always been unpopular amongst Company employees, predominantly because he had spent his entire career railing against fraud and corruption. Company funds were often used to finance private ventures, a practice that should have brought immediate dismissal. But this illegal system was so widespread, through every level of the administration, that the very senior officials whose job it was to root out malpractice, were themselves the worst culprits. Hastings had taken a heavy-handed approach that had been widely criticised. There was limited support for his reforms and his personal reputation was attacked at every turn, even if his own missteps were much less significant than the chasms of corruption committed by his accusers.

There had, of course, been the earlier scandal of his relationship with Marian, the former Baroness Imhoff, but since he had finally married the lady, that was no longer quite so outrageous. Furthermore, compared to most Company men (with their countless mistresses and local women), Warren Hastings was a devoted husband who did not appear to have a particularly licentious nature. Yet society affected shock at his peccadillos with little regard for its own. The current outrage concerned the trial and execution of one Nanda Kumar, a local governor who had dared to accuse Hastings of accepting bribes. Hastings had counterattacked: Kumar had been accused of forgery and brought to trial. A rival Council member, Mr Philip Francis, who had a long-standing enmity with Hastings based on jealousy, old grievances and his own unrequited affection for the Baroness, had taken up Kumar's cause, propelling their personal antipathy onto quite another level.

Hastings had connived with the chief justice to have Kumar found guilty and executed, a singularly excessive penalty for forgery by any standards. The Indian gentry was outraged, for Kumar was a highly respected Brahmin. The British community was aghast at Hastings' flagrant abuse of power, with no apparent sense of irony. Philip Francis appealed direct to the London Headquarters. In retaliation, Hastings cast public doubt on Francis' own probity. In a letter sent in August, Hastings had gone so far as to call into question the other man's reputation both in public and private life on the basis of his lack of 'both truth and honour in all things'. Such slander was a step too far. Philip Francis had no alternative but to call out the governor-general.

Calcutta was still dining out on the subsequent duel that had taken place in the grounds of Belvedere. The ramifications rumbled on and on. That the governor-general would sink so low as to risk everything upon an exchange of handgun fire! He had even arranged a huge loan from a local Nawab to ensure that Mrs. Hastings would be well-provided should she be widowed. Luckily for the governor, Francis' shot missed its target, while Hastings hit his opponent in the side; Mr Francis survived but his injuries were serious enough for him to drop his complaint and plan his return home when sufficiently recovered. The Bengal Gazette had been full of the salacious details; daily, further indignations were revealed to the eager public. Since the duel, Hastings had retreated to his Belvedere palace and was seen even less in public than formerly, apart from weekly Council meetings.

It was easy to forget, amidst the local blather, that the British administration was in the midst of a mighty conflict. Hastings had committed two armies to fight in Bombay and Madras, and was facing the prospect of a simultaneous French naval blockade along the Coromandel. The Dutch had refused to limit trade with Britain's enemies, thus bringing another enemy into the fray. They had declared their support for France. The more that Light heard about the pressing issues of the day, the less sure he felt that he might persuade Hastings into a venture across the Andaman, particularly one that might mean further military engagement. Luck was against him yet again just as he was poised on the brink of success. As the days passed, he became more disconsolate. Would he chase the unattainable pearl forever, just like the dragon around the vase?

And then, quite against all hope, an official invitation arrived, summoning Light to attend Governor Hastings at Belvedere Palace.

***

The drive south to Alipore, along pleasant boulevards flanked by porticoed government buildings in the Neoclassical style, gave way to lush open parkland created from the tropical landscape in the image of a temperate homeland far away. Belvedere was an astonishing edifice, a country seat amidst a deer park, as grand as any palace in Europe. Light felt anew the familiar inferiority that had stalked him as a younger man in the grander homes of Suffolk. He did not belong amidst the halls of the great. Dusting off his best outfit, he steeled his nerve against his self-doubt. Hastings was offering him a chance to speak. What was there to lose? He had heard the word 'no' many times before and should no longer fear it.

Despite the grandeur of his surroundings, when Light was ushered into the great man's actual presence, he found himself in a small study, sparsely but well furnished, much like the man himself. Hastings was lean, on the edge of gauntness, but with a look of wiry strength. His angular face was fresh and clear, his eyes were keen, and his demeanour open and approachable. Light had expected a remote, standoffish man, but Hastings was nothing of the sort. The governor rose from his desk as Light entered and proffered his right hand.

'Captain Francis Light, at last we meet! I feel I know you already for the mountain or correspondence you have remitted to my office over the years! How are you enjoying Calcutta?' The welcome took Light by such surprise that he was momentarily put off guard. To cover his discomposure, Light muttered a few inane compliments about the city and its great buildings, the theatre and the coffee houses, quite like London, and so on and so on, until his abilities in the social niceties had quite dried up.

Tea was served in paper-thin China cups with tiny almond dainties on the side. Light took the opportunity to sip and nibble, and gather himself. After some uncomfortable minutes, Hastings set down his cup with an exactness that indicated that the necessary social discourse was done and they were about to talk business.

'I expect you've heard about recent developments concerning this office, both public and private?' he began without a trace of embarrassment. 'There's no need to pretend otherwise, sir. I'm familiar with the tittle-tattle. To be perfectly honest, much of it is true, adorned with the inevitable embellishments one would expect in Calcutta where vultures perch on every rooftop eager for fresh meat. It has been quite a season and no mistake.' There was even a wry grin on Hastings' face.

Light nodded with solemnity. 'I had heard, sir. War on several fronts and internal conflicts in the Council. It seems you are quite beleaguered.'

Hastings laughed ruefully, acknowledging Light's unsuccessful attempt to pretend that he had not heard about the scandalous duel. 'Men such as yourself, who conduct the actual business upon which this Company depends, face many dire problems to be sure, but there's a certain clarity in what you do. You buy, you sell. You make a profit or you lose money. Everything rests upon your own ability – and the vagaries of wind and weather. But for those of us in the senior administration, matters are more obfuscate. Although it is my function to oversee the entire operations of the Company in India on behalf of the London Directors, those same gentlemen perversely fear nothing so much as a man who achieves his brief too well. Since the very beginnings, London has contrived to drive wedges between its senior councillors, for bickering and rivalry ensure that no one ever feels completely secure; there is always someone willing to blight your reputation at home. My whole career has ever been thus. Pay no heed to the outrage and scandal. It means nothing more than I am doing my job. Inordinately well.'

There was bitter satisfaction in Hastings' words. Light remained in silence, unsure whether he was meant to venture an opinion or no. Instead he merely nodded and took another gulp of tea.

For what seemed a very long pause, Hastings stared straight at him, his scrutiny boring into Light's soul. 'Captain Light, I think I may owe you an apology.'

'Apology, sir?' Light gasped. It was another unforeseen direction.

'I listened to the negative reports of Monckton and his crew back in Queddah. Even at the time, I was unconvinced by their ramblings. It was obvious that the failure of the mission could not be set entirely at your door. But you made mistakes, Light, as did they. I very much hope that you've learned in the interim.' Hastings's manner was now more severe, the self-mockery having quite vanished.

Light contrived a contrite expression. 'I certainly have, sir. I was a lot younger then.'

'Good. You've done well since then, I agree. This relationship with the King of Siam is most promising. You do well with these local potentates, Light, a singular advantage that very few of our people ever achieve. I respect a man who has local knowledge and takes the time to master their tongues and cultures.' He paused, biting on his lip as if deciding how much he might reveal. 'Let's not waste time dilly-dallying around the houses. I know why you're here. You want me to approve an establishment in Jangsylan. Is that the measure of it?'

Light took a deep breath. 'That is the measure of it, sir. I have the trust of the island. It's a fine emporium, free of Dutch and Bugis nuisance. There's an excellent haulage route across the narrow peninsula that would preclude our sailing for weeks through the dangerous Straits to reach the China Sea. For a relatively small investment in men and money, we would have a safe base from which to conduct China trade and to supply India with vital resources, commodities that have never been more needed than today.'

Hastings nodded sagely in agreement. 'I cannot argue with your reasoning, sir. And you are correct in what you say. The question of a British port in the Straits has vexed me for some time. We should have acted sooner. The French attack will be devastating, even if we repulse it, although that is by no means sure. Are you aware that the British government has refused the Company any financial assistance, in either the local conflicts or the French engagements? Everything must come from our own revenues. Meanwhile the London Directors are already baying at my heels on account of what they regard my "profligate" expenditure. Do you understand what that means as far as your request is concerned?'

The silence was profound. Light's crestfallen face revealed he understood too well. 'There's no money for a venture in the Straits, no matter how important.'

Hastings nodded his agreement, his sombre expression showing that he wished it could be different. 'Correct. Until this war is won, I have neither men nor money in my back pocket to spare, and if I did, the Company would be down upon me with the sword of Damocles. I am very sorry, Captain Light. This is not the right time. I cannot accommodate your proposal at this moment. Furthermore, I am not entirely convinced that your relationship with Jangsylan is presently as it once was. I'm not insensible to the events in Siam, and most particularly Jangsylan where it seems your local currency has fallen of late. The King of Siam is becoming suspicious of foreigners and you have been forced to move to Queddah, despite your agency still being located on the island, in the hands of Captain Scott, that irascible rogue. I do not think you have been entirely honest with us in your recent missives. What exactly have you done to lose favour on the island?'

Hastings was, of course, well-informed. Light should have expected that he would not be able to pull the wool over his eyes. 'I have run afoul of the Royal Superintendent of the South, Chao Phraya Khang Seng, as monstrous a rogue as I have ever met. He is hated on the island and by the governor, who is my close associate and relative by marriage. I assure you that the people of Jangsylan welcome the English. They are eager to throw off the Siamese yoke.'

Hastings' eyes narrowed as he pursed his lips in thought. 'We will not tangle with the Siamese, that is indisputable. Unless Tak Sin falls. Which is a distinct possibility, or so I have heard. Your assessment, Captain?'

'It is as you say, sir. Siam is on a knife edge. Only Tak Sin was able to reunite it. If he is deposed, the tinder will catch fire and there will be opportunity for us. The south yearns for independence. Burma and China lurk on the northern borders. Cochinchina is chomping at the bit for freedom. In those circumstances, we would be entirely welcomed to bring economic security to Jangsylan and keep supply lines open. It is but a matter of time.'

Hastings placed his hands down on the table. He had come to a decision. 'In that case, our course is clear. As soon as the current hostilities are over, we will return to this matter. Until then, we await developments in Siam. I have also received a proposal from your good partner, which we should also keep upon the table should Jangsylan ultimately prove unworkable. Captain Scott has raised the matter of an island off the coast of Queddah, Puloo Kesatu, or some such name. It is uninhabited but has fresh water and a benign climate. He deems its location conducive. Given that your stock is now raised with the new sultan, might this be a viable alternative?'

'Indeed, sir. The island is known colloquially as Pulau Pinang. It was once offered to me by the previous sultan as a marriage gift.' That fact was not strictly true but was a convenient fiction that he and Scott had considered in the past. Muhammed Jiwa was long dead. It was well known that he had been inordinately fond of Light. Who could contradict his assertion? 'Scott and I have both spoken of its potential and believe it to be an ideal proposition. Of course, it would take investment to develop into a settlement, whereas Jangsylan is already a thriving trading post. But I concur with Scott it has great merit. And Sultan Abdullah is ripe for manipulation. He's much more desperate than his father, the old sultan. I am sure he would bestow it upon me if I approached him in the future. May I also point out that my wife is a member of the royal family of Queddah?'

Light was unsure quite where the idea of mentioning Martinha's family connections came from, unless it had been germinating ever since Fairlie had summarily dismissed Martinha as nothing but his local mistress. As soon as he uttered the words, however, the half-truth solidified into fact. He *was* intimately connected to the highest families of both Queddah and Jangsylan. That would not only raise his wife's status, but also his own. It gave him nobility by association, something no other British officer could claim.

'I thought she was related to the governor of Jangsylan?' Hastings inquired.

'On her grandfather's side. Her grandmother, however, was a Malay princess.'

Hastings paused, resting his chin on his joined hands. 'You seem to have extremely fortuitous connections in the Straits, Light. Most interesting. Is your wife a Mohammedan?'

Light shook his head. 'No sir, a Christian lady. Her father was of Portuguese ancestry ...'

'... I'd keep that quiet if I were you. The rest, however, is alluringly exotic. Bring her over to Calcutta when all this is over. Mrs Hastings would be intrigued to meet the lady, as would I. You're a fascinating fellow, Light. Full of unexpected surprises. Not your typical merchant captain.'

Hastings stood up; Light fumbled with his chair and found his feet. With an amicable hand on his back – Hastings did not reach Light's shoulder – he saw him to the door where the two men shook hands. 'Between now and then, Light, we need supplies on the Coromandel. The French aim to blockade and starve our settlements to surrender. Gather all your contacts and run the gauntlet. All the basic food stuffs. There's money to be made. The price of rice is already soaring. That should give you and Scott plenty to occupy yourselves until the peace. I have much enjoyed our meeting, Captain Light. It was most productive. I wish you a pleasant stay in Calcutta and a safe voyage home. Please give my regards to Mrs. Light. Good day, sir.

And with that, the audience was at an end. Light made his way back to the *Bristol*, his days of leisure now at an end. It was time for the other officers to enjoy Calcutta, while he had much to occupy his mind. His final objective might be as distant as ever, but he was closer now than he had ever been. For Hastings was won over.

23

Little Georgie

Kuala Bahang, Queddah. 4th April 1783

It was Lent and the household was fasting, or at least those Christians amongst them. On a whim, as much to escape the confines of her humdrum daily life as for any other reason, Martinha took a trip downriver to the port on the pretext of purchasing cloth for Easter outfits, accompanied by her maid Esan and a few sturdy bodyguards. The early morning sail was a boon to her spirits; cool breezes and the tang of the sea a restorative in itself, although they brought Francis to mind even more vividly than ever. Somewhere, across that body of water, the same spray broke against his ship and the same sunlight warmed his face. Martinha prayed he was safe and making his way homeward.

At Kuala Bahang jetty, she called on Felipe at the agency office to avail herself of funds for her shopping expedition. They kept little coin at home. The visit also provided her an opportunity to catch up with her brother. The siblings had not spent much time together in months, for with Light and Scott almost permanently at sea these days, the main responsibilities for the company now rested entirely on Felipe's shoulders.

Her brother was a man full grown, as tall as her father had been and developing a similar paunch, the result of his love of food and spirits, another legacy from Martim Rozells. His appearance was pleasing more than handsome, enhanced by a ready smile and hearty manner, but he was a worrier, too. Felipe took his responsibilities seriously. As Francis often wryly observed, Felipe Rozells did his worrying for him, leaving him entirely free of any stresses or encumbrances. Privately, Martinha and her mother thought it high time her brother should marry and have a family life away from the company, but Felipe claimed he was too busy to find a wife. No doubt the task of locating a suitable girl would fall to them before long. There would be no shortage of candidates for the eligible young bachelor.

Martinha also wished to enquire if Felipe had any recent news of her husband, perhaps snippets of information gleaned from other captains recently in port. It was over five months since Francis had sailed, with scarce any news the entire time, itself unusual, for he always sent word when he was able. Of late, his absences had been particularly protracted and Martinha lived in fear of hearing the worst. The war between the British and the French still raged in India; now the Dutch had entered the fray, openly assisting the French with supplies, ship repairs and all manner of support. The Straits was fraught with danger, the Andaman even more so. Francis was running French blockades along the Coromandel while Scott was darting in and out of Dutch waters in the south, carrying goodness knew what contraband. They could be hanged if they were caught. All for the sake of profit.

As they took a simple Lenten breakfast of soupy noodles and a few stringy green vegetables on the upper balcony of the company offices overlooking the busy harbour, Martinha quizzed her brother. He was sure to know more of her husband's whereabouts than he was prepared to say. Felipe was his usual

vague and vacillating self, having no doubt been warned by
Francis not to 'worry' his sister. His dithering only troubled her
more. Francis was expected 'soon'. He had recently been in India
but was most 'probably' in Thalang by now, picking up tin and
the usual commodities. He was expected back in Kuala Queddah
for Easter, 'most likely'. If weather and winds permitted. Likewise,
Captain Scott who had been over to Riau but would be heading
back to Thalang at this time of year. Perhaps. Martinha was not
to worry. Captain Lindesay had recently been in port; he had met
with the Captain on his way to Madras. Soliman had just arrived
from Malacca with news of Scott, but these reports were months
old. Nothing more than 'should' and 'maybe'. Martinha was none
the wiser. In fact, she felt very much worse.

Called away to deal with a client, Felipe left his sister on the
balcony, where she sipped tea and gazed idly out over the jetties,
on the men loading and unloading, swarming over the motley
collection of vessels with the industry and purpose of an army
of ants. Her thoughts were far away, her hands idly stroking the
restless burden in her belly. She was pregnant again, over six
months' already. If Francis returned for Easter, she could share
their good news. The south-west sailing season might then keep
him closer to home. Or was this another child she must bear
alone? Martinha prayed daily for a son. Perhaps then Francis
might spend more time with them, or was that mere fancy? Her
husband had a wanderlust. Not even love – or a male child –
would keep him home.

Her reverie was suddenly interrupted, a flash of the here-
and-now intruding on her inner world, when her eyes fixed
upon a woman making her way through the crowded wharves,

accompanied by a servant carrying a basket of provisions. Something familiar about her shape and form alarmed Martinha most peculiarly. The woman was lithe, with generous curves evident through the worn folds of her baju and sarong. She wore her hair bound with a cloth, as was the custom, but walked with a hauteur lacking in the other lowborn women on the street. Perhaps it was her carriage that caught Martinha's attention, head held high, striding forward with a prideful gait, a woman confident of attracting the gaze of other people, especially men. A beauty.

Amdaeng Rat. Martinha stared, leaning over the balustrade for a better look. There was no doubt. That Siamese girl who Francis had once received as a debt wife? What on earth was she doing in Kuala Bahang? He had sent her back to Tharua years ago. Or had he? Without contemplating what she might do or say should they actually meet face-to-face, Martinha charged back into the upper office, grabbed her money purse, and shouted a quick apology to her brother. She would return later.

Down the stairs she dashed in unseemly haste, with little Esan hardly able to keep up with her. She ran out on to the street below, past where her guards were lounging, and then took to her heels in the direction where her nemesis was heading. Ignoring her companions' pleas to slow down, Martinha continued her charge until she sighted the lady in question, now only a short distance away, having stopped to buy some fruit. Catching her breath, bending double to ease the uncomfortable stitch in her side – much to the consternation of Esan – she indicated to her people that she was following *that woman* and that they should stay by her. Esan and the men exchanged knowing looks but obeyed, encircling her close all the while.

Amdaeng Rat dawdled for a while longer before heading out of town towards a pleasant kampong in a clearing about ten minutes' walk. Set on a slight rise above the road, the settlement was far enough from the harbour to be free of the coastal stench. It had a charming view of the coast and was cooled by fresh sea breezes. A certain type of resident essential to any port town resided here – the wives and children of visiting merchants and traders. The locals knew it as Concubine Village, or its equivalent in several other languages, for it was home to both local women and settlers from Siam, India, Java, Sumatra and beyond. Children were raised there in a vibrant stew of languages, religions and cultures, free from the abject want and squalor common in port towns. These women were well provided for. Their men had pockets full of coin when they were home.

Tracking her prey to a neat and well-appointed wooden house, Martinha waited in the shadows as Amdaeng Rat climbed the stairs to her door, calling out gaily to neighbours, who waved back. The woman had lived there for some time, for she was well known, a further twist of the knife to Martinha's heart. There could be only one rational explanation. Francis had never returned the girl to Tharua as he had promised, but had instead established her here as his mistress.

Martinha's shock was profound yet underlain with a bitter sense of realisation. She should have known. She had often wondered if her husband visited whores while on his travels. Her mother had – in her subtle and nebulous way – more or less told her to expect and ignore such things. She herself had come to accept that he most probably did. It was how men coped on long sea voyages, and few would blame them. But to keep a mistress only a few miles from home was an entirely different matter.

Esan stood by, observing her mistress, well aware what was going through her mind. Truth be told, she had known that the Siamese women now lived in the harbour town. Little remained secret in such settlements, but no one in the household had expected the mistress to find out. Now her heart fluttered with uncertainty and guilt. 'Nona, Nona, take no notice. She is just a kept woman. Nothing to do with us. Come, let us go and look for cloth!'

Martinha shrugged away her hand. 'The Captain keeps her here, I'm sure of it! I will not leave this place until I know for certain.'

'It will do no good! Please, Nona! Better not know,' Esan pleaded but her entreaties fell on deaf ears. Martinha's mind was made up.

'Wait here. I am going to pay a visit on Miss Rat,' Martinha said with vehemence, dropping the polite title of Amdaeng; the little whore had forfeited all rights to be respected.

On the threshold, Martinha grasped her courage and knocked forcefully. After all, she had no cause for shame. This woman was the sinner, not she. The door opened cautiously and the same young servant peeped out.

'I wish to speak to Rat,' Martinha announced firmly. 'Bring her out here.'

The door closed for a few seconds and then was swung open with force. Amdaeng Rat stood there boldly, her hands on her hips.

'I wondered if you'd have the nerve,' she announced, her lips scarcely able to contain her amusement. 'I saw you on the balcony back there, looking out like the queen of the world. Not so high and mighty now, *Than Phu Ying* Martinha ...' Rat used the Siamese honorific with a sneer. She really was a most unpleasant woman, Martinha thought, *proud that I have stumbled upon her dirty secret.* Her hopes plummeted. No woman would behave this way save one who felt she had already won some twisted form of victory over another. Or another's husband.

'Why are you living here, Rat? I was told you had returned to Tharua long ago,' Martinha spoke with a cool disdain that she did not feel. She did not intend to give the woman further satisfaction by displaying her distress.

Amdaeng Rat shrugged nonchalantly. 'I did not wish to go back to my husband. He's a pathetic little man. I asked Captain Francis to take pity on me – and he did. He found me this house and keeps me in much comfort.'

Martinha stared straight back at her, refusing to allow the taunts to reach their mark. 'You will have no choice but to return when your husband finally pays his debt.'

Rat laughed out loud. 'You don't know anything, you little fool! That debt was paid long ago. But Captain Francis didn't want me to go. So, he returned the money and I stayed here –'

Martinha gasped, unable to hold back her disbelief. 'He refused to send you back? That is not possible! It is a grave offence. There would be consequences.' But even as the words fell from her mouth, Martinha understood what should have been obvious all along. Three years ago, Francis and Scott had been driven from Tharua along with many other foreign traders. Now trade was running smoothly again. Scott had returned to their old office and yet Francis had never set foot back upon the island, still trading from his ship when in port. His lands and properties at Tharua had been forfeited. She had believed his story about the inexplicable wrath of King Tak Sin – but that had been a lie. The people of Tharua had turned their backs on him because he refused to return a free woman of Siam to her home as custom demanded.

'He tossed away his rights to reside in Thalang for me, Martinha. I may call you that now, I presume? Seeing as we're almost sisters.' Amdaeng Rat pushed her blade home.

'I don't believe you!' Martinha protested vainly. 'My husband would not behave like that. He is an honourable man!'

Amdaeng Rat whispered to her servant, who disappeared inside while the two women stared each other out. Moments later, the girl passed a small child to her mistress, who turned back, the cold smile of triumph on her face. 'This is *our* son, Nona. He is why your husband risked so much for me. Perhaps you should pray in your fine Christian church that the baby in your belly is a handsome boy like my little Georgie. We named him for the King of England, of course.'

It was too much. Horror-struck, Martinha backed away, before turning on her heels and staggering down the steps, the cruel taunts of Amdaeng Rat ringing in her ears long after she had left the kampong far behind. 'Two daughters is not good enough, my dear. A man wants sons. You are no different from me, Martinha Rozells. Just another girl from Ujung Salang. Except I give him boy. Remember that.'

24

Running the Gauntlet

The Blake, Coromandel Coast. December 1782

It had been a long voyage, a circuitous route made necessary by the French squadrons swarming the seas between Madras and Cuddalore like mosquitoes on a swamp, requiring weeks of extra sailing to enter the Coromandel from the north. Light was on the *Blake*, Scott's lively little grab; speed was essential in such hostile waters and she was roomy enough for the large rice cargo intended for Fort St George, where supplies were alarmingly low. They had sailed in a convoy to offer an element of protection and kept mostly to the high seas where French warships were less likely to patrol. But they could not stay at sea forever.

Perhaps there was an element of over-confidence as veterans of so many successful runs. The weather certainly played a part in what transpired. Light had hoped for storms, common at this time of year, for heavy rain would conceal them as they ran the blockade into port. Up on deck on that December evening, Light watched the sunset, the blue-sky day dissolving into purple night. A magenta glow framed in rose-gold stained the horizon, casting a glimmering amaranthine shadow upon the sea. Dark billowing clouds swirled in fantastical shapes, advancing from the west to swallow up the day. An idle observer would have rejoiced in the beauty of the evening, but Light felt the first prickling warnings of alarm. Like bruises on the skin, skies this colour warn of violent movements within. All they could do was make speed for land, and hope to skirt the approaching tempest.

Which for the most part they did. The storm, when it broke, was savage: heavy vengeful seas pitching and tossing the ships like children's playthings in a tub. Thankfully, they were on its edge and not in its fierce heart, in which case they might have been overcome, so heavily laden were they. But the winds inexorably drove them south, far further than they wished to go. There was nothing to be done. It was enough to save the ships and hope the French had found shelter in port themselves.

All night they laboured, sailors lashed to the rigging against being swept overboard while they struggled to save the sails. Dawn at last, the winds finally dropped and they found themselves floating on a serene morning sea, last night's tempest quite vanished from sight. Barely any evidence of the typhoon remained, other than the flotsam of trees and coconuts bobbing past. How southerly was their position? A far-off smudge revealed distant landfall with no means of knowing exactly where they lay. The only choice was to head north by day and take a reading from the stars by night.

And then they saw the fleet. Specks at first, mere dazzles in the distance, but moving at a speed that could only indicate one thing. Warships. They could not outrun them. Too far away to ascertain their allegiance, the sailors of the small cargo ships endured the intervening hours of waiting, praying to their gods that they had stumbled on a British squadron.

The ships were French, Admiral Suffren's fleet on the way from Cuddalore to Aceh where they intended to winter. It was their bad luck that the storm had driven the convoy straight into their waiting arms. The four ships and their valuable cargoes were seized. French officers and marines poured aboard, demanding bills of lading, helping themselves to whatever they fancied, declaring the vessels war prizes. They were courteous enough but gloated, with more than a touch of relish, that the British had already lost the war at sea following the battle of Trincomalee back in September. It was even worse than Light had feared. The French assured him that India would soon fall. The British would be driven from the East for good.

Summoned aboard the *Héros,* the flagship of Admiral Suffren, Light requested that he might be allowed to dress appropriately before meeting such an august person. His captors accorded him the right to change to a frock coat and clean breeches, donning hat and boots, clothing he had not worn in many a day. Suitably attired, they were escorted by marines to the transfer to learn their fates, together with the other captains.

Suffren was not at all what they had imagined. Instead of an elegant French nobleman, Comte Pierre-André de Suffren de St-Tropez for all his aristocratic titles had the look of a fat, vulgar English butcher, or so Light remarked. He was short and extremely obese, with a big round head, totally bald on the crown but thatched with thick grey hair at the back and sides, and a short rat's tail of a queue straggling at the nape of his neck, bound up in coarse yarn. Light need not have bothered dressing to impress. Suffren was shabbily attired, in old blue breeches, dirty sweat-drenched linen shirt, sleeves rolled up for business. He wore no waistcoat, no cravat or stockings, and his feet were shod in worn slippers.

The admiral's English was only passable, sprinkled with a healthy smattering of his own language; Light remembered little of his own French – but tried his best. Some of the other officers had a better grasp of the English tongue, so together they reached mutual understanding. The ships were now war prizes, the men were prisoners, and their cargoes were forfeit, notwithstanding that they were private traders. Even the ship of Petersen the Dane was impounded, for he was openly trading on behalf of the British, sailing in a convoy of English traders, and carrying cargoes meant for Company ports. No exception would be made for his neutrality.

Yet, the admiral was a gentleman for all that. It was not his intention that they should suffer personal indignities, especially as their crews comprised local lascars with whom the French had no quarrel. Suffren intended to burn and sink the three smaller ships, which would slow down his fleet after transferring their cargoes, while the faster *Blake* was co-opted as a supply ship. The sailors would be absorbed into the French crews. While Light could keep his men, he would become part of the French squadron, although relieved of his command. Lieutenant Jean-Louis Régnier was to assume the role of captain of the *Blake* with a detachment of marines. The captains of the other ships were sent to Cuddalore where they would be under house arrest; the *Blake* was despatched to Trincomalee as a cargo vessel serving between the two ports during the winter season.

It was a bitter blow, even if Light felt fortunate that his ship was not to be scuttled and that he was to serve his captivity aboard. The worst fate he could imagine would be a French prison, or even house arrest for what might be several years. From the deck of the *Héros,* the four captains were forced to watch as the empty ships were fired. It was a harsh lesson. The vessels were privately owned; entire fortunes had been invested in them and their cargoes. Nor could they expect compensation from the British government for the losses they had incurred on their behalf. Their involvement was regarded as a personal risk in the pursuit of profit, with no allowance given for the service they had provided to the British forts.

Once restored to the *Blake,* Light's ship joined a small squadron that now broke from the Sumatra-bound fleet to deliver their prizes to Cuddalore and Trincomalee. For the indefinite future, Light would bring the benefit of his knowledge of the local waters to the French, grateful for his life and that of his men.

The new French captain, Lieutenant Régnier, was a genial young fellow, fluent in English and quite the Anglophile. An amity steadily grew between the two men, which made Light's captivity more bearable. Each evening he was invited to dine in his erstwhile Great Cabin on food and wine that were a considerable improvement on the fare he had previously endured. Régnier had been slightly wounded at the battle of Trincomalee and still carried his left arm in a sling. He believed it had been broken and badly set; it still gave him much discomfort. 'But I am fortunate I did not lose it,' Régnier observed. 'That would have been the end of my career.'

After a few days, Light ventured to ask if he might take a look at said arm, explaining how his naval career had begun as a surgeon's assistant, and that he had some experience in the setting of broken bones. Régnier was more than happy to allow him. Decent surgeons were in short supply in the fleet.

'I was knocked off my feet by cannon shot. My elbow bore the weight of my landing. Is it possible to repair?'

After a careful examination, during which Régnier's groans indicated that his discomfiture was indeed great, Light rubbed his chin in thought. 'The elbow has settled out of place. I have seen such injuries before. It is possible to reset – but a very painful process, I'm afraid. I could try to resolve it but not without sedation. Would you agree to opium? As you know, we carry it aboard.' Light grinned, aware that it was part of the cargo that had been confiscated. 'Do you trust that I will not take advantage if I have you under my knife, so to speak?'

Régnier sighed. 'I would trust the devil himself to find relief from this fiendish pain, Monsieur le Capitaine. I believe you are a gentleman. But I shall also have an armed marine standing by, just in case!'

The two men laughed. The procedure was performed. It took Light longer than he would have wished to finally reset the elbow for he was woefully out of practice and poor Régnier, despite the heavy dose of opium, roared and bellowed through the pain. But in the end, it was achieved. The arm was bound, and in a few days the swelling subsided, leaving the limb almost as good as new. Thus, the friendship between the two adversaries grew. Light had made another valuable comrade.

The weeks passed by, during which life returned to something approximating normality as they shuffled back and forth between Ceylon and the Coromandel. Christmas passed, celebrated in Popish style in Cuddalore, and the New Year was ushered in. It was months since he had left home. How was his family faring? Had they any inkling of what had happened, or maybe they already feared the worst? It was unlikely any news had reached Madras, but his absence would alarm them. But then, he was often away for months on end; Martinha was used to that. She probably presumed he was gallivanting somewhere in India while waiting for the winds to change. It was all he deserved. For that is indeed what he usually did when away from home.

One evening in late January en route to Ceylon, Régnier and Light were enjoying a game of chess and a glass of brandy after dinner when the conversation turned to family. Régnier was unmarried as yet but hoped, once this war was done, to return to France and marry the girl who waited for him in Toulouse.

'You must miss your wife and children, Francis,' Régnier observed.

'I do. More than ever. In truth, I have been an unworthy husband, like many men of my profession. I am hardly ever home. My little girls barely know me. I live as a bachelor most of the time, if you take my meaning. Yet now, facing God knows how many years in this maritime gaol, I cannot help but wish I had been a better man for them. Martinha deserves so much more. She is an exceptional woman,' Light murmured, sufficiently in his cups to be maudlin.

'She is not British then?' the lieutenant asked tentatively. The name sounded Portuguese. In these waters that inevitably meant mixed race.

Light laughed, before draining his glass. 'She is not British, sir. Martinha is – to be frank – hard to define. She is a little bit of everything of the Indies. She is Siamese and Malay and Portuguese and Indian. I believe her great-grandfather, was even French, a Catholic priest to boot!'

Régnier chuckled. 'Then, she is the East! And, you, mon capitaine, are the West. A very compelling combination, *n'est-ce pas*? A beauty, I presume?'

'A beauty beyond words, far more than I deserve. My daughters, too. Most handsome children. I am a fortunate man, indeed. I was born an unwanted bastard but adopted by a good man of standing who raised me as a gentleman. Life may have thrown obstacles in my path but all-in-all I have been lucky. Finally, I understand that! The loss of my freedom makes me realise my blessings. God gives to us but we take his gifts for granted until those self-same gifts are taken from us. Only then do our minds gain clarity. All our trivial ambitions seem as nought.'

'You would be with your wife and daughters again more than anything?'

Light nodded sadly. 'More than anything. I would accept my humble home in Queddah and the life of a local trader if I could but end my days with them, *mon chèr* Jean-Louis.'

Régnier poured another glass. 'To freedom and returning to those we love! This war will end, sir. You will return home. Of that I'm sure.'

Light clinked his glass but his thoughts remained far away. It was not his absences alone that he regretted. It was his mistakes. His infidelities. And the damned catastrophe of Amdaeng Rat. What had he imagined when he had settled her in Kuala Bahang? Why had he allowed himself to lose the support of Tharua in the misguided belief that he could be a decent father to a misbegotten son? How could he ever have thought the little *luk kreung* child might ever be an English gentleman? The example of Soliman should have taught him. His own invisible father had done the right thing. If you cannot be a father to a child, then find someone decent who can. To imagine that a child brought up in Concubine Village by a simple girl from Jangsylan could ever be his son in anything but name had been a fantasy.

And for that he had risked Martinha's trust. If he ever got out of this mess alive, he swore to put it right.

***

In March, whilst moored at Trincomalee, the Blake found itself side-by-side with the frigate *Consolante,* which had brought in an East Indiaman, the *Fortitude,* captured in the Bay of Bengal. Régnier invited its new captain to dine. The affable Captain Mallé had news of the war: Madras was under siege, the soldiers in Fort St George reported to be starving and disease-ridden. The writing was on the wall for British India. Light listened in, hardly able to believe it possible. Hastings would not allow Bengal to fall! The army would prevail. He must not let French bombast dishearten his spirits. It was surely just the rhetoric of war. Most likely the British were saying much the same about their chances. The adventure in the East could not be over!

The following day brought new orders and two more prisoners to the *Blake,* a husband and wife by the name of Hickey. Suffren's fleet had returned from wintering in Sumatra and the final push was on. Lieutenant Régnier spent that evening dining on the *Héros* with the admiral, while the English captives were left to their own devices. Supper had been laid for them in the Captain's cabin.

The Hickeys were an unlikely pair. William was in his early

thirties, handsome in a weak and dissolute fashion, his long hair worn loose, his flamboyant clothes elegantly tailored, with something of the fop about him. Light immediately judged him a charlatan, a charmer who used smoke and mirrors to win over his audience. From Hickey's potted history, he was the son of a successful solicitor, born in Pall Mall and educated in Westminster School, no less, but with telling gaps in his narrative that suggested his life story was not all it seemed.

Hickey claimed to be a lawyer, although there was little evidence of academic study, for since the age of twenty he had been travelling here and there about the world. He told lurid tales of earlier voyages to India, China and even Jamaica, then back to England again, journeys apparently made for little other purpose than amusement. A few years earlier, however, he had taken up a post as a Solicitor and Proctor to the Supreme Court of Bengal (how did these wastrels secure these posts, Light wondered?) He had recently been in London on official business during which time he had met and married the lovely Miss Charlotte Barry. But on their return journey – on a Portuguese ship, no less! – they had had the misfortunate to be taken by the damned French, who insisted on holding them, even though their ship had not been aligned.

Light listened to the pompous young man and his tedious empty life, whilst observing the behaviour of his 'wife' with amusement. Mrs. Hickey was very young, probably little more than twenty, but in no ways the blushing bride. In fact, Light doubted whether she was a wife at all. He knew women. This little *demi-mondaine* was a lady of fortune, who for reasons known only to herself had attached herself to the dissipated Hickey. She would no doubt ditch him just as quickly if a more amenable 'husband' chanced along. India beckoned with all its rich English gentlemen spread out before her. Charlotte Hickey spent the evening making eyes at Light across the table, tossing back her auburn curls and gushing with fake charm at every comment he made.

The couple had undoubtedly spent an eventful time at sea: Charlotte's maid had passed away not long after they left Lisbon of some ailment or other, their ship had almost sunk in a storm, Charlotte had near died of fever, and then had come the humiliation of their capture. It was indeed a pitiful tale. Nevertheless, their treatment had not been too bad for all that: Charlotte peppered her conversation with tales of Christmas parties and riding excursions in Trincomalee as the guests of the French and Dutch residents there, and the beautiful clothes and goods that had been supplied for them *gratis*, since they had lost almost all their personal belongings in the storm.

Despite Hickey's best efforts, Light refused to open up to questioning. He was just a British country trader out of Madras who had had the misfortune to have been taken by the French. Beyond that he would not say. Soon enough the Hickeys dismissed him as a man of no consequence, a fellow of the lower classes, someone hardly worth cultivating, although no doubt a sterling Englishman for all that.

The Hickeys stayed aboard the *Blake* for the next few weeks as they crossed to the Coromandel. When they were finally transferred to Cuddalore to be released and returned to Bengal, Light breathed a sigh of relief, glad to be free of their tedious aggrandizement. He made a mental note not to look them up on his next visit to Calcutta, whilst promising faithfully to do so.

Mrs. Hickey gave him one last doe-eyed glance over her shoulder as she made her way to the conveyance, licking her rosy-pink lips in a disturbingly feral way. That way lay danger, Light thought to himself, rather proud to have escaped her clutches unscathed. He'd rather chance his luck with the French than that little vixen. Perhaps he was learning at last?

Thus, March gave way to April. It was already nearly Easter. Soon it would be six whole months since he had left. Surely his family would be alarmed? Scott would speak to merchants who had been in India; the possibility that he was a prisoner would begin to be mooted.

Their circumstances had deteriorated of late. The French fleet was being hunted down by British naval forces under the command of Admiral Sir Edward Hughes, the loser at the great sea battle of Trincomalee. Hughes was eager to restore his reputation. What if they should run into the British fleet in these waters? Light's knowledge of sea battles was extensive from his Navy days. He well knew their haphazard nature. A small snow like the *Blake*, if caught in the midst of a bombardment, was sure to be at great risk. Speedy as she was, she could not outrun British warships of the line. He might be looking at a watery grave after all.

One early April night, the fleet sailed into unusual conditions, a misty haze that sometimes blew off the land at the turn of the monsoon. As a result, the night was deep dark, visibility poor, with dense drifting clouds that obscured both the moon and stars. The fleet was scattered, the smaller supply ships bringing up the rear. Late on, the *Blake* all but ran into an English 74-gunner, itself probably sailing nigh on blind. It was the *Superb*, flying the pennant of Rear-Admiral of the Blue. By the damnedest of damned luck, they had come across the flag ship of Sir Edward Hughes, the commander of the British fleet in the East Indies.

Initially the signal sent out from the warship was a mere acknowledgement; to all intents and purposes, the *Blake* was a friendly trader, a British country ship, albeit in enemy waters. The admiral would not be expecting trouble when he ordered the *Blake* to draw about. An officer was preparing to come across.

On board Light's ship, panic reigned. Régnier and the officers were debating how to proceed, their consternation so great they even invited Light to join their deliberations. 'We should fire upon them. We have the element of surprise and might inflict a mortal wound,' Régnier suggested. 'Our fleet is close. The noise will draw them to us,' he assured them.

Light was having none of it. The British warship – with all guns trained on them – would blow them out of the water if they dared fire even one round. Régnier might be ready to be a martyr for France, but he was not. 'The entire British fleet is in these waters. This is the flag ship of the Admiral, dammit! The rest cannot be far off. Nor do we have any way of knowing their numbers or how they are placed. If we fire, there is a distinct possibility that it will draw the rest of the British in no time. We will be destroyed either way. Do you wish inadvertently to fire the first shot in a decisive battle that the French might lose?' Light cautioned. All eyes turned on him.

Silence reigned whilst Régnier re-assessed. Light was correct. He had no authority to engage the British. Should this prove a disaster, he would be court-martialled, if he hadn't already drowned or sustained a fatal injury in battle. Suffren was known for his rigid adherence to protocol. Senior officers had already been sent back to France for execution for failures in carrying out exact orders.

'On consideration, I concur,' he replied sharply. 'Then it seems you have your ship back, Captain Light, and that I am now *your* prisoner,' Régnier said forlornly. 'May I say that I could not wish to lose my command to a better fellow,' he added, bravely.

But Light had not finished. 'Hold your horses, Jean-Louis! That is not at all what I meant. If you surrender to the British, then the jig is up. They will know the French fleet lies close by, still ignorant of their presence. I, for one, have no desire to be caught in the midst of the subsequent mêlée. The *Blake* would never survive the assault. You must trust me again, sir, as you once did with your broken elbow. You and your men are to stay below, well out of sight. Let me handle this my way, if you please. And with God's good grace, we may yet see another day.'

Régnier was aghast. 'You would betray your country? You would chance that your own people would catch you in a lie? If so, you would be shot for a traitor!'

Light was unconcerned. 'Either I die or I am killed, you mean? There has to be a better way than battle, lieutenant. I am not a soldier. I left the Navy years ago. I am an independent merchant who has lost a lot of money in the service of my country, which will surely refuse to remunerate me for my loss. I must look to my own endeavour to salvage what I can of my ship and my life. With luck, when this war is over, I shall be left with both. So, pardon me, sir, if it is worth the risk!'

Up on deck, it took only minutes to convince the English lieutenant, who had come aboard with a few marines. They suspected nothing. 'Your name and details, sir?'

'Francis Light, trader out of Jangsylan and Queddah. We are returning to the Straits after delivering rice to Madras. Bloody hell, sir, it was a desperate journey getting past the Frenchies, but the Fort was damned glad for our supplies.'

'You're very far south, Captain Light. Surely you ought to have sailed further north to avoid the French convoys?'

Light borrowed from the storm that had led to their original capture, so that his lie might be grounded in some truth. 'Hit a nasty tempest out of Madras, sir. Blew the little *Blake* right off course,' he said, affecting the speech of a man of the lower orders, an adventurer made good out east.

'Well, you're damned lucky, sir. We were told the place is crawling with Frogs.'

'No, sir. It's as quiet as the grave out here. Passed a local boat earlier. They said most of the French had withdrawn to Trincomalee for refitting and water. The rest are still huddled down in Cuddalore till the storms pass. It can be unpredictable this time of year.'

The captain's ears pricked up. 'You're sure of that? By God, we could pin them down, and mayhap trap Suffren himself and his entire fleet like sitting ducks! This is sterling information, sir. Good man. May we assist in any way?'

'No, sir. Thank you, sir. We just want to catch the winds and get home, if we may. God speed, sir. You blow those Frenchies out of the water for good King George, eh?'

It was easy done. The British warship sailed away, unaware that within a few leagues the entire French fleet lay stranded in the mists, like Easter lambs for slaughter. Régnier and his fellow officers crept up on deck to watch until the last vestige of the enemy was swallowed in the haze, and they were alone again. '*Mon Dieu*, but that was close!' Regnier laughed, slapping Light upon the back. 'We owe you much, my friend. You are a shrewd man. A man of peace.'

At that Light spun round. To Régnier's utter astonishment, he was armed, having pulled a pistol from his jacket. It was now trained on the lieutenant's heart at near point-blank range. '… Not exactly a man of peace, my dear Jean-Louis. I'm afraid your initial instinct was right. I *will* be taking back my ship tonight. But there will be no violence or unpleasant consequences, unless, of course, you try to be heroes. Look around you, gentlemen, please. Observe!'

Light's entire crew, that mismatched motley of lascars culled of every Asian origin, now encircled the hapless French entire. Each man was bearing weapons, and was ready to kill, if necessary. It would only take one word from the Captain. 'Whilst you were sweating down below, *mon chèr Captaine,* my men were liberating our arsenal. Do you surrender, sir?'

Régnier shrugged. His men threw down their weapons. '*D'accord*. I have no choice. What now, sir?'

Light grinned, shoving his pistol back into his belt and gathering up the scattered weapons. 'Have no fear, lieutenant. We'll set you down in a launch off Jaffna. From there, you can make your way back to Trincomalee. Tell your people that the British re-took the *Blake* but that Captain Light insisted no harm should come to you. They allowed you a jolly boat to make your way to land, for they were uninterested in taking prisoners. You'll have time at sea to devise a suitable fiction. So, I think that we are now even, Jean-Louis? Come, I say we open a bottle of your

excellent cognac and pass the grog around the men. Let them fight
their wars, sir, if they may. But for us, we shall agree to part as
friends!'

PART FOUR

A Family of the Straits

(1782-1785)

25

To the Four Winds

Ban Takkien, Thalang. October 1782

Nine long years had passed since he had last set foot on the island of his birth, nine brutal years of endless campaigns interspersed with the harrowing intensity of court life. His face was testament to the toll, the youthful unlined beauty having given way to a rugged masculinity that rendered him almost unrecognisable. Where once there had been near-feminine softness, now hard-etched lines were carved on weather-beaten skin. Gone was the androgynous slenderness. Lord Thian was now muscled and spare, his brow lined, the first hint of grey prematurely dusting his temples. Lady Chan – a woman not given to sentiment – was taken aback at the sight of her eldest and best-loved child. If this was what the world had done to him, she wished he had followed his heart and retreated to a monastery long ago.

Lord Thian had arrived home exhausted to the point of collapse, clothes mud-spattered and torn. He had travelled a distance, that much was clear, and asked only for sustenance, water to wash, and a bed. For the next two days, he kept to his room, showing no sign of life other than the empty bowls of food placed outside the door. No one dared disturb him. The earthshattering events that had taken place in Thonburi – to which Lord Thian must have been a close witness – were common knowledge. The swirling rumours were vague and contradictory. Little hard fact was known. The household waited impatiently for the truth.

Early one morning, on the third day after his arrival, Lord Thian stepped out into the cool air and sat upon the bare earth of the gardens, deep in thought. There Lady Chan found him. She took a seat on a nearby bench and waited, unwilling to break the silence of his meditation, the interval affording her the chance to observe her son and learn the changes that the years with Tak Sin had wrought upon her beautiful boy. She mourned the passing of his youth and the callous pressures she herself had placed upon his shoulders, forcing him to prove himself as a man rather than embrace the yellow silk and spend his life in scholarly and religious pursuits. But it was too late now for regrets. That boy had gone forever, another casualty of her many mistakes.

Finally, Lord Thian opened his eyes and lit the morning with his gentle smile of welcome. In that moment, Chan saw the child he had once been, bringing a rare smile to her face in response. She supposed he found her changed, too – and much aged. Such was the passage of time. 'Mother –' he whispered. 'It is good to be home. This place is such an idyll of peace and beauty.'

'It is good to see you, my son. You have been sorely missed,' Lady Chan replied warily. She would not force him to speak until he was ready.

Thian bowed his head in acknowledgement of her words. 'Know that I would have visited long ago had I been able. But the times were dangerous and I feared my presence might be misconstrued. Paranoia has reigned these past years. The south was suspect. I stayed away to save us all.'

Lady Chan advanced towards her son, placing her hands on

his shoulders. 'When you are ready, son, please tell me how it was. I wish to share your troubles. I also need to understand what has happened in the City. But in your own time. And only share what you can bear to reveal.'

Thian nodded, placing his own hand upon his mother's, looking up at her, his eyes moist with unshed tears. 'But what is truth, mother? There are many ways to tell a story, each true and false in equal part. No two people ever see the past the same. The only surety in which we may ever trust, is that in this moment, I am here with you in this place and at this time. The past is lost forever. The future does not even yet exist.'

His opaque reply was troubling. Something tormented him enough that he could neither look back nor forward. Hardened as it was to disaster, Lady Chan's adamantine heart was pierced through by his dilemma. 'We have heard such rumours! But I would not wish to believe everything I have heard, for I know how false such stories can be. But if it is too painful for you to speak of it –'

Thian rose to his feet to tower over her tiny frame, and placed a gentle finger against her lips. 'You deserve to know, dear mother, and I swear I will be honest with you, as far as it is possible. Tonight, at dinner with the family, or at least those old enough to bear the details, I will speak. But until then, let us spend a quiet day. There is so much of the mundane affairs of our family and the island that I wish to know. I welcome the chance to hear of such matters, far away from the horrors of the past few months.'

Lord Thian was true to his promise. That night, after they had eaten, he gave account of the momentous events that had shaken the nation. The rumours they had heard were largely correct, although he added the detail that brought verisimilitude to the wild speculations. It was a terrible story. No wonder it had left him traumatised.

'The news arrived when our armies were in Cambodia, whose king – a vassal of Thonburi- had been deposed and killed by rebels. It was while we were deep in this war of attrition that the dread news from the City reached the Command. A revolt had broken out, led by a general of a famous house, one Phraya Sanka, who had gathered a coterie of disaffected nobles about him. Taking advantage of the absence of so many army commanders, they had stormed the palace, where they met little opposition. All those surrounding King Tak Sin simply melted away; there had been no one left who cared enough to defend him. The courtiers and servants, the guards and officials had seen the writing on the wall long since. The once mighty, but now pitiful, king was dragged off to imprisonment.'

'Lord Duang acted quickly, retreating as fast as possible, desperate to act before it was too late, arriving outside the gates of Thonburi in the early days of April. There we pitched our tents, an army laying siege to its own city! Fortunately, the sight of battle-hardened troops on the doorstep was enough to drive fear into the hearts of the rebels, and to bring some much-needed sanity to the situation. They threw themselves upon the mercy of Lord Duang, offering him the throne, claiming it had never been their intention to tear Siam apart.'

'Brushing aside their obsequious protestations, Lord Duang demanded to know the whereabouts of the king, at which the prostrate nobles shook with fear. Great Tak Sin had already passed on, they said. The general's rage was palpable; he leapt from his horse, seizing Phraya Sanka with his bare hands, and bellowing in his face. 'What have you done with our Great King, filthy worm?'

Shivering in the presence of such great wrath, General Sanka revealed the tragic story. The king had initially accepted his imprisonment with great humility, asking only to be allowed to retreat to a monastery to spend the rest of his days in prayer. But the rebels had refused his request. A figurehead such as King Tak Sin might become a pawn in the hands of the enemy, both home and abroad. Lurking unchecked on the fringes, he would always be a threat to any new government. Furthermore, was it possible to trust the king's word? Tak Sin might say one thing today in his lucidity, but just as easily relapse tomorrow into madness and launch an attack to reclaim his throne. It had thus been decided that Tak Sin must die, much as it had pained them all to take the awful decision.'

'It was decided that his death must befit a royal prince, whose blood must never fall upon the ground or be shed by the hands of lesser mortals, following the death meted out to King Trailok long ago. Thus, His Majesty was tied inside a sack of velvet and beaten to death by clubs of sandalwood. In this way, the velvet sack held both his body and his blood, and the ancient tradition was upheld. Then, to prevent a public outcry, the body of the late king, still wrapped in its velvet shroud, was quickly buried in an unmarked grave within the palace grounds.'

'Lord Duang could not contain himself at the outrage perpetrated on the same king who had delivered Siam from the Burmese and reunited a shattered kingdom against all the odds. He ordered the immediate beheading of Phraya Sanka and the other nobles involved in the rebellion and execution of their king. Their families were also put to death and their fortunes seized. The subsequent bloodletting went on for weeks. The people rose in praise of Lord Duang, whose courage and virtue were indisputable. He was right in his actions. Siam owed the great Tak Sin much more than a lonely, bloody death and an unknown grave, even if it was generally agreed that his fearsome reign must end. And so, the Siamese people welcomed the coronation of Lord Duang, who styles himself King Rama, the first ruler of the Chakri dynasty.'

Around the table, a shocked hush greeted Lord Thian's moving story. Tears pricked at their eyes, for who could not feel sorrow at the fall of the great man? To have ascended such heights only to lie forever in an unmarked grave seemed the cruellest reward for the magnificent service he had given to his country.

It was Lady Chan who first broke the silence, with an observation entirely typical of her. She had not let her feelings blind her to the facts. 'King Rama was crowned three months ago, my son. Where have you been since?'

Lord Thian winced imperceptibly. 'The purges went on for a long time,' he muttered, unwilling to expand. His family did not push him further. They knew only too well the inevitable consequences of such a violent aftermath. If Thian had been a present – or indeed the commander – he would have witnessed the slaughter of entire families. It was unimaginable.

Lady Chan continued to observe her son closely. He could not hide from her. She doubted that his ambivalence was driven by disgust at what had been demanded of him. For all his spiritual purity, Thian would never baulk from his duty, even if it meant the massacre of innocents, should he believe that it was the right course of action. He had been a soldier for many years. There was already much blood on his hands. No, she thought to herself, her son was lying, of that she was sure. And his duplicity was adding to his discomfort, for he could never easily tell an untruth. Whatever had happened at Thonburi, this was no more than the 'official' version of the rumours. Another truth lay hidden that he chose not to reveal.

'Dear Thian,' Her voice was faint but all those at the table turned to heed her words. 'What now? Must you return to Thonburi and the wars? Or is it possible that you have at last returned to the bosom of your family, satiated to the full by the world at large?'

Her son stared straight at her, with eyes that told a different story from his lips. 'Neither of these two paths will be my future, mother. First, I will rest here for a short time, and then I intend to leave behind this world of cares and sorrow. It is my intention to travel to the far north, to a kingdom in the mountains where I may retreat to a remote monastery. There I shall spend the rest of my days. Know that I leave in order to keep you safe. You will be forever in my thoughts and meditations. As you have always been these many years apart.'

It was all he would say. No entreaty would sway his resolve. Lord Thian would travel to the Himalayan mountains to study at the feet of learned Mahayana monks. He would follow the way of the Bodhisattva. It would be a lifelong journey.

On the night before he left Ban Takkien, Lord Thian did not sleep. Instead, while the rest of the household slumbered, he committed to record the true details of the fate of Tak Sin in all its terrible glory. He wrote of conspiracy, retribution and revenge, far more shocking than the public record. Once his chronicle was complete, he rolled it, setting it in the copper crucible of an incense burner. There he lit a fire and watched as the pages flamed, curled, burned, and turned to ashes. Then he placed the incinerated remains inside a tiny box inlaid with mother-of-pearl that he concealed upon his person. Sometime in the future, on a high mountain overlooking the world, he would cast those same ashes upon the four winds. Some trace of what had been done must survive lest he go mad with the hidden knowledge. He owed Great King Tak Sin that much.

To the Great Winds: My Testimony

It began a long time before it ended. For who could recognise the first discordant note amidst the cacophony of adulation? The king had ascended so far above us that his idiosyncrasies were to be expected, indulged, and even adored. We were each and every one of us unwitting participants in what followed. Does our ignorance absolve us from blame? From my very first meeting with General Tak Sin, I observed aspects of the man distasteful to me, yet I chose to find a thousand justifications to excuse my instincts. I wanted him to be the god that he became. In the light of what we now know, the signs had always been before our eyes. We were as complicit in the creation of the monster as he, perhaps more.

It was with relief that we departed for the campaigns in Cambodia, merely for the chance to escape the random *horrors of the court. Not long before we left, a singularly appalling act took place that should have propelled into action those who truly cared for the king. It began innocently enough. A large rat ran through the private quarters of the king's favourite wives, the Lady Ubol and the Lady Chim. Their maids called a guard to enter the inner rooms and catch the rodent, an episode that proved more challenging than it seemed, for the wily rat was difficult to trap. Thus, the guard, a tall and handsome fellow, reputed to have Portuguese-Indian blood, spent some time in the forbidden areas.*

What happened next is unclear. Somehow, the king was informed of the presence of the guard where he was not allowed. He flew into a terrible rage. Whether by malicious gossip or his maniacal caprice, the King decided that the two pitiful women and the hapless guard had been involved in shameful impropriety. Nothing would persuade him otherwise. The three unfortunates were summoned before the entire court to be flayed alive. One of his wives was pregnant, but even that was not enough to sway the king. The terrible penalty was carried out in public view, the entire court witness to the piteous screams of those three innocents. But still they did not die. Their torment was endless. Eventually even the King himself could tolerate the dreadful shrieking no more; he rose from his throne, seized a sword, and put an end to them himself in the most horrific manner: by hacking off their hands and feet, even slicing off the women's breasts, whereupon they bled to death.

The court gazed on this outrage in shocked silence, each noble afraid even to move or speak lest the king's wrath be visited upon them in its turn. Such horror makes cowards of even the bravest generals. To our shame, we stood and witnessed this orgy of violence – and did nothing. But the memory could not be so easily put aside. It reminded us of our own vulnerability. Not one of us was safe.

So, off we heroes went to war, embracing the opportunity to be free of the terror of Thonburi. But evil followed us nonetheless. It was not long before Lord Duang learned that his own son had been executed for the most trivial of reasons: he had not bowed before the urn containing the mortal remains of the king's parents. The general was devastated, but outwardly revealed no enmity towards the king. Yet all those who knew him were not fooled by his show of self-discipline. From that moment on, the bell was tolling. The officers to a man threw in their lot with Lord Duang. The insanity must end.

The particular details of the conspiracy are unknown to me. I was not party to the intimate discussions that decided the fate of the King. I surmise that Lord Duang, or his brother Lord Boonma, made secret approaches to the most disaffected parties at court; General Phraya Sanka had been a companion of both in the past. When the news of the overthrow of King Tak Sin reached the camp, it came as no surprise. The frantic march back to Thonburi on the pretext of saving the king was no such thing; it was merely the next step in the conspiracy. When Phraya Sanka threw himself upon his knees and offered the throne to Lord Duang, that was no spontaneous action, but a well-planned performance. The conspirators expected to be showered with rewards for their service in no way anticipating the general's next act.

Lord Duang had planned meticulously. Siam might once again be thrown into chaos and disunity by the rebellion. Every achievement since the fall of Ayutthaya might be destroyed. And so, from that very moment, Lord Duang – now King Rama – began to create a new narrative, in which he was the heroic saviour of Siam, and in which each dire consequence meted out was just punishment for those who had dared to murder the hero of the nation.

Thus, the rebels and their families were summarily executed, removing any witness to the conspiracy, and absolving King Rama from blame. It was also a definitive warning to those who might think Tak Sin's fall meant open season for revolt. The first problem dealt with, King Rama now turned to the matter of the former king who, contrary to public opinion, was still at that time very much alive. Surely Tak Sin could not be allowed to live, the danger of his mere existence presenting too great a threat?

Yet, at this final moment, even King Rama hesitated, the only time I ever witnessed weakness in his resolve. Tak Sin and he had been bosom companions since boyhood. They had shared the deprivations of many *campaigns. Together they had built a new future for Siam. The new king was honest enough to recognise that, without the genius of his former friend, none of what they had achieved would have been possible. Even the unjust murder of his own son was not enough to convince him to pronounce the final sentence.*

Whilst the new ruler of Siam turned over this matter, Tak Sin sent a message from his prison cell. His mind was in a current state of clarity; his gruesome deeds now haunted him. He was resigned to death, for he well knew he deserved it. Had guards not stayed his hand, he would already have committed suicide. It was right that his life should be forfeit for the sake of the future peace and stability of Siam. But he had one last request: that he might bid farewell to Duang, his brother, before he left this world. The poignant appeal, typical of the courage of the man he had once called friend, was enough to bring King Rama to a decision.

With tears visible in his eyes, he waved away the messenger and abruptly left the hall, indicating that a few of us should attend him in his private rooms. We expected to be told that the punishment was execution, and that we ourselves were to be responsible for the deed. With sombre faces, steeling our resolve, we followed him inside to learn King Tak Sin's fate.

As all the world now knows, the former king was beaten to death in a velvet sack after which his body was immediately buried in an unmarked grave. Speed and secrecy were essential. The populace must be kept in

*ignorance to calm the turmoil. This method of execution,
rooted in protocol and tradition, would ensure that no
royal blood would be spilt upon the ground to honour and
respect the former king. It brought another overlooked
advantage.*

*The poor unfortunate victim was not Tak Sin, but
a palace servant, chosen for his proximity in height and
weight. The sack concealed the true identity, as did the
secret burial. This misdirection hid the fact that King
Rama could not bring himself to do actual harm to the
king's person. It was enough to depose him and seize his
throne. One day in the future, when the body has decayed
to nothing more than an assemblage of bones, the king
will publicly exhume the corpse and Great King Tak Sin
(or rather his dead servant) will receive a burial worthy
of his name. A great monument will be erected over his
mausoleum and the citizens will prostrate themselves at
this shrine. Siam will then be ready for a new story to
justify the cruelties of its past.*

*But what of Lord Tak Sin? Where is he now? Still
lingering in some hidden dungeon far below the palace?
Only one person in this world knows for sure and he
is soon to be lost to Siam forever. King Rama bade me
deliver Tak Sin to a monastery far away in the forests
and tell no one his true identity. It would be enough that
he was a monk who had lost his mind and was given to
flights of fancy that he had once been the king of Siam
and could fly amidst the heavens. My task achieved, I was
to be allowed one last visit home, on the understanding*

that not one word of my involvement was ever to be spoken. Then I, too, was commanded to retreat forever from the world into exile from my native land. It was only King Rama's love for me that prevented him from closing my lips forever. For whilst I live, he takes the risk that someone knows the truth.

Or do I fool myself? Now that my task is done, and I have made my last farewells, will assassins steal upon me one night to remove the only man alive who knows the whereabouts of King Tak Sin? We shall see. I leave my destiny in the hands of fate.

26

Reunion

Around the large teak dining table, a motley gathering was assembled, each with more than Christ's Nativity to celebrate. It had been a particularly tumultuous year, having brought a number of singular challenges: Light himself had survived capture by the French; Scott, imprisonment by the Dutch; Martinha, the birth of another daughter; and other guests each had their own prodigious stories to relate. Therefore, it came as no surprise that the jovial company spent much of the day's festivities catching up on each other's exploits, whilst raising copious toasts to God, the King and any other saviour they had called upon in their hour of need.

Of course, centre stage stood Light's own daring escape from the jaws of the French fleet, a story that only improved with each retelling, the original narrative already taking on the embellishment of epic. Not to be outdone, however, was James Scott, whose brush with mortality in Malacca made for another compelling yarn.

A few months beforehand, about the time that Light had sailed home when all hope for him had nigh been lost, Scott himself had fallen into the hands of a different, some might say deadlier, enemy. With Light absent from the scene, the full burden of company business had fallen to Scott. He had been much overburdened, continuously at sea for months. Either because exhaustion had caused him to lower his usual caution or whether desperation had driven him to take one too many risks, he had unwittingly sailed into Malacca waters. Almost at once, as if primed for Scott's proximity, his ship was surrounded by an entire Dutch convoy. Scott had been arrested on suspicion of dealing in armaments meant for use against the VOC on behalf of the Sultan of Selangor.

'I jolly well hope you were,' Light joked, 'for I would not like to think my profits suffered further in my absence by a scarcity of gun trade!' He howled with laughter, as much at his own witty remark as his enjoyment at pulling the wool over Dutch eyes. Light's riposte was received with a ripple of hilarity around the table, for the Hollanders were despised by all.

Scott grinned back. 'Dear God, man, of course! We'd been stacked up to the rails in guns until only hours before! But, fortunately for us, the contraband had recently been offloaded to the vessel of our good friend and ally, Juragan Soliman ...' He tipped his glass towards the young Malay across the table '... whose nippy little bark had been able to slip past the Dutch blockade, for they deemed him naught but a lowly local trader. And so, whilst I was hauled up by the bloody Dutchies, Solly here was no doubt already feasting with Sultan Ibrahim in Kuala Selangor!' Soliman responded to Scott's comment with a mere acknowledgment of the head. He seemed to be the only diner not entirely amused by the tale.

In truth, the situation had been no laughing matter, the humorous version told by Scott disguising the very real danger he had faced. The Dutch were much beleaguered by their Bugis enemies, mostly based in Riau, from where they constantly raided VOC ships and made general nuisance of themselves. Recently, however, the confrontations had escalated; the Bugis had several times dared to attack Malacca itself. The year before, the Dutch had sent an army of retaliation into Riau, but it had been near impossible to prevail in an archipelago of a thousand tiny islands against an enemy as proficient at the game of hide and seek as the Buginese. Malacca was in steady decline; the Dutch stomach for the Straits was waning fast. Yet an injured animal is always at his most dangerous. Tension had reached boiling point, awaiting only a tiny spark to set it off.

Scott's ship, the *Prince Henry*, had been boarded and he roughly mishandled by marines searching for the guns they believed to be on board. Their examination proved futile, so their mood grew more aggressive, threatening Scott with even more violence if he refused to admit his involvement with the Bugis and the illegal trade in weapons. Scott launched into a description of the scene with gusto, fuelled by his day-long carousing on fine wines and spirits.

'They took me by the arms, those scurvy cheese eaters, and searched about my person, divesting me of anything they perceived to be a weapon, whilst taking every opportunity to get in the sly punch here and there. Naturally, I objected to their ungentlemanly conduct, calling them out for the miserable, beer-swilling Calvinists they are.'

'Thus, speaks a Scottish Presbyterian,' Light chuckled, always the foil to Scott's Celtic hyperbole.

'A different thing, entire, man!' Scott replied with glee, warming up nicely to this captive crowd. 'Where was I now? Ah yes, says I: "Let me go, you damned dogs," or some such thing, for I would not wish to offend the ears of the good Fathers here with my actual words. For some such reason, the Dutchies took offence and decided then and there to clap me in irons, my arms lashed behind my back no less, like an animal for the roast! I didnae take too well to that, as you might imagine. And so, I let forth a right old string of curses for which pains I was heavily cuffed about the face and knocked quite off my feet by their filthy seamen. One waved his fists in my face, saying that if I did not hold my tongue it would be at my own peril. Grudgingly, I accepted defeat, asking him (quite politely, or so I thought) to render me assistance in getting back upon my feet, whereupon the cur told me to go to the devil for he would spit upon me first before he ever extended aid. Now what do you think of that?'

There was general tutting around the table, as well as a modicum of head shaking. If events had transpired thus, Scott had been a fool to attempt resistance. But then, he was known for a hothead at times, especially when in drink. Which he usually was.

The result was that he had been taken to Malacca gaol pending trial for suspected gunrunning. There was no evidence, of course, but the Dutch authorities hoped to secure proof in time. In the meantime, Scott was chained up in abysmal conditions; a Dutch prison is as close to hell as any man can get and live (sparing the cells of the French, which are known for their particular vileness). For two long months, Scott had festered in the filth and squalid heat, fed on food that rats might refuse. He claimed to have shrunk to a mere shadow of his former self, although he appeared as hale and hearty as ever. The experience evidently hadn't done him permanent damage.

In the fullness of time, Scott had been brought before the court, which, in the absence of evidence, dropped the main charges. He was, however, fined the extortionate sum of two thousand Spanish dollars, a reprehensible penalty for the trivial charge of 'entering Dutch waters without leave.' Despite the dire encounter and the silver coin it cost him, Scott was jubilant at his discharge. Nevertheless, he was pursuing the matter further with the British authorities. He would write a stern letter of complaint about the treatment of a British subject merely going about his 'honest' business in the Straits. Even if he was ignored, it would alert the authorities to the growing menace that British merchants might face.

'It's all grist to the mill, Francis. Every insult to British sovereignty only gives emphasis that an English factory here is vital to protect our shipping –'

'And every gun sold to their enemies weakens the damned Dutch monopoly,' Light added with feeling. The assembled guests nodded in agreement. If there was ever a time to challenge Dutch supremacy it was now – and the Bugis were the key.

As the afternoon progressed, and the drink flowed freely, even the more conservative guests found themselves becoming more expansive. Martinha had invited Bishop Joseph-Louis Coudé and Monseigneur Arnaud-Antoine Garnault, Missionary Fathers based in Kuala Queddah since they had fled Siam in fear of their lives. They were much beholden to the Light family. The captain had taken up their cause with Sultan Abdullah, who had granted them permission to rebuild the old mission chapel of St. Michael's at Alor Setar. Martinha and Lady Thong Di worked tirelessly for the thriving Christian community and the many new families recently arrived to swell the existing flock.

The two churchmen had their own enthralling tale of escape from the clutches of Tak Sin back in '80. Before that time, they had been most welcome at the court in Thonburi. The axe had fallen quite without provocation. The king had decreed that all Christians were under a total ban. They must depart the country at once, or suffer execution. At that time, the two men had been based at the mother house in Ligor, from where they fled in the company of the then bishop of Siam, Olivier-Simon Le Bon, who had sadly not survived the arduous journey, yet another Christian casualty of the final years of Tak Sin. From there, inevitably, the talk fell to the recent demise of the mad king of Siam, and the rise of the new Chakri dynasty.

Lady Chan had written, so the family was well versed in the official story. The two priests had their own independent sources. Conflicting rumours still swirled. Some even asserted that Tak Sin was alive, possibly in a monastery, and that he would one day rise again to retake his throne. Whispers even said that reports of the king's descent into madness had merely been the invention of Lord Duang, who had conspired all along to displace him. But few paid any attention to such fantasies.

'There was a time,' remarked Bishop Coudé, 'when the Fathers were honoured guests at Tak Sin's court, so we can bear witness to his gradual decline. Sometimes, he would welcome us, but at other times he would suddenly find fault and exhibit inexplicable anger at our presence. Even then, we knew he was a sick man, sad to say. The time came when he stopped inviting us to audiences. We heard that he had devoted himself to prayer, fasting and meditation in order that he might fly in the air. The poor man was quite insane. All those surrounding him merely pandered to his crazed notions. For who dared contradict the mighty Tak Sin?'

Monseigneur Garnault continued the sorry witness. 'We even took up the matter with Tak Sin's own son after the decree of banishment. We reminded him that, in the past, the king had defended the religious freedom of his foreign guests. But his son had merely replied: "It is true he did once support your faith, but my father is much changed these days.' It was the closest that anyone ever came to admitting that the king was no longer the man he had once been. After that, we knew we were abandoned. Thus, we advised our faithful to flee as best they could. It was a pitiful time. Many died along the way. Our hearts are still heavy at the cost.'

'Do you think he was indeed executed? What of this notion that his refuge is some distant monastery?' Scott inquired.

The priests both shook their heads. 'He is surely dead. For that is how such matters are ever resolved in the kingdom. The Siamese are gentle people for the most part, but are capable of extreme and hideous violence at times. Nor is new king Rama likely to leave any threads hanging in the new tapestry he is weaving for his realm.'

'Was he in fact the driving force behind the conspiracy all along? One could hardly blame him,' Light wondered, his own memories of the terror of the later years at Thonburi still fresh in his mind.

The Fathers thought not. 'For there could be no more loyal servant than Lord Duang. It is unthinkable that he would in the end betray his lord and friend.'

Light and Scott, however, were not as convinced that any man close to power is quite so lily-white, but kept their thought to themselves. The Siamese mindset was ever complex to western understanding. Even Lord Thian had demonstrated his private concerns about King Taksin, if only by his utter silence on the matter. And who more likely than someone close to the king to be the instrument of his ultimate removal?

'Perhaps your Cousin Thian might know some juicy morsels from behind the scenes?' asked Scott, eager for more gossip and sure that Light was holding back on the subject.

Martinha shook her head. 'Sadly, I am afraid we no longer have contact with my dear cousin for he has left this world,' she murmured, the first time that she had joined the conversation.

'Dead?' Scott gasped. 'My God, did he fall in the purges?'

'No, not at all. Thian had always been a protégé of Lord Duang, quite as much as Tak Sin. In recent years, he had been exclusively in the general's service so remained with him during the terrible events. After the bloodletting was finally done, Thian found that his heart had been sundered by it. He decided to take the yellow silk. My cousin does not intend ever to re-enter this world again –' Her voice wavered as she fought against the tears that always threatened at the thought of the loss of dear Thian. Such a terrible waste.

'Bad times,' Light sighed. 'Not only for Siam, but for us all. Rama is no Tak Sin. He will not deal with the Company, for he intends to hold the entire kingdom in his iron grip. I'm afraid, whilst there is still much money to be made in Thalang, we must accept that we will never gain a British stronghold there.' They drank even to that disheartening news, much as they drank to everything on that Christmas Day.

Meanwhile Soliman, who had listened but so far taken no part in the discussions, suddenly broke in. 'If not Thalang, Captain, then where? For surely the need has never been so great for your Company, nor the time so ripe?'

Francis held up his glass, swirling the contents, a veiled look upon his face. 'Where, indeed, clever Sol. But you have it in a nutshell. The moment is here but where to place the flag, eh?' Light flashed a glance across the table at his partner; Scott raised his own glass by way of reply. Whatever was in their minds, they were not yet ready to share the knowledge. That they had a plan was crystal clear, however, if only from their dissimulation.

When the gathering finally broke, and the last of the revellers staggered home full of festive cheer, Light indicated for Soliman to stay behind and join him for a last drink. Soliman declined the brandy; Light had noticed he had taken no strong drink all day. His boy had changed. He now wore his hair long and unbound, held back by a cloth *dastar*, in the Malay manner. He dressed in loose tunics and sarongs, and was never seen without his keris, thrust into his belt of silver coins, the signs of a man of means in these parts. It seemed to Light entirely right and proper that Soliman had decided to become what he, in fact, had always been: a Salateer of the Malacca Straits.

'You had us very worried there, sir. I thought for sure we had lost to you to the French, or even worse, to the deep,' Soliman said with a smile of relief. His English was unimpaired by his years away. He still spoke it like a native, even with a slight Suffolk twang that amused Light no end.

'It was close, to be sure. But a few of my nine lives still

apparently remain to me,' Light joked.

'Nine lives? Soliman was confused; his English did not extend to idioms of this type.

Light laughed. 'Merely an old saying from my home country. A cat appears to have nine lives because of the facility with which it escapes the jaws of certain death. And so, it seems, do I!'

The two men settled down on the steps, looking out at the clear, starry night. It was a typical hot night in late December in the Tropics, nigh on impossible to conjure up the cruel winters of his childhood Christmases. Light found his thoughts often strayed to memories of home these days. He had begun to miss England in a visceral way that had never troubled him before. What were his chances of ever spending time in Suffolk again? The dream of returning with a fortune large enough to buy a fine country manor was as vivid as ever. But if it was to be realised, it still lay somewhere ahead of him, as ever just beyond his fingers' grasp.

'I hear you've been in and out of Riau selling guns. What news?' Light asked.

Soliman rubbed thoughtfully at his wispy beard. 'Business thrives, Captain. There are never any shortage of buyers in that particular commodity. But the Dutch are prowling with menace. They fear the Bugis mightily, especially now they're snapping at the gates of Melaka. It is a dangerous run, even more so now than ever,' he observed.

Light concurred. 'As our dear friend Scott has found out to his cost.'

At the mention of James Scott, Soliman's face darkened. 'He has used me ill, Captain. I carried his guns – for which he has still not paid me – knowing full well that had I been taken, the Orang

Belanda would have strung me up, and all my crew besides. We mean nothing to him. He does not value our safety one jot. I will not work with Scott again, sir. Any guns I sell from this time on, the risk will be mine alone, as will the profits be,' he insisted.

Light had no illusions about his partner. Scott was an unscrupulous friend at best and, despite his respect for Soliman, would have no compunction at sacrificing the lad for his own end. 'I agree with you, Sol. You must only take chances for yourself, never for others – and that includes me. I do not wish to leech upon your profits. What I need from you, is information. You must have gleaned some whispers of what is to come. What do you know of Bugis intentions?'

Soliman leaned back against the wooden treads, staring up at the clear night sky. 'There is man with whom I have built a relationship. He is the key to Bugis plans, but he trusts no one. He cannot afford to, for the Dutch would pay a king's ransom for knowledge of his whereabouts. It is possible I can persuade him to accept an approach from you. That is all I am prepared to promise at the present time. If he discovers that I have so much as mentioned his name to a Feringghi, then my own safety will be compromised, for he has killed men for much less, I can assure you. And he loves the orang Inggeris no more than the orang Belanda.' Soliman reverted to Malay at the mention of the foreigners; the words had a derogatory edge, not lost on Light. He suspected it reflected Soliman's personal opinions with regard towards Light's own compatriots in general.

'I would be grateful if you could champion my cause with this fellow. I can offer him support as well as armaments. Since my Siamese contracts have dried up, I have a vast store to hand; he is welcome to take his pick. Remind him that the British also hate the Dutch, now more so than ever. Tell him that "his enemy is my enemy" and in this fact lies the best way of forging an alliance, one of mutual benefit. On a related matter. How stands my esteem with Selangor these days? There was a price upon my head in that kingdom not too long ago!'

The young man shrugged his shoulders. 'Their preoccupation is the Dutch. I think they have forgotten you, sir. Salehuddin is long dead. His son, Sultan Ibrahim, has no interest in past quarrels. He looks to the future. The old Bugis enmities have been set aside. Riau-Johor and Selangor have joined in alliance to strangle the Dutch in a vice between them. They will move from the north, the south and from the sea. I doubt he will object to an approach from you. I will make your case, Captain. Trust me. If anyone can win them to your cause, it can only be me.'

There was more than a hint of arrogant swagger to Soliman's assertion, although Light knew it to be a fair assessment of his chances. He enjoyed the lad's conceit, for it was based on conviction rather than braggadocio. Furthermore, it was exactly what Light had hoped for. Siam and Burma would soon be at war again. The Dutch would either be wholly occupied or driven out. That would leave the ailing throne of Queddah, riven with internal conflicts, and ripe for alliance.

'Good God, Soliman, you're a genius! What would any of us do without you? But take care not to fall into Dutch hands. They would be merciless if they knew who you really were.' Light threw his arm about the young man's neck and drew him close. 'Let no one know of our relationship, not because I am ashamed to be your father, the very opposite. For I love you dearly and would not wish harm to a single hair on that handsome head of yours!'

Soliman's smile stretched ear to ear. 'I am just a humble skipper with a small craft plying my trade. I run back and forth into Melaka and they suspect nothing, for the Dutch are stupid fools who do not believe a Malay can even think, let alone plan a conspiracy against them. They are condemned by their own self-importance.'

'All the same, take care. For people talk. There are those who would sell such information to the Dutch, even should it be a betrayal of one of their own. We live in a faithless world, my boy.'

As the year waned, Light found his optimism for the future quite renewed. Over in India, the British had finally prevailed and the French would soon be driven out of the region for good. It was time for the Company to once again look East.

***

Although Martinha had enjoyed the occasion, she had contributed little to the merriment, busy as she was organising food and drink and tending to the children. Her third daughter, Mary, was now four months old, a demanding baby, given to colic and difficult to feed. Thong Di believed the child's problems were the result of the prevailing state of Martinha's mind during her pregnancy. Her daughter had been distressed by her husband's blatant infidelity, and then further shaken by his apparent disappearance. Martinha had been convinced that her husband was dead and that what lay between them would never be resolved. An expectant mother should be calm and peaceful, not fired up by tempestuous emotions; it was well known that such passions were detrimental to the baby's health. Happily, Mary had arrived safely enough, for all that. She was a hale and hearty child, but bad humours lingered, and made the little one restless and unhappy.

Martinha had her own opinion. Throughout the months since her meeting with Amdaeng Rat, she had prayed night and day for God to bestow on her the gift of a son, for she believed that only a boy could re-instate her in her husband's heart. She had then been plummeted into the depths of a deep sadness by Francis' unexplained absence. And just when all hope seemed lost, he had returned, as ebullient as ever, fired on by his unlikely deliverance. Home in time for Mary's birth, he was as happy with his daughter as he would have been to welcome a son.

Yet Martinha herself had not found it so easy to accept. The bond that had been forged at birth with her other daughters did not this time take place. Instead, there was only dissatisfaction, tinged with bitterness. In her heart, she now believed in this lay her child's discomfort. The little girl sensed her mother's lack of maternal affection. Martinha's milk had been slow to come in and, even when it did, was deemed insufficient for the baby's needs. A wet nurse had been found, further distancing her from her child. This was the burden Martinha carried, ashamed even to discuss with her mother. Not to love your child enough was unnatural and obscene. It cast a light even on this happy Christmastide, for the Nativity story was a constant reminder of her own inadequacies as a mother.

Nor had her relationship with her mother recovered from Thong Di's response to Amdaeng Rat's presence in Kuala Bahang. Her dismissive reaction had convinced Martinha that she had known about it all along – and had chosen to keep the truth to herself. Perhaps everyone had been party to it, except her. Had she been the one naïve fool, a silly girl lost in a fantasy of a romance that had only ever existed within her dreams? The realisation stung deep. What else did she not know? Was this a tiny rock on the surface of the sea, concealing a huge underwater mountain beneath? And would she be broken on its jagged edges?

Whilst entirely sympathetic to her daughter's plight, Thong Di's motherly advice had largely comprised of 'pay no heed'. Although Francis was a good man, he was still a man for all that, and keeping mistresses behind a wife's back was what men did. Even Martim Rozells had maintained other women here and there in his younger days. If there had been children from those liaisons, then Thong Di had neither known nor cared. Martinha should follow her example. She was Francis' wife, that was enough to ensure her status.

In time, Martinha herself had indeed come around to this way of thinking. Compared to the lives of most, her marriage was perfection. Francis was a kindly man, with a sense of humour and a fondness for his family. He was also a passionate lover. She knew the place she held in his heart. Besides, during those awful weeks when she had feared Francis might have been lost at sea, his imperfections had seemed insignificant. If the Good Lord ever brought him back to her, she would readily forgive all else. And God had granted this request for which she was eternally grateful. Thus, she had slowly resigned herself that she might never have a son – and that Francis would always have a wandering eye.

His time as a prisoner-of-war had wrought changes on her husband. Whilst he might relish the opportunity to narrate his daring adventures before an audience, Francis had been deeply shaken by the experience. He had expected, at the very least, many months – even years – of confinement, and quite possibly death in a sea battle. Such brushes with mortality inevitably bring clarity. Francis had returned with a renewed appreciation for family life. His utter delight at little Mary's arrival appeared quite genuine; she was his unexpected, unlooked-for gift. At the time of her birth, he had even gone so far as to say that it meant nothing to him should he never father a son, for in his experience, the best people he had ever met in life had been of the female gender, saving Squire William, of course, the very best of men.

Not long after his return, Amdaeng Rat had returned to Thalang. Since her fateful discovery, Martinha had arranged for the lady to be watched, determined no longer to be the dupe kept in the dark. Thus, she had discovered that her love rival had been forced upon one of Light's vessels and transported back to Tharua, where she was now reunited with her family. Her pathetic husband – who had offered her for trade in the first place – subsequently refused to take her back now that she was encumbered by another man's child. Amdaeng Rat had been fortunate indeed that her parents hadn't thrown her out. Nona Light took great comfort from the fact that her chief rival was removed; she had won that particular battle. In future, Francis would never dare to flaunt a woman so close to home. Yet she had learned much from this sorry incident and would never be the gullible fool again. There would be other women, of that she was sure.

Despite her husband's declarations of love and promises to be a better man, Martinha knew her tiger was not about to lose his stripes. The conversation around the Christmas table attested to that. Now that the war in India was drawing to a close and the British victory had been won, his sights were once again set on the far horizon of his dreams. Nor would she wish to hold him back. She had no desire to change him. Francis was what he was. The pearl he had chased these many years was finally within reach. Perhaps, if he achieved his goal, he would find peace at last.

But all the same, the next time that he sailed to India, Martinha intended to go with him.

27

Raja Haji

Kota Malawati, Selangor River. Early February 1784

It was the most clandestine of ventures, quite as dangerous as his many forays through French-infested waters in the Coromandel. The southern Straits was on the brink of a mighty conflict and enemies lurked everywhere. In the midst of this uncertainty, Light sailed from Queddah on the pretext of a regular trading visit to Thalang, No one knew his real destination, not even Scott. So much for his promises of candour to his wife.

The *Bristol* rendezvoused with the *Harimau* in a glistening cove lying in the embrace of a tiny forested islet off the north coast of Perak. While the scattered denizens of nearby Pangkor island may have noticed the large privateer and a small local vessel, two ships passing on this busy maritime route would cause little suspicion. Furthermore, it was unlikely anyone had observed them dropping anchor in the impossibly lovely emerald bay that looked outwards to the open Straits, providing the ideal secluded anchorage for a ship that wished to be concealed.

In the tranquil natural harbour, Light instructed his men to spend a day or two enjoying the crystal waters and plentiful fishing grounds, whilst he boarded the *Harimau* dressed in the flowing gown and turban of a Chulia merchant, grateful for his sturdy beard growth. In naval fashion, he was rarely hirsute, so his disguise was well-judged. The journey south was short, skirting the Perak coastline until they approached the wide swampy estuary of the Selangor river. Even so, Light kept to the small cabin. He might pass for a light-skinned Indian at a distance, but his blue-green eyes would give the game away up close.

It was early evening when they neared their destination, the new fort at Bukit Malawati rearing up with menace above the river's winding reach. The wharf below was a riot of gaudy perahus festooned with strips of garish cloths, their bows carved as brightly painted birds. High above this scene of sleepy indolence, woolly clouds of silver-grey frothed in the orange-red setting sun that cast a glistening golden shadow across the pewter waters. But it would have been wholly unwise to let the glory of the evening relax their vigilance, any more than they would have lowered their guard in the dense jungle that clung to either bank. Their every move was watched; the fort's cannons were trained upon them.

Silent warriors, Bugis keris tucked proudly in their belts, emerged to line the wooden jetty. Soliman exchanged a brief word with their leader; he merely scowled by way of reply. Light disembarked, forced to walk the gauntlet of the hostile guard who menaced but did not impede his progress. Their aim was to intimidate – and they were successful. From now on, they were reminding him, Light was at their mercy, walking into the tiger's lair, with only Soliman to intercede for him. One Englishman alone amongst a horde of Buginese, and his only defender a mere Malay.

No time was wasted. They were led up a steep stone staircase to the fortifications fringed by an impressive platform of cannonry, from where the view of the river over the thick mangrove to the shimmering sea was breath-taking. Seated cross-legged on a pile of cushions in the shade, smoking on a pipe of tobacco, Soliman's mysterious contact awaited. Although Light had never met him, he recognised the man instantly, partly because he had already presumed his identity, but also for his similarity to his older brother, whom Light had known passably well.

This was Raja Haji Fisabilillah, the younger sibling of the previous Sultan of Selangor. The two brothers were of a similar type: stocky, fleshy Buginese with the stature of hardened warriors. Light approached with respect, bowing: 'Yang di-Pertuan Raja Muda. Your Majesty.'

Light's assumption had been correct. Ten years ago, the self-same Raja Haji with his Bugismen had driven old Sultan Muhammed Jiwa from his capital at Alor Setar, ransacking the palace and raiding the Chulia ships in the harbour. Raji Haji had thus been the spark to the tinder of almost everything that had then occurred. This enigmatic man had his tentacles looped around the entire decade.

Now the onetime warlord was Yamtuan Raja Muda of the Johor-Riau Sultanate, the true power in the southern Straits, presiding over a veritable golden age of Bugis trade that had recently eclipsed Dutch pre-eminence. He was a fascinating character of contrasts, the link between the previously estranged Bugis groups, unusually able to garner support both from Selangor and Johor, effectively trapping the hated Dutch in a vice between the two states. The Dutch greatly feared him. That alone was enough to make him a person of great interest to the British.

But Raja Haji was much more than a Bugis adventurer with

fortuitous connections. It was generally agreed that Raja Haji was a learned man, a visionary, who had travelled far and wide and had absorbed wisdom from many sources. And now he was determined to rid the Straits of the Dutch menace for good.

Raja Haji smiled in response to Light's respectful address, but without much visible warmth. 'So, the notorious Captain Light, we meet at last! I have long been curious about you.' The Bugis leader set down his pipe, beckoning Light to move closer. 'No need for too much formality, Kapitan. You may refer to me as Yamtuan for, despite my name, I am no king.' True enough, but all the same, he was the real power behind at least one throne.

Light gave another gracious bow. 'Most respected Yamtuan, I thank you for welcoming me at such a momentous time for the Bugis alliance. I understand you may be wary, for my relationship with your brother, the late sultan, was not always an easy one. I believe, however, that today we live in a different era, and that our interests are now closely aligned. To set aside the past and look to a mutually beneficial future would be in both our interests.'

Raja Haji chuckled at Light's attempt at formal Malay address. 'Perhaps we should set aside the clever words, Kapitan. I do not have the time for protocol. It is to your good fortune that the Inggeris now assume the position of friends of the Bugis for the simple reason that we are both enemies of the Belanda. Yet, you are evidently far from comfortable in this setting, that much is plain to see. You do not trust me. And may I say, I do not trust you either. Which makes us both sensible men. By the way, your outfit is ridiculous. It fools no one. You may be able to speak the language of the Straits, but you will never pass for one of its people.'

Light threw off his turban, tossing it to Soliman, in recognition of his tawdry attempt at masquerade. 'I quite agree. We westerners look utter fools in native garb. Let's be candid with each other, Tuan. You're a long way from home with the Dutch baying at your heels, despite being an honoured guest in your nephew's kingdom. Thus, you cannot afford to be overly choosy in your friends these days. This is my offer: a quantity of weaponry and a plentiful supply of rice. Furthermore, I promise to render no help to the Dutch or their allies. Know this, however. I am here in an independent capacity and do not speak on the behalf of the Honourable Company, or indeed my nation. I can assure you this much: although the British will not fight on your behalf, they will be more than happy to harry Dutch shipping in any way they can. Whatever you have heard about me in the past, I think you know I am a man who keeps his word. So, may we talk business?'

Raja Haji listened carefully, his attention fixed. 'A man who keeps his word? Perhaps you are, or at least as much as any of your kind is able, I suppose. But the word of a Christian is very unreliable commodity. It is a pot with many holes. Do not take me for a fool like that little prancing cock, Abdullah. I know that you are useful to me, or you would not be here. I also know that I am crucial to the future plans of your Company. So, let's not pretend that either of us is doing the other any favours, eh?'

Unusual in a negotiation with a local leader, Raja Haji had come straight to the point, where it was generally the custom to dance about the houses of politeness and pretence. Light decided that he rather liked the Yamtuan. He also decided not to accord him a single inch of leeway. 'I would hazard a guess that however much the British desire alliance with you, your need of us is so much greater. I take it you are planning to lay siege to Melaka? Quite a daunting ambition, if I may say so.' Light dangled his bait.

Raja Haji shot a withering glance towards Soliman standing in the rear. 'Are you a snake in the grass, boy?'

Soliman dropped to his knees. 'I told him nothing, sir, I swear!'

Light continued. 'He did not need to reveal your plans, Yamtuan. They are obvious. You must either launch an attack on Melaka soon or hide in Riau until the inevitable arrival of an armada from Batavia, or perhaps even from Amsterdam!'

Raja Haji indicated for Soliman to stand, turning his attention back to Light. 'You are very astute, Kapitan Light. It makes no odds if my plans are now revealed, because we attack any day. The Sultan of Selangor, my nephew Ibrahim, has assembled his forces. The Minangs of Rembau are with us, and, of course, the armies of Johor. Together we will strangle the Dutch vermin in their nest. I want any guns, powder, cannon and foodstuffs you can supply. But speed is of the essence. How long will it take to fulfil my request?'

'But, Tuan, you haven't asked my price,' Light retorted with wry amusement.

Raja Haji countered bluntly. 'You'll take what I pay you, Kapitan, for the true reward is in what's to come.'

Light let his response hang in the air, maintaining his sardonic face, playing out his various gambits. Finally: 'Men say you are a mystic with supernatural abilities, able to control men's minds, and even look into the future.' It was impossible to tell if this was meant as mockery or praise.

This time, Raja Haji's eyes crinkled; he was genuinely enjoying the back-and-forth. 'What men "say" about me, I have found, is generally enough. I do not need to defend my reputation if it has already preceded me. Like you, Kapitan, I am a clever man. Yes, I have many and varied gifts. But it is up to you to decide for yourself wherein my real abilities lie,' was his equally oblique reply. 'Now, how long will you take to supply my weapons?'

'They are waiting for you but a day's sail away off Perak.' Light had been expected this conclusion. For what was the chance that a warmonger would not require weapons of war?

Well satisfied, Raja Haji settled back, an expression of approval on his face. 'It suits us very well that you Inggeris care more for commerce than for conquest. That is the very reason we are prepared to trade with you.' Raja Haji motioned over to his men, who carried forth an open chest of silver Java rupees. 'How fortuitous that the warship *Welvaaren* lingered awhile before it sank beneath our Riau waters. There was time for us to relieve it of some of its cargo. It seems fitting that my enemy should pay for the instruments of its own destruction.'

The deal was quickly done. Neither man had time for further pleasantries. By nightfall they were back at sea, in the company of Bugis vessels. The commodity exchange was completed by morning. Light and Soliman watched from the *Bristol* as the Bugis ships sailed away, now much lower in the water, loaded down with armaments as they were. 'A good day's work, Francis,' Soliman observed, his eyes set firmly on the departing ships, deep in thought.

Light concurred. 'The real benefits, however, as Raja Haji so acutely reminded us, will be in the times to come. This is a singular moment, Sol. Imagine should they achieve their aim and drive the Dutch out of Melaka and back to Batavia? The Straits will once again be free for all traders without constraint!'

Soliman did not appear quite so convinced. He patted his benefactor fondly on his back as he made moves to take his leave. 'You don't believe that any more than I do, Captain. For the British are waiting on the horizon to sweep down like eagles from the clouds to snatch up the tastiest morsels. Don't take us for fools, sir. We know the way the land lies. What is that thing you say? Ah yes, "betwixt the devil and the deep blue sea". Which will you English prove to be, I wonder?'

Light placed a restraining hand on Soliman's arm as he swung his legs over the side. 'Then, why are you on my side, Sol, if you do not trust my motives?'

Soliman grinned back, still the honest and affectionate boy of old. 'I trust you completely, at least as far as my own life and safety go. And as a trader, I know if I invest in you, I will one day be a rich man. But you are not the Company, sir. Nor do you really care about the fate of my people. For this, I do not blame you. Nor do I blame the Bugis. Or even the Dutch for that matter. People come into these waters. It is how it has been for all time. Every man must make his fortune as he may. But nor do I shut my eyes to what is happening. The Straits is changing. It will never be the same again.'

'You either change with it or be left behind, Sol,' Light warned.

'Indeed, sir. Know that you will always have my support. For you are a good man in a bad world. Like Raja Haji. *Sama sama.* You have both earned my loyalty. Always, sir.'

The two men embraced. 'You took a risk for me today. My eternal thanks, Sol.'

'No risk. I knew the Yamtuan would take to you. Everybody does,' Soliman grinned.

'Then perhaps I raised you in my image after all, for it is clear he holds you in high regard, lad!' They both laughed as Soliman skimmed deftly down the ladder towards the waiting skiff. 'Take care, Sol. Don't get embroiled in the coming fight. You are not a soldier. Leave that to those who are.'

Soliman saluted to his stepfather, jumping lightly into the boat that barely rocked at his deft landing. 'I have no intention to be part of it, Captain! I head north to Mergui. I do not plan to be anywhere near the south for the next few months. And you? Where is your next port of call?'

'Thalang. I need to justify my untruth. Watch out for Burmese up in Mergui. Rumour has it they're on the move again. Perchance we'll meet in Tharua anon? I look forward to it, Sol!'

Even as the *Harimau* sailed away, Light doubted that the next few months would see the end of Holland's sway. The Bugis would poke their stick at them, lay siege for months, damage VOC trade significantly, but in the end, the Dutch would prevail. They had time and armies on their side – and the confidence that the Bugis alliance would never hold for long. That was the winning card in every game in the Indies. The local peoples' volatile independence would always be its downfall.

It made no odds. Either way fed his own vision for the future. Dutch weakness offered an ideal time for the British to assert their authority; Dutch strength would provoke Calcutta into necessary action to protect their interests. All that was needed in this rich stew pot was a stick to stir the brew.

* * *

By April Malacca was under siege, the Bugis encroaching daily on the outer perimeter until the very town itself was nigh on breached. It was only a matter of time until every dog and rat was eaten, and the city forced to surrender, held back only by the stout defence of the local people, who, despite their own reservations against their foreign masters, had no wish either to fall to Bugis marauders. Better the devil they knew than the one that they did not. The siege held through May and into June until fate decided the result. A passing rifle shot from the battlements struck Raja Haji; he died later that same day.

The strength of the coalition had rested solely on the mercurial personality of its leader. No sooner was he gone than the entire alliance collapsed. The Minangs sued for peace; the Sultan of Selangor fled into exile; the Bugis retreated back to their island archipelago to select another Yamtuan and lick their wounds. Even the young Sultan of Johor chose this moment to flex his fledgling muscles, offering support to the Dutch in return for freedom from his Bugis masters. The sun was setting fast on the Golden Age of Riau.

And just as Soliman had predicted, the British watched and learned. James Scott wrote to Warren Hastings with a colourful rendition of his dreadful treatment at the hands of the Dutch, a complete outrage against an innocent British subject. He urged the Governor-General to look to Penang, a little jewel of an island off Queddah, for the British in the Straits, who had been much wronged, needed a solid base from which to protect their trading interests more so than ever, or such travesties would continue.

And Hastings proved true to his word. A delegation led by one Captain Thomas Forrest was sent out to test the water at the court of Queddah. Forrest was impressed by the possibility of a British base on the 'Arekanut island' of Penang, even compiling detailed maps with observations. But Sultan Abdullah preferred his own trusted representative to conduct the negotiations. And waiting in the wings was Captain Francis Light, ready to step forward on the stage to claim the applause of all.

28

Anna Maria

Calcutta. October 1784

The crossing of the Andaman Sea to Bengal was a miserable interlude for Martinha, having never before made a journey longer than up or down the coast. The open sea terrified her. The ploughing progress of the ship, the sudden onset of fierce storms, the total absence of landfall in an endless watery horizon, and the claustrophobic, uncomfortable world of men, left her unsettled and ridden with gloomy premonitions.

She had left her daughters at home. They were safe, of that she had no doubt, but, almost as soon as the familiar coastline of her home had disappeared from view, she was assailed with a dark conviction that she might never see her children again. Her determination to stay close to her wayward husband had blinded her to her duties as a mother, which responsibility ought to be her primary concern. It was too late now to change her mind. There was no escape from fate.

Intense relief at attaining the wide entrance to the mighty Hooghly river and their anchorage at Kedgeree kept her fear of the return journey temporarily at bay. Her feet would soon attain dry land; the first half of her torment would be at an end. But even then, anxiety nibbled at her soul. This was a foreign land where her status was unclear; she was neither local nor a respected visitor. Francis was his usual optimistic self, delighting to be back in town. His attachment to Calcutta was strong. With a jarring sense of shock, she realised that her husband had a separate existence amongst his British countrymen of which she knew nothing. In no small measure it was as if he had returned home to England. Martinha saw a very different side to him as he plunged back into familiar ways.

No sooner had they arrived than her husband sent for seamstresses to fit Martinha with suitable western attire for various public engagements. She for her part remained ambivalent; it was unlikely in the eyes of the condescending British residents of Bengal that a mixed-race woman from the Indies would be acceptable in society. But when she voiced her concerns, Francis brushed them aside. 'You are not a *Bibi*, Martinha! You're a Christian woman of noble birth, both in Siam and Queddah! Why, your name itself is Portuguese! Once dressed in western garb, you'll look the very image of a refined gentlewoman!' Martinha wished she could share his certainty.

Arrayed in unfamiliar European dress, Martinha had further doubts. She found the clothes cumbersome and constricting, wholly unsuited to the climate and uncomfortable to wear. Yet when she caught sight of herself in the mirror, the woman staring back already seemed immeasurably altered. She was a different lady, elegant and beguiling. But would Calcutta see the same thing?

At first, her fears appeared unfounded. When they drove around the astonishing city to visit its many wondrous entertainments, Martinha observed rich women, many of them native, dressed both as English ladies or swathed in the exotic saris of India. They were accompanied by their British 'husbands' even in public places, with no apparent disapproval. While her apprehensions remained, she vowed to do her best for Francis' sake. This trip was of the utmost importance. She must not let him down.

One afternoon they were invited to dine at Belvedere with the governor-general himself. Such an invitation was an honour extended only to those in the highest echelons; Francis believed it to be an indicator of his future status, an introduction to the most influential families in the city. Light and Martinha attended in the company of William Fairlie, now a stalwart of the Bengal Council, whose star continued to ascend in the Company firmament. They were Fairlie's houseguests. He was Light's patron in Bengal, eager to introduce the experienced Captain Light as a man in whom the Company should put its trust. Fairlie was proving to be an expedient ally.

Martinha disliked the pompous, self-satisfied Scot on sight, nor did he show her even the least interest, save for an unctuous bow whenever she entered a room. Beyond that, Fairlie neither addressed her directly, nor behaved as if she was even present. Francis seemed not to notice this disregard, or if he did, he accepted Fairlie's discourtesy as a matter of course. That unsettled her. Was this how Englishmen treated their wives in society? During the elegant carriage ride out to Alipore, while Francis and William chatted idly about the ever-expanding city, Martinha mulled over her near-invisibility and what it augured for the social gathering ahead.

Her misgivings were temporarily set aside as they crossed the extensive deer park and approached the magnificent white palace that was Belvedere. Astonishment drove all other considerations from her mind, even if disquiet still curdled in the pit of her stomach at such unimaginable grandeur. Chancing a glance across at Francis, she was disconcerted all the more; his utter pleasure in his whereabouts demonstrated the gulf that lay between them. This was the world to which her husband aspired.

Dinner was an ordeal. The food was pasty and bland, swimming in pale, tasteless sauces, heavy with dry meats, and served in a bewildering complexity of dishes. Her place setting was laid with a multitude of intricate cutlery, the function of which was quite unknown to her. Only by paying careful attention to the behaviour of the others did she select the correct utensil and discover the proper way to proceed. But as her appetite had quite deserted her, she found herself merely nibbling at food and sipping on her glass of sweet wine.

Francis was seated further down the table, as peculiar British etiquette demanded, while she had been placed between two strangers, a man who ignored her and a woman who spoke about her as if she was not there to another lady across the table.

'She doesn't eat much, does she?' the lady across the table commented to her neighbour. 'No doubt that explains her undernourished size.'

Martinha realised with a start they were speaking of her. Did they not realise that she understood English?

'Scrawny, as all these girls in the Indies, although not unpleasant to look at. Fair enough in the skin, too. Their children will be attractive, no doubt,' the lady next to her replied, without any sense of embarrassment. Women in Martinha's world could be scathing and cruel to an outsider, but it was rarely that such a public display of rudeness was voiced. It would be considered uncouth to be so openly discourteous.

At first, Martinha ignored the remarks, concentrating on the intricacies of her food, but then decided she ought to indicate she understood their language, rather than lead them further into impoliteness.

'You stay longtime in India, Ma'am?'

Her simple inquiry, the archetypal opener at any table in Calcutta, was received with blank incomprehension. The women looked about them with knowing expressions as if she had quite spoken out of turn. 'My word,' her neighbour muttered. 'Is that some foreign tongue?'

Her friend tittered cruelly. 'I think she's trying to speak English, my dear. But I couldn't for the life of me construe the sense of it!' They both laughed heartily.

Martinha dropped her head. It was impossible she had been misunderstood. They meant to wound.

The meal continued on and on, course after groaning course. Martinha set her face in a rigid but demure expression, and sat out the excruciating experience. All the while, further down the table, Francis himself was as merry as a lark, completely insensible to her predicament, basking in the attention of those seated by him who eagerly lapped up his supply of stories.

Finally, the ladies rose, as if by some unseen signal, gathering their purses, rearranging their attire, and giggling at the gentlemen, those naughty boys who were to be left at table for who knew what further indulgences. Martinha looked in askance towards Francis, whose head was turned away from her; he was deep in conversation offering farewells to a lady seated nearby. Martinha was left entirely unsure what next she ought to do.

'Come, my dear,' murmured a voice from behind her, and a gentle female hand was placed upon her arm. 'Let's leave these fellows to their brandy and cigars, whilst we retreat for fresher air and more genteel conversation!'

The breezy invitation took her quite by surprise after so long a time as a pariah. She allowed herself to be swept from the room and into another smaller chamber beyond dominated by huge glass doors opening out onto a deep shady terrace, refreshed by a cooling breeze. The other women settled themselves within on the well-upholstered silk chairs, eagerly accepting glasses of port, but Martinha found herself steered towards the garden itself by the same mysterious woman who had rescued her.

Once outside, amidst the riot of flowers and greenery, the two women took seats by a fountain crowned by twin cherubs spurting spouts of water that were captured in a huge stone leaf. 'I must apologise for prevailing upon your attention, my dear, but it seemed you were somewhat forlorn. As your host, I am wholly to blame. I should have given more thought to the seating arrangements.'

Until that moment, Martinha had believed her English fluent. It was not a matter of the individual words the lady said, but more the way they were pronounced that confounded her. Her accent was strangely guttural and flat to her ears. Yet something of the woman's manner told her that her attentions were kindly meant, so she smiled back, and waited expectantly for enlightenment to come.

The lady beamed. 'Forgive me, Mrs Light. You do not know who I am! I had quite forgot that my reputation does not precede me everywhere in the world. I am Marian Hastings. My husband is the governor-general, Sir Warren.'

What followed was the only bright spot in a day of abject misery. Lady Hastings was a charming and benevolent host, although it was only much later that Martinha came to appreciate how fortunate she was to have secured this lady's support. At first, they chatted amiably on inconsequential matters in a simple English that Martinha could follow, settling her into the conversation. It was evident that Lady Hastings was well used to putting others at their ease. 'Your English is exceptional, my dear. I thought at first you had not been able to follow the dinner conversation. Now I realise to my distress that you followed it only too well. May I apologise for the arrant rudeness of those ladies. I am not insensible to their prejudices but I had imagined that on such an occasion good manners might prevail over narrow-minded intolerance. But I should have known better. For there is nothing that these empty-headed people love more than a victim upon whom they can pour their vitriolic ridicule. So much the better if she is a beautiful foreign woman married to the most handsome man in the room!'

Lady Hastings spoke with passion, almost as if she herself had tasted similar rancour in the past. Martinha blushed at the unexpected compliment, looking down at her lap where she twisted her hands together nervously. 'I didn't understand everything, my lady. My English not so good as it should be,' she added softly.

'Nonsense!' Lady Hastings disagreed. 'It is perfectly adequate! English is a most ridiculous language. Even one who understands it perfectly can find oneself lost in a conversation. For it is not the words themselves that are complex but the labyrinthine manner with which the sentences are put together. Why, half the time they appear to say the opposite of what they actually mean! What sounds like a compliment is in reality the gravest insult. What comes over as offence was meant as an hilarious joke. It is the damnedest language to comprehend. The English seem wholly incapable of saying simply what they mean. Or meaning what they say, for that matter,' she added, with a bitter note of resignation.

'Are you not English then, Lady Hastings?' The woman's solidarity suggested she was speaking from an understanding of Martinha's plight.

'I most certainly am *not* English, my dear lady! I am German, and, despite the fact that I share this honour with King George himself, I am regarded by the British as something of a coarse savage with an incomprehensible and crude language, a source of mockery to them. Furthermore, although I have been sedately married to my husband for many years, I am considered a shameless harridan, quite an achievement amongst such a gaggle of harpies, I can assure you. You see, I am a divorcée. Which in society makes me akin to a loose woman, never to be forgiven for my earlier transgression, even though my first husband was a brute and Mr. Hastings is the most devoted of partners. Yet I shall always be portrayed as the seductress, the woman of ill-repute who brought shame and scandal to the office of the governor-general. Only the fact that my husband is the most senior statesman in the entirety of British India forces them to grovel and fawn in my presence, which makes them hate me all the more, of course!'

Marian Hastings did not at all appear to be discommoded by this state of affairs, chortling gaily to herself. She was still a handsome woman, although Martinha presumed her to be of quite mature years, at least thirty-five, if not older. She was a good few inches taller than her diminutive husband, slender with narrow shoulders and the whitest of complexions. Her pallor, however, was enlivened by the flame-red tumbling curls that framed a narrow face saved from plainness by large liquid green eyes and the vitality of her expression.

Martinha had never seen such colouring in her life, and found it hard to tear her gaze from the russet loveliness of her hair. It was even more mystifying that this noble woman, one of the great figures of the age, should suggest a kinship between them.

'You are too kind, my lady,' was all that she could muster by way of reply. 'I do not believe I can be accepted by these people. They speak as if I were invisible. I fear I shall be an embarrassment to my husband.' Martinha exclaimed.

'Not at all!' Marian Hastings replied with vehemence. 'You are already the talk of the town, dear Martinha. Of course, they will be catty towards you, sharpening their talons to wound. For how else would you know you mattered in society? If they thought you insignificant, they would pay you no mind at all. Is it so very different amongst your people? I hear the citizens of the Indies are remarkably courteous and polite.'

Martinha relaxed, replying with a smile. 'They do pretend to courtesy, that is true. And I doubt there would be insults around a dinner table. But they can be just as cruel, I can assure you. For people are placed into ranks with such rigidity that those below are all but invisible.'

'Aha!!! So, the caste system thrives there just as here! Every society has its own particular ways to wound, it seems. Let me give you some advice, my dear, before we return and join the others. First, acknowledge that you will always be an outsider. They will not accept you as the wife of an English gentleman. Although they might tolerate you as his mistress.'

'But Francis and I are married!' Martinha added. 'In a Nuptial Mass!'

Lady Hastings tutted. 'I wouldn't make too much of that. Mrs. Light. Popery is worse than Hindooism here, my sweet. Better to let them think you are an exotic Malay queen than a mulatto Catholic!'

Martinha stared back in utter surprise at the very concept. How could that be? Were they not all Christians, after all? She found these English people almost impossible to understand.

Lady Hastings was amused. 'I know, it is quite nonsensical, but the British are the most intolerant people on God's earth – with the possible exception of the Germans, that is, who are equally as wooden-headed in their prejudices. My dear Martinha, I have enjoyed our little conversation today. We must meet again before you leave! There is much for you to learn. I cannot expect you to grasp it all in just one day.'

The conversation had already given Martinha much to think about, even before Lady Hastings moved on to her final piece of sisterly advice. Rising from the seat, indicating that Martinha should do the same, Lady Hastings announced her intention to return to her guests.

'That dress suits you perfectly, but if I may suggest one thing? It matters not at all to these women how becoming your frock may be. To put it very bluntly, they would most cruelly remark "you may put a silk dress upon a goat, but it is still a goat." Particularly if you wear their fashions and outshine them. I recommend that instead of aping English gentleladies (who for the most part are neither gentle nor ladies), you should accentuate the part of yourself that is different. Or they will always regard you as a mere exhibit in a Cabinet of Curiosities. Display yourself and give them something to twitter about! Wear those beautiful fabrics of your native people and flaunt your exotic beauty with pride! Make them face the truth: that you are a beautiful foreign woman, and you sleep in the bed of the most desirable man in the room. While they may never like you, my dear, nor will they be able to ignore you.'

And with those words of wisdom, no doubt handpicked from the benefit of her own personal experience, Lady Marian Hastings swept into the withdrawing room. As they approached the gathering of ladies, all curious to know quite what the illustrious first lady might have had to say to the little native upstart, Madame Hastings whispered to Martinha under her breath: 'And do call me Anna Maria in future, my dear, for after all, that is my given name.'

29

Pooloo Pinang

The Council House, Esplanade Row, Calcutta. October 1784
A few days later, Light met with Sir Warren Hastings himself in his rooms at the Council House. It was four years since they had last met and time had weighed heavily on him. His hair was now completely grey, carefully coiffured around an entirely bald dome. His etched face was thinner and more lined, although his colouring was fresh. The light still gleamed in his eyes. Whilst not a sick man, his responsibilities had taken a heavy toll. There was but eight years in age between them, but it might have been eighteen.

'It has been too long, sir,' Light began with a bow, extending his hand.

Hastings replied, with a hint of a wry smile. 'That is the very nature of time, Captain. It passes quicker than we are able to run after it, I fear.'

They shook hands and settled down, the formidable teak desk between them. 'I'll not beat around the bush, Light, for we know exactly where we stand. When last we met, I promised you we would revisit the matter of an establishment in the Straits after the war was done. That time has now come. Recent events have made it even more pressing that we proceed. I had high hopes this Raja Haji fellow might rid us of the Hollanders, but it appears he is now dead and the Dutch have reclaimed their primacy. Are you aware of Captain Forrest's recent mission?'

Light had met with the celebrated Thomas Forrest a few months earlier in Queddah. Forrest, a former Navy man and captain of a Calcutta syndicate, was well known as an intrepid surveyor of the lesser known waters of the East. Fluent in several languages, he was held in high regard. It spoke of the serious intention of the governor-general that he had sent out such a representative to lay the ground work for alliance. Forrest was no Monckton.

During his travels north through the Mergui archipelago, Forrest had framed the notion that there lay the perfect location for a British settlement, untrammelled as it was by the issues of the southern Straits, but in easy reach of India. Having presented his findings to Hastings, he had been sent back with credentials to present himself in Riau: Hastings had been interested in supporting Raja Haji in the hope that the Dutch would be driven out.

But the Yamtuan was already dead by the time he had arrived. Instead Forrest had withdrawn to Jangsylan, meeting with Lady Chan and James Scott, whom Forrest called 'a very sensible and intelligent gentleman'. Scott must have been on his best behaviour, Light had remarked when he heard Forrest's impression of his unconventional friend. It was at this time that Forrest had first learned of the island of Penang – and had been subsequently most impressed at its suitability.

Hastings pointed to a series of papers laid out before him on his desk. 'Captain Forrest has been most assiduous in his reports. He has recommended a joint settlement – two bases, one in the Mergui archipelago and the other on the island of Penang. He believes that Sultan Abdullah may be amenable if approached in a sensitive manner. Your thoughts, Light?'

Light's courtship of Thomas Forrest had clearly paid off. Initially, on being informed of his arrival, Light had been affronted that Hastings has sent out another officer above his head, but on meeting the man, Light had quickly come to realise that the honourable and forthright Forrest was the best hand he could have been offered. Naturally the Company would send out one of its own to make the first approaches. Forrest's impartial acuity and local knowledge had already led him to the conclusion that this region was most suited to British interests; it had only taken nudges from Light himself, his friends in Jangsylan – not to mention the self-interest of Jamual in Queddah – to convince.

'Captain Forrest is a remarkably astute fellow, with a vast knowledge of the Indies and beyond. It was a pleasure to meet him,' Light answered. 'I believe he was favourably impressed with the island of Pooloo Pinang. In the light of recent developments in Siam, I would entirely concur with him that it would be in British interests to negotiate an agreement with Sultan Abdullah.'

'But what of Mergui? Forrest was much taken with the area.' He held a paper close to his eyes, searching for a line. 'He refers to it as "The Remarkable Islands of Mergui".'

'In truth, Mergui is exactly as he describes. A wondrous place, rich in resources and almost entirely unoccupied. The problem, however, is the politics of the nearby kingdoms. Burma has risen again and appears to be on the cusp of another devastating attack on Siam. Both kingdoms claim the wealth of Mergui. It would not be an advantageous moment to chance an incursion.'

'Indeed, indeed.' muttered the governor-general. 'We do

not wish for another war. Anything but that!' He rolled his eyes heavenward. It was unclear whether 'we' meant the Company headquarters in London, or if it was a reference to his own career. Despite his victory against the French, the reputation of Warren Hastings was at an all-time low. He had spent too much money. Now that the war was won, the huge drop in Company profits to pay for it was the only consideration. It was a thankless reward for his mighty efforts.

'And you yourself fully believe this island Pinang to have as much potential as Forrest and Scott?' Hastings shot the question at him, a swift change of direction, possibly meant to catch him off guard. 'You were once in favour of Jangsylan. What has caused this radical change of opinion? I hear it is a largely uninhabited isle. The cost of settlement – and the time it will take to make it viable – might make it a prohibitive prospect.'

But Light was ready for this objection. He knew that he must justify his volte-face. 'I have not changed my mind, sir. Of all the places in the region, I still believe Jangsylan to be the most perfect location. But Siam has become a different place with the accession of King Rama. He would never agree to it.'

'Burma and Siam will clash. How can he prevent us if the people of Jangsylan invite us in?' Hastings argued, the devil's advocate.

'Should we make a move we would find ourselves trapped in the very local warfare you so wish to avoid. If Burma wins, Jangsylan will fall. If Siam wins, Rama will attack. Much as it pains me, I have had to accept that the window of opportunity has now closed on Jangsylan.' Implicit in his response was a note of culpability directed at Hastings. They should have moved earlier.

The governor-general did not shirk his responsibility.

'Of course, you are right. This matter should have been resolved years ago. I do not hold you responsible in any way for our tardiness in this regard. But will Queddah give up the island easily? Or will they demand all manner of impossible terms?'

Light had prepared what he believed was a compelling proof of the ease with which he might negotiate the delivery of the island of Penang into British hands. It had begun as a fancy of James Scott's, way back at the time of his betrothal to Martinha. Sultan Muhammed Jiwa had arranged the marriage. Scott had suggested he might ask for the island of Penang as dowry. At the time, Light had dismissed it. He neither wanted the island nor believed it appropriate to ask. But several times since, Light had implied that the grant had actually been given until he had almost begun to believe his own untruth. The sultan was dead. Who could contradict him?

'I am sure Sultan Abdullah will have all sorts of ridiculous demands at first. It is always the way in these circumstances. He must save face, after all. But he needs us desperately, assailed as he is both home and abroad. In the end, he must bow down to the inevitable. There is also another ace in my hand regarding Penang island. His father, the old sultan promised it to my wife as part of her marriage portion back in '72. Abdullah is fully aware of this, although there was never formal ratification. But this is why he is inclined to hand it to me – because, in a sense, I already own it.'

'Good God, man! That is a turn up for the books. I had no idea. And you think the sense of honour that surrounds such bequests, especially from a deceased sultan, will tip the balance in your favour?' Hastings questioned.

Light nodded sagely. 'I do indeed, sir. Much is placed on the royal word. It will also be easier to convince the court at large. The island is being presented as dowry, not given away as a foreign concession.'

'Legally, it could be returned.'

'Just so, sir. Although I would like to see them try to reclaim it from us in years hence.'

Hastings grunted in satisfaction. 'You've thought this all out, haven't you, man?'

'For years, sir. For years.' Light replied with relish, again reminding his superior how long this establishment has been in the making. 'And as to the matter of the time and cost, the subsequent rewards will be incalculable, my word on't. Nothing ventured, nothing gained, sir. We cannot waste this golden opportunity.'

The governor-general rubbed his forehead in thought. Light knew Hastings wanted to agree but his natural caution was holding him back. Then, as if his mind was made up all in a flash, he sat back up straight and gave Light the full benefit of his piercing gaze.

'So then, sir. If you have been planning this for many years, what then is your opinion on how we might proceed?' Once convinced, he went straight to the point.

This was Light's chance. It was a speech he had been rehearsing for weeks, tossing and turning the words over in his mind, writing and re-writing his thoughts throughout the long sea crossing. He took a deep breath, composed himself, and launched into the gambit that he believed might be the most important discourse of his life.

'This is a singular moment in the Indies, sir. For the first time in over a century, the Dutch are in disarray. They may have won the struggle with the Bugis but it has been at great cost. They are severely hobbled; it will take years to regain their previous dominion. Furthermore, the Bugis themselves received a mighty blow and have retreated back to Riau to lick their wounds. The Sultan of Johor is taking advantage of this unexpected gift to extricate himself from their yoke. To the north, the imminent clash of Burma and Siam makes all the rulers of the Peninsula nervous. They worry that the winner will view the vacuum in the Straits as ripe for the picking. Never was there a better moment for the British, sir! They all look to us for support because we are known, not as empire builders or land grabbers, but as merchants who believe in free trade for all. Wherever we go, we create markets and fortunes, not just for ourselves but for those in alliance with us. I believe the Sultan of Queddah will be open to a serious proposal, but with one important caveat …'

'… We will never offer him military assistance, Light. That is not a matter for negotiation. We will not send troops to defend him from the Bugis, the Dutch, the Siamese or the Burmese!' Hastings broke in, thumping his fist on the desk at the mention of each rival.

Light nodded his head in full agreement. 'That is incontrovertible, sir. It would be a most grievous error to become embroiled in their internecine conflicts. No, that is not the caveat to which I refer. These Malay sultans are proud, Governor-General. They are unconvinced by the British, for they do not trust those of the Christian faith. They also have a very intricate court protocol. Even the most innocent comment may rile them in a fury enough to run wild and damage their own interests. There is a word in their language for a peculiar indigenous response, impossible to render in our language for we British do not suffer from this particular condition. The word is 'amok'. The wrong approach – no matter how beneficial the alliance – might inflame the sultan with the result his people would run 'amok' and slaughter all their perceived enemies.'

Hastings paused, long enough for the silence between the two men to raise the tension in the room. 'And only one man knows these local rulers well enough to walk the precarious path between British good sense and Malay cultural sensitivity. Is that the measure of it, sir? Are you making a case for yourself, Captain Light, as the only man capable of engineering a suitable outcome?'

Light bowed. When he raised his head, his smile was clear to see. 'There is no intent to play you for a fool, sir, but I cannot see anyone more perfectly positioned to conduct this delicate negotiation. I understand these people and the politics of this region like no other Englishman. Queddah is my home. My very future is staked on the peace and prosperity of the Straits. Who better than I to broker the deal? Sultan Abdullah trusts me – why, he even calls me Dewa Raja and brother! These people seldom put their trust in the foreigner. I alone have cultivated that relationship. Yet, I am first and foremost an Englishman, a servant of the Company and a loyal subject of King George. I can be your representative and I can also put the sultan's case fairly to the Council.'

Hastings chuckled at the florid speech. 'Captain Light, I had not thought you such a wordsmith! Whilst I take your point, and wholly concur that there are few with your singular skills and connections, some might say you are the servant of two masters, wherein your primary concern might be confused. How does any man represent both sides at once in any meaningful way?'

This was the gamble Light knew he must take. The Company did not entirely trust him, for he had always been a lone wolf operating on the fringes of society. Pretence was useless to a man such as the Governor-General. Hastings would see right through him if he tried for unctuous platitudes.

'For it would be no such thing. I would, of course, honour the wishes of the Company. Nor would I be contemptuous of the sovereign rights of the sultan. But you ask whom would I represent first and foremost? Why, myself, of course! For who has more to gain and more to lose? The very safety of my family rests upon the outcome, as does my entire fortune. In my experience, there is no better incentive to peaceable resolution of implacable problems than when a man works in his own best interests. Is that not the very philosophy of the Honourable Company, an association of independent merchants cooperating for the better good by conducting their own private business?'

'Good God, Light, you're a rogue and no mistake! Who but you would dare to set your stall out so blatantly! But you're right, man. I am heartily sick of pretence and backstabbing. Of course, you will find the best way forward if it is in any way possible. And by the same token, I am convinced that you will twist and turn and spin any yarn that best serves your aim. Better that I never know the details, eh? Just give me this Pooloo Pinang. I will take a chance on you, Light. But if you fail, it's on your damned head. I will not back you up in any circumstance. Are we clear on that?'

It was agreed. Nothing concrete set to paper, but Francis Light was confirmed that day as the official Company representative at the Court of Sultan Abdullah of Queddah with a precise objective: to secure the offshore island of Penang for a British trading base.

30

Nagas

It seemed that year as if the entire Peninsula held its breath, each player scrutinising the other, waiting for the first volley. For the most part, no action was taken, the state of determined irresolution that is often the choice of most nations. Meanwhile, the Siamese and Burmese faced each other off. The invaders had twice as many men as King Rama; this news encouraged some of the sultans of the Peninsula to throw off their yoke. Malay troops from Patani, Kelantan and Terengganu prepared to march north and join in the Burmese pincer, while, down in the south of Siam, the passes that led to the narrow neck of the Peninsula were already well guarded. Everyone was primed, yet nothing happened.

Sultan Abdullah preferred any policy that involved burying his head in the sand in the vain hope that the mounting crisis would simply disappear. After all, preoccupied with external threats, his enemies at court were unlikely to retain the appetite for insurrection, thus the home front would be quiet for the time being. Why then should he commit prematurely to British proposals if it was to prove he had brought in outsiders for nothing? Possible alliance with the British Company was unpopular in Queddah, where any talk of ceding land to foreigners was anathema. In the coming war, either Siam or Burma would eventually emerge triumphant, at which point Sultan Abdullah would send the *bunga mas* to whomever was the new master. The better plan was to risk nothing and sit the moment out.

A perfectly timed occurrence allowed further prevarication. News trickled through from Bengal that the governor-general had unexpectedly stepped down from office. The great and powerful Sir Warren Hastings – who might as well have been a king for the power he wielded – had either resigned or been removed! Reports said that he was already on a ship home, his enemies in London sharpening their knives to have their revenge on his return. Abdullah grasped this most welcome breathing space. With the British in disarray and the Peninsula in stasis, perhaps he could now defer any decision about Penang until further down the line. Despite his promises to Light, if he could possibly avoid ceding any of his territory or influence, that would be his preference. Wait and see, were his watchwords. Wait and see.

Francis Light was near apoplectic with rage. For days he thundered about the house, or stormed outside to sit alone by the edge of the sea, ruminating on the utter frustration of it all, impotent energy coursing through his body. This could not be happening! Not now, not when he had almost had his fingers on the very prize, the dragon's talons curling around the elusive pearl, only to have it jerked from his grasp and recede into the distance, yet again. What was to happen next? Who might be the new governor-general? Would he respect a decision taken in the dying embers of the old regime, or might he desire a new broom to brush away every stain of Hastings, sweeping the leavings of his policies into the gutter?

In desperation, Light had written to one of the few men he trusted to supply impartial intelligence. It had been many years since he had met with Captain Andrew Ross in person, but his old friend – and regular correspondent – was now elevated to a lofty role on the Madras Council. It was hardly the outcome one might have expected twenty years before when, as a green young man Light had bumped into the dour captain in a scurrilous Madras punch house – and the Scotsman had saved his life. To his intense relief, his reply came back in less than two months. It went some way to settling his troubled mind.

> *Dear Francis,*
>
> *You are not alone in your annoyance at the devastating turn of events. Hastings will be sadly missed by those who wish for some probity in the matter of Commerce and Politics in India. But the former Governor-General was not loved by Company officers, and his loss is mourned by few. I would not envy his position on his return to London. The knives are out.*
>
> *We are currently in a state of Flux, the finances of the entire Presidency in the direst straits. A new Governor-General has been suggested. He is a worthy appointment, although it is unlikely he will be installed for at least another year. In the meantime, we have an Acting Governor-General, one Sir John Macpherson, a decent enough fellow, somewhat lacking in imagination and never one to rock the boat. Many think Macpherson a nonentity, a man who rarely puts his head above the parapet. In my experience, he is just the sort of fellow who can easily*

be persuaded, for he will be eager to leave a mark in his short Residency. Imagine if this Interregnum heralded the establishment of the long-awaited Indies settlement after all? Such a minor triumph is beloved of inferior men, who generally ride upon the coattails of others.

Do not falter in your Determination, my dear Francis, for this may be the very moment when an inadequate governor might jump at terms at which a more perspicacious administrator would baulk. If you take my meaning.

As to the new Incumbent. It is to be Earl Charles Cornwallis, the commander in the recently lamented American war. Whilst many hold him entirely responsible for the loss of the American colonies, he does have his supporters in London. Should Lord Cornwallis' appointment be ratified, however, I doubt he will be an easy man to deal with for the likes of you and me. Cornwallis knows as much about the Indies as you know about Embroidery. My advice would be to move with all haste. A small window of opportunity lies open – and then all may be lost. Strike while the iron is still hot, so to speak.

God speed, Francis. I believe you are near to achieving a great service for the Nation as well as the realisation of a lifelong Ambition. If the fools that govern us do not bar the way, that is. My regards to your family and that disreputable countryman of mine, Jamie Scott.

Your friend,

Andrew Ross, Captain and Member of the Council, Madras Presidency.

Ross had given him much to think on. He was right. A weak governor-general with aspirations to prove himself would be many times more malleable than Hastings had ever been. An agreement acceptable to both sides would require an act of legerdemain, given the entirely different visions held by the two negotiating parties. But, it might not be so difficult to pull the wool over eyes that did not look too carefully. Light's bitterness receded notch by notch until he found himself quite reassured. A new stratagem was required, however. It was exactly the sort of conundrum he enjoyed. For who was more devious than he or could devise a better tale to confound?

For the next six months, Light carried on the double game, penning constant updates to Macpherson, framing Penang in the most positive of lights. Meanwhile, his audiences with the sultan continued, despite the prevarication, with Light stressing the eagerness of the British to accommodate the sultan's wishes. He even proposed that this was the very moment Queddah should take advantage of a weak governor-general and the Honourable Company's concern that if a settlement was not secured soon, the Peninsula might be lost for good.

Received by a plethora of courtesies, every issue raised was agreed upon in theory, but nothing by way of concrete terms was settled. The sultan would wait until external events became more manifest. There was even whispers of a Burmese alliance of the east coast kingdoms; Queddah was considering joining. Why then would they have need of Britain?

Notwithstanding, Light's inducements slowly began to make an impression on Abdullah – or more importantly the real power behind the throne, Jamual, who was becoming ever more concerned for his personal safety. He feared assassination, with some justification, and had held several private meetings with Captain Light, thus introducing a third faction to the complex machinations, proving himself an unexpected – if dangerous – ally. By the end of the year, the sultan finally succumbed to persuasion and drew up a document of his demands. He was not prepared to give an inch of Penang soil without specific British concessions: a huge annual rent of 30 000 Spanish dollars and military support against his enemies, both at home and abroad. If Light could deliver, then a treaty could be agreed. If any of these prerequisites were not forthcoming, then not one parcel of land would be conceded.

A formal document was prepared in Jawi; Light oversaw its translation into English. The Bengal Council invited Light to make his presentation in February of the following year. The sultan meanwhile settled back to await the outcome, convinced that he could not fail. Either he gained the British alliance on his terms, or he chased the foreigners away and proved to his own people that he was no puppet of the westerners. The Company anticipated this timely opportunity to snatch a perfect gem of a location in the most preferential of terms. Neither party appreciated that they were at the mercies of their intermediary, Captain Light, upon whose translation and interpretation the entire matter rested.

* * *

Martinha's year had similarly been one of increased anxiety and momentous decisions. Whilst her husband might view the political climate as an opportunity, she was faced with the realities of what might transpire if the worst should happen. Francis' position in Queddah depended entirely on the patronage of the sultan; if Sultan Abdullah was removed, her family was in a precarious position. Their very lives might be at risk. Yet if they had to leave, where could they go? Thalang was on the brink of chaos. Her aunt's recent letters were most disturbing. Uncle Pimon, her frail husband was on his deathbed. When he finally passed on, the family's political prominence died with him. Many enemies were waiting to pounce.

Furthermore, there was the Burmese threat. No, Thalang was the last place they might look to for safety. Neither did Martinha relish the other options: India, some godforsaken outpost like Riau, or perhaps return to England? Her foretaste of British society in Calcutta did not lead her to view that particular prospect with much regard.

The Catholic community of Eurasian families was another concern. Both she and her mother worried for their future should hostilities break out. This hapless group of settlers was always the target for the worst retribution in these parts, for they represented the Christian world no matter that they were as much a part of the indigenous fabric of the Straits as any others. But everywhere the Serani became the scapegoats. Thong Di and Martinha vowed to protect them with what little influence they might have. They would not abandon them to the cruel hand of fate.

But most of all, it was as a mother in which Martinha's deepest fears lay. The future happiness and security of her three little daughters concerned her mightily. What was to become of them in Queddah? They would never find a place in the communities along the Straits that either she or her husband could accept, even though they had been raised to speak three languages and were as much at home with local Malay children as their Siamese cousins. Sarah, Lucy Ann and Mary were not as other offspring of such marriages as hers. Both she and Francis believed their children would only thrive as English gentlewomen. Yet that very society would never accept them, unless their upbringing was vastly to change.

During their recent trip to Calcutta, when the realities of English society had been so manifestly revealed to her, Martinha had been given the opportunity of considering an alternative. Francis had taken her to a most charming location in Chowringee, a house with shady colonnades set in pretty gardens. It was an Anglican school for girls, staffed by missionary teachers from England. The purpose of this enlightened institution was for the betterment of the children of Company employees. It housed a number of girls of mixed parentage for whom it was deemed essential that they be removed from any taint of racial degeneration caused either by their mother's inferior parenting or their acquaintance with Catholic belief and superstition.

Mrs Hedges, a well-known benefactress and Calcutta resident for many years, was responsible for its establishment. She was a kindly woman, driven by the best of charitable intents who employed several teachers from England and Scotland whose zeal was unquestionable. These ladies were on a mission to ensure that British values were upheld in communion with the Protestant faith. As a result, the Lights were assured, their daughters would one day be admirable debutantes into Bengal society, and their marriage prospects much enhanced.

'It is essential for country-born British children,' Mrs.

Hedges observed in amicable confidence. 'By means of a rigorous education in the British tradition, there will be no subsequent question that the values of the "lower orders" might dilute the purity of our future citizens. Of course, I speak only of daughters. It is still preferable to send sons back to England.'

The whole experience had been a further blow to Martinha. The notion of sending her daughters across the sea to be educated in an alien world by strangers of a different race and religion was something quite beyond her ability to comprehend. One sent boys to study at a monastery – but this? For his part, Francis was also sobered by the reality ahead, although more accepting of its necessity. He himself had left home at fourteen. Boys in his world often spent their entire childhood in the hands of strangers. Girls, however, were a different matter.

'Calcutta is not so far away, Martinha. We can visit every year,' he had weakly attempted to convince.

'Every year? My daughters will be strangers to me! I will never be with them when they need maternal care! Not to mention how these English teachers will make them disdain their very origin. Our girls will look at me and, instead of a mother, they will see a native woman of whom they should be ashamed,' she protested.

'Stuff and nonsense!' Francis replied. 'You shall always be their beloved mother. The girls adore you! You will write to each other regularly and they will long for your annual visits. Martinha, while it is not what we would wish, do we have an alternative? Look around you. Who knows what may come to pass in the next few years? In Calcutta, they will be safe. Is that not enough reason to make this great sacrifice?'

Martinha could not argue with his reasoning. Her mother

had a further perspective on the matter, one that was equally persuasive. 'From the very moment you make an alliance outside of your own people, these challenges are unavoidable. Look to your own family! Your grandmother ran off to Thalang to escape an unjust husband – for that she lost her first son and saw all her future children raised in an alien culture to which she never belonged. When I was left a widow and forced to remarry against my will, I sent my children away in the hands of a stranger because it was the only way I could ensure their safety. Thank God that man was Francis. He saved us all. Martinha, this is your cross to bear! What you must do, you do for their good and, just as you always thanked me for it, so they will never forget your sacrifice. Be assured of that.'

It was a compelling argument. A child must be something in this world to survive: to be stranded on some halfway shore between neither one world nor another would ultimately destroy them. Even young Soliman had had the sense to understand that harsh reality. The best that she could do for her beloved little ones was to accept that her children must outwardly be British. And that meant sending them to India.

Francis and Martinha planned a journey in the coming year when he could meet with the acting governor-general to present his proposals for Penang again and she could settle Sarah and Lucy Ann in the boarding school. Two tiny girls alone in an alien world, leaving her only little Mary for consolation, at least for a few years more until she too was old enough to join her sisters. It almost broke her heart to think of the moment of parting, no matter how congenial the school and how kindly the teachers.

But even that opportunity was denied when Martinha

discovered she was pregnant again. By the time Francis planned the Calcutta sailing, she would be too far advanced to travel. She must say farewell and watch her little daughters board a ship, to sail without her across the wild Andaman Sea to Bengal.

This pregnancy was more trying than her previous ones. Nausea consumed her, until she could barely eat enough for sustenance, spending much of the last few months before their departure lying in a darkened room, wasting the precious moments which she might have devoted to her girls. Thong Di believed that the reason for her daughter's weakened state was that the child she carried was a boy; they were always more troublesome. Martinha disagreed. Despair was the root of her malady. She might never see her darling girls again. And one day the child within her womb and little Mary would share similar fates.

***

The Governor of Thalang was dying, although it seemed to his long-suffering wife, Lady Chan, that the old man clung on far past his welcome and should hurry up with the wretched business. On the other hand, one indisputable benefit arose from his indecision: whilst he lived, he remained governor. Or rather, she did. On balance, Chan was grateful for his stubborn refusal to depart the world.

The first hint of dark clouds on the horizon had come as early as July, when rumours spoke of the mobilisation of Burmese armies. Attack in the north was now almost certain. In response, Siam had begun its own preparations. The south, as usual, lay low, expecting as usual to be observers to the action. Lady Chan, like many others, saw as much advantage as concern in the imminent war. But the Burmese king had other plans. He raised an army of 140 000, which he divided into nine separate units, each one aimed at vital targets in Siam. Two of these forces, 10 000 men in all, were poised to sail from Mergui to the Andaman coast: the supply lines that would feed the Siamese army must be cut off.

A summons from the royal army reached Tharua ordering Lady Chan, the *de facto* governor, to present herself to the southern military command stationed on the mainland at Kokkloi, at the junction of the trans-peninsular routes to the south and east. No explanation was given, but the terms of the missive were curt and brooked no opposition. With a complement of local militia, the redoubtable lady – now in her fifties – obeyed, sweeping into the headquarters with her usual imperious authority.

Without time even to rest or refresh, she was immediately brought before a general who did not deign to introduce himself, but she knew to be Phraya Thammatrailok. His mood was sour. He seemed insulted by her presence, either because she was a mere woman or because he deemed Thalang an insignificant annoyance at such a time of national crisis. Lady Chan, however, suspected that his anger was the mask he wore to hide the hopelessness of his situation. The south felt abandoned. The promised relief army had not arrived – and some believed it never would. It might already be too late.

'You are here to answer charges of long-standing tax irregularities. Until the money is paid, you will be held prisoner,' the general informed her without even as much as an introduction, and then indicated for guards to remove her from his sight.

Lady Chan raised her hand with authority, stilling the

soldiers in an instant. She would not be dismissed so lightly. 'I am not the governor of Thalang. I am merely his wife,' she replied emphatically. 'I am also an old lady who has made the difficult journey here to deliver troops for the war effort. How dare you treat me in such a disrespectful manner. If King Rama knew, he would have your head! Do you know that my eldest son, Lord Thian, was one of his most trusted generals?' she declared, challenging him to oppose her.

The general frowned, his stern face now even darker. 'Don't take me for a fool, Madam! You hold the power in Thalang and have done so for many a long year. I have no time for your nonsense. Our coffers are empty with the cost of provisioning our armies. Pay up or linger in a prison cell, the choice is yours. Our patience is quite exhausted by your corruption and prevarications!'

The general had a point. Thalang had never remitted the required sum in taxation; their fiscal evasion was legendary. But that was hardly a matter Lady Chan intended to give consideration. 'And exactly how would my incarceration assist at this current time? Forgive me if I read the situation incorrectly, but are we not facing an impending Burmese assault of such magnitude that it is unlikely the south will prevail? And you want to lock up the only person in the region who may be able to keep open your supply lines? Are you a damned idiot, man, or is this just a poor attempt to frighten me?'

The general's mouth fell open in shock. Never in his life had any woman – few men, for that matter – spoken to him in such terms. He was quite unable to reply, giving Chan the opportunity to take charge of the discussion.

'I think we need to start again, sir. I agree there is the matter of unpaid taxes. And this is how we shall resolve the matter. Number one: I have already delivered a force of 300 men to the regional command. I can spare no more, for Thalang must do all it can to fortify itself should this line fail. And fail it will if you are not adequately provisioned in food and armaments. Which brings me to number two. Thalang hereby undertakes to guarantee rice and livestock, plus as many weapons as we are able to lay our hands on, save those we reserve in our own defence. The island will bear a huge financial burden, far more than any paltry tax irregularities that your grubby Treasury officials have uncovered. In return, I expect the slate to be wiped clean. And no more nonsense about rough handling of your local allies!'

The beleaguered general considered the offer laid upon the metaphorical table. The lady had seen through his desperate ploy and pre-empted any argument he could possibly employ. General Thammatrailok was exhausted and on the edge of despair. Her proposition was the first positive news in a long time. For once, he was too desperate even to attempt to save his own face.

Nodding brusquely, he accepted, changing the subject to cover his embarrassment. 'I hear Phaya Pimon is ill? I wish him a speedy recovery.'

'He is dying, general, and may well be dead by the time I return home. Which leaves Thalang without a governor. I doubt that Bangkok will be bothered in the circumstances? We are abandoned, general, so we each must look to our own survival in the coming days. The governor of Ligor has led his people into the forests. I promise you Thalang will not flinch. But there are no guarantees. I have no idea how long we can continue to support you.'

'We are grateful for your effort such as it is. We hear you have foreign contacts, who can bring in cargoes from India and the south?'

Lady Chan shook her head. 'They will not sail into a Burmese fleet. I have a few loyal friends, but even they must look to their own. But I will try, and so will they. It will cost, though. Even friends expect to be paid well for risks taken. War makes paupers, but it also makes men rich.'

General Thammatrailok was astonished by Lady Chan's courage and her acuity. His former arrogance quite vanished; he was, like most men, now ready to eat meekly from her hands.

'You speak the truth, dear Lady. We thank you for your good sense and your aid. In return, we promise to hold the passes and keep Thalang safe at least from land attack.' They both knew that the island's strength – as well as its vulnerability – would always be the sea. The south was now in the hands of fate.

That night, Lady Chan wrote from Kokkloi, to appraise Captain Light of her situation. If anyone would help Thalang, it would be he.

***

During the tedious months of inaction and fruitless negotiations, Light swallowed his frustrations and soldiered on with his day-to-day business, plying his merchant ventures through the nervous Straits at this uncertain time. War was coming either way. Markets were eager for weapons and rice, opium and tin. Everyone was stockpiling. That, at least, was something he might control. Whilst he waited out the ambiguous future, he could make some money and increase his reach over the trading networks of the Straits.

During one quick dash into Thalang in early December, where the atmosphere was charged with foreboding, he attempted to meet with Lady Chan. She was not, however, on the island, having been summoned to Kokkloi in mysterious circumstances. Her husband was very ill, the family's fortunes were waning, and her enemies were on the move against her. Everyone knew she had been holding the reins of the administration for years and now, apparently, she had been accused of tax evasion. The accusations were serious. There were even reports that she would be imprisoned at Kokkloi, the camp where the royal forces of the south were based. Light decided not to linger on the island. If his benefactress was about to fall, he did not wish to be brought down in the avalanche. Then he received a brief letter from her. Lady Chan did not seem her usual composed self.

> *From Than Phu Ying Chan to Latok Kapitan Light,*
> *The governor has reached his final days. We are now quite abandoned. It is known to us that your dealings with Thalang on my behalf have caused you to lose your profits and brought you so many difficulties. My agents tell me you are about to leave as the news is not good. The Burmese are coming. It cannot be long. But I have one last desperate request to make of you. You are the only post left for me to cling to!*
>
> *We need rice. We need weapons and powder. The local men who will be our only defence need opium. I beg of you to prevail upon Kapitan Sakat to bring up at least ten bales. Or come yourself, if you are able.*
>
> *Dispatched Tuesday, December 6th 1785.*

Lady Chan was openly begging for his help, acknowledging his recent losses and only able to promise similar debts in the near future. Her untypical desperation revealed the bleak prospects waiting for the island. His business done, Light left assurances that his company would not forsake them if the worst should happen, but he did not tarry further. Promising that he would do his best to keep them supplied with necessities, he removed himself as quickly as he could from the scene.

A short distance from the Tharua roads, however, he spied the familiar sight of Soliman's boat heading straight for his position. The two vessels stopped to greet each other. Soliman was not his usual cheery self. His face was grim, his eyes alarmed.

'Why the haste, Sol? Burmese?' Light shouted over. Everyone had an eye to the horizon expecting warships any day.

'Aye, captain. Only a few outliers, to be fair, but they were warships. Scouts, perhaps?' His words, however, were not commensurate with his panic.

'Off Mergui? Perhaps heading for Tennasserim?' Light guessed.

Soliman shook his head. 'No, much further south. Heading this way. It may only be a scouting expedition, but I doubt it. I think the war is about to start, for the seas are teeming with terrible portents. Something dreadful is about to happen. Flee back to Queddah now, before we are overtaken by the evil!' he shouted over.

Light was astonished at Soliman's words. He was not a lad given to the superstitions common amongst the local people. Something had severely shaken him.

'What did you see, Sol? What has afrit you so?'

'Nagas, sir! Thousands upon thousands of huge serpents, writhing in the waters like a vision of hell! We barely escaped their clutches. They extend for league upon league to the very end of the horizon!' Soliman's voice broke.

'Sea snakes? They're not uncommon in the Straits, lad! You've witnessed them often enough, even in large shoals!' Light reasoned.

'Not like this, sir. Never before like this! I swear it was like the end of the world! It is beyond nature. They are creatures of hell!' he answered back in horror. 'See, even now we have not outrun them!' Soliman indicated the far horizon, where a dark, stormy patch of sea was advancing. It was hard to be sure at that distance, but the waters had the appearance of something solid, yet alive. There was already a murmur rising from his own crew, driven no doubt by the alarm of Soliman's men.

'Good God,' Light muttered. 'What the devil is that?'

'We must go, Captain. This little boat will not survive them!' Soliman was already moving off. 'Do not tarry! Make for Queddah without delay! We must outrun them!'

Driven by curiosity, and less concerned for his ship's safety for it was a large cargo vessel, Light ordered his men to approach the churning body of sea. His sailors although mightily disturbed being already entirely alarmed, grudgingly obeyed. As they neared the floating mass, the swell increased, caused by something other than deep-sea currents. It was as if a preternatural force was stirring up the turbid waters.

And then he saw them. First just a few, then more, next – within moments – the sea was suddenly alive with the squirm of snakes: long, thick, venomous serpents, monsters from an ancient myth. The impact of their writhing rocked the ship with an abnormal intensity; the sound of their bodies colliding against the hull resounded in repulsive, fleshy thwacks. The men peered down in horror at the ophidian maelstrom through which they now sailed.

These snakes were of the type commonly caught in nets by the fishermen in these waters, or washed ashore along the beaches. A hideous reptile, with none of the iridescent beauty of the coral snake, these ugly, grey-brown brutes were the length of a man full grown, thick and lumpy, their bodies stout and misshapen, with rippling dorsals crossed in broad dark bands. Their tails, like paddles, beat powerfully against the water and each other as they thrashed and surged in an involuntary frenzy. Here and there one reared up above the swarm, as if driven by some powerful instinct to survive, its gaping mouth, long-fanged, screeching out a silent curse. It was impossible to witness without a shudder of revulsion.

Light tore his eyes from the repugnant spectacle to look out at the waters beyond the shoal, only to find that what had initially been a patch of darker sea, now filled the entire surrounding Straits until the far horizon. Soliman had said 'thousand upon thousand' but it was an underestimate. What they were witnessing was a vast corpus of sea snakes numbering in millions. He had never before heard of such a phenomenon, nor seen anything of its like in all his years at sea. Where had they come from? In what waters had these numbers spawned? What drove them in their desperate, headlong journey south?

Although he was a Christian gentleman with a healthy regard for science and reason, life aboard and in the East – where he had witnessed many wonders that defied all logic – had taught him to keep an open mind. He did not doubt that the natural world held mysteries unfathomable, but never so much as he witnessed that day. There were indeed more things in heaven and earth than were dreamt of in his philosophy, just as wise Will Shakespeare, who had himself never left old England's shores, knew all too well. Light and his crew stared into the very maw of hell. It could only mean one thing. This was a portent of momentous events to come. The seas were warning of a terror that would sweep all in its path.

'Raise sail, men! All speed. Back to the Tharua roads. We must warn them to prepare...for the Burmese are coming!'

PART FIVE

Pearl of the Orient

(1786)

31

Halcyon Days

Calcutta, January. 1786

It proved to be the most amenable of voyages, crossing the Andaman in pleasant weather in the company of his two young daughters. Although they had always been his delight and joy, during this period of enforced closeness, Light realised that in truth he hardly knew them. Fate had now afforded him this singular opportunity to redress that sorry situation, it would seem, ironically at the very moment when he was about to part with them for a very long time. The days were fine, the seas were calm, and the winds were in their favour. His men could sail in these conditions almost without a master, thus there was little for the captain to do but entertain his girls. It was the merriest of times, the only cloud in the sky being the reality of the separation to come.

At the onset of the journey, his girls had been subdued. Although accompanied by their grandmother and some maids, the ship was an alien world to them and the sea a frightening environment. They also suffered from the loss of their mother, during which painful parting they had wept profusely, whilst Martinha had kept a stern composure. She had remained aloof, almost indifferent, brushing off their tears and instructing them to be less emotional, more lady-like, not to embarrass themselves or bring shame to their father. The only concession to affection as they took their leave was a cursory peck on each of their cheeks with a fussy reminder to behave, eat well, be polite, remember their prayers and wash regularly. Martinha's behaviour had confused the girls, who were used to a happy, loving mother, now mysteriously replaced by this distant, hectoring matriarch. They did not understand how she could be so unfeeling on the last morning they would spend together.

Light was not fooled. Cloaking herself in the armour of propriety was the only way his wife could face the loss of her two daughters. One single concession to emotion – and she would have collapsed in grief. It was a typically Asian response, he thought, one of those occasional moments in their married life when he realised with surprise that Martinha's internal responses did not match his own. He was already dreading the day when he would deliver the girls to their new school; he fully expected to blub like a babe.

The journey brought home to him the full cost to his family of the wandering existence he had chosen, an occasional few days at home, and then off again to foreign parts. Even when he was 'home', he generally spent more time at the port or the palace than with his little ones. Here and there, he would pass an hour or two with them, they would be paraded before him to show off some new talent, or for a kiss at bedtime – but as people in their own right, Light did not know them at all, to his absolute shame. That part of their lives had been left entirely to their mother and grandmother, viewed as women's business. That his children might be small humans with their own personalities, hopes and dreams, had never even occurred to him. Children were just another commodity that one acquired – albeit a most adorable one – a necessary stage in life's passage. But during those long days aboard, with little else to do but spend time with each other, it was as if he met them for the first time – and fell more in love with them than ever.

Sarah, the elder, was seven years' old, a quiet, obedient child with an intelligent mind, who gave the impression that she was older than her years. She already took the responsibility of her younger sister very seriously, and was often overly anxious for her wellbeing. But beneath her sensible exterior, she hid a lively and spirited nature.

The younger Lucy Ann, was a clumsy, playful child, just turned six, endlessly curious and always laughing. There was something of the tomboy in her, for she was ever in places that she should not be, picking up oddities that fascinated her, diving headfirst into trouble with no thought to consequence. Nor did she have much patience for her studies. Whether she was ungifted academically, or simply undisciplined, he could not say. Perhaps she was indeed more like her own father had been as a boy? Now that was an idea that intrigued him. Both of the girls were pretty: Sarah, willowy with dark blond wavy hair and Lucy Ann, sturdy and blessed with a tumble of unruly raven curls. It dawned on him quite out of nowhere that he loved them so much that it pained his heart.

At the outset, the girls had been restrained in the company of their father, clinging to their grandmother for comfort. But in the close proximity of shipboard life, unfamiliarity soon disappeared, and their natural temperaments emerged. Soon enough, they were jumping up and down with glee when their father emerged on deck each morning. The girls would charge around the deck, making friends with all the sailors who treated them like little princesses until they were in danger of being thoroughly spoiled. The men were forever slipping them gifts: a whittled toy or a piece of scrimshaw fashioned into a necklace or plaything.

One had a pet monkey dressed in breeches and a tiny, red waistcoat, with a little woollen cap upon his head. The animal was a clever creature, an able mimic, always playing tricks upon the sailors. The men knew him as 'The Dutchman', 'Dutchie' or 'Orang Belanda', because of his western garb but the girls – who all but adopted the monkey as their own pet – took to calling him 'Captain Scott'. Light laughed heartily, but was puzzled as to why.

Sarah had her answer ready. 'But it is obvious, Papa! For, although he chatters incessantly and is endlessly amusing, everything he says is quite unintelligible!'

And little Lucy Ann chipped in further '– and he wears the clothes of a gentleman but they are so dirty and full of food stains!'

Their wit and sharpness utterly enchanted their father. His beautiful daughters were two vibrant characters already. How much he might have missed had this unique few weeks not been granted him! Light vowed to make more effort with little Mary and the new baby when he returned home, that he might build a close relationship right from the start, for all too soon he would lose them, as well. He also vowed to write regularly to his girls in India. He did not wish to lose this precious budding intimacy.

And so Light spent those few weeks of the crossing learning at last how to be a father. He showed them games that he remembered from his Suffolk childhood: scotch-hopper and skip rope, fashioning spinning tops and whirligigs to entertain them, and games of quoits and nine pins. He taught them the basics of the sailing of a ship, how to identify common marine birds and fish. He read to them in the sleepy afternoon heat, all three curled up under shady awnings beneath the endless sky. And what better place than a large cargo ship for playing hide and seek?

One day a school of dolphins joined the ship, prancing and diving before and aft the vessel to the utter delight of the girls who all but fell over the side to view them better. Light had to keep a firm hand on each, particularly rambunctious Lucy. Through them, he saw the world anew with younger eyes. Although they were sad to leave their mother's side, they were excited and curious to embark on their new school life. It was a grand adventure, one denied to most girls, who never normally left the compounds of their homes. As young as they were, Sarah and Lucy Ann were keen to know the world outside their little Straits existence.

He was intrigued that his daughters already had strong notions of who they were in the world, although he had never consciously discussed it with them. If asked, they proudly announced that they were 'English girls', and that their father was a 'famous English sea captain'. One day, they hoped to go to London and see all its wondrous sights and visit Suffolk to see the places where their father had spent his boyhood. Martinha and he had made the right decision. These girls already belonged in a wider world than the little home in Queddah where they had been raised. Whether the rosy glow of later memory painted those days in golden light, or perhaps the skies had indeed been relentlessly blue and the seas a gentle wave, nevertheless it was a halcyon time for all, one that stayed forever in their hearts.

The clement sailing also worked its magic on Lady Thong Di,

awakening the part of her that had long been repressed. Although a constant feature in Light's life at home in Queddah, his mother-in-law always kept a discreet distance, ever warm and friendly, but never pushing herself forward. Light observed this change with great affection, for he had strong feelings for this courageous woman without whose hand he never would have found this family life that meant so much to him. Thong Di, similar in age to him, was still a handsome woman, although she seemed much older, having settled into mature widowhood, dressing in a sober, matronly fashion. It was hard to imagine that he had once considered her a potential wife. She now not only behaved, but also looked, like a mother to him.

Yet Lady Thong Di – affected by some freedom of wind and wave – began to shed her more formal shawls and costumes, preferring to appear on deck in simple sarong and kebaya, often barefoot, with a bright scrap of cloth tied round her hair. The sun brought a golden tinge to her skin, her eyes sparkled, and errant tendrils escaped from the tight confines of her bun, until the memory of the once-beautiful woman emerged from the gracious older lady. There was a lightness to her mood; this was an unexpected adventure that she could no more resist than her granddaughters. Something of the girl still remained, or rather the woman of distinction who had once led a mission across the sea as ambassador for the Sultan of Queddah to meet an unknown English sea captain.

What qualities blessed his children, inherited from their rich and varied lineage! They were surely the future of the East, a part of the rich blend of cultures and religions that existed in symbiosis together. But despite that conviction, Light intended to take no chances. He must ensure that the rest of the world – or rather, the rest of the world that mattered – saw them foremost as British subjects. He was not naïve enough to think such things could be disregarded. They were more important now than ever.

When the day finally came to deliver Sarah and Lucy Ann to their boarding school, it was with deep, abiding sadness. They parted with kisses and hugs, tears and gifts, promises to write and visit often, then Light watched them go, dabbing at the tell-tale signs of his own sorrow trickling down his cheeks. Lady Thong Di placed her hand upon his arm and squeezed fondly. 'They will be well cared for. It is the right thing to do. I am relieved that they are out of Queddah and the madness that is now upon the Straits. Their safety is assured. Take heart, dear Francis!'

'But they are such little things to be so far away from home!' he cried, his voice gruff as he struggled with the overwhelming tide of his emotions.

'The girls are stronger than you think. They also know that they are loved, which is more than most children know in this sorry world,' she reminded him gently. 'The coming year will pass by in a moment. And when Martinha is recovered from her confinement, we will all return and make merry as a family in this beautiful city. I have never seen anything quite like Calcutta in all my life, not even in my imagination. Is London anything like it?'

* * *

Light met with the acting governor-general later in the week, in a formal office at the Council House, in preparation for the Bengal Council's consideration of the proposal for a British establishment on the island of Penang. Whatever approaches he had planned in the days leading to this official audience, however, he soon disregarded when in the presence of Sir John Macpherson himself. The new governor was no Warren Hastings. Andrew Ross had been correct in his evaluation of the man.

Macpherson was a hearty, handsome Scot of the Isles, tall and broad with the solid muscularity of the soldier. His eyes were pale blue and his cheeks were ruddy, giving him an easy, genial appearance. He dressed soberly but of expensive cloth and wore a neat and well-powdered wig. At first glance, Sir John gave the impression of an administrator of both good humour and probity, a compelling combination, for it suggested he was a good leader. But appearances can be deceptive. The impressive outward façade concealed a much less remarkable interior.

Light had done his research, primed by Ross's information, and knew that the governor-general was, in fact, a man given to vacillation who relied heavily on his subordinates, and at all times looked for the easy route to accomplishment. He was also eager to restore his reputation, somewhat tainted by an earlier entanglement with a local nawab whose suit he had unwisely espoused to the ire of some of the leading figures on the Madras Council. His appointment as governor-general had been received with lukewarm response by the merchant society in general. Thus, Sir John Macpherson had urgent need of a cast-iron certainty to prove himself. He seemed already convinced that Light was offering such a prospect.

'At last, we meet, Captain Light! I feel we know each other well already, on account of all the correspondence we have shared. I trust you have the relevant documents in order for the Council?'

'Indeed, sir, please take receipt of sufficient copies of my translation of the original documents. As I am sure you will appreciate, the papers were prepared by the court scriveners in Jawi, the script of the Muslim Malay courts, which is wholly unintelligible to Company officers. I have taken the liberty, however, to translate them into the King's English, so that you are fully comprised of each and every proposal. Have you had time to read through the copy I sent you earlier?' Light handed over a wallet of papers that would soon, he hoped, bear the joint signatures of both sultan and governor-general.

'I have indeed read through the document. It has furthermore been overseen by my impartial advisor, Mr Joseph Price, one of the worthiest of Bengal merchants whose expert opinion I greatly value. There are a few matters, however, that I would like to clarify to enhance my understanding of the terms. Am I correct in assuming that these proposals are merely the opening gambit and that the sultan expects to further negotiate?' Macpherson questioned. Light wondered who had put that idea into his head. Probably Price. But he was ready to sidestep the issue.

'Most certainly, sir. It is the way of all business in the East. One places a vastly exaggerated demand upon the table, allowing substantial concessions subsequently to be possible for both parties, so that dignity and face can be saved on either side.'

Macpherson approved of Light's response. 'Thank God we have a man who understands these heathens, eh? We are most appreciative of your efforts and endeavours on our behalf, sir. Let's take a closer look, shall we, and venture where they might yield to our advantage.' He consulted his notes. 'My initial concern rests in the cost of this endeavour, Captain Light. The Company finances have been left in a parlous state by the former governor-general, I'm afraid to say. The coffers are empty, due mostly to his mismanagement. You were acquainted with Sir Warren Hastings, I believe?' Macpherson inquired, innocently enough, but Light was not fooled. It would do him no good to be overly associated with yesterday's man.

'I would hardly claim that we were acquainted, sir. I sent my regular reports and had audiences with Hastings several times when I was in Calcutta, just as I have done with you. The former governor-general was a singularly difficult man to know, in my opinion, and not an easy man to deal with. His ideas were very fixed; he would brook no opposition.'

Light felt his way bit by bit, observing Macpherson's reaction to each sentiment of veiled criticism; his words were well received so he continued with more gusto. 'I believe that, if Sir Warren had been less obdurate, a settlement in the Straits might have been established long ago, with significant implications in the wars against the Dutch and French ...'

Macpherson almost leapt from his seat, relishing the attack upon his predecessor. Light recalled Peter denying Christ, an unlikely but not inappropriate comparison. He had admired Hastings almost more than any man he had ever met, and yet here he was falsely mauling his reputation, merely for the sake of ingratiating himself into the confidence of his successor. Light shook away the shame. Nothing he might say or do would save Hastings now. He must look to his own future.

'I entirely concur, Captain. And may I add, I fully intend to put right what Hastings so signally failed to do during his time in office. There *will* be a British settlement in the Indies by the time this year is out, my word on't! But if I may return to the matter of the cost of the expedition. The King has asked for an extortionate sum, an annual rent of 30 000 Spanish dollars. You must realise that this could never be agreed, even should the Treasury be as rich as Croesus!'

Light concurred heartily, making sure to commend Sir John's good sense. 'The figure does not signify, Sir John. These people have little understanding of the value of coin, being mostly barter traders. They also have scant regard for accuracy in numbers, merely picking out a figure from the aether that means little more than "a large amount". In the same way, they speak of armies of tens of thousands when they mean "a lot" of soldiers. It is a figurative way of speaking, typical of their nature. It would be a small matter to secure a somewhat more reasonable sum.' Poor old Sultan Muhammed Jiwa must have turned in his grave at the arrant insult to the business acumen of the Queddah court. It was the second denial.

'I thought as much. The Indians are much the same, always inflating with hyperbolic quantities. We can return to an exact figure at some later time in our discussion, should the Council see fit to approve your proposal. Now, let me move to my next point of issue.'

They both shuffled papers for a moment, gathering their thoughts, and then Macpherson moved on. 'As I see it, the treaty rests on a few salient particulars upon which we must insist. Article One: "*The Honourable Company shall be the Guardian of the Seas for Queddah. Whatever enemy that may attack the King shall be an enemy to the Company, and the expense of engagement should be borne by us ...* " I must say I disapprove of this commitment. Else we shall be liable for every damn entanglement they incur!'

'I beg to differ, Governor.' Light was quick to dissuade Macpherson from this line of thinking. 'One needs to view this particular article from an alternate perspective. If we are to be "Guardians of the Seas", this entitles us to sole control over all the waters, rivers, bays and islands, all bounded by the local sea. We shall have complete ownership of every aspect of the seas: who may enter, who may buy or sell, who may water or victual, who may fish or help themselves to wood, not to mention anyone who enters for the purposes of mining and the profits therein. I am not entirely sure that the sultan and his minister have realised this deeper implication. Another, perhaps more important consideration, is that this article precludes all other foreign powers from any presence save that which we allow. I would judge this article as one of the most valuable aspects of the treaty entire. It would be well worth the cost incurred of small defensive engagements. Of course, we would only ever engage when it was in our interests to do so. Which is always the case wherever British privileges are granted.'

To this sleight of hand, Macpherson gave accord, his eyebrow raised in recognition of the acuity of Light's argument. 'Well said, sir. It is always in these apparent concessions that our true authority must lie. And I am greatly amused that they have entirely missed the point! They will concede much that would be devilish difficult to reclaim at a later date should they discover their error in judgement!'

Light indicated his agreement, complimenting the governor on his quick appreciation of the deeper issues. 'You have probably noticed that I have also submitted a paper of remarks to accompany the original proposals, which may I say the sultan himself only refers to as "desires", not demands. I hope the Council will find them useful in unravelling the complex twists and turns of the Sultan's mind.'

'Capital, sir, capital! You have done our work for us, man, by interpreting his meaning! Now, if I may refer to Article Five of said document, where the sultan states, rather dramatically in my humble opinion, that *"any enemy of this country, be he Son or Brother, shall become an enemy to the Honourable Company as long as the Sun and Moon endures* ... " Does the sultan think to embroil us with his local rivalries, a situation wholly repugnant to us?'

Light shook his head and chuckled. 'They do love their poetic allegory, sir. Everything is coached in terms of fable and the language of epic. It is merely the strict form of their court protocol. A central matter does lie here, however, one of the greatest importance, cloaked in the rhetoric. Whilst I agree, we must phrase the terms of our treaty with the utmost caution to ensure that we do not become entangled in their native quarrels, this can also be interpreted as referring to *our* mortal enemies, the European powers who are pressing their intent in the region. To the Malays, the Dutch and the French are our "brothers", for they find it difficult to distinguish between us. We are all "Christians" or "Ferringhi" – which means Frenchman – or "*Orang Belanda*" – which means Dutch. They cannot tell us apart, by God! This Article is essential for it ensures the support of the Malay kingdoms should the British see fit to proceed against their European rivals! To better understand this, may I appraise you of some recent developments? The Dutch have reinstated themselves in the southern Straits and Riau, and are beginning to look to Perak and Queddah with renewed confidence. The French for their part, while they may have been chased out of India with their tails between their legs, have now set their sights on Burma and Cochin-China. Should the Frenchies worm their way into those courts, we may find ourselves facing an even greater French threat than that posed of late by their alliance with Tipu Sultan!'

Macpherson banged his hand upon the table. 'By God, man, we need your understanding of the situation! This is all new to me! So, when Article Six demands: *"...If an enemy attacks ... "*, this refers as much to possible future attack from the Dutch or even the French?'

'Indeed, sir. The Siamese and the Burmese are currently having one of their usual tussles – they go back and forth with monotonous regularity, rarely achieving much by way of change to the status quo. This time, however, the Burmese appear to be in the ascendancy. Should they succeed in driving back the Siamese, they may very well take it into their heads to make a move on the northern Straits from their base in Mergui. There is a historic interest in this region, contested by the Siamese and Burmese over centuries. It rarely comes to much – but if the French should add their naval might to that of the Burmese – well, I do not need to indicate to an administrator of your experience what might be the consequence of that, sir!'

With one fell swoop, Light had raised and dismissed the real threat to his proposal. The war between Burma and Siam might well engulf the entire Peninsula for years to come, and yet he had consigned it to the level of a minor border skirmish whose only threat lay in some vague and undefined putative French involvement. Had he gone too far? Should he perhaps never have mentioned Siam and Burma at all? Light waited in anticipation of Macpherson's counter. Warren Hastings would have seen through this arrant fiction in an instant. But it failed to arrive; the governor-general had gobbled up his explanation, because it was what he wished to hear.

'I am so very glad you have explained this to us, Captain Light. For the issue of Siam and Burma has been mentioned at Council, and was the main objection to an establishment in Queddah. There were those who were concerned that the kingdom of Queddah was too close to the fighting. But in the light of what you have now said, this casts a wholly different complexion upon the matter. This is a most important consideration, perhaps the single most significant point of all.'

Light bowed graciously, lowering his head to hide the grin of delight that threatened to spoil his unctuous expression at the success of his complete obfuscation. Macpherson was a fool whose eyes were so firmly on the prize ahead that they failed to see the huge chasm right in front of them. Now all he had to hope for was that the Council would be equally blinkered, or that Macpherson made a good enough appeal to win his case.

'Sir John, I am indebted to you for your sympathetic deliberation. Please give my good wishes to the Council and my gratitude for allowing me to set these proposals before them.' This was the time for the ritual grovelling that so pleased men like Macpherson who could now play the gracious governor, basking in his bounty and administrative skills before a subordinate officer.

The meeting wound down to its most satisfying conclusion,

Macpherson priding himself on his keen grasp of the issues and Light equally relieved that he had navigated the reefs of impediment that lay between the two opposing ambitions. They shook hands and Light took his leave, a sense of lightness flooding through him at this chance to finally lay his hands upon the prize. 'I hear you settled your girls in Mrs Hedges' admirable school? Excellent idea, if I may say so, Captain Light. It answers the one question hanging over your character, you know? The matter of this Catholic half-caste woman you've been associating with ... you must look to the future, sir. If you are to become the administrator of a British possession, you have to follow the rules, if you take my meaning.'

A prickle of annoyance momentarily froze Light's genial smile into a rictus, the muscles of his cheeks twitching as he sought to keep from expressing his anger at the insult to his wife. He should have expected this response. Calcutta was awash with prejudices of this nature these days. It mattered not how many local women you kept in your home and how many children you had scattered about the place. But to flaunt one as your wife, and a Catholic to boot? That was unacceptable. He tamped down anger and reached in his bag of half-truths for the old saw he had dangled before Hastings in the past.

'My relationship with Martinha Rozells has some bearing on the success of these negotiations, sir, if I may say so, one that might shed a wholly different light on the way Calcutta views the liaison. She has a personal connection to Pulau Pinang. The late sultan, father of Abdullah, gifted her the island as part of her marriage portion when we went through a ceremony of sorts at his court. Unfortunately, Muhammed Jiwa passed on before he could make good on the grant but his son is disposed to honour his beloved father's wishes. I would hazard that this is the driving force in his willingness to deal with us at all, sir. I doubt he would be so inclined to alienate land to the Company else.'

Macpherson's eyes gleamed with satisfaction. 'So, your controversial alliance with this woman of the Malay court at last comes to fruition in our favour, Light! This will go a long way to allaying any residual doubts against your appointment as superintendent of the new settlement. It is indeed a masterstroke of diplomacy, sir! Good man!'

It had taken only an instant for him to make up his mind and relegate his marriage to little more than a lever in his political ambitions. What did it matter? His private life was nobody's business but his own. How did it signify if he danced to the Company tune when the greater victory would soon be his? 'But you are correct, Sir John. My girls will be English gentlewomen, you may count on that. Demure Protestant ladies, able to present themselves in society, proficient in music, painting and the gentle arts. I will never permit the accident of their birth to be detrimental to their station in life.' There, he had said it. The third – and worst – denial, relegating Martinha to some mistress of no importance other than how she might advance his career. He almost heard the cock crow three times.

***

Two weeks later, Light was taking breakfast in the company of Lady Thong Di on the verdant terrace of William Fairlie's new mansion, even grander than his original home. Fairlie himself was absent, out of town on business, leaving them the run of the grand palace with its dozens of willing servants. A manservant, perfectly turned out in his whites with a carefully folded gold-edged turban, appeared at his side, bearing a silver platter on which lay a communication embossed with the Company stamp and embellished with artful calligraphy:

Captain Francis Light, Esquire

Light set down his tea cup with precision, trying to still the slight involuntary tremble in his right hand. He dabbed at his lips with his napkin, then calmly took his leave of Lady Thong Di. Standing, on legs that were as unstable as his hand had been unsteady, he bowed: 'I must deal with this matter privately, my lady, my apologies.' And withdrew.

He had to be alone for this moment. After twenty years of never-ending struggle chasing the invisible prize, here in this envelope lay his future. How would he contain his utter dejection should he discover that he had reached the final hurdle, only to have failed? There had been too many disappointments over the years, too many times when it had seemed he had succeeded only for his hopes to be dashed. If this was to be another such disappointment, he needed to be alone.

Yet, if it should be good tidings, the achievement of his lifelong dream, then nothing would prevent him behaving like a giddy child, thumping out at the air in triumph. The walk from the room, across the entrance hall, up the stairs, along the long wide corridor that led to his chambers, all the while clutching the instrument of victory or disaster within his sweaty palm, took a veritable age. He willed his legs to move without shaking, his face to maintain the expression of cool control, his roiling stomach, which now regretted the indulgence of his large English breakfast, to settle.

At last he reached his door, wrenching at the handle and slamming it shut behind him. As he tore at the seal, his trembling fingers struggled with the carefully folded sheet, ripping the edge in his haste. And then, he scanned for the answer he had anticipated for so many years.

Thursday, the second day of March, in the year One Thousand Seven Hundred and Eighty-Six The Council House, Bengal Presidency, Calcutta

The Bengal Council this day has voted to accept the King of Queddah's offer to the Company for the Harbour and the Island of Pooloo Pinang. It has been generally agreed that the Harbour would be a particularly suitable location for Company's ships travelling between our ports on the Indian coast and China. It will also provide a harbour from which His Majesty's naval vessels might venture to protect our interests throughout the Straits and the Andaman waters. As the Dutch have re-established their ascendancy in the southern waters, Penang will afford an Emporium for our trade in the East Indies, particularly for the commerce in Opium.

On account of the exceptional endeavours of Captain Francis Light, his facility with native languages and scripts and his singular relationships with the Sultan of Queddah

*and other local potentates, the Council appoints him as
Superintendent of our future establishment at Pooloo
Pinang ...*

The sheet slipped from his hand, the final commendations left
unread. Light slumped to his knees, his fists clenched and his face
contorted with the effort of containing the shock the words had
brought him. Then he raised both arms into a gesture of victory
and roared like a beast who has vanquished his rival. The noise
carried out to the garden, where Lady Thong Di still sat serenely
on the veranda, sipping at her cup of tea. She smiled to herself
with pleasure at Francis' exultant cheer. She understood far more
than he realised about the real purpose of his visit to Calcutta;
her daughter always confided in her, no secrets lay between them.
Thong Di breathed a deep sigh of relief. They must still be vigilant,
however. It was not finished yet. Much was still to be achieved
before the island of Penang might become their new home.

   But this much was certain. If the Captain made this happen
then they would all be safe for ever. And who else in this world
but Francis Light might achieve this impossible dream?

32

The Heroine Sisters

Ban Don Fort, Thalang Province. February-March 1786

For many years Lady Chan had nurtured a secret longing that her aged husband would die, so often had he been a liability both to good governance and to her own plans. Since the onset of his final illness, Phaya Pimon had several times hovered at the brink only to miraculously revive and return to his habitual status of ailing burden. Yet his expected death shortly after her judicious retreat from Kokkloi came as a profound shock. She found herself inexplicably saddened by his passing. Wandering his deserted chambers left her utterly bereft, scarce able to hold back her tears.

Her despair was also rooted in pragmatism. The governor had chosen the worst possible moment to go, leaving her entirely alone in the face of the coming Burmese storm. With Phaya Pimon as a sacrificial victim, there had always been a chance that Lady Chan could negotiate an arrangement with the Burmese command, for surely a person such as she, with great local knowledge, might be a valued asset in their reconstruction? But now, isolated and the only person of note connected to the ruling house, there was a distinct possibility that she herself might be the chosen scapegoat. Chan had enough local rivals who would gladly hand her over to Burmese justice.

Thus, Lady Chan accepted that she and her people had been

abandoned to their fate. Her eldest son had retreated to some faraway monastery, her husband was finally dead, Captains Light and Scott were nowhere to be seen, and the Siamese forces had deserted her. General Thammatrailok had apparently died in the Burmese assault; the remaining officers had fled into the forest along with most of the Phang Na population lucky enough to escape capture. Kokkloi and Pak Pra had already been ransacked. Rumours were even abroad that Bangkok itself had fallen – or was on the brink. There would be no royal army.

Their future, such as it might be, now rested solely in her hands, much as almost everything else in her life. Not one of the many men she had known – be they relative, husband or lover – had ever protected her in her hour of need. She had never been accorded the luxury of playing the helpless woman or of taking refuge in a man's safeguard. On balance, it was probably for the best. She had yet to meet the man who was her equal. Thus, with her characteristic equanimity, she set herself wholly to the task.

Lady Chan sat down at her escritoire to set down her predicament in writing as was her custom whenever confronted with an intractable problem. First, she stated the many challenges that beset her and the options that remained. Then she listed the family members and retainers who relied upon her and upon whom she might herself rely. Finally, she estimated how many peasants were dependent on her. A goodly number might have fled already, but, as nowhere safe was left for them to go, she included the entire number.

Captain Light had once told her that the entire population of Thalang was about 14 000, of whom less than 2 000 were warriors, although this sum had been depleted by the complement she had left in Kokkloi. With a strike of her pen, she crossed the figures out. It was impossible to save them all. In attempting to do so, they might all be lost. Instead, she would concentrate on those from her own clan and the surrounding areas, perhaps five or six hundred souls, the majority women, children and old people.

Sending out messengers to the surrounding villages, Chan summoned a meeting at the old French fort outside Ban Don village set in the heart of this region, about three miles from Bang Tao Bay in the west (where the Burmese would most probably arrive) and a similar distance from both her own ancestral village of Ban Takkien and the port of Tharua. This area was to be her focus; she encircled it upon the map.

At the appointed time, Lady Chan and her household made their way to the fort. They found a sea of frightened people burdened with all their portable possessions ready to flee, skittish as deer who would take flight at the least hint of danger. Inside the dilapidated stronghold, from the top of a staircase overlooking the central ground, the redoubtable lady struggled to make herself heard. From every side clamours of panic rang out: pleading, despairing, begging, screaming. Her people were ready to abandon all hope. Their doom was already upon them.

Furious at her inability to gain their attention, Lady Chan tried several times to quieten them, even banging on a small gong, but the sound was lost amidst the pandemonium. She glanced around forlornly towards her family members, at her three youngest children – the eldest only fourteen – and to her faithful sister, Lady Mook, who was surrounded by her own daughters and their families. Chan's face betrayed the hopelessness she felt. These villagers were a stampeding herd of animals. There was no reasoning with them.

As Lady Chan began to give up all hope, salvation arrived from the unlikeliest of sources. Perhaps it had always been within her, or maybe she recognised that her sister's mighty resolve was finally failing, for Lady Mook, Chan's loyal and gentle sister, often the butt of her elder sister's acerbic mockery, stood forward – and took command. Snatching at a rifle held by one of her own guards, she raised it to the skies, firing above the heads of the crowd. At the loud report, the seething mob caught its communal breath, eyes rolling back in fear, like one giant terrified beast, ready to believe that the Burmese had already arrived and that this was their death knell.

Seizing her moment before all hell broke loose, Lady Chan began: 'People of Thalang! Listen to me! Our fate is in our hands! Today we face the worst threat in living memory. What we do from this moment on will decide whether we survive or perish. There will be no army from Phang Na. We are abandoned. The Burmese are even now sailing for the island –'

'Then we must flee!' shouted one voice, backed up by general agreement. Lady Chan shook her head.

'Flee – to where? To the sea? You will be taken by the Burmese into slavery – or thrown overboard to drown if they deem you too young or too old to be of use. To the interior? They will swarm over this tiny island like a plague. Not one village will be spared! Do I hear you say that you will run for the mainland? It has already fallen!'

'Then we are doomed!' shouted one man. 'Let each man put his family to the sword and kill himself, rather than let the Burmese devils have their way with us!'

This suggestion brought another round of shrieking and panic. Lady Mook was at her sister's side now, still holding the rifle, her sturdy body, feet square-planted, in startling contrast to the willowy elegance of her sister. She fired another shot, following it with a bellow of surprising force, quite unlike her usual soft voice: 'Shut your mouths, you stupid fools! Listen to my sister! Only she can save us!'

And astonishingly, it worked. The crowd fell silent. Of course, Lady Chan would have a plan! When had she ever been bested by anyone?

Chan looked across at her homely sister with a smile of real appreciation tinged with shock. Lady Mook nodded back in response, her own pride in the moment clear to see. 'My sister and I swear this day that we will do whatever is in our power to protect you. We cannot save the island entire, but we might save ourselves. If this is to succeed, however, I need every one of you. Every single one! Man, woman, old, young!'

'But how, my lady?' shouted one young woman, her baby bound to her breast by a sarong. 'How can we succeed where even other armies have failed? We are so few! Not enough men!'

'You are right! How can we think to drive off the Burmese on our own? The answer is, we cannot do so. They will come and, of course, we cannot fight them! But what we can do is make this fort as difficult as possible to take. Think on it! The Burmese troops, perhaps a few thousand men, are far away from home, and out of contact with their forces on the mainland. They have little food, relying on seizing supplies from the villages they take. Even their armaments will be rationed. For they are expecting to fall upon an unprotected island and feast upon its spoils. In most areas, that is exactly what will happen. So, we must give them what they don't wish to receive. We will make their lives so miserable that they decide we are not worth the trouble – and leave us well alone!'

Her suggestion was greeted by a puzzled silence. Groups of villagers turned to each other to discuss her words. Some realised her plan had merits and were trying to convince the others; some thought it a hopeless endeavour. Chan gave them a short while to mull it over, before speaking again:

'First, we gather our food and livestock and bring it to the fort. Carry all your most valuable possessions, too. We may be confined for many weeks, so must ensure that we have enough to hold out without deprivation. I have already sent to Tharua for weapons and supplies. The farang captains have brought us much guns and powder, and many sacks of rice. We are well stocked! We can last out a long siege. There is also opium!' At this, a loud cheer rang out. At least if they were to die, their pain might be eased in the peaceful dreams of the poppy.

'Then we burn our lands! We destroy everything that you have worked for these many years. We set fire to boats! Raze houses! Throw cargoes into the sea! It is a terrible cost – but it might save us. For what good is Ban Don to the Burmese if it is a wasteland?'

'They will massacre us! At least if they take us as slaves, we may have a chance!' One unconvinced voice shouted out. Others agreed. They were poor people. Perhaps it would not be so bad in Burma?

Lady Chan gesticulated fiercely. 'Are you fools? Do you think that they will take your mother for a slave? Or your grandfather?

Or your little babies? No! They will put them to the sword before your very eyes!' She pointed out vulnerable people in the crowd as she spoke. No one disputed her. The Burmese were known for heartless cruelty. 'Are you willing to sacrifice the past and future of your line, merely to earn a few miserable years on a slave ship or be worked to death in the rice fields of Burma? I, for one, would rather take a stand and die here than a fate such as that!' Lady Chan shouted vehemently.

A chant of support rose up from the listeners. 'Stand or Die! Stand or Die! Stand or Die!'

The two sisters smiled; Lady Mook slipped her arm around her sister's waist and drew her close. Together, the two women raised their hands out to the people. 'We will hold the line, like warriors together. Each of us will take our turn to patrol the walls, with courage in our hearts and rifles on our shoulders – and if there are not enough guns, then we will whittle them from palm fronds! It will be enough from a great distance to give the impression that a large number of soldiers is stationed within, for the Burmese will never imagine that the simple people – the old men, the women and the children – had the wit and courage to stand against them! We have the element of surprise. We also have a fortress, which will take time and cost lives for them to storm. Above all, we have cannonry, large and powerful European cannons, ranged along our walls. What will they have? A force on the move, that does not expect resistance? They will bear little more than muskets and rifles. I would not be surprised if the majority of these wretches only carry swords and knives, for they are the lowliest of the Burmese troops. They will be no match for us, for we are the people of Thalang!'

And so, it came to pass. The Burmese landed at Nai Yang beach in the north of the bay and then sailed down the rivers to the interior. Meanwhile, other forces attacked the rest of the island. For four long weeks, Ban Don fort resisted a Burmese throng of 2 000 men, who found a barren desert where they had expected the wealth of a prosperous trading community. They laid siege to the fort, but it was at a great cost. Whilst the people of Thalang stayed inside, well fed and safe, the Burmese broke themselves on their large guns. Four hundred died against very few Siamese casualties. Furthermore, the Burmese had no food, so it was not long before starvation and disease began to take a further toll. By March, they had had enough. When the news reached them that the armies of King Rama had triumphed and that Ligor had been recaptured, the spirit of this southern force was broken. The island of Thalang was not worth it. They would withdraw with the bounty that had been raped from the rest of the island.

Yet freedom came at a great price. Vast areas had been virtually depopulated; thousands of islanders had been taken to Burma as slaves, and as many had been slaughtered. Entire districts had been stripped clean of everything of value. Buildings, homes, temples, crops, ships and warehouses had been destroyed. Those left were in desperate straits; there was little spare food and not enough people to replant the crops. Tharua, Ban Takkien, Ban Lippon and Ban Sakhu were in ruins.

And yet the island survived, although it would be many years before Thalang returned to its former prosperity.

33

Stratagems

Queddah. April-May 1786

In the fort at Kuala Bahang, Sultan Abdullah sat brooding over the many insults he had suffered of late. His court was the usual snake-pit, nobles fawning to his face while whispering discontent behind his back. Whatsoever he did for these people, it would seem, it was never enough to satisfy their appetites. And then there were the godforsaken Burmese, who could not even win a war with nine armies! King Rama was already reclaiming Siam, battle by battle. Furthermore, his attention was already turning back towards Queddah.

To prove his loyalty, Sultan Abdullah had been ordered to present himself in person to one of Rama's generals. It was unthinkable that he should be summoned into the presence of a mere soldier! Instead, Abdullah had sent his brother-in-law, Laksamana Tunku Ya, as his representative, but he had merely been sent back. Not good enough for the Laksmana of Queddah, a relative of the sultan himself, to meet with a Siamese officer? Who did these dogs think they were? Furthermore, when he dispatched his own son in his place loaded with gifts, the same general had forced Queddah to declare war on Burma, send perahus to Mergui, food to Ujung Salang, and cannon and cloth to Siam as if they were lowly subjects, instead of noble vassals!

If not for Jamual, the sultan dreaded to think what might have happened to him. His loyal advisor, himself assailed with all manner of threats, had persuaded the sultan that for his own good he should abandon the palace and take refuge in his recently strengthened fort. Not only was he protected by stout walls and cannons, his sanctuary also afforded speedy access to the sea if the unthinkable was to occur. So here he was, shut up like a prisoner in his own kingdom, with only Jamual to defend him from his many enemies.

Where was the English captain with his promise of alliance? Now, when he had never had a greater need of British support, apparently Light was dragging his feet in Calcutta. After over four months, surely enough time had elapsed for a journey of such importance to be accomplished back and forth across the Andaman Sea? A Dutch delegation offering financial and military support in return for permission to settle Pinang island had recently made their approach. They promised a port to rival Malacca and Batavia, from which the sultan would personally greatly benefit. Abdullah was close to accepting. The faithless, vacillating English Company deserved nothing more than to lose out after dangling Queddah on a rope for so many years.

The sultan's rage was unpredictable. One day he favoured peace with Siam, on another he suggested alliance with Burma; today he might be sure of British aid while tomorrow he was looking to the Dutch who would at least protect him from his mortal enemies, the Bugis! But Jamual persuaded him not to act too hastily. Would it really be preferable to create an even greater monster of the Orang Belanda? He suggested that the sultan might give Captain Light a little more time. The English company was still their best hope.

Meanwhile in his own chambers in the fort, Jamual found himself equally beset on all sides. Unlike the timorous sultan, however, this was his preferred position. For years, he had been building his house of cards, a vast unwieldy complex that rested on the shakiest of grounds, held up only by the mutual antagonism of its separate parts. Most people hated him – with good reason, he had to admit. Few men of note in Queddah did not hold a grudge against him. Jamual made no attempt to cultivate the friendship of such men. They never let him forget that he had once been a humble *kuli* from India who had dragged himself from the gutter and made a fortune, mostly from their greed. He had ledgers full of the names of those same lords, all owing him money. Jamual had no illusions about his unpopularity and the many enemies who wished him dead in any number of foul ways.

It was of no consequence. These same men who hated him, hated others more. Of that he made sure. Each day he pushed the boundaries of his influence a little further, spinning his webs and spreading his lies. Whilst they might resent – even despise – him, the Queddah nobles needed him. As did the sultan, of course, now completely isolated and entirely under his control, a hostage who had willingly handed himself over to his captor, convinced by the carefully conjured falsehoods and deceits he himself had planted in his febrile mind.

Dragging his attention back to the discussion around the table, he listened as his Chulia brethren articulated their own particular grievances. Yet another dissatisfied and angry group to be appeased.

' – and now he entertains these Orang Belanda, falling for

their blandishments just as before he licked the hand of the Company! You cannot let him sign away trading rights to any of these infidels! It will destroy our business – and if we suffer, so does the entire Peninsula! We are trade in these parts! Without us, there would be nothing but opium and guns, for that is all these Europeans care for. To them, the Straits is just a waterway that leads to somewhere else! They have no stake here. They will destroy the traditional way of life!'

Jamual had heard every argument a thousand times before. In one sense, they were right. But in another, they were just another group of self-interested merchants exploiting the local kingdoms. He breathed deeply, his annoyance swallowed down. 'You are quite right, brothers. We cannot let this happen. Have no fear. Abdullah will never put his seal to any agreement with the Christians. But let them dance around him for a time. While they do, it keeps our others rivals at bay. Or at least looking away from us, which amounts to much the same thing.'

'So, no Company settlement on the island, either? You can assure us of this? For you know what happens if you allow these Europeans even so much as a toe upon the carpet – the next thing they are lords of all they survey!'

Jamual held up his hands. 'My word on it. I would rather lay down and die than cede one tiny square of ground to any of them. But it serves its purpose to keep them as the immediate enemy as far as the Malays are concerned. That ensures our safety. Trust me. When have I ever failed my fellow countrymen?'

Grudgingly, they accepted his reassurances, although not entirely convinced by his protestations. Even his own people did not entirely trust him, it would seem. Yet, in the main, their interests aligned, so they trudged compliantly out, still muttering their concerns. For his part, Jamual knew they were no fools. What they said and what they did were two very different matters. Even now, they – just as he – were preparing for a number of eventualities. The traditional way of life? What did they care for the harmony and peace of the Straits? No more than he did. They were merchants. They would sell to all comers. If there should one day be an English port on a nearby island, they would be over like a shot, setting up their bazaars and making money from it. Just as he planned to do. The writing was on the wall. It would only be a matter of time before his neck was on the block. And he intended to be long gone by then.

'Before you go, friends –' Jamual summoned them back. 'Above all, we must look to our future interests. The English may be our enemies for now, but if the situation deteriorates, then we must be prepared. Better the devil you know than the one lurking with a keris in the dark of night. You know who the Malays will come for first if they rise up? It will be us. So, have a care not to close every door with the Company. We may have need of them yet.'

***

The months of April and May brought Martinha many blessings. In April she welcomed the birth of her long-awaited son. At last she had the male child to complete their family, the baby who gave her the affirmation that her husband himself had never demanded of her. Not once had Francis ever reproached her for their lack of a son. It had been her own preoccupation that had eaten into her soul since the loss of her first stillborn boychild all those years ago. Her joy was now complete. The baby thrived – smaller than the girls but an easier delivery for all that. Mary delighted in her newborn brother, who bestowed on her the rank of 'big sister' now that her elders were away, and the little three-year-old bustled about like a mother hen to tend to her charge.

Then in May came the return of her husband and mother carrying precious letters from her daughters, as well as the best of tidings from the Bengal Council. The perilous fate that had haunted her for months began to recede into the distance, with the offer of a bright new future on the island of Penang. The tensions that had hovered above the household for so long were easing: Martinha was safe, the Captain was back, Thalang had survived, and there was hope of a new settlement where they could all be safe.

One look at her mother alone quelled the worst of Martinha's fears. Lady Thong Di seemed quite renewed by her trip. She had enjoyed Calcutta and was at peace with the decision to leave her granddaughters there. During the weeks of her stay, she had visited the school regularly; the girls were settling well. Now, with the safe delivery of the baby, Martinha and she could look forward to another visit, perhaps later in the year when all the business with the sultan was achieved.

Francis, although simmering with positive energy and pride in his achievement, was more circumspect. A long road still lay ahead before they could rest on their laurels and take possession of the island. Whilst he was confident that agreement could be reached, it would take time – a commodity in even shorter supply now than ever.

Matters in the kingdom had deteriorated rapidly in his absence. The Dutch were sniffing around, alarmed at the prospect of a British port to rival Malacca, and were offering all manner of inducements to draw the sultan away from alliance with the Honourable Company. Anyone with any good sense ought to understand that the Dutch would not deliver what they promised, but with Sultan Abdullah's fondness for the easy option, coupled with Jamual's villainous cunning, the damned Dutch had made headway. The sultan also now had another bargaining tool to throw at the Company, should he deem the offer on the table too unpalatable. Then there was the old fox, Laksamana Tunku Ya, Abdullah's brother-in-law, either the sultan's best friend or stirring up the court against him. Not to mention Jamual. Who knew what he was planning? Light took a deep breath and prepared for an uphill struggle.

With his tiny son in his arms, however, Light felt the turning of the tide. One by one, all obstacles had been surmounted. Every recent development had been in his favour. Now this little boy, the son who carried on his name, would grow up in the knowledge that his father was a man of importance, a British officer who represented the great East India Company and, with God's good grace, the founder of their stability and authority in the Straits. A new golden era dawned. Francis refused even to contemplate anything else.

The baby's name had never been in any doubt. He was to be William, named for dear Squire Negus, whose surname he might never carry, but whose memory would live on through him. Light also chose a second name with an appropriately imperial touch, fitting for the first son of a new dynasty in the East.

The letter Francis wrote to his mother informing her of his recent abundance of good fortune contained the ink print of a tiny foot and the legend:

'from your loving grandson, William Julian Light, born April 27ᵗʰ 1786.'

***

A merry band gathered in the Light family house, summoned from all parts to a meeting in which Captain Light – now bearing the official designation of 'Captain of Marines' with a blue and gold jacket to match – was part celebratory, part council of war. A strategy was urgently needed to address the task in hand. Scott had recently returned from Tranquebar where he had spent the first quarter of the year after abandoning Jangsylan to the Burmese. Since then he had made a quick trip there with much needed aid and was enjoying the role of official raconteur of the miraculous repulse of the Burmese. The story, no doubt already highly embroidered by Lady Chan in the first place, was now entering the realms of mythology in Scott's florid style.

'In the face of a countless horde of ravaging Burmese, the ladies of Thalang patrolled the walls with palm fronds shaped like muskets –' he proclaimed, mincing along the imaginary battlements, with a large leaf jutting out from under his arm.

There was great hilarity at his antics. 'Good God, Jamie, not even a Burmese would have been fooled by that carry on!' Light observed. 'I'm sure the good ladies wore headcloths and marched like their sons and brothers, not like that, you nincompoop!'

'Aye, I expect they did, but a good story always needs a little tailoring to enhance the telling,' Scott added with a grin.

'Not this one,' added Soliman, who had also been in and out of Tharua of late and had his own opinion on events. He did not approve of Scott turning the story into a party piece. 'Many people dead already in Ujung Salang. Many taken for the slave market. How can a few hundred people stand against a Burmese invasion? This was a feat of wondrous bravery! Lady Chan is a remarkable woman. Her sister, Mook, also played her part. Lady Thong Di, you come from a line of courageous ladies. Nor should we be surprised, for we have witnessed your bravery and that of Nona Light so many times already!'

'They are in dire straits though for all they drove the Burmese off,' Thong Di reminded them. 'My sisters have written of the devastation. They have no food, nor can they even plant crops with so few left to labour. We must do everything we can to assist.' Lady Thong Di spoke up, where normally she would stay silent. It was the least she could do for her homeland in the face of the great sacrifices of her sisters.

'We will help them, have no fear,' Light promised. He did not add that the unexpected bonus of this terrible tragedy, however, was that, should his new settlement come to fruition, the only trading centre in the region that might have rivalled them had now been crippled. One could not ignore that sad irony.

'I am procuring ships and cargoes daily,' Felipe broke in. As the only male member of the Ban Takkien clan with the wherewithal to assist, he felt it was his duty to lead the relief effort. The captain's priorities understandably lay elsewhere at this time, but he would not forget his people. He raised his glass.

'To Lady Chan and Lady Mook! To my mother's safe return from India! And to my dear, dear sister, who has passed through her own trials and bestowed upon our family another beautiful child – and a boy to boot!'

Sometime later, when the women had taken the children off to bed and the men sat on amongst the leavings of their celebratory meal, the talk turned to the serious business of where they went from here.

'I've written to the Company with my heartfelt praise for their excellent appointment of a man of local knowledge and great experience to lead our new settlement, begging them to permit no interference and defer to your better understanding of the parties involved, at least until the early days have passed,' Scott informed them.

'Steady on, James,' Light replied. 'There's still much work to be done before we clap ourselves upon the back. But I thank you most sincerely for your words. Now, let us review our position –'

Light consulted the official papers set out on the table before him, flicking away food crumbs and moving empty glasses to clear a space. 'Macpherson has been parsimonious with his provision for the expedition, as befits a penny-pinching Scot.' Light tipped a wink to James Scott, who feigned a wound to his heart at the remark. 'Thirty thousand rupees entire, a paltry sum, so we must be thrifty and imaginative in our outlay. I also managed to squeeze out of him a chest of worthless coin, mere one-*pice* bits, but they at least contain the Company stamp on one face, so have the mark of authority, even if there was no time to fashion King Georgie's face on the reverse! I'm sure I can find a resourceful usage for them by and by.'

'Did he offer any troops or ships?' Soliman questioned, aware that the sultan expected a significant force, whose sole purpose was to protect his position. 'Sultan Abdullah is locked up in the fort waiting for the British to save him from his own people.'

'And the Siamese. And the Dutch. Imagine their reaction when they find he has granted the island to the British from underneath their noses,' Scott wryly added.

Light swore. 'Jamual is pulling on the Sultan's strings. I'll warrant he's stirred up the court with lies, merely to give him reason to hold Abdullah hostage to his own malevolent intent.'

'One day, he will be caught in the nets of his own lies,' Scott added. 'He has too many enemies not to come to a reckoning sooner or later.'

'Perhaps,' Light considered. 'But, unfortunately, he is also the key to Abdullah, so we are at his mercy. Men like Jamual spend their lives mired in shit, but more often than not, when better men perish, they emerge smelling of roses. Such realities test a man's faith in the wisdom of the Almighty,' Light added. 'But let us not be diverted. Soliman is correct. Abdullah wants an army, so we must give him the impression that military assistance is on its way. Macpherson is sending a ship, the *Emily*, expected in a week or so. It carries one hundred Bengal marines, a crew of lascars, a small troop of artillery and a number of British officers –'

'One vessel?' Scott scoffed.

'Three to be exact. The *Speedwell* and *Prince Henry* have also been commissioned and fitted out.'

'But they are ours! Thank you very much, your High and Mightiness. We are directed to act in the name of the Company, and must use our own cargo vessels in lieu of warships!' Scott fumed.

Light shrugged off his complaints. 'They have promised others later. Ours are here on the spot. To be fair, we cannot not wait for months while other ships are commissioned. Our boats have guns. They dwarf theirs. It will do for an opening salvo. Macpherson also sends official gifts for the sultan. I think we're ready now to make our bid. Is there anything I have overlooked?' He shuffled through the papers, setting aside what he had already mentioned.

'I've been scouting the island as you asked, sir,' Soliman spoke up. 'I located three existing settlements. None appear to be pirates. Since old Sultan Muhammed drove them out some years ago. The new settlers are mostly Minang migrants, fisherman or small traders with no love for Queddah, for their perahus are often preyed upon by men from the mainland. I spoke to one Minang, Nakhoda Kecil, who claims to be some sort of headman. He welcomes the British. I don't think there will be any problems from that quarter.'

'How many settlers?' Felipe inquired. He was taking notes, ever the faithful secretary.

Soliman hunched his shoulders. 'Not sure. Nakhoda Kecil said fifty-eight persons but I think he means men. There were women and children, so there could be three or four times that number. But they will work for us. They will clear land and build huts. I say we do business with them.'

Felipe agreed. 'They have much to benefit them. Men working to better their own lives will be more useful friends than passing traders and soldiers from a foreign land. And these fishermen mistrust the Queddah people. That is always useful.' He grinned and the others nodded their agreement.

'Divide and conquer, I believe the Romans called it,' Light laughed. 'Jamual isn't the only one capable of that. Good work, Sol. Keep them sweet. Drop off the odd sack of rice, a few bars of tin or a bit of opium – anything you can spare. You know best how to oil the gun.' Soliman grinned back. It was exactly the sort of task he enjoyed most.

The four men talked well into the night, planning for every eventuality. They made note of those on whom they might rely or those they might approach with offers of a safe haven on the island in return for support. Success would ultimately lie in their ability to galvanise the vulnerable communities to form a powerful bulwark against the hostile elements that surrounded them. One of which might ultimately be Queddah itself.

At last, the men called it a night, well into the small hours. Light tossed back the last of his brandy and stretched out his long limbs. 'Gentlemen, the waiting game now begins for a few more weeks, at least. I will approach the sultan for an audience when the Company ship is here. Until then, we send a letter, explaining that we have a promising offer from Calcutta and will present it formally when our forces arrive. Meantime, we see to the needs of Thalang. And I get some long overdue time with my family. For I have damned well earned it!'

34

Treaty Talks

The Emily, Queddah Roads. Late June 1786

The rain poured down incessantly, a grey curtain on an angry sea, the soporific calm of the noon waters a distant memory. Light was aboard a small barque conveying him from the fort at Kuala Queddah to the *Emily*, his newly appointed flagship, anchored portentously midway between the mainland and Penang. The weather was a fitting reflection on his progress over the past few weeks, the wretched elements mirroring the churning emotions he was struggling to contain.

To say his negotiations with the sultan and the duplicitous Jamual had proved unproductive would be an understatement. Several weeks of frustrating back and forth had followed his letter of proposal. For a week or two, there had been no response at all, a worrying state of affairs given the recent contacts between the sultan and both the Siamese and the Dutch. What was he to make of that? During his absence in India, had they decided to exclude the British altogether? Or were they simply reminding him that he was nothing but a lowly *wakil* who must wait upon the pleasure of the king?

Finally, on the last day of June, a formal order had arrived, requesting that Light attend the palace with his marines. Abdullah required evidence of the provision of Company troops before he was prepared to proceed further. Well, two could play at that game, thought Captain Light. The following morning, accompanied by Captain Glass of the *Prince Henry,* Lieutenant Gray and a dozen of his most imposing Bengal marines, together with Artillery Captain Howell and a complement of riflemen, Light set off for the palace, where the party was initially received with a promising fanfare: kompang drums and banners, honouring them as visiting dignitaries.

Yet, instead of being ferried to an audience with the sultan, they were taken to the house of Laksamana Tunku Ya where both he and Jamual were waiting. Under a canopy in the grounds outside, Light formally presented the British Company letter and the gifts from Calcutta. A volley of guns accompanied the presentations, courtesy of the artillery. The gifts were laid out for inspection, an impressive display that included as centrepieces a set of decorative blunderbusses with ornamental gold and silver barrels and silk brocades heavy with gold and silver thread.

Sultan Abdullah was nowhere to be seen, for which absence the Laksamana made profuse apologies, with some vague excuse of the sultan being discommoded, no doubt a euphemism for the fact that he was still locked up at the fort down river. Attention then turned to the gifts, before Jamual announced curtly that they simply would not do.

'I beg your pardon?' Light asked with incredulity, for it was tantamount to a gross breach of protocol to respond in such churlish fashion without at least the pretence of polite acceptance. 'In what way are these gifts insufficient?'

'They insult us! Two old fashioned pieces and a few rolls of sari cloth?' Jamual sneered.

'It is a ceremonial gift, not a trade item, sir,' Light reminded him tartly before restoring his expression of composure. 'Then, may I inquire what would the sultan consider to be "acceptable" in the circumstances?'

Jamual fixed Light in his gaze. 'Guns. You promised guns. He wishes to see some evidence of weapons.'

Light bowed and retreated with as much courtly grace as he could muster. It would serve no purpose to give vent to annoyance. That would be exactly what Jamual desired.

The next day, he returned with a hundred muskets. The additional offering was finally deemed acceptable, and the negotiations continued.

'Has the sultan perused the Company's terms of proposal?' Light inquired, hopeful that time-wasting objections were now at an end. He was mistaken. Again, Tunku Ya and Jamual consulted each other in private – no doubt a tactic agreed well in advance – and they shook their heads.

'We are uneasy with the language used. Or perhaps it is your poor translation?' announced Jamual, in tones heavily laced with sarcasm, either accusing him of intentional falsehood or a general insult on his abilities. Either way, it might presage a serious problem.

'The letter is addressed, I believe, to Sultan Abdullah, not to his ministers,' Light reminded them, well aware his complaints were futile. Nothing reached the king's eyes without passing through these two men.

'Some of the words are couched in terms akin to threats to his Majesty,' said Tunku Ya. 'The sultan will not accept language that demeans his authority or treats him like an ignorant child.'

'I assure you, no such intention was meant, Tunku,' Light replied in as calm a manner as he could manage. 'Perhaps it is merely the more direct terms in which the English language is invariably phrased?' he offered as a compromise.

'Or perhaps the Company thinks the sultan is a native idiot?' Jamual retorted in as direct as fashion as any insult could be. Light held his tongue until he had gained control of himself, relieved that the English officers did not understand the conversation, for they would have demanded some sort of apology – and the impasse would continue.

'May I suggest that we prepare an *alternative* translation for the sultan, one that offers a less *abrasive* rendering of the terms?' Light suggested. It would waste even more time, but as least he could counter the longer delays that their original contention raised.

Tunku Ya nodded his agreement while Jamual's irritation at Light's adroit turning of the tables was indicated by the narrowing of his eyes. Light might have trumped him but he had no intention of allowing him to win the entire argument. '*Two* other versions, I think. One provided by each party. For purposes of comparison.'

'That seems amenable,' Tunku Ya agreed. 'At the moment, there is a general vagueness concerning the rights that the Company might in future claim on the mainland that are contingent on possession of the island of Pinang. We see a certain "looseness" in the language that might at some later time be misinterpreted.' Tunku Ya was an astute administrator with a sharp and incisive mind. He had immediately spotted the ambiguities that Light and Soliman had purposely inserted in their flowery translation concerning the rights the British would have to armed patrols of the waters around the island and 'the adjacent coast of Queddah'.

An adjournment was inevitable while two translators with sufficient skills were located from the local community, new versions of the documents prepared, then rendered in calligraphy worthy of a treaty. Finally, they would have to pass Light's own thorough perusal, for he was alert to the danger of new demands being slipped in at this late stage. Thus, it was ten days before Light was summoned again, this time to the fort itself. Finally, Sultan Abdullah himself was ready to receive them.

The entire party shuffled nervously into the audience: Light and Scott, Captains William Lindesay of the *Speedwell,* James Glass of the *Prince Henry*, Lt. Holcombe of the *Emily*, and the military officers: Captain Howell, Captain Trapaud and Lt. Commander Gray. It was an impressive show of Company military command, enough to allay any fears that Calcutta might not fulfil the Sultan's demands for support against his enemies.

The meeting opened with the usual prayer. Then the subject of the gifts was revisited: the sultan was fulsome in his praise of the guns, but wondered when the rest would follow.

'We are awaiting Company ships, your Majesty,' Light deftly sidestepped the question. 'It could be a few weeks yet. They are dependent on the weather, which has been unseasonably stormy of late.'

Abdullah seemed to accept this answer, for he moved on to the matter of the document itself. The new versions had proved satisfactory; fears of any British interest in the mainland as a buffer to the island's security had been allayed. Now, the sultan fixed his mind on his other main obsession: money.

'There is no reference to the actual payment in coin. We

must have full restitution. The British will dominate our trade. Queddah demands compensation for our future losses,' Jamual insisted; the sultan affirmed his agreement with much nodding of his head.

'It is a very large sum, Tuanku. In the first instance, the Company must make a huge investment in the island for the purposes of establishing a settlement. The costs will be substantial. It is unlikely that we will see a profit for several years, during which Queddah will be mostly unaffected in terms of its volume of trade,' Light argued skilfully.

Abdullah nodded. 'We may be willing to accept less initially. Perhaps twenty thousand dollars. Or even ten.' Light watched Jamual's face for disapproval, but saw no sign of dissent. It surprised him.

'Does the Company intend to monopolise the sale of tin?' Sultan Abdullah added.

Again, Light glanced across first at Jamual. This time the king's merchant was listening intently, but his face still revealed little. 'The Company does indeed intend to trade in tin – as do I myself, Tuanku. Every person in these waters is at liberty to buy and sell freely, for it is the English custom to encourage free commerce. Furthermore, the Company is more than willing to share evenly the profits in the most lucrative goods, namely tin, rattan and opium. Naturally, this is only extended to the local people in view of the great friendship and alliance between our nations. Cargoes from foreign ports would not be included.' The Dutch and the Bugis could go hang if they thought to muscle in on the tin trade.

The questioning went back and forth for some time in this

fashion, a laborious interlude for most of the British party, who were completely lost in the torrent of courtly Malay. Scott tried his best to mutter now and then at least the gist, but he was mindful not to offend the sultan's dignity by talking in his presence. At last the king and his advisors withdrew to consider the particulars. Light and the Company men were asked to wait in an anteroom where refreshments were served and they might take the opportunity to sit down after hours upon their feet.

It was not until late in the afternoon, when the rain had yet again set in and they were still packed together in the stifling space in almost complete darkness, that an envoy summoned them back into the royal presence. Fearing the inevitable announcement of further impediments, they all filed glumly back, only to find that at last progress had been made. All of a sudden, the veil of indecision and objection had been raised.

'We give our consent,' Sultan Abdullah pronounced. 'A temporary agreement may be drawn up, awaiting ratification from Calcutta. Let it be known, however, that my seal depends entirely upon the complete agreement to all terms by the governor-general on behalf of King George III.'

Light raised his joined hands in supplication and was allowed to approach the sultan, whereby he lowered his head to kiss the ring of Sultan Abdullah's extended hand. 'Most respected Tuanku,' he said reverentially. 'With your permission, I shall now proceed to the island with the purpose of making my preliminary investigations.'

The sultan held up his hand. 'The Company response may take many months. Surely, it is needless to incur expense on the island which might prove wasted if the treaty is rejected. Perhaps you should wait?'

Light had feared this reaction, the usual prevarication. It must be pre-empted. 'The greater expense has already been incurred, Your Majesty. It makes little difference to the cost should we remain in Queddah or Pulau Pinang and in the interim, we must live somewhere.'

At that Jamual interjected, with his usual poisonous dart, aiming for the heart of the matter. 'Ah, but would you then quit the island willingly if the directors should find the sultan's terms unacceptable?'

The fawning smile faded gradually from Light's face. He was unable to answer the direct question with any honesty. His mind raced with possible counters before he grasped upon the only one he could employ. 'Such initial possession would by its very nature be temporary, Tuanku. For we would not yet have ratification – and who can act without a formal agreement?' It was mere rhetoric. It promised nothing, yet Sultan Abdullah gave a nod of approval – and Jamual raised no objection. Which in many ways said everything.

***

The company of British officers and merchants wasted no time in embarking upon their task. The next day, after an evening aboard the *Prince Henry* which rendered them with exceedingly bad heads the next morning, the serious work commenced. In the captain's cabin on the *Emily*, Light sat down with the with James Scott as his righthand, Felipe Rozells his secretary and accountant, and Soliman his local agent. He felt justly proud of the team that would be the basis for the new administration.

Out of politeness, and because he wanted to ensure he had their complete support, Light had also called together the military officers supplied to him for the expedition. Lieutenant Gray, commander of the Marines, was a hard-headed young officer with a world-weary manner, usually inclined to the negative opinion, as if positivity might direct extra work his way. With one hundred Bengalis under his command, he was a seasoned marine himself, but this particular mission meant nothing more to him than a stepping stone in his career. Gray was not prepared to go the extra mile for an insignificant port in the middle of nowhere. Captain Howell of the Rifles, however, was a more a decent, upright officer, one with little imagination but a man who could be relied upon to do his job all the same. It was unlikely, however, that he would ever step outside the square or take a chance.

Captain Elisha Trapaud of the Engineers was a different kettle of fish. From a Huguenot family of Kent, Trapaud was a cultured and affable career soldier with some pretentions as an artist, rarely seen without a sketch block in his hand. Eager to please and always ready to learn, he was constantly making designs and jotting down notes, even drawing in the margins of his documents. Trapaud was captivated by the region and the many wondrous sights of sea and land. Most of all he was willing, unlike the surly Gray or the punctilious Howell, and possessed the imagination to realise the potential significance of the moment in which he found himself. He had high hopes of being a vital part in the new establishment of a British outpost. Moreover, Trapaud fully understood that, to realise this ambition, they would all have to be 'creative' within the terms of the agreement. As a result,

Light made a special point of drawing him into his inner circle. Trapaud was a useful advocate who would have his corner against his fellow officers and Bengal. Regaling him with tales of his own dear Huguenot relative, Aunt Margaret Negus, and his much-loved Kentish captain John Amherst, Light won over Trapaud's trust; the younger man for his part lapped up the attention with a puppy-like need for approbation.

The commanders of the three ships were men of a type familiar to Light and Scott: competent and experienced sailors with naval backgrounds and a natural interest in all things mercantile. Their opinions were of great value, although Holcombe and Light discovered they did not work well together. Scott felt similarly about James Glass, in command of Scott's own ship, the *Prince Henry*. It was the natural competition of rivals for a ship they both claimed as their own. Lindesay of the *Speedwell* was another matter. He had worked with Light for years and was a tried and trusted colleague.

Within a few days of the granting of Abdullah's approval, a committee for the settlement of Pulau Pinang was formed. It was immediately a hive of activity, embarking people and provisions to the island, reconnoitring the best landing points, liaising with the native settlers and drawing up plans for the initial base. The fort would be sited on the north side of the island, at a triangular promontory called Tanjong Penaga named for the tall and stately trees that grew there. Unlike much of the rest of the coastline, this cape was sandy rather than mangrove, so provided a safe and ideal landing place. By the middle of the month, Gray and the marines were already busy clearing the thickly wooded area for the building of the first stockade.

The astonishing speed of Light's actions took the court of Queddah by surprise, for they had expected months to pass before such activity commenced, time during which they might decide to withdraw support, ally with another party, or learn Calcutta had changed its mind completely. The Malay court preferred the never-ending long game, which provided endless opportunities for backtracking. To be put so abruptly on the spot was a matter of consternation. The court conferred, sent envoys to the sultan; Abdullah held council with his closest ministers, who in turn consulted their own spies. It was decided that the British must be scrutinised at all times.

A conciliatory embassy was dispatched in the guise of partnership. The sultan wished to 'take interest'; he was 'eager' to view the progress of the new establishment. This unwanted intrusion, however, did not deceive the Company men. Light had fully expected to be watched like hawks, so he allowed a small embassy to visit and observe. He also gave instructions to his officers to oversee the watchers themselves at all times, to tell them nothing – feigning lack of Malay language – and to ensure that, apart from the official party, not a single Malay or Acehnese with a keris was ever allowed to set foot on Tanjong Penaga. He did not intend to be caught napping should the sultan suddenly change his mind. And so, the two sides remained – in an alliance, but with a healthy mistrust for each other nonetheless.

35

The Rubicon

Light Residence, Alor Setar, Queddah. Early July 1786

As is the way when existential crises threaten, the truth has a way
of taking on a life of its own, aided and abetted, no doubt, by
the lies and rumours purposely circulated. The Light household,
in their Queddah home above the river not far from Alor
Setar, were soon alarmed by the change in their standing in the
neighbourhood. Only the Malay servants would now venture out
to the market or to the jetty to buy fish, for an unpleasant attitude
was developing towards the family of Captain Light and their
retainers. They represented everything that the locals felt was
wrong: they were the evil Christian Company which was cheating
Sultan Abdullah; they were hand-in-glove with the hated Chulias;
they were pro-Siamese and would support King Rama. The list of
grievances went on and on.

It was only a matter of time before the mutterings turned into
something darker. One night, arson in the grounds of St. Michael's
caused damage to a few graves, although thankfully the fire was
doused by vigilant guards before it reached the chapel itself. A day
or so later, an unwise revenge was taken, no doubt by some young
Serani boys still seething at the attack upon their sacred ground.
A pig's head was thrown over the wall of a mosque, the most
grievous of insults that achieved little other than fomenting more

violent responses. At this point, Light intervened. His family was
too isolated so he moved them down to Kuala Bahang where they
squeezed into Felipe's small atap house by the harbour.

After only a few days there, however, Martinha stepped in.
The household was even more vulnerable in this tiny dwelling by
the port, where they were even more accessible than behind the
walls of their home compound. She sent an urgent message to
her husband. The immediate family – and their servants – would
be joining him on the *Emily*. It was far from ideal: his wife, her
mother, two small children and a host of maids and servants in
the midst of a military operation? Yet, Light himself recognised
the danger. He could only fully guarantee their safety if they were
with him aboard ship.

On the afternoon of the 13th July, a small boat drew alongside
the *Emily*. On board was his family, some servants and Father
Arnaud-Antoine Garnault, bishop-in-waiting since the death of
Bishop Coudé the year before. The Catholic priest had heeded
the warning of the fire at St. Michael's. As a European he was an
obvious target for the mob.

'Should we have stayed, they might have massacred us!' Fr.
Garnault explained as he was helped aboard. Light offered shelter,
but wondered who now would look out for the priest's flock left
behind with little support or succour? This was the second time
the missionary had abandoned his parishioners to their fate.

'Nor are we guaranteed safety here. We hear rumours that
Jamual plans a raid upon your ships at night!' insisted Garnault.
Light merely nodded, being far too occupied with his family to
bother with their rumour-mongering

'We are well armed, sir, and the watch is posted. I doubt his perahus would be a match for our cannon. And to what purpose? Jamual has more to lose than most if this alliance fails,' Light argued, irritated by the implication that the two priests might have a better understanding of the situation than he did himself. While Light had no doubt that such a rumour had been flying about, it was just as likely to have originated amongst the Malay opposition – or even from Jamual himself, trying to force his hand. He hardly needed lessons in diplomacy from an aged holy man.

'If you will excuse me, Father, my men will see you to your cabin once we find a spare corner to put you. It will not be grand nor can I guarantee a berth on the *Emily*. It will likely be one of our other vessels. I must now look to my family, if you will –' Light strode purposefully away, ushering Martinha and the others below, leaving the French missionary glowering his disapproval at his lack of perceived respect for his office. What else did he expect from an English Protestant?

The priest was not Light's only problem. Lieutenant Holcombe's face revealed his disapproval. It was thunder, tight-lipped with quivering jowls and a high colour. 'I beg your pardon, sir?' he demanded. 'Am I to understand we have just boarded a party of women, children and an old man! This is a Company ship on Company duty. It is not a pleasure barge!'

Light rounded on him, more than ready to unleash his temper – and Holcombe was the perfect foil. He had been struggling to keep a civil tongue in his head for weeks with the man. 'And you are a Company sailor under my command. If I ask you to jump, your only question should be "into the sea or will the deck be sufficient, sir?"' There was a pause while both men stared each other out, a mere whisper away from taking this to blows.

In the end, Holcombe had the good sense to accept defeat. 'My apologies, sir. I only meant to say we are not best suited for woman and children at the present time, being so primed for defending our position here.'

Light grunted. 'What are we defending if not the future of the settlement? My duty here is difficult enough without fearing for the safety of my family. Of course, it is not ideal! But neither would a violent assault upon my home! I have no choice, nor do I believe it is necessary to justify my decisions to the first lieutenant of my command vessel!'

The tetchy interlude did little to improve their relationship but it did at least clear the air. Both men now knew where they stood. Holcombe, whilst privately seething that this former country ship captain had outraged his dignity, also accepted that Light was quite within his rights to take him to task. The lieutenant marked it down, however, in his mental catalogue of grievances. Should Light fail in this endeavour, which given the growing opposition might very well occur, he himself would have much to reveal about the arrogant would-be superintendent in his report to Bengal.

***

In the cramped quarters allocated to the ladies, Francis enjoyed an hour or so of family time, supping with little Mary, whilst jiggling a fractious William on his knee, leaving Martinha with her women to organise the space. It was always a wonder to him with what speed and thoroughness women left their mark upon a room. His cabin had never been more crowded – or better organised.

'Come, Martinha! Sit here awhile. Your girls can do the rest.

You're barely out of confinement!'

Martinha huffed and puffed, tucking back stray strands of hair into her headcloth. 'You sound like Mother. I am perfectly fine, Francis. Giving birth is not a sickness. We simply cannot live in this cabin until we sort things out.' But she relented, giving instructions to her girls in rapid-fire Malay, then sitting down beside him, reaching for William and settling him at her breast. The baby ceased his grizzling, and nuzzled down. Light placed a fond hand on the little bald head, caressing both scalp and the swollen breast of milk.

'A glorious sight! A mother and her babe. How I have missed you all these weeks, Martinha! While not a comfortable berth, it is for the best. My fears are much relieved now you are all here. Was it very bad at home?' he murmured.

She gazed across at him and sighed. 'Bad enough. Every noise in the night and I feared a mob was coming. So many silly stories are flying around and stupid people believing anything. How could our very neighbours think that we might turn from friends to enemies?'

Light rubbed at his temples; he had the beginning of a headache behind his eyes, a tight band constricting his skull. For weeks he had been storing up anxieties, only to thrust them deeper and deeper down inside. The pot could only hold so much. Some days he feared it would burst. 'There are too many conflicting interests at stake. Here in the Straits, we live in apparent harmony with one other, each religion and race together. But it is a fiction, my dear. The moment the fragile bonds are challenged, then the weak foundations are revealed. You saw what happened in Siam? The entire edifice of the Straits is on the brink of collapse. That is when the true face of society shows itself. Every man for himself. Each group turning inwards. Those who are not with us, are against us. It is a story as old as time.'

Martinha gave his words some thought. 'It is true. This I know. We always know. We laugh and joke about our differences but amusement hides our true feelings. We don't like each other very much. Malays resent Chinese and Indians, Chinese look down upon everyone, Indians care only for their own, and so it goes. Same, same in Siam. And no one cares about the Serani! I'm glad we sent the girls away,' she sighed deeply, and held her baby close. A tear trickled down her cheek, but she wiped it away. 'I'm not going to cry. It is the milk. It makes me weepy!' she excused herself.

He knelt before her, holding both in his embrace. 'It is good to cry. Sometimes I lock myself in my room and kick the furniture, or drink a jug and toss it overboard in temper!'

'That is not crying!' Martinha laughed at his foolishness.

'It serves the same purpose to me. I never cry, my dear, I do not know how. My emotions are expressed in quite a different way. If I could punch Holcombe in the nose now and then though it would do me very well, but I have so far restrained myself from indulging in that particular fantasy,' he grinned. They both smiled; it eased the moment considerably.

'I think maybe laughing is better than crying, Francis?' she observed.

'Perhaps it is, dear girl. Is it worth it, I often ask myself? All these years chasing a seat at the Company table? Is it worth it for what I may have brought down upon us all? For this may fail, Martinha. The sultan wants what the Company will never give. I can hold him off for so long but should the Malays rebel against him or the Dutch join the fray – three ships and a small detachment will not protect us from the wrath of those who seek vengeance. In the dark of the night, I shudder to imagine what would happen should it all go wrong!'

Light choked off his words and grimaced. It was exactly what he did not wish to say. Whilst Martinha had been at home and he could frame his thoughts in a carefully composed letter, he might keep her unawares of the gathering storm. But in her presence, after only a few words, his true emotions had come pouring out. It was unmanly of him. His poor wife was already on the verge of tears, with two small children and her mother to protect. His admission of despair might drive her quite over the edge.

As was often the case with his wife, however, the very opposite occurred. She stretched out a hand and gently stroked his head, much as he had fondled his little son moments before. 'Dear Francis, take heart. Of course, it is worth it! For what else are we to do? Our fate is already written; it is left for us merely to live it. Everything in our lives brought us to this moment. You, a poor misbegotten lad from England and me, a girl from Ujung Salang with as many races in her as the Straits itself. What else lies ahead for us but a place of our own to shape in our singular image? Where else could we go? Back to England? Calcutta or Madras? Do you really think we could be happy there? We must either make our own world here – or die trying. Think of my two aunts. They saved Thalang! Sometimes, you must let fate have its way –'

He had never loved her quite so much as at that moment nor had he fully understood the great gulf that lay between their worlds. Martinha was a strong woman from a lineage of proud ladies, and he had underestimated her. She was not just his wife. She was his partner. Together they would see this through.

Light cleared his throat. His eyes were moist. Martinha's eyes crinkled in a smile. 'Why, Captain Light, is that a tear I see in your eye! The man who cannot cry is moved by the words of a mere woman!' she teased.

'No mere woman, Martinha, my dearest love. You are my heart. You and the children. But you are also my strength. I promise you, I will not fail. One day we will sit together in the grounds of our own mansion, and we will remember this day. I will deliver the island for us both – and we will build a world for ourselves!'

'Or die together in the act!' she whispered. 'Although, please God, it does not come to that!'

***

The act of safeguarding his family had an unlooked-for result which brought the already brimming pot to the boil. The tension generated in all quarters had reached fever pitch. What was about to happen if even the English captain no longer thought it safe upon the land? The next morning, a number of small boats pulled alongside the *Emily*, a motley collection of barely seaworthy vessels. Holcombe was in the act of chasing them away when Light came up on deck, disturbed by the commotion.

'Who the devil are they?' Light shouted as he caught sight of the raggle-taggle fleet.

'Damned if I know,' Holcombe replied. 'Some locals whining

to be taken aboard. It seems they think we're carrying passengers,' he added, with a sneer. Light ignored the reference to his family, and lent over the rail to address them. He recognised their leader straight away, a Eurasian cloth merchant with a small shop in the town. 'Is that you, Mister Thomas?' he shouted. 'What brings you out?'

'Captain Light, please help us! We wish to go to the island. It is very dangerous in Queddah. Even our priests have fled! Please, don't send us back. We are Nazareni. We will be killed first!'

They were a pitiful bunch, crammed onto the unsteady barques overloaded with possessions, livestock and bags of supplies. Whatever had driven them from Kuala Queddah, the situation must be deteriorating. How could he ignore their pleas? It would be inhumane to do so – and what would Martinha and Lady Thong Di have to say if he left their own folk to the wolves?

'Thomas, we have no room aboard! And the island is uninhabited. There is nothing to sustain you there!' he replied.

'We do not care, sir. We have food and animals. We can work. Please sir, let us go across and we will work for you, too. Do not abandon us, I beg of you!'

What was he to do? Could he deny them a safe landing on an uninhabited island? They might be humble people, but Thomas was right. They were self-sufficient and they understood hard work. Soon enough it would be people like these whom he would welcome to the fledgling settlement. If he brought them in at the very beginning, then they would be his most trustworthy supporters.

'God speed, Thomas. Take your people to the island and may God help you all. There is plenty of water and an abundance of trees. As soon as we are landed, we will do our best to add to your supplies. Until then, there is fish!'

A cheer rang out from all the refugees. They shouted out his name, thanking God for his good grace. And then they were off, bobbing dangerously over the water heading for the island. Light instructed a small launch to follow at a safe distance, in case any of the boats should get into difficulty. Holcombe was aghast. 'But you have no right to land civilians! Calcutta has not yet ratified the treaty!'

Light gave him the benefit of his sternest gaze. 'Are you questioning my decisions, sir?'

Holcombe backed down, stepping away and giving his superior the most cursory of bows, adding another transgression to his growing internal list of complaints.

That was just the start of the evacuation. A few days later, a sturdy junk pulled by with a few sampans in tow. It was the local *Kapitan Cina*, a bullish old merchant, Khoh Lay Huan, known everywhere as 'Old Khoh'. His role as Kapitan was to intercede with the Malay government on behalf of the Chinese trading community. Although he could probably speak perfectly adequate Malay, no one had ever heard him do so, for he always communicated through a translator. Some said that Khoh's apparent inability to speak the local language was a ruse he employed, all the better to fool the other party into underestimating him. Whether this was true or not, Light did not know, but nor had he ever heard of any occasion on which this wily old campaigner had been bested.

Which was why Light was surprised to be addressed by Kapitan Khoh in fluent, if heavily accented, Malay. 'Good morning, Kapitan Light.'

'Good morning to you, Kapitan Khoh. How may I be of assistance?'

The old man gesticulated to a sampan to come forward, accompanied by a torrent of Hokkien. 'This for you, sir. Plenty fish for your men. Nets also. And some fishing boys. They help you catch more fish.'

Light was bemused by the unexpected gift. 'That's very kind of you, Kapitan. Is there anything we can do for you in return?' There had to be a reason for this sudden bounty.

Old Khoh's mouth widened in a gap-toothed smile. 'Chinese people want go island. Can or not? Queddah very dangerous place. Queddah people no like Chinese. Chinese people very hardworking, Kapitan. We make money for British company.'

Another embassy seeking refuge? This was a community that Light would be a fool to refuse. 'You wish to settle on the island? Do you understand there is nothing there? You would have to build everything anew. Are you sure you wish to abandon Queddah?' he enquired.

Khoh nodded, the deep-etched lines of his face solemn. 'Queddah finish for Chinese. My people want stay with British. British people strong. They also good traders. We promise work hard and build new town. Can or not?'

Yes or no. Khoh was not one for dancing around Straits-fashion when discussing business. 'How many are you?' Light asked curiously. There must be more than these few boats.

Khoh gave the matter some thought before answering. 'My family. Maybe twenty persons. Then the others come – maybe fifty, sixty? Next week, some more. Enough to build Chinatown.

Then the rest come over. Maybe six hundred peoples by the end of the month?'

Six hundred? Light almost burst out laughing. The energy and ambition of these Chinese settlers was legendary. He had no doubt that by the end of the month there would indeed be a rudimentary Chinatown. How could he turn his back on industry like that? 'Then I invite you to cross to the island and make haste. You have much work to do, Kapitan Khoh, and little time in which to achieve it. I thank you for your generous gift. We will talk more soon, on the island.'

**

Later that day, as the afternoon rains lashed the deck obscuring both the island and the mainland from his view, Light stood beneath a canopy and looked out across the water. What next? There was still no sign of the Company reply. With the best will in the world, he could hardly expect one for several weeks. The sultan's treaty had only just been dispatched and it was unlikely it would result in an immediate acceptance of Abdullah's terms. Meanwhile there they sat, offshore from an island daily filling up with the flotsam and jetsam of Queddah, wretched people all hoping for a sanctuary where they might be safe.

A few years earlier, a British ship moored off Langkawi Island, the inappropriately named *Friendship*, had been boarded at night by a band of marauders. The British captain and crew had been hacked to death. It was unclear quite how they had upset the local Malays, but the memory of that chilling episode lingered. He had many more enemies than poor Captain Coston of the *Friendship*.

Perhaps Jamual – or some other Malay adversary – would storm their ships one night. Perhaps the Dutch would turn up with a few warships of their own. Perhaps Abdullah would renege on his agreement and demand his island back.

Already, in a sense, they had staked their claim. His men were clearing Tanjong Penaga and other settlers were busy putting together their own simple shelters. Had the die not already been cast? Should he take the chance and cross the Rubicon? On the safety of the island, they might have a better chance of defending themselves should the worst come to pass. But to take that decision would mean acting without the formal sanction of the Bengal Government.

Light was suddenly a boy again, standing on the rails of a sinking ship, the visions of those he loved rising up before him, this time alongside those he feared. He was approaching another such reckoning. For if he did not move soon one way or another, there might be nothing left to gain. In truth, his mind was made up already or he would not be entertaining such thoughts. As soon as the ground was ready, he would occupy the new territory, the Company be damned. If he should make a success of it, then Calcutta would jump aboard. If he did not, they would all be dead anyway.

36

The Box of Coins

Tanjong Penaga, Penang Island. August 1786

There was much work to be done and not a moment to lose. Already the settlers had made a sizeable impact on the clearing of the perimeter, whilst on the cape itself construction had begun on a few rudimentary buildings and a temporary stockade. The local Malay fisherfolk had proved their value in providing the materials for the wall. Soliman had made a mutually satisfactory offer to Nakhoda Kecil and his people: for every one hundred nibung palm trunks felled, they would receive one silver dollar, a fantastical amount of coin for these humble fishermen who knew little more than barter trade. By means of their sterling efforts, the deployment of the Bengal marines, and the labour of the settlers, progress was impressive.

Light had relocated to a tent on the island alongside the military encampment, each passing day transforming him step-by-step from merchant captain to island governor. It set a positive example for the superintendent to share the hardships of the men, but it was more than that. Light was now a Company officer of the highest rank in the region. He was crossing the gulf between one existence and another that had taken many years to reach but was being realised in mere weeks.

One morning, after inspecting the building works at the fort, the superintendent wandered along to the northern border that already bore the absurdly lofty name of Light Street, when it was actually little more than a beaten mud track leading to the western edge of the cape, the site of the diggings for a deep well, a work of great import. The streams and water sources of the cape itself were inadequate, being stained red by the roots of the Penaga tree thus the need for a plentiful local supply was paramount. Whenever he passed by any settlers involved in their various activities, Light stopped and offered encouragement, genuinely astonished by the speed in which they had already marked out their zones and were toiling away to erect their wooden shanties. It was indeed already possible to make out the future alleys of the future settlement in the areas surrounding Lebuh Cina and Jalan Melayu.

But to his great annoyance on his return to the cape, Light discovered that his marines had downed tools and were cavorting on the beach, running in and out of the surf, clad only in their undergarments. They had been directed to the clearance of the dense interior forests beyond the promontory, the intended site of the settlement's vital farming lots. Summoning Lieutenant Gray, Light demanded to know why the men were wasting time when they ought to be extending further inland, for farming land was a matter of urgency.

'Different species of trees, sir. The trunks are hard as rock once you leave the sandy cape,' Gray observed. 'Our axes can't shift them. The blades are bent and broken on the trunks.'

'And so, you let the men play about all day? Surely there is something else they can be put to? Furthermore, I observe that the native people have no difficulty felling the ironwood trees. Perhaps it is a question of industry, sir? I have sent to Malacca for native axes better suited to the task but, in the meantime, surely at least an effort might be made? It's bad for morale to allow men too much idle time on their hands. Before you know it, mischief will occur.'

'It is not only a manner of effort, sir,' Gray began, with a sour edge to his tone, annoyed at this public reprimand. 'They hear the natives have been well paid to fell trees. They feel that they should receive the same, for they are marines, not native sea folk!'

Light could barely believe what he was hearing. 'They are paid the King's shilling to do the job that is required of them! And their immediate task is to clear this infernal forest. The local fishermen are freely employed by us to compensate them for the time they must spend away from earning their own livelihoods. Is it usual to pay soldiers extra for doing their damned duty?' He barked back.

Gray dropped his head, acknowledging Light's objection. 'I have told them so, sir. This morning, however, I allowed them a day of ease that they might rest their blistered hands and strained muscles, on the understanding that they must return to their duties tomorrow as usual. I deemed it easier to cajole them if I showed some sympathy for their plight. But they're a headstrong bunch, sir. The Bengalis are renowned for it. Even if they return to work tomorrow, they will drag their feet and make heavy work of it. You know how soldiers are. Little progress will be made if they have a mind to be difficult.'

Light refrained from suggesting that a dose of corporal punishment might effect a change in attitude for, as a former sailor himself, he well knew the many ways military men could confound their superiors if they wished. 'I will give the matter some thought, Gray. But these men will be back to work tomorrow and there will be progress. Ensure they fully understand the potential danger we all face if this island is not secured with the utmost speed.'

'Yes, sir. Tomorrow will see a return to normal, I guarantee. If they were British lads, I would be more hopeful.' Gray added, with his usual air of pessimism. He would do what he could, but these were Indians, and who knew what to expect with them?

Light considered the matter during the remainder of his morning tour, which for the most part was an encouraging inspection. How might he persuade the marines to put a shoulder to the wheel without compromising discipline? Early in the evening, back in his cabin for a family visit, the idea came to him from a most unexpected source. Inquisitive little Mary had discovered something of infinite interest whilst snooping around his cabin. Light paid her no mind since he was engrossed in reading reports. Suddenly Martinha darted forward to pluck the little girl out of a wooden chest of small brass coins. The tantrum as Mary vented her annoyance to be so abruptly torn from her treasure finally disturbed her father from his work.

'Goodness gracious, Mary, has someone been murdered?' Light asked with a stern but amused expression. He had not even noticed she was there. Mary pursed her lips in feigned annoyance, frowning comically up at him.

'Francis, she is playing in a box of coin right next to you! I was afraid she would put them in her mouth! Look, they are scattered everywhere! Do you not hear the children even when they are right next to you? Must I supervise them at every moment?' Martinha grumbled at her husband, who surveyed the scene with the typical surprise of a man who supposes that a woman will inevitably attend to such distractions.

'Good Lord, it's the box of *pices* from Bengal. They're damn near worthless. I keep thinking that eventually I will find a use for them –'

And there it was. The perfect solution. Leaping from his seat, Light picked up Mary and danced with her around the room, much to Martinha's consternation.

'Have you gone quite mad, Francis? Why this levity? How can you reward a child for misbehaviour?'

He returned the now giggling child back to her mother's arms. 'The bloody Marines want paying to chop down trees, the lazy dogs. They object to the fishermen receiving a silver dollar for a hundred trunks. I've just realised how I might give them the fillip to kick their useless arses into action, and be rid of a cumbersome box of worthless copper at the same time.'

The following morning, an urgent message was relayed that all inhabitants must assemble on Tanjong Penaga by the foreshore. Cannons would be firing volleys of coins into the thick ironwood of the interior. Once the cannonade had ended, logging would resume, and the rest could return to their occupations. Any one was then welcome to join the marines in felling trees and keep any monies that they came across in the undergrowth for their pains.

The bulk of the coin had little value, one *pais* coins, known by the British as pices, each a mere hundredth of a single rupee, but Light had added a few handfuls of silver dollars to whet the appetites. Soliman ensured that a Malay boy came across one of these treasures early in the day's felling, thus increasing the general fervour of the work. For the next few days, enthusiasm for the logging was mightily increased. Most soldiers found only the copper coins, but enough silver dollars were found to satisfy them; they worked with renewed vigour, determined that they would not see any more of the booty fall into the hands of native settlers. A race between the different groups ensued in which an extraordinary progress was achieved, quite surpassing Light's best hopes. While no actual payment had been given for their service, the marines felt rewarded equally, thus placating their wounded pride. Face was saved all round. By the end of the week, sufficient headway was made for the settlers to begin planting basic fruit and vegetables plots.

Scott had even more ambitious ideas. One evening on the *Prince Henry*, he showed Light some plans he had been working on. 'The interior is ideal for agriculture. We can always source our rice supply from the mainland or from Jangsylan, so it seems to me that rice as a crop is not so vital. I believe that, whilst we should encourage the settlers to occupy themselves with their small holdings, that we ourselves should organise the clearance of vast spaces for the purpose of largescale plantations. Imagine if we were self-sufficient in nutmeg, mace, cinnamon, pepper and the like, here at the very port? We might one day steal the spice trade from under the noses of the Dutch! For who would need to venture further into the Straits to Malacca, Sumatra, Batavia – or beyond – when spices could be safely and cheaply bought in the port itself?'

Light was unsure if Scott was not moving too fast, too soon. 'But it will take years before any lucrative harvest would be possible,' he reminded him.

'All the more reason to get a move on. What are we waiting

for?' Scott retorted.

'Coolies? How may we work plantations with a mere handful of settlers, each fixed upon their own endeavours?'

'The poor will flock over in their dozens if they know we need workers, you can bet your boots on that, Francis. In the meantime, we can bring labourers from Calcutta and Madras. But once the word goes around, there will be influxes from everywhere. It could be as valuable as the trade itself.'

Light sat back down and took a deep swig of his brandy. 'Good God, but we are committing ourselves and no mistake! Are you ready to become a farmer, Jamie?'

Scott chuckled, filling up his own glass with a large measure and topping up his friend's. 'I'm ready to make money, Francis, whatever the manner may be. We will own this island, you and I. Let's stake our claims before some other interlopers do. Mark my words, once this port is open for business, it will be a little goldmine. Our little goldmine, Francis. This is what we deserve for all we have done to achieve this possession.'

It was undisputable. No Company man would expect other. There had to be some compensation for the danger and the deprivations they had borne.

37

The Prince of Wales

Pulau Pinang. 10ᵗʰ August 1786

On the morning of the 10ᵗʰ August, two ships were sighted, sails billowing white as they hove towards the island, unmistakably East Indiamen by their draught and lumbering gait. Their distant promise sent a frisson throughout the region, both island and coast. Was this the long-awaited response from Calcutta? Were these vessels carrying the promised weapons? Light knew the answer even before the ships pulled alongside. There was not a chance that the Council could have given an affirmative response in a mere four weeks. On the other hand, it would not require two East Indiamen to deliver a mere 'wait and see.' At the very least, they would be carrying supplies.

And so it proved. The two captains, Thomas Wall of the *Valentine* and Richard Lewin of the *Vansittart* had been despatched from Madras and were on their way to China by way of the Malacca Straits. The governor of Madras had directed them to call in at Penang island to give support to Captain Light, observe his progress in the negotiations, and to deliver some supplies, whilst stocking up on necessary local provisions. There was a great deal of interest in the merits of this putative new base, and the captains had been sent to reconnoitre for the future. Light silently gave thanks to Andrew Ross on the Madras Council, for he knew his old friend must have spoken in his favour, which had spurred this unexpected embassy. The *Valentine* carried a personal letter from Ross himself confirming his suspicions, and its warm support gave him much heart.

> ... *I suggested to Governor Sir Archibald Campbell that it might be a great utility to let company ships currently in Madras, call upon you for water and revictualling although General Orders state that ships should not make landfall in the Straits of Malacca. However, he had decided he would allow some leniency where the island of Pooloo Pinang is concerned, especially as it lies so directly in the plotted course of our Ships so that little delay would be incurred. He also observed that it might stand you in good stead with the Natives if it was demonstrated how favourable the establishment might be in attracting eastern bound trade, thus affording you a better chance of both convincing the Court of Directors of your suitability and winning local support for this endeavour ...*

At a welcome dinner that night on the *Emily*, a most optimistic – some might say disingenuous – report was delivered by the future Superintendent Light, who avoided any mention of the lack of official ratification or the dangerous rumblings emanating from Queddah. Instead, he waxed fulsome on the advantages of the island, its abundant natural resources, the plentiful local trade, and the remarkable advancement achieved in the construction of a colony in so short a time. There were already several hundred settlers in amicable partnership with the Company forces raising the settlement as he spoke.

It was during dinner, after Light had promised to escort the party of officers and merchants to visit the island the next day, that it occurred to him. These East Indiamen would be in port for but a few days, a week at most. What better time to make an official declaration? The very presence of the Company ships suggested to the mainland watchers – and to the migrants on the island – that agreement had been reached. The great activity and progress of the settlement implied official recognition to the guests. Letters had been delivered to Captain Light from these arriving vessels. Who could say exactly what they contained? Perhaps the excessive amounts of alcohol imbibed that night contributed to Light's epiphany, but nevertheless, he came to a momentous decision.

The food was laid out on deck around a table set beneath the balmy evening sky, a spectacular panorama of purple licked with gold and red that framed the serene beauty of a silver moon. A fragrant breeze was wafting from the land. The weather gods had at last decided to favour them. It was a night of sheer perfection, making of their location a paradise on earth, a moment to remember down the years. The stars were all aligned, or so it seemed.

Rising to his feet at a suitable pause during the convivial after-dinner conversations, tapping on his glass, Light called the party to attention. All eyes fixed on him, no doubt expecting the usual loyal toast. But before he raised his glass to the King far away, Captain Light had a portentous announcement to make.

'There can be no better time than the present, when good fortune has brought such elevated guests to bear witness.

Tomorrow noon, on the field of Cape Penaga, I order that the flag be raised by which the Honourable Company might take formal possession of the island of Pulau Pinang. May I extend an invitation to all to attend the hoisting of the Colours in the name of His Majesty George III? My friends, please raise your glasses to the King and to the bounteous future of this, the latest acquisition for Britannia across the waves ...'

There was a scraping of chairs and stools on wood as everyone found their feet, raising their glasses with a rousing cheer. Scott gave Light a questioning look; Light shrugged back with a smug smile. The following day would bring the validation that would brook no further doubt. These visitors would carry the report of the formal possession of Penang throughout the Indies, all the way to China and anywhere else they put in, together with their glowing accounts as witnesses to the historic occasion. It would be a *fait accompli* by the time, months hence, it reached London and the rest of the world.

'A very fitting choice, Captain Light,' added George Smith, a Calcutta merchant with the punctilious certitude of the perennial sycophant. 'I presume you're aware that tomorrow is the eve of the Prince of Wales' birthday? A most appropriate date for such an occasion, if I may say so. It is wholly fitting to take advantage of the symbolic moment, for this island will now be added to his inheritance.'

It seemed to Light and Scott – who both commented on it later when they were alone – that heaven itself was smiling, adding its own ratification to the deed. For neither man had had the faintest notion of the date of the future king's birth until that very moment. Yet, what luck, eh? Too good a bonus not to claim as further credit.

'My thoughts exactly, Mr Smith. In fact, I intend to rename the island in his Majesty's honour,' said Light with a flash of further inspiration. After all, a new possession would require renaming. Why not call it after young Prince Georgie and win the approval of court?

* * *

By the early evening of the day in which the Prince of Wales Island was admitted into the British Crown, all the guests finally retired to their vessels, exhausted by an historic occasion under a burning hot sun, with the promise of a great feast the next day in honour of the event and the island's namesake. Superintendent Francis Light took advantage of the quiet evening to wander around his new domain, with a sense of ease such as he had not experienced in a very long time. Wherever he walked, settlers treated him with the greatest of respect, even fondness, for the people who had come to him for succour now saw him as their saviour. He would never need to watch his back against an unknown foe with such humble folk surrounding him. For they would be watching it for him, out of both loyalty and dependence. Already he felt a strong paternal bond with his islanders; in future he would protect them as if they were his own.

The fort was in the first stages of construction, the perimeter of the stockade growing daily, built of sturdy nibung palm. In its central ground, where the Company troops and officers were billeted in tents, several structures stood complete: a simple *atap* house for Light's own family in the rear, a wooden building to house the officers and their mess in the middle ground; and, in the far distance, the almost finished wooden chapel that would become the island's first Christian church. Approaching it, he came upon the camp where the French father was now based, supervising the construction of his religious establishment.

'Good evening, Father!' Light called out as he neared the compound.

'Bon soir, mon Capitaine! Or rather should we now say *Supérintendent*! Many congratulations. It was an honour to attend the proceedings,' replied Father Antoine Garnault.

'My pleasure that you were able to bear witness to the occasion. I observe progress on the chapel continues apace.' He indicated the rising walls of their new house of worship.

'Indeed,' continued Father Antoine. 'We hope soon to have the consecration of this site at which you will, of course, be guest of honour, along with your wife and her mother, who have been such pillars of support for our community.'

'I would be honoured,' Light replied, more out of form's sake than genuine respect, for he was personally disapproving that the Eurasian settlers had been forced to slave to build this chapel for the missionary priest at the expense of their own urgently needed dwellings. 'When do you intend to hold this blessed event?'

The curé joined his hands as if in prayer. 'The fifteenth of August is the feast of the Assumption of Our Blessed Lady. It is our fervent hope that with God's good grace we will be ready by that date to bless the Church of the Assumption, for there could be no more fitting name for this Holy Ground!' he exclaimed.

Light could not help but be impressed. 'The island only four days' old and a Christian chapel will be ready for public worship!

That is indeed a great achievement –'

'A Catholic chapel, sir, not simply Christian. I doubt Englishmen would regard the building of a Protestant establishment as a priority,' Garnault jibed, still smarting somewhat from what he perceived as lack of support for his holy office from Captain Light.

It was the dart Light needed to give vent to his true opinion. 'I would agree with you, my dear Père Antoine. An English parson would be more than happy to hold a church service under the pleasant shade of one of these great trees for many months, considering the benign climate of this island. He would instead regard the comfort and wellbeing of his flock as his major priority. I wish you a pleasant evening, Father – until the fifteenth then?'

Light moved away, well pleased with his rejoinder. He was the superintendent now; no more would he hold his tongue to insults as in the past, now that he had no need to pander to the whims of others. That was as long, of course, as Martinha did not learn of his upbraiding of her beloved priest. Then there would be hell to pay from the one person in his life whose opinion he truly valued.

As he strolled towards the lantern, now recently lit upon the threshold of his family home, a sudden movement to his right from behind a tree made him turn his head abruptly. And there he came upon the most unlikely new arrival to his island, whose appearance shocked him so profoundly that instinctively he reached for a non-existent weapon. A moment later, however, he realised that the man was not a threat, being held firmly by wrists bound in rope by none other than Soliman.

'We caught this ugly fellow trying to come ashore on a little sampan,' Soliman grinned. 'It took a while before I recognised him without his fancy silks and turban.' It was Jamual himself, dressed in shabby clothes and simple chequered headcloth, his thick beard shaved to a swarthy shadow.

'Good God, if it isn't the old devil himself! What brings you to *my* island, sir?' Light laughed.

Jamual scowled, struggling against Soliman's grip. The younger man was stronger than his slim build suggested, for the bigger man could not throw him off. 'Let me be! I came to see Captain Light with news he needs to hear!'

Light stepped into the concealment of the trees. 'Then speak, you dog. I warn you, however, to remember you are on my ground now, and must play by my rules. What brings you here anyway? Do you not recognise the danger you are in without my leave, in the dark, with no witnesses? I could have you slit and thrown into the sea, with no one ever the wiser.' Gone was any pretence of civility to this man who had fomented mistrust over the past years to muddy the waters of alliance.

Jamual chuckled. 'Yes, you could have me killed, but hear me out first, for I have done much to make this "illegal" settlement possible, if you but knew. I have fled Queddah with a price upon my head. Sultan Abdullah has announced that the recent instability has been wholly the result of my machinations. He has declared that I have been holding him against his will at the fort, issuing orders in his name without authority, whilst driving wedges between the court, the king, the traders, the people of Queddah and the British Company.'

'So, the sultan has come to his senses at last?' Light threw back at him.

Which comment amused Jamual even more. 'Every word that emanates from the mouth of the sultan has been put there by me. These are no different. He spouts only what I have told him to say to save his own position, for he has no policy save what wiser men devise for him. For months, I have been working to assist your endeavour in ways you cannot even begin to imagine. Without my involvement, there would have been no crisis, so none of the settlers upon whom you rely so much would have left the mainland. Nor would my Chulias have accepted the value of a British port, and thus we would have danced around for ever more between the court and Bengal until the damned Dutch swooped in and swallowed us whole. Now all at once, with the arrival of British trading ships and the new settlement growing daily, everyone looks to his own advantage. Suddenly, they all wish to be a part of what is to come. But how to reconcile the enmity of the past? Very simple. It was never enmity at all but only the dark deeds of duplicitous Jamual, who lied and twisted everyone to mistrust each other. The evil advisor has now fled, or else we would have strung him up! Thus, we can embrace each other in friendship from now on. I have saved your lives, Kapitan!'

Light could scarce believe the man's sheer audacity. 'So, we have you to thank for achieving this masterstroke, I presume? Jamual, you're the slipperiest snake I have ever had the misfortune to encounter. Let me put it to you another way. You have continued to conspire against all parties to make a fortune for yourself, but when you realised that the tide was turning, you offered Abdullah a way to hold his throne and achieve his desired alliance with the British, whilst holding on to your own worthless neck. Do not for one moment allow yourself to believe that I am in any way in your debt. Should our interests have aligned, it is mere coincidence. Get off my island and out of my sight, for should I ever hear from you again, I will order your arrest! And then, I will hand you over as a gift to Queddah to call your damned bluff. It would be satisfying indeed to hear that your execution had been ordered by Abdullah himself with Tunku Ya smiling on. Let him go, Sol, but watch him carefully every second until he leaves our waters.'

Jamual shrugged off his captor, rubbing at his bound wrists. 'I'm on my way to Madras, just as I promised Abdullah when I took my leave. His position is now secure. I believe you will see the tension between your two sides diffused, at least until your Company makes its mind up. Soon you will receive a delegation from the Chulias who desire to open a bazaar here. I have managed to convince them to change their minds. You will not refuse them either, for they will bring a magnitude of trade in your direction.'

He took a step forward; Soliman lunged as if to apprehend him but Light held up his hand. Jamual did not intend to attack. Moreover, he was curious to know what else the rogue had to say. Now face-to-face, Jamual hissed his final words, his lip curling with disdain. 'We shall never be friends, Light, but know this. We are men of the same ilk, even if you cannot see for yourself – with your arrogant British sense of virtue – that you are quite as devious a puppet master as I. Furthermore, I *shall* return to these waters one day when the future is settled. And you *will* let me trade here, for I still have great influence amongst my people and it would not be wise to offend them. But for now, I am here merely to tell you that you are safe for the time being. There will be no attacks at dead of night. Beyond that, is up to you. Let's see what manner of man you really are, eh?'

And then he was gone, off into the dark night, as unrepentant and assured of his own entitlement as Light was himself. The superintendent shook his head with incredulity at the turn of the day's events. But the battle was now a step closer to being won. He could not deny Jamual's ultimate role in that.

***

Martinha was sitting on the stoop, staring out at the darkening sky, the first time in the busy day that she had taken a moment for herself. It was their first night on the island. The family had crossed over in the early morning before the ceremony and taken residence in their tiny new home. She glanced upwards at the flag pole in the midst of the central ground, wondering at the significance of the piece of striped cloth that fluttered against the night. How could such a tawdry thing contain so much meaning for those people who had attended the formalities today? They had demonstrated the same kind of reverence for it as the French Fathers showed to the cross of Him who Died for mankind.

She had not attended the days' proceedings, nor any of the gatherings recently held to entertain the visitors from Madras. Nor would she join the dinner tomorrow to celebrate the birthday of the English King's son and the Honourable Company's formal possession of the island. Francis had not asked her so to do, nor had she any wish to be there anyway. These were not her people. This was not her business.

Yet this place was to be her new home, this beautiful virgin island with its future still unwritten, free from all the complexities that had beset her native soil in Ujung Salang for so many years, and the tensions that had threatened to tear apart the peace of the mainland. This island was the best chance for her family to plant new roots and watch them grow without the tangled forests of complication that bedevilled elsewhere. As she meditated on her past, this present and the future they might build together, Francis himself returned from his evening walk, joining her on the step under the moonlight. He slipped an arm about her waist and drew her close. Together they looked up at the starry heavens.

'This is all I have to offer, Martinha. A clear sky and fair weather ahead, at least for a little while. This humble home, the lowliest you have ever known – and as wretched as the poorest hovels of my life – is all I now have to offer, even after these many years together. I've always asked much of you, my dear, and returned so little. I fear I must ask even more before we are finally done,' he whispered, acknowledging the formidable task ahead.

Martinha turned her head to face him square. She intended to be honest. 'I hate it, Francis. I hate this place! The house is small and hot and dusty and wholly inadequate. I fear my babies will fall ill and we will be helpless to provide for them. I worry that my mother will not be able to stand such a fall in her estate, for she was born the daughter of a noble house. I cannot sleep for thinking of the many things we must achieve, even to have the simplest of lives – but, I cannot blame you for all of that. For such is life. No other path remains to us. So, we must make of it the best we can.'

Light sighed, burying his face against the thick abundance of her hair, ever grateful for her calm support, as cool and serene as the nacreous moon above. 'I swear one day I will raise you from this squalor. You will be the lady of a great estate as fine as Belvedere. I will build for you a palace on this island and you will be its queen!'

Martinha smiled. 'Belvedere? I think even Superintendent Light may be reaching a little too far in that ambition! I do not wish for a grand palace, Francis. A pretty Queddah house will be enough!'

'Well, perhaps not Belvedere, my love, but at least a fine manor, with a tinkling river flowing past, and there *must* be deer! I insist on it!' He grinned and her heart sang.

'Then so shall it be, Francis Light, for there is nothing under earth or sky you cannot achieve once you set your mind to it. This I know.'

Light rose to his feet, pulling her along with him. 'Then we must abed, my pearl, for it is time for us to rest and renew. The morrow will bring many challenges. Yet, perhaps the night still has a final few pleasures in store, perchance? Once more, do y'think, to celebrate the day?'

Martinha threw back her head and laughed with delight at his nonsense. 'They must be silent pleasures, Francis, I beg of you. For we have but a thin board wall between us and the rest of the household. We do not have the lofty halls of Belvedere quite yet!'

Epilogue

Melton Manor, near Woodbridge, Suffolk. April, 1787

'Read it again, James, read it again, my dear lad! For I shall never hear enough of it!'

James Light poured another drop of sherry into his mother's glass. She would never ask, nor would she ever refuse, a tipple of her favourite beverage, particularly today of all days. The parcel had arrived post-haste in Mr George Doughty's own carriage, for it had been delivered first to Martlesham Hall along with a similar missive addressed to him. It was more than the usual longed-for letter for it contained both a personal correspondence and a longer official report; there was even a sketch by way of illustration.

The etching was only adequately rendered, in James' opinion, but all things considered, it was a remarkable witness of the famous event. The report comprised copies of the actual Articles of Possession of the Prince of Wales Island, along with a detailed personal account of its founding ceremony from the diaries of Captain Elisha Trapaud, himself a signatory to the treaty.

Feigning exhaustion and the loss of his voice, James insisted on a break to take a further sip of brandy, until Mary Light begged for him to resume, laughing at his time-wasting, for she knew he was teasing. He sifted through the pages to find his place, taking his own sweet time, licking a finger as he turned back each fragile leaf. Then, finally ready, he settled back to re-read from the very beginning:

'... *At noon, we assembled under the Flagstaff, every gentleman present hoisting the British flag, and took possession of the Island in the name of His Majesty George III, for the use of the Honourable East India Company, agreeable to the Orders and Instructions from the Governor-General and the Council of Bengal. The artillery fired a Royal Salute and the Marines three volleys. I named our acquisition 'The Prince of Wales', it being August 11th, the Eve of his twenty-fourth Birthday ...'*
Written this 11th Day of August 1786 ...

'Did you mark that line, James: "orders and instructions"? Francis now has orders and instructions like a proper governor!'

boasted Mary Light.

'He is a proper governor, mother! The superintendent, no less!' James replied smugly.

'How do you say its name again? These foreign words are the very devil on the tongue!' Mary laughed, her face a high colour and her manner as giddy as a girl of sixteen. Mary Light deserved this glorious moment for all the years that she had waited. Her beloved son had never returned but the news of his great triumph had. It was the next best thing.

'I'm beggared if I know, Mamma. Something like Pooloo Peenang, I assume. Not that it matters anymore. From this day forth it is the Prince of Wales Island, and we can all get our tongues around that with little problem!'

Mary clapped her hands in glee. 'D'you think that the Prince – the King even – will hear of it?'

'To be sure, mother. It is a significant achievement. I wouldn't be at all surprised if Captain Light isn't soon enough dubbed "Sir Francis Light"!'

Tears ran down the old woman's cheeks that she mopped ineffectively with her kerchief. 'He always were a special boy, James, I so wish that you had known him! One of these days, I'll ask Mr Doughty to tell him all about you, for it is high time you met.' Mary reached for James; he embraced her heartily.

'No, mother. Not just yet. There'll be time enough for such meetings in the years to come. First, I must complete my medical studies and second, I refuse to leave you alone and sail away across the sea. You've already lost one son to the East. You will not lose another!'

Mary stroked his head fondly. 'You're the very best of boys, dear Jamie! You have a very different nature from my Francis. He couldn't wait to leave, I fear, for he was always the reckless adventurer. How fortunate I have been in my two handsome sons!'

James Light patted her gently on the back. He had been blessed, just as his Francis Light before him, with the unfailing love of his stepmother Mary and the fond protection of his dear departed guardian Squire William Negus. Without these two people, he would have had nothing but an orphan's fate. He would do anything for Mary. Yet, despite his fascination for the now-famous Captain Light, part of him disapproved of the heartlessness with which his adoptive brother had abandoned his responsibilities to his mother and uncle in their old age in search of his own ambitions. He himself intended to remain by her side as long as she needed him.

'When I am gone, James – now, don't look like that, none of us are immortal and I am old and cannot have many more years left. When I am dead and gone, you must go to this Pooloo island place and make a life for yourself. They'll need a good doctor on a desert island, to be sure. And Francis would never turn his back on you, for he above all knows what a trial it is to be in this world without benefit of a decent name.'

James smiled, knowing she was right, but hating to hear her say it all the same. 'But I do have a name, mother! I have your name and it is a fine one that you gave to both of us. Now the whole world knows what a name it is indeed! One day, my brother Francis and I shall meet and I dearly hope for it to be a fond reunion. But that day is still some years away, maybe more, for you are hale and hearty and may very well see us all out. For now, I take pride in his wondrous achievements.'

Mother and son settled back again as he resumed his reading, the descriptions of the beautiful island paradise quite putting their imaginations to flight. Outside, the Eastertide weather was typical of April – sun and showers, with blustery winds dancing through the green shoots and the budding spring flowers. Within these pages lay a very different place of relentless sun, skies of azure blue, air heavy with humidity, and of the soporific hum of jungle sounds set against the thump of wave on white sand shore.

> '... *It was the hottest time of the day, when the sun lies directly overhead and there is not an ounce of air undrenched in moisture. There we were, drawn up in Ceremonial Attire, a great discomfort in the heat, but an impressive display nonetheless. It was a small but worthy gathering, representative of the Honourable Company, the British military forces and the merchant community of Madras and Bengal for whom our humble Port will be a vital anchorage on their long China voyages. The gathering included Artillery, Marines, Engineers and Lascars, alongside the Merchants ...*'

'Pass me the sketch, Jamie for I would look upon the scene as you read.' James handed over Trapaud's engraving, while Mary squinted at the picture, her eye glass close, the better to see the details.

'That man there, he is your brother Francis! There's no

mistaking him. He were always tall and skinny. Looks like he still hasn't filled out much!' Mary cackled in delight to see her son in the flesh, stroking Francis' image fondly. 'Under that tree, there – perchance is that a native? He holds a musket, I think. Would that be safe?' she wondered.

James glanced across. 'A Bengal marine, mother. They are experienced troops, most loyal to England, so have no fear. The two men sitting under the tree might indeed be natives, for their dress is somewhat fanciful, and they wear some manner of turban on their heads. In the distance, can you spy a woman with a pot on her head, in the Indian fashion?'

'Let me see, oh, let me see! Could that be Francis' lady wife, Martinha?' Mary squinted some more, wondering as she always did, how her son could have settled for a native woman when he might have had any woman that he chose.

James shrugged. 'I don't think she'd be carrying pots like a serving wench. Yet, mother, it is unlikely that Francis is married in our meaning of the word, you must understand that. But he has been a loyal husband, that is well proven. They have four children now–'

'And the little boy born just a few weeks before, according to Francis' news! They call him William after the squire. Mr Negus would have been delighted, the poor fellow, had he lived to see this day.'

James remained somewhat pensive, dwelling on one uncomfortable aspect of the matter. If Light had never married this lady by proper rites, weren't his children also bastards, just as he and Francis had been, with the added stigma of a dubious heritage? He supposed his brother loved them anyway. James himself would never condemn his own children to such a station in life; he intended on a decent career as a doctor and to make a suitable marriage, so that he might slough off the lingering threads of low birth.

Mary was oblivious to James' introspection, still mulling over the conundrum of the enigmatic Mrs Light. 'Perhaps Martinha was still recovering on that day so soon after the birth? She might be within one of the tents or buildings? Although I have heard tell these native women are very hardy, that they give birth and go straight back to the fields,' Mary added, parroting the platitudes gleaned from local gossip about the strange ways in foreign parts.

Her son smiled overindulgently. 'I am sure Francis would not expect that of his mistress. Martinha is a woman of good birth in those parts, so there must be some allowing for her higher class. I expect she may be aboard ship with the children.'

Mary frowned. 'You know, I worry that she is a Catholic, Jamie. It is a strange how-de-doo, for all that. I cannot pretend to understand. Why hasn't he settled down with a woman of his own kind?'

'She is a Christian, mother. With Portuguese blood, Francis says, so not so very far away from us. She must be civilised at least. Take heart from that. And Francis loves her. It must be enough.'

The old lady nodded her head. 'In truth, I do not care if his wife is a kitchen maid as long as he is happy! Who am I to cast doubt on her good name? I'm nothing but a woman of the common folk myself, granted good fortune in this life!' she added.

James shook his head. 'Common folk? Why, mother, you are a paragon amongst women for all the blessings you have bestowed on us poor unfortunate boys! I will not hear you demean yourself so! Now, let me return to the letter –'

'Is that their home, do you think?' Mary perused the sketch. 'Back there in the distance? It looks like a thatched cottage on stick legs. How strange.'

'I believe such dwellings keep out snakes and vermin. Floodwaters, too. I read an account of life in these waters,' James informed her. He devoured anything he could find concerning the exotic Straits of Malacca, where he surely did intend to one day go, as if by learning of it, it might bring him closer to his brother.

Mary shuddered. 'Snakes? I cannot abide them! Not even little grass snakes. Francis was always catching them in the summer. You never knew quite what was wriggling about his room –' She disappeared into her memories as she so often did when Francis' name was mentioned. The past was all that she had of the boy who had been absent for many more than the fourteen years he had spent with her. Francis would be a stranger to her now. Mary preferred to remember him from the time he had been wholly hers.

And so, the afternoon passed by in their close reading, over and over again, of the letter and report that had taken many months to reach them from half a world away. Francis had made sure that they would be amongst the first to hear the details, which Felipe Rozells had carefully copied from Trapaud's own notes, with additional embellishments from the superintendent himself. Trapaud had made several versions of his original sketch, so that there would be a pictorial memory for the families at home to cherish.

It was the least that Francis could do for his dear mother, whom he presumed was quite alone now. He had never been informed of the baby boy Mary had adopted after he had left. No one had thought to tell him in their letters. Mary herself, of course, could neither read nor write well. She cherished a secret hope that one day Francis would return to Suffolk and her sons might come to know each other as brothers. Now it seemed any plans he might have had would be delayed for what might be many years. By then it would be unlikely she would be alive to hold him in her arms again. At least she would have this memory of his triumph, and proof that the dream of her beloved son had been realised at last.

Francis Light, man of substance, whose name would echo through the halls of the great and powerful. The boy from Suffolk had finally snatched his pearl.

Terima Kasih

I'm an avid reader. No page of a book is ever turned unread, particularly the Author's Notes, which I enjoy quite as much as the books themselves. Yet now that I am in the position of an author, such notes have taken on a deeper significance. A creative work never reaches the light of day on an author's labours alone. A host of other contributors and supporters have made it possible. Thus, it would be wholly remiss of me not to make mention of those who have played their part in transforming my fledgling ideas into this finished novel.

There simply isn't sufficient space to list the many historical works that I have used for inspiration on the 18th-century world. I have made full use of the standard authorities and journal articles about Light and his times, some written over a hundred years ago, some much more recent. To those authors I would like to offer a thanks for their scholarship and research that has enabled me to climb upon their shoulders to write this story of mine. I would, however, like to cite by name a few books that may not be generally known and yet have been enormously helpful. Thank you to Colin Mackay for *History of Phuket*, a veritable goldmine for the island and the Light period; Ian Morson for *The Connection: Phuket, Penang and Adelaide*; Chris Baker and Pasuk Phongpaichit *A History of Ayutthaya*, and *Lords of Life* by HRH Prince Chula Chakrabongse. Francis Light spent many years in Phuket and his association with the island ran deep. It is a fascinating part of his life that is sometimes overlooked.

The much-maligned internet has been a magnificent resource,

especially during Covid when travel for research was impossible. I have voyaged all over the world courtesy of maps, personal blogs, art galleries, virtual tours, and websites too numerous to mention, all of which have helped me recreate places I have never visited or that are now lost to us, as well as people whose stories are forgotten. I have accessed portraits, records, diaries, letters, newspapers, private papers – now available at the simple touch of a key. One such favourite – *threedecks.org* – is a veritable cornucopia of information about the navy, painstakingly collated. An entire novel could be written from just its data!

I must also give a nod to those authors whose historical novels originally drew me to write my own. A well-researched and richly imagined historical novel can be just as informative – and arguably even more enlightening – than a history book. Such works bring the past to us alive and immediate, allowing us to relate to people and events despite the different worldview of an earlier time. I have been a fan of Patrick O' Brian for many years. I defy any historian to demonstrate a deeper knowledge of the maritime life in the early modern age than he and freely admit that some scenes in both *Dragon* and *Pearl* are an homage to O'Brian's novels and the hours of pleasure they have given me.

Thank you to all these many historians and authors – with the necessary proviso that, although I may have used your work as reference, any errors or false assumptions I have made are entirely my own.

To Marianne Khor – with me from the start of this journey; Nisha Dobberstein whose early feedback gave me confidence that I was on the right track; Judith Kveton and Joaquina Testa, my dear friends from Indonesia, who regularly Whatsapp me for updates; Karen Loh and Maganjeet Kaur, my collaborators in museum publications, whose encouragement and advice has spurred me on; Ro King who answered my call when I did not know what to do next – and led me forward. To Marcus Langdon for answering my questions with such kindness; Wong Chun Wai for helping me publicise my work; Dennis de Witt for his support; Sue Paul for her thoughtful contact and comments. And to all the many others who have sent me such generous messages. Never underestimate how important feedback is for any writer.

An enormous thank you, of course, is due to Philip Tatham at Monsoon Books. I certainly did not imagine that I would ever find a publisher with whom it was such a joy to work. I have learned so much from him already that I believe is making me a better writer. He has worked tirelessly on my behalf with good humour and friendship throughout this process. I look forward to more collaborations in the future.

Finally, to my family: my Mum and Dad, who recognised since childhood that I nurtured a desire to write and always believed that I would do so. Mum taught me to read at four, Dad taught me to love history. This book is particularly for them. To my darling husband, Henry, who has probably read the manuscripts more times than I have and is my greatest fan – if far too generous a critic! To Zoe and Andrew, Daniel and Juria, Dominic and Yvonne – your enthusiasm and love has been vital. And to Esben and Séamus, who already love books as much as I do and are so proud of their grandma.

Terima kasih banyak semua!
Rose Gan, Kuala Lumpur

Dragon

(Penang Chronicles, Vol. I)

The forgotten years of Francis Light –
before Martinha and Penang

The 18th-century Straits of Malacca is in crisis, beleaguered by the Dutch, the Bugis, and the clash between Siam and Burma. Enter Francis Light, devious manipulator of the status quo. From humble origins in Suffolk, Light struggles against the social prejudices of his day. As a naval officer and country ship captain he travels from the Americas to India, Sumatra, the Straits and Siam, enduring shipwreck, sea battles, pirate raids and tropical disease. But Light's most difficult challenge is his ultimate dream: a British establishment in the Indies on behalf of the East India Company. *Dragon* charts the colourful adventures of Francis Light in the decades before the settlement of Penang, the first Company possession on the Malay Peninsula.

Pearl

(Penang Chronicles, Vol. II)

Francis Light, the enigmatic Martinha, and the island of Penang

The eponymous pearl, Martinha Rozells, embodies the rich and diverse heritage of the Straits in the 18th century. Her husband, Captain Light, is the dragon in search of his elusive pearl: a British settlement on the Straits of Malacca. Through their eyes we experience the rich culture of the region and its tumultuous politics. From the courts of Siam and Kedah, to capture by the French and Dutch, from the salons of Calcutta through gun-running in the Straits, *Pearl* takes the reader on an astonishing journey culminating in Captain Light questioning where his allegiances lie if he is to outmanoeuvre the Sultan of Kedah and raise the British flag on Penang.

Emporium

(Penang Chronicles, Vol. III)

A possession must be held: the struggle for Penang

A paradise on earth. Penang – the Pearl of the Orient – has fulfilled its promise, becoming the most vibrant port in the Indies in a few short years. But paradise comes at a price for Francis Light and his family. Penang's meteoric rise from deserted island to thriving port attracts unwanted attention from both the Dutch and the French, while the Sultan of Kedah rages at the treachery of the British. As the 18th century draws to a close, Penang must fortify and prepare for war, and Light's partner, Martinha Rozells, learns to negotiate the murky waters of colonial prejudice and corruption for the sake of her family.